LARK
SONG

LARK SONG

JANE BAILEY

LAKE UNION
PUBLISHING

Published by Lake Union Publishing, Seattle

www.apub.com

Amazon, the Amazon logo, and Lake Union Publishing are trademarks of Amazon.com, Inc., or its affiliates.

ISBN-13: 9781477805121
ISBN-10: 1477805125

Cover design by Emma Rogers

Printed in the United States of America

For Anna and Lucy

A family, a beautiful, fragile family, full of life and laughter and affection. He gazes at his blurred horizon. All this could have been his. Well, not Wales, obviously. But that life, that reason for waking up in the morning. And yet he has betrayed no one, has lied to no one, and all he ever wanted was the truth.

There are muffled sounds behind him, but the wind is in the wrong direction for him to make them out. He hopes no one will come up to him with a yappy dog and comment on the view. He has no tissue and snot is running over his lip.

'Good to see the long view, isn't it?' It's a yappy man instead. 'I like to think I get the bigger picture up here.'

Duncan wipes his nose on his sleeve and tries to see the bigger picture. At least the shadows of clouds leave sunshine behind them, not the trail of waste he has created. He is terrified the man will see his tears and show sympathy. He moves away down the hill, as if human kindness might scorch him.

THE LONG VIEW

Duncan stands on top of the escarpment and surveys the Severn Valley. On the right of the horizon is the breasted silhouette of the Malvern Hills, and ahead is the dark blur of the Forest of Dean and the faint blue line of the Black Mountains in Wales beyond. Giant shadows cross the fields below him, the grass an improbable green and separated by trees and hawthorn puffed out by late spring. Everything is swollen and full and ready to burst. His head is leaden and his eyes well up. It must be the wind, he tells himself. There has to be a way back, a way to put things right. He can't believe what he has done to those children; it's hard to put any sort of border around the enormity of it.

He can't understand how the tears come like this. There is usually a mechanism, some switch to stop them and drive them into a knot in his throat instead. But now they run down his cheeks and scald his skin, the same hot shame he felt when he wet his trousers in the school nativity play, aged five. It is all his fault. A terrible secret has been unearthed, not accidentally, but doggedly and deliberately. And now the damage is irreparable. He had told himself that he was helping Freya in the name of truth, but he has just bulldozed all the obstacles in his way, and in the process, he has ruined the path. The wild cherry is weeping its blossom; the cloud shadows mock him, swooping over the hedges and the houses and the fields, slick and smooth, slithering over everything in their way, transforming themselves and then reshaping, but damaging nothing.

PART ONE

1

A TASTE OF THINGS TO COME

The house smelt of autumn, as if it had breathed in wood smoke from the surrounding fields and was sighing it into the upstairs rooms. Jack sat on his bed with his laptop, stuffing Milky Ways into his mouth. He had bought a bumper pack from the mini supermarket, and had only intended to eat one every now and then, but he found that each one beckoned him just as the last one was being chewed. He barely had time to savour the final mouthful when the need to tear the paper off the next one took over. He was powerless, which was briefly a good feeling, but suddenly it was not. He was shoving the blue papers under the bed where they joined some balled-up red ones, and he realised that he'd done the same thing last week with Maltesers. He wouldn't do it again. He left two Milky Ways in the bag. He wouldn't eat them. He had will-power. He was going to get fit and look like Warren Gifford in his class. All the girls liked Warren; he played football and said cool things. He was witty. Jack was going to be witty. He typed in 'Things to say to girls'.

You smell great. Could he really say that? He tried to imagine Ellie Chapman's response to this, but it wasn't good. *I lost my phone number. Can I have yours?* Ugh! *Do you have a plaster? I scraped my knee falling for you.* He tried to imagine what she'd say to that and shuddered. *Do you know what this material is? (Feel own shirt) That's boyfriend material!* He smiled. He could imagine saying that one day, but not now, and not to anyone he knew. He could imagine Warren Gifford saying it. Some guys were just funny. Some guys could just pull it off. His dad, for example. His dad used to be funny around people. He knew how to make people laugh. It was so slick. He made it look so easy. How come they shared the same genes?

The image Jack saw in the mirror was so different from the way he felt. He should have been seeing a noble nose and a square jaw. His brows should be thick and straight, his shoulders broad, his look intense and commanding. What he saw was a boy with a softness that didn't suit him any more. He wasn't fat. He might have been heading for plump. No, he *was* plump. Plump, plump. Pullump, pullump. It sounded like an elephant lumbering around. He wasn't going to be able to compete with Warren Gifford any time soon. Anyhow, he didn't actually want to *be* Warren Gifford because Warren Gifford was a knobhead. He just wanted to be more attractive to girls. He knew what his problem was because he'd googled it over and over. His problem was *metabolism*. His metabolism was not up to scratch. This wasn't his fault, but he could change it. It *was* possible to flick a switch and kind of turn it up. He just needed to build up some muscle because muscle burnt up more calories than fat. If he did some weight training and then jogged to school every day . . . but then everyone would see him and think he was a dick, *and* he'd arrive at school all sweaty. No. There had to be a simpler way. He would do ten sit-ups before tea and ten before bed.

Sophie opened his door. She stood there expectantly, holding her fluffy otter toy, which was wearing an outfit that Mum had made.

'Go away, I'm doing sit-ups.'

'No, you're not. You said you'd play.'

'I have to do exercises.'

She moved to stand in front of him.

'It's execution day. You said so.'

He looked at her bald eyelids. There was something desperate about his little sister pleading like this, with no eyelashes. He didn't know why she pulled them out. He wasn't supposed to ask her, but whenever he did, she simply said she had to. She was just weird like that, but it made her look pathetic, and like those children in medieval paintings who didn't seem to have eyelashes either.

'Only if I can execute the ducks.'

'No, not the ducks! Matilda. You can do anything to Matilda. You can hang her if you like.'

'She's already dead.' He pushed the door to with his foot, and there, hanging from the door-handle by the neck, was a Barbie doll covered in red biro marks.

Sophie explained that he could torture Matilda and execute the grown-up ducks, as long as the ducklings were spared. He pretended it was a tough decision, then gave her a friendly swipe and agreed.

After tea, he positioned himself for ten sit-ups, did three and gave up. It had been a long day, and he was going to start the new regime tomorrow. He hated himself for being weak, and ate the last two Milky Ways so that there were none left to tempt him.

2

THE RESCUE

A few hours earlier, the autumn rain was tipping down, splashing back off the pavements to make ankle-height crystal fountains. Wide puddles were spreading out from the kerbs. People were sheltering under awnings or making their way doggedly from shop to shop, head-down and hooded. Duncan was standing in a charity shop doorway when the car went past. The spray was like a sheet of glass, a wave of clawing water. It soaked a passer-by and threw her sideways, so that she toppled to the ground. It was an undignified movement, the sort of dancing stagger that made Duncan hold his breath, hoping and believing she might right herself before the contact with the ground. He rushed over. He had thought her elderly, but when she looked up from under her hat, he saw that she was a youngish woman, and she looked mortified. He helped her to her feet and could tell from her heavy leaning on him that she was struggling. Her green woollen coat was sodden. A middle-aged lady stopped and asked if she could help.

'No, no, I'm fine – really. Thank you.'

But Duncan stood his ground. 'You're drenched. And you're hurt . . . Are you hurt?'

'No, really. I'm all right.'

'Look, I only live round the corner. Let me take you back and you can dry off.'

She looked at him directly and frowned. What a stupid proposal. He could be anybody. What was he thinking?

'I'm perfectly okay. Bit bruised – mostly in the ego area. It's really good of you, though. Thank you.' And she ambled away.

Duncan watched her go and felt uneasy. The rain subsided, and he bought a newspaper and some chicken Kievs for later. As he walked back down the row of shops towards home, he saw the woman sitting on a bench, her head in her hands. He stood and looked for a moment, unable to think how to approach her.

'Excuse me,' he tried. 'Um . . . Look, I know it's none of my business, but, um, are you okay?'

She looked up and sighed. 'Yes, I just missed my bus, that's all.'

'You really do look wet through. Look, I'm sorry I suggested taking you back to my place earlier – that was stupid of me. But please, at least let me buy you a coffee or something. Give you a chance to get dry before the next bus.'

She smiled then, a full and lovely smile with big teeth, he noticed, especially the front two. There was a coffee place just a few shops away, and they made their way there with barely a word.

'There,' he said, when they found a table for two near an open fire. 'Let me take that coat off you.' She obeyed, and he took his own thick coat off and placed it round her shoulders.

'Oh!' she said, but didn't stop him. Her acceptance of this simple gesture gave him a shock of excitement – of triumph, perhaps. She smiled. 'Are you sure you won't get cold?'

'Not at all. Not in front of this fire. Now, what can I get you?'

'There's no need. I can—'

'I insist. A hot chocolate? A latte?'

'A hot chocolate would be so good! Thank you!'

He returned from the counter with two hot chocolates and a plate of biscuits, and he saw that she had slipped her arms into his coat.

He was so surprised by this gesture that he felt heady with tenderness for her.

'You look better already,' he said. 'Bit of colour in your cheeks.'

She touched her cheeks. 'This is so kind of you. I feel such an idiot.'

'Why? That driver was well out of order. He should've stopped.'

'I don't think it was the driver's fault. People just don't realise how quickly the puddles form. They don't think.'

'You're very forgiving.'

She smiled again and looked about the coffee shop. He had thought her plain. Now that he could see her clearly, he was taken aback. There was something so extraordinarily gentle and unspoilt about her that he could hardly stop staring. He could feel his hands trembling suddenly. 'Do you have far to go?'

'Just out to Stonely. Do you know it?'

'A little village to the . . . south?'

'That's it. Only twenty minutes away by bus. When you can catch one, that is!' She looked at her watch. 'I can't stay too long. I have to be back to pick up my children from school.'

'How old are they?'

'Well, Sophie's five – almost six, Jack is eleven, and Will is seventeen.'

'You must've been a child bride.' Oh God. Did he really say that? 'I mean, you can't possibly have a seventeen-year-old.'

'Actually, I almost was a child bride, but not quite. Got pregnant as a student. Had to give up my degree, so I was twenty when Will came along.'

He pictured her home. It would be chaotic, bohemian, full of scattered toys and rugs and children, and he envied it.

'What was it, your degree?' He should stop quizzing her, but he wanted to know everything.

'Botany. It was fascinating. I loved it.'

'Did you ever finish it?'

'Unfortunately not. Bringing up a child seemed to take over. I just work three days a week as a school classroom assistant at Sophie's school now. And what about you? Don't you work on a Friday?'

'I have Fridays off. One of the perks of being in a partnership. There's two of us. Architects. So . . . do you think you'll ever finish your degree?'

She laughed. 'I did have plans to go back when Will started school, and my mum was going to look after him, but then . . . well, she died.'

'I'm sorry. What an awful time to lose a mother.'

She smiled and shrugged. 'Never a good time, I suppose. What about you? Do you have children?'

'No, sadly not.' He felt as though someone had placed an enormous steaming-hot pie in front of him, full of things waiting to fly out. And when the pie was opened . . . 'I was married, about ten years ago, but we didn't have children. I would have liked them.'

'I'm sorry. Did you lose your wife?'

This sounded odd to him. For a brief moment, he wondered what it would have been like if he had simply mislaid his wife, forgotten where he'd left her. But perhaps there was just something about him that made him look bereft.

'No! Um. We divorced. Amicable divorce, really. Long time ago.'

'What was her name?'

He hesitated. 'Serena.'

'And you haven't been tempted since?'

Did she mean by the prospect of love or of children? He needed to steer things promptly. 'Actually, I have tried online dating.' He could hardly believe what he'd said. He had never admitted this to anyone.

'Oh really? What's that like? I mean, is it scary, putting yourself out there like that?'

'Yes.' He laughed. 'I'm hopeless at it. I obviously don't say the right things about myself, or read the subtext of other people's profiles well enough. There must be a knack, and I haven't got it.'

She was unwinding now, and her cheeks were aglow from the fire. The smell of damp wool from her own coat hanging over the back of a chair, where he'd positioned it in front of the heat, was wintry and comforting. Her eyes opened wide. 'Oh, have you had lots of really excruciating dates?'

'Well, a few. Nothing terrible.' What with the fire and her expectant, warm face he felt like opening up a little. 'But, the thing is, I *mind* that they turn out to be ten years older than they claim because I want an honest woman. Is that too much to ask? And I mind that they don't care about architecture or New Wave cinema or Radio 4, when they claim they do. I mind that they don't really give a toss about walking along cliff paths. Not that I demand any of these things, but because they *lied*, and because I would like to have one tiny thing in common with them. And I mind that they say they are ready for love and "maybe more" but spend the first two hours running down their ex-partner or spouse with such vitriol it is hard to concentrate on anything but getting home to a good cup of tea, a digestive biscuit, and the cat. Mr Simpkins doesn't talk about anything, and he's fine about the Nouvelle Vague.'

She spluttered over her mug.

'Mr Simpkins?'

'Yes. British Shorthair.'

'Well, I think you're right to have high standards.'

'Just standards.'

She grinned, and looked at her watch again. He started to panic.

'So . . . your children span quite an age range . . .'

'Yes. Bringing up Will was quite all-encompassing, somehow, and I wanted to enjoy him. And then when he went to school, I toyed with the idea of going back to uni, but then Mum died and Jack came along. And Sophie wasn't planned at all, so she just came along almost six years ago – but a lovely surprise, of course.'

She made it all sound so random. Her children just 'came along', as if joining an impromptu street party. He imagined her daily life:

cluttered, chaotic, and alluring. It tantalised him. His own life was so tidy, so uneventful, so clean. The nearest thing to chaos was a cat bowl encrusted with flakes of hardened food, or bits of tuna-in-jelly flicked on to the floor around it.

'Your husband's a very lucky man.'

She looked down at her mug, and for a few seconds he longed and hoped for her to say she was divorced. But she didn't. She circled the rim of the mug with her finger and pulled a strange face.

'I think he was. I think he was a lucky man.'

'I'm sorry, has—?'

'He died in an accident.'

'I'm so sorry. That was so thoughtless of me.' He was sorry. Sorry and a little thrilled.

She looked up, almost indignant on his behalf. 'Don't be daft. How could you possibly know?'

'Was it recent?'

'Two years, now.'

'Still quite recent, then.'

'I suppose so.'

'That must be hard, having three children and dealing with their bereavement as well as your own.'

She gave him a grateful glance. 'Actually, yes. That's the worst bit, what it's done to them. I mean, Will is all over the place, like most seventeen-year-olds, but he was fifteen when it happened, just the age when you need a bit of male guidance, and he . . . well he . . . well, he has issues, which I won't go into, and Jack, he's developed a sort of eating disorder. I don't know if it has a name: he kind of comfort eats – but he's *not* fat – and I know that started when Reuben died . . .'

Reuben.

'. . . And Sophie . . . oh, poor little Sophie, she pulls her eyelashes out. I mean, to be fair, she was quite an anxious little girl before he died, but the eyelash-pulling . . . that all started after he died. Oh, it breaks my heart. Some days I just feel . . .'

There was a silence that wasn't silence at all. It was the low, deep murmur of a busy coffee shop on a wet day. It was him remembering her face in her hands. It was her remembering so many years he knew nothing about.

'I really must get back.'

'Let me give you a lift. My car's right here – in the next road.'

'No need. There's a bus due in two minutes.'

They made their way to the door together, and as soon as they walked out on to the street she started running.

'It's here! Goodbye – thank you! Thank you for the drink and everything!'

And then she was gone, and Duncan stood for a good few moments in the cold breeze before he realised she was still wearing his winter coat, and he was holding hers.

3

THE COAT

It was the act of sitting down in the bus, something about the action itself feeling so subtly different, that made her realise she was still wearing his coat. She pulled open the lapel and looked inside the lining pocket. Nothing. No wallet, no piece of paper with any clue at all about the owner. She sunk her hands into the deep pockets and her fingers found some small dog-eared cards bundled together with an elastic band. She pulled one out and studied it. *Duncan Swan, SwanRobins Architectural Design Services, R.I.B.A. Chartered Practice.* There was a personal email address and an address and telephone number for the practice. She looked out of the window at the passing fields. Blackberries were swollen to their full ripeness along the hedgerows and dark purple sloes dotted the yellowing blackthorn leaves. There were tatty sheep with their heads down, their backsides in need of a tidy-up before the November tupping. It was still raining heavily, and the edges of everything shifted and bent through the glassy rivulets on the windows. Two birds: swan and robin. SwanRobins. Was Robins a woman or a man? How did this Robins like working with Swan every day? Duncan Swan. Now she would have to see him again. She would have to return his coat.

For the first two days, she did nothing about it. She hung the coat in the hall, and the next time she saw it was on Will, as he twirled around the kitchen.

'Hey, Mum, what do you think? Cool, eh? Whose coat is this? Was it Dad's? Can I have it?'

She put down her chopping knife and stared at him, open-mouthed.

'You'll have to take that off now. It's not mine. Someone lent it to me.'

Will moaned, as if it weren't fair, and she promised him one for Christmas, although she guessed it was beyond her price range.

'Cool guy, anyway. Who is he? Someone we should know about?'

She told him then about the incident in the rain, how kind the stranger had been, and how he now had her manky old coat instead of his.

'The stuff of romance!' said Will in a husky, dramatic voice, and she turned back to the chopped carrots in case she betrayed any feelings she wasn't yet sure of herself.

After that she hung the coat on a hanger and put it on the back of her bedroom door. She pressed her face into it and breathed in deeply. It smelt slightly of wood smoke and something else – a cologne, perhaps – that she remembered from his nearness when he had placed the coat around her shoulders. Then she put her arms around the coat's waist and squeezed hard. It was soft and collapsed under her pressure, and she was shocked at her disappointment. At night, when the children had all gone to bed (or in Will's case, gone to his room), she tried the coat on again. She lay on the bed with her hands deep in the pockets and drifted off to sleep. At three in the morning she got up and removed it, arranging it tenderly on its hanger before going to the bathroom.

She had fantasies about turning up at his flat with the coat and of him inviting her in. (She assumed it was a flat because in that elegant Georgian area of town where they'd met, there were no houses.) Once inside, he gives her coffee, and there is a log fire again, and one thing leads to another. And in this fantasy the children are all taken care of – off doing something with someone. There's nothing to think about but the gentle smell of his cologne and the touch of his skin. But, of course, she couldn't turn up at his flat because she had no idea of his address. Turning up at his practice presented more difficulty. He would have to be alone. Robins would have to be out on a project, and there would have to be a visitors' couch somewhere – perhaps in a foyer that wasn't open to the public. Or perhaps she bumped into him again on a Friday, his day off.

It was no good. She would have to phone him or email him or take it back, with or without Robins present.

It had been a while since she had heard the familiar *I'm so sorry* about her husband's death, and even longer since she had delivered the teary, pink-eyed thank-yous. There was something shabby about the way she missed those frowns of concern, even though they could be exhausting. But there had been something solid and steady about the consolation of grief, and now that its reliability was slowly being eroded, she felt giddy by what she saw in its place. There was a gleam in the shifting sands, and she feared that if she dug too deeply she would see something far more shiny and troublesome. More shameful than relief: joy, perhaps, at new possibilities. Excitement, even. Freedom.

Of course, there could be no freedom with three dependent children, and she would not acknowledge such shocking thoughts. But still they sparkled.

Two nights had passed, and on Sunday evening she sat down at her laptop and emailed him:

> *Thirty-seven-year-old woman (my friends tell me I look eighty-seven) seeks companionship with kind, intelligent man. Three dysfunctional children (5–17) and one dysfunctional cat. Widow of two years. Utterly exhausted. Not much to offer, but likes gardening, and currently owner of very nice coat. On the plus side, lots of love to give and very tactile.*

She pressed 'Send' before she stopped to think about it, then bit her lip in horror. She waited, staring at the screen. Nothing happened. Life would go on, and whatever humiliation she had made for herself would pass in time. Whatever had she been thinking? She knew nothing about New Wave cinema, and didn't even know how to mingle at parties. She had spent her youth wondering how other people did it. Her sister, Rachel, had had to ration her parties so that she could fit in homework. Freya always imagined that one day her sister (who was nearly two years younger) would show her how to develop a facility for make-up and flirting. Meanwhile she sat in her room drawing the crest of a lark, painting hedgehog quills or trying to find the exact colour for a robin's breast or a fox. She grew tomato plants from seed and made patchwork quilts and kept caterpillars. She was going to study the environment and protect the world from global warming.

She cringed. Duncan wouldn't look at his work emails until Monday morning. She snapped the laptop shut and went to watch television with the children, wishing Sophie were older so that it could be *Pride and Prejudice* and men with brooding brows, instead of weapons and explosions and loud, gory death scenes. Sprawled on the sofa next to Jack, Sophie didn't seem to care. She took her otter with her wherever she went, and no doubt the stories in her head too.

At bedtime Freya gave the coat a coy glance. It didn't seem to mind. It wasn't laughing at her or hiding from her, and when she went in close to sniff the collar, it didn't back away. At eleven thirty she flipped open her laptop. Nothing. She couldn't sleep, and tried it again at midnight and at one o'clock. Then at one thirty she saw that a message had been left at one sixteen:

What's your cat called?

She smiled. Then frowned. Maybe this was an embarrassed reply, an attempt to deflect her blatant flirting. (Had she been blatantly flirting?)

Well, he certainly couldn't think her desperate. She had appeared to wait over fifteen minutes to reply:

> *Chunkables. He started off as Constable Chunkables, but there were some unfortunate diminutives, which I don't think my youngest understood at the time. Is your cat of good character?*

He came back straight away:

> *I think we should meet and discuss my cat and other matters.*

The coat on the back of the door tried to look nonchalant, but it had never looked sexier.

4

ON THE OUTSIDE LOOKING IN

Will had a growing feeling that everything he did upset someone in some way. He was a source of hurt. And it wasn't always accidental. He was not a nice person. He could see swallows and house martins lining up on the wires along the lane, ready for their hazardous migration flight, and he envied them. He wished he could just disappear. Sometimes he felt like a dam about to burst, and other times he was just lugging badness around with him that spread like a virus. He just had to interact with someone for a few seconds and they were doomed. He had pissed off his father just days before he died by calling him a bigot, for example, although arguably he had deserved it at the time (a possibility which Will tried not to think about now, since his dad had assumed the squeaky-clean perfection of a dead person). He regularly hurt his little brother by calling him 'fat boy', even though he knew weight was Jack's nemesis, and he even upset his little sister by calling her 'baldy', quite unnecessarily, when he knew she was obsessed with trying to grow her eyelashes back. And now he had upset Mum. And this was really stupid because she hadn't done anything – *yet*.

He'd just passed her bedroom quite innocently, and happened to see her lying on the bed in that coat. The coat the man had left. And he knew – without any more details – that she was starting to fall in love with this mystery guy, and that would lead to a whole series of things that weren't okay. For a start, she would be going out in the evenings, and who would be babysitting? He would, of course, and that would put limits on his freedom. But, of course, that didn't matter. The fact that *he* might be in love with someone and *he* might want to go out in the evenings was not even considered. His father's inconvenient death had left him as adult number two in the house. Not that it was his dad's fault. He didn't want to think that. But sometimes he hated his father for being so selfish as to pass on a baton that Will had not been ready to take. But his father hadn't been selfish, he knew that. In fact, he had been the most unselfish person in the world, what with all his charity work and blah-di-blah. It was just Will who was being selfish. But . . . but, but, but . . . he was *also* thinking of his siblings here. If she started getting all lovey-dovey with some new guy, there'd be all the upheaval that went with it, and that would affect everyone in the family. Granny Sylvia had warned him not to let any men come sniffing around his mother too soon (she meant 'ever'). 'They'll all be after your father's life insurance money. You wait and see. They'll be queueing up – and I'm not going to sit here and watch some other man slip into my son's shoes. No siree! I'll die first.' Whilst Will hoped that she *would* die, her words had nonetheless troubled him ever since.

How would Sophie feel about a new man watching television with them? How would Jack feel about strange shoes in the hallway and embarrassing mealtimes with questions about school from a total stranger? And then he'd be moving in, and then there'd be all his stuff in the bathroom and mortifying grunts from the bedroom. Didn't Mum *realise*? But when he had laid this all out for her, told her what he was worried about, she had asked him where on earth he'd got all these ideas from and he'd told her about the phone call, how he'd heard her all murmury and blushy on the phone after she thought he'd gone to bed, and then she'd gone ballistic, and her voice had gone right up, and she said she felt like she was living in a bloody goldfish bowl. When did *she* ever get any privacy? *He* had his privacy. He could go out with his mates and say and do what he liked and she had no idea or any wish to pry, but *she* had to get permission to make a date, and even a private call wasn't possible any more – even waiting up till gone eleven to make it, since he now went to bed at some goddamn unearthly time and lived like a creature from another planet, while everything she said and did was open to scrutiny by everyone. A bloody goldfish bowl!

Will had felt momentarily bad about that, but mostly because he was slightly afraid when Mum got angry. Not of her, of course, but the fact that she was all that stood between life as he knew it and orphandom. The thought of losing Mum, or Mum's goodwill, struck him as too unbearable to think about, so although he pretended to be laid-back about her outburst, it made him experience an anxiety that he couldn't quite control.

'Just promise me you won't go marrying him,' he said at last, affecting a benign and avuncular stance across the kitchen table whilst the others were watching CBeebies.

'Well, I hadn't planned on marrying anyone, least of all someone I've only just met.'

'Well, that's all right, then.'

'No! No, actually, it's not all right. I can't *promise* anything, and I shouldn't be asked to.'

'Why not? Have you no sense of loyalty to Dad? Have you *any* idea what it would do to Jack and Sophie if you brought a dummy dad into the house? Hmm?'

'I'm sorry, but you can marry who you like, you can go and fall in love with whoever you want—'

'Oh, really?'

'Yes, really. And no doubt Sophie and Jack will find someone to love and go off and marry them, or do whatever people will be doing by then, but *I'm* not allowed to find happiness again. Is that what you want for me? Am I supposed to grow old with a bunch of cats long after any of you give a damn about this house, or who's living in it, because I've got to wait until you've all left and my jowls are swinging around my shoulders before I so much as think about my own happiness? Is that it?'

'Well, at least you've *had* your romance.'

'Well, I won't be having any more, will I? Not living in this greenhouse!'

'Goldfish bowl.'

'*Goldfish bowl!*'

He had upset her a lot, and he was feeling it now. If she knew half of the things he got up to, she would be far worse than this. She might even withdraw her love altogether. Strange that she should feel that she couldn't hide. He often had the sense that he was invisible. He felt like someone looking in on other people's lives, as if there were a sheet of glass between himself and reality. He behaved as if he were Cool Will, the arty, well-dressed older brother, but he was just a peeping Tom on the world, and he longed to be on the other side of the window.

5

TAINTED LOVE

They started seeing each other that autumn. Each time Duncan saw her, he was taken aback by something new and lovely that he hadn't noticed the time before. Once, he just had to stand and stare at her unobserved in their agreed meeting place, the coffee shop where he had first taken her to get out of the rain. She was sitting in a corner with her glossy mud-coloured hair loosely tied up. He loved that looseness, and hadn't really noticed it before, or wondered how long her folded hair must be beneath the casually placed grip. Tendrils of it hung about in an untrained fashion. There was nothing harsh or tight about the hair or about her. Her movements were fluid and gentle, her voice had no edges to it, and she smiled easily. He found something endearing about the way her smile showed her gums. He wanted to take out that loose grip and shake down her shiny hair. He wanted to watch her put it up in the mornings. He wanted to stand behind her and kiss that neck where the little mousse of baby hair strayed out of control.

The conversation each time they met was easy. There were no awkward silences, and to Duncan's surprise they seemed to laugh a lot – *giggle*, in fact. They giggled like children and kept finding new things to giggle about. The first time they parted they hugged goodbye and kissed each other on the cheek, breathing each other in. The second time – a lunch – they kissed like hungry lovers, and the third time he took her back to see his flat rather than go anywhere else, and they couldn't keep their hands off each other. He touched her bare skin and she touched his, clothing came off frenetically, but then she was adamant that it was all too soon, and he backed off. Her heart wasn't in the refusal, though, he could tell.

'I don't mean too soon after Reuben. I mean too soon for *us*. I mean, we've barely met.'

'Well, we're both adults. Neither of us is betraying anyone.'

'I know. It's just been so long since I . . . I don't know . . . I feel so . . .'

Her face was flushed and she continued to hold him, and there was an understanding between them, he was certain, that next time they met, she would be ready.

The next time was Friday at her house. It was Sophie's birthday, although she was at school and having a proper birthday celebration and a party the following day with all the girls in her class invited round. Even so, Duncan felt awkward. He thought he should probably give her a present, so he had bought her a fluffy crocodile with an endearing face. It had been an interesting shape to wrap, but it looked exciting in its mauve paper.

He had been invited over on the Friday morning, so he and Freya would have some time on their own first. The house was made of greying Cotswold stone, in places revealing its once creamy-gold splendour. It was low and set back from the lane which led into the village of Stonely, the poorer sister of Up Stonely, which contained a far greater proportion of double garages, 'studios' and grotesque conservatories. Duncan knew this because he had often been called upon to design them. He always tried to make them more architecturally in keeping with the local vernacular, but since a conservatory of any kind on a Cotswold cottage was a complete anomaly, he struggled with their design. Perhaps for this reason he had a soft spot for the poorer sister village with its tatty, unkempt cottages, its working farms and local

Co-op store. It had kept its fair share of grandeur, with a smattering of Londoner-owned houses unoccupied for most of the year, but the pub still had outside toilets and was frequented by locals who tramped in mud from the fields.

Freya's house had flaking metal window frames that hadn't been painted for years, with a patina of black mould along the edges of their panes. The old metal guttering was leaning away from the roof and a downpipe had become detached from its rusty hinges. The front door was covered in broken blisters of paint showing years of different colours underneath the top layer of dark red. Over the doorway the stone was carved with the name 'Menabilly'. The gravel in the driveway, which went down the side of the house to the rattling back door, was bald in many places. He felt it could do with a comb-over.

'Where does the name come from?' he asked.

'It's the big house in Cornwall that Manderley was based on – in the book *Rebecca*.'

'Ah yes, I know. I saw the film.'

She was right about the dysfunctional cat. Chunkables attacked his ankle as soon as Duncan set foot inside the kitchen. He calmed down a little when Duncan didn't make a bee-line for the remains of his tuna-in-jelly, but he did draw blood.

Freya opened the back door to put the cat out, and an enormous creature rushed at the doorway. Before he realised what was going on, Duncan heard a skittering sound on the linoleum and found himself butted out of the way by a wide and shaggy sheep. Freya sighed. 'Oh, Gloria! You weren't invited. Can't you go and join the others. There's really nothing here. Oh – this is Duncan.'

Gloria nuzzled her head against Duncan's thigh, quite forcefully. 'Hello, Gloria.' He had to step back to avoid toppling over.

'We brought her up as a lamb – she was rejected by her mother so the farmer over there sent her to us to see if the children would enjoy feeding her. She's eighteen months old now, and will probably have lambs of her own in the spring.'

'Well, she looks big enough for them.'

'She is pretty hefty – can only just get through the door. Trouble is, she thinks we're her family, so she's always trying to reunite with our 'flock'. There's a large Gloria-sized hole in the hedge at the bottom of our garden."

'I don't blame her.'

By now Duncan was patting her deep-pile head and feeling sympathetic towards the sheep. 'Can I feed her something?'

'Absolutely not.' She bustled Gloria out of the back door as deftly as a sheep farmer. 'Sit down in the living room, I'll make you tea.'

Freya put on some Spanish guitar music and went to fill the kettle. Duncan was too curious to sit down just yet. He went over to the bookcase and tried to work out what it meant. Scores of books on botany and plants. Great hardbacks of rare field flowers and oriental species. A few books about setting up your own business, a couple of rows of respectable novels, a pile of music sheets with spiteful little black crotchets far too close together to be easy reading. Someone played well. And there, on the opposite wall, a large family portrait. He made his way over and inspected it at close range. There were two boys, one much older than the other, slim and attractive. The younger one was smiling anxiously. Next to him was a very young girl with brown curly hair and the same wistful expression – sad, almost – he had seen in her mother. And there was Freya, smiling at the camera, with a male arm over her shoulder. It was Reuben's arm. There he was: a tall, solid, dashing-looking husband and father, beaming the beam of a man who has it all.

'Ah, you've spotted the family photo!' She stood in the doorway, waiting for the water to boil. He could think of nothing to say, so she went to the picture and pointed out each of her children, adding, at the end, 'And that's Reuben.'

'A handsome man.'

'Yes. He was.'

There was a silence, which Duncan assumed was full of rememberings.

'What was he like, Reuben?'

She gazed at the picture. 'He was . . . gorgeous. He was perfect.'

All right. Steady the buffs. 'I mean, what was he like as a person?'

'Oh, he was . . . well, he was full of life, full of fun. Everyone liked him. He really was the life and soul of the party. He used to make us laugh so much. And *good*. He set up a charity supplying clean water to developing countries.'

'You must miss him a lot.'

'Yes.' She went to finish making the tea.

When she came back, she had a tray with biscuits and a garish teapot, and sat down beside him on the sofa.

'A teapot.'

'Yes. It was Reuben's. He always insisted on a teapot. I usually just dunk a teabag in a mug.'

The teapot somehow announced Reuben's presence more acutely than his beaming photograph. At some point Reuben had gone into a shop and seen this implausible teapot with its colourful 'ethnic' design, and said, 'That's the one for me.' Duncan felt a shock of outrage at the teapot. As though Reuben had managed to wheedle his way into their presence and was spouting forth about supporting arts and crafts in developing countries.

It was a simply furnished room with a very 'lived-in' look to it. There was a pile of books on the floor in the corner, a rucksack and a pair of trainers. The sofa was covered in a battered patchwork throw (clawed by Chunkables no doubt) and various crayons were wedged between the seat cushions. The piano was home to hair scrunchies, headphones, school books and a family of toy otters. From where he sat, he could see another picture, even larger, of Reuben. This one was a giant mug-shot of the man, shamelessly grinning at the camera and happily taking up a quarter of the surface area of a dresser.

'Oh, that's Reuben too.' She stood up and went to fetch the framed picture, as if Duncan might want a closer look. 'He *was* very handsome.'

'Absolutely no doubt. A fine-looking man.'

But dead.

'You know, people used to really envy me – women friends, I mean. They used to say, "God, Freya, you're so lucky. He even remembers all your anniversaries and birthdays *and* he brings you flowers sometimes, just for no reason but to be romantic." And he was, he was just like that. I *was* lucky.'

'What did he do for a living?'

'Oh, he did lots of things. But for the last few years he was working for a charity, Children First. Perhaps you've heard of it? He spearheaded the setting up of water sources in drought-ridden villages in Africa. He used to travel there quite a lot. He even . . . he even gave some of his own money to the projects if there wasn't enough available, and set up his own charity. He was a wonderful man.'

Duncan swallowed. This was to be expected. He was pleased, of course he was, to see such loyalty from Freya. 'Who plays the piano, then?' he asked, trying to change the subject.

'Oh, that's a sore point. No one, I'm afraid. Jack did have lessons but gave them up last week. Getting him to practise was like pulling teeth. Will, my older son, gave up after "Home on the Range" years ago. And Sophie hasn't shown any interest yet. I'll never sell it, though. Reuben used to play beautifully. Every Christmas we used to gather round and sing carols, but when we were all whacked out and full of turkey, he would play classical pieces to die for. I mean . . . Well, he was so . . . And the *cello*. My God, when he played "The Swan" on the cello. It used to make my toes curl. You would've felt just the same if you'd heard him.' She stroked the photograph frame, then got up and replaced it reverently on the dresser. 'It's still hard to believe that we'll never hear him play again.'

Duncan sipped his tea. It was too hot and it burnt his lip. 'I'm afraid I don't play anything. Well, I say anything, but I'm being far too modest. I used to be able to play "The Ash Grove" on the recorder. When I was eight.'

'Child prodigy!' She laughed and showed her gums. 'Look, I hope you don't think I haven't moved on.'

'You sure?'

'Absolutely sure.' And she put her mug down and cupped his face in her hands. Then she knelt on the floor in front of him and moved her hands down his body.

He cleared his throat. 'When are the children back?'

'I don't pick Sophie up till three. The others get home at half past.'

He allowed her to touch him a little longer, and then he stood up, lifted her into his arms and took her upstairs.

It was everything he imagined it might be. Her kisses alone sent such shock waves down his spine he could barely believe she was human. There was so much tenderness in them, and so much warmth. By the time they had taken off their clothes, the sheer contact of skin on skin was overwhelming. She felt like silk, and smelt of sandalwood and roses and washing powder (although that might have been him) and . . . oh, Lord, she smelt delicious. He had never known lovemaking like it. He moved inside her, his head ablaze with craving. She fixed him with her intense blue eyes and he held them with his own. His breaths grew deeper and more frantic and he closed them briefly and oh . . . when he looked up . . . oh . . .

And there he was again. Bloody Reuben, beaming down at them both from above the bed. The previous lover, overseeing the new one. *Nice one, mate,* he might have been saying. Or maybe he was feeling a bit smug at Duncan's lack of imagination. *Missionary? Is that all you can think of?* Duncan let out a long, deep sigh. He flopped down by her side and pulled her towards him, gasping for air. She was wonderful. He wanted more of this. More and more and more. He wanted Freya, but he wanted Reuben to get lost. Preferably in a sock drawer.

They lay back and dozed, except that Duncan couldn't quite drift off. He watched the close horizon of Freya's skin as it rose and fell next to his cheek, and he breathed in the musky scent of her. Around her neck was a pendant. He had noticed it when they first undressed, but now he saw it up close and he inspected it carefully. A four-leafed clover encased in a clear disc, attached by a short gold chain to another chain around her neck. He touched it and she lifted her head.

'For luck?' he said.

'I am lucky.' She smiled.

'It looks special.'

Why did he say that? He knew it would be Reuben who had given it to her. He knew he was simply prompting more revelations he didn't want to hear. Or maybe he did. Maybe he wanted to get it all out of the way as soon as possible, just to see if he could live with it.

'Yes, Reuben had it made specially for me. It's a real four-leafed clover that he found. And the chain is twenty-two-carat gold.'

He could think of nothing to say. She may have caught his mood, because she said, 'Do you mind me wearing it?'

'Of course not.'

He touched his nose, maybe to check it wasn't growing.

He could tell that the children were eyeing him with interest, although when he tried to establish eye contact they tended to look away. She had introduced him only as 'Duncan'. They sat around the kitchen table chatting amiably enough to each other about this and that, but he felt like the elephant in the room.

'Are you Mummy's boyfriend?' asked Sophie, infused with birthday confidence.

He opened his mouth to speak, but Freya interjected.

'Duncan is an architect. He's come to look at our kitchen and see if we can extend it a bit.'

What?

'Phew!' said Will, as if the last thing they wanted in their lives was another man.

'How old are you?' asked Sophie.

'Um, forty-one.'

'That's *old*.'

'It is. I've always thought six was a good age. How old are you?'

'Six today!'

'Wow! How cool is that. Are you having a cake?'

'Tomorrow.'

'Your proper cake is tomorrow,' said Freya, 'but as it's your real birthday today, I've made you a little cake as well.'

Sophie beamed. 'Yay!'

After the candles were blown out and the cake distributed, Duncan produced Sophie's present.

'As it happens, I heard it was your birthday, and since I won't be coming to your party, would you like a little present from me now?'

The little girl was ecstatic. He watched her semi-bald eyelids as she directed her concentration at the unwrapping. She was so excited that Duncan felt quite moved that such a simple gesture on his part could produce such rapturous results.

'It's a crocodile,' he said helpfully, since the fluffy creature, apart from having a wiggly smile, looked very little like one.

There was an eerie silence. She held the toy at arm's length and her smiling face turned into one of horror. Her mouth went down at the sides, she dropped the animal on her crumb-filled plate and, with a piercing scream, ran from the room. The two boys and Freya exchanged glances. Loud wailing could be heard from the playroom across the hallway. Duncan could not imagine where he had gone wrong.

'God!' said Will in disdain. 'That was clever!'

'It's not your fault, Duncan,' said Freya quickly. 'You weren't to know. I should've said.'

'What do you mean? Said what?'

Will sighed in exasperation.

'Our father was killed by a crocodile.'

'Eaten by one,' added Jack.

'That's enough,' said Freya, getting up and heading in the direction of the crying. 'Duncan wasn't to know. How could he possibly have known?'

Murmuring and comforting sounds could be heard across the hallway.

'Are you really an architect?' asked Will.

'Yes.'

'Good. Because the last thing we need at the moment is more upheaval.'

'Oh, I don't think Freya is planning any structural changes immediately.'

'No, I mean, if you were her boyfriend, we wouldn't want her marrying again or something.' He studied Duncan knowingly. 'So that's a relief.'

Duncan nodded quietly, lost for words. A *crocodile*. Then Freya appeared, and he asked if he might go and have a quiet word with Sophie himself. He didn't want the little girl to think of him as some sort of ogre. As he put his hand on the door-handle, he sensed that this was the most terrifying thing he had ever volunteered to do. He had no idea what to say.

6

HEAVY HEAVY

Mummy is the first to come in. She kneels by the sofa and strokes Sophie's arm.

'He didn't mean any harm, sweetheart. He didn't know about the crocodile. He just wanted to give you a present.'

She strokes Sophie's hair and wipes the tears with her cool knuckles. Sophie reaches out to her, and Mummy's arms around her are like reaching dry land. She heaves and pants. She squeezes and clings. It is relief and agony. What if Mummy dies? What if the man takes her away? Bad things happen. Bad things happen.

After Mummy leaves, Sophie feels all heavy heavy. Like she did when she started to give out the maths books at school. The pile was thirty books fat, and it was hard to lug around. Each table made it lighter: Caterpillars, one, two, three, four, five . . . then Frogs' table, one two, three, four, five . . . She gives out the books in her head, feeling the pile go down, feeling the slow lightness, until she reaches Butterflies, her own table, and there are just five to go. The books are a faded red, and some are so tatty, the covers all fluffed up and dog-eared – she doesn't know how people let them get like that. She likes to keep hers neat, but Henry Topper bent one corner when he leaned over her to borrow a pencil. It will never be the same again. And her work is neat. She doesn't like to cross things out. But sometimes you have to cross things out. She has a white pen that she used once, but Miss Dowling doesn't like white pens. She said she wanted to see their mistakes. She said it was important to see their mistakes because then she could see where they went wrong and what she had to teach some more of. But Sophie doesn't like crossings out at all. She doesn't like mistakes and she doesn't want anyone to see them.

Now the door from the kitchen is pushed open again.

'I made a mistake. I'm sorry.'

It is the dunking man. He comes in and crouches on the floor beside her. Heavy heavy. She picks up an otter and strokes its head without looking at him.

'He's a handsome chap. What's his name?'

She doesn't want to say. So she doesn't. But then the silence is heavy heavy, so she says, 'Peter.'

'Peter? Hello, Peter.' Silence. 'You like otters then?'

She can see him casting about for things to say, scanning the floor for other toys to talk about. He picks up a hedgehog. 'Wow,' he says. 'Big hair. What's his name?'

'That's Esmerelda, and she's a mummy.' Isn't it obvious? She's wearing a dress. 'Daddy hedgehog is called Prickles and he's in the prison with the duck family.'

'All of them?'

She nods, annoyed with herself for having given this much away. The ducks aren't bad people.

'What have they done?'

Sophie shakes her head and folds her lips. She doesn't want to say that the ducks have stolen food and the hedgehog has made people cry, because he'll think that's childish, and he might laugh or, worse, he might want to join in. Sometimes she likes it when grown-ups join in. Sometimes they make it funny, like when Daddy played with her once or twice, but she can barely remember that now. Sometimes Will plays with her for a bit, but he always puts people in prison and Jack always arranges executions. She doesn't think Dunking would hang her animals or be cruel to them, but she doesn't want him being nice to them either. She doesn't want to like him too much.

'Which are your favourite animals?' he tries.

'The otters.'

'I see. And have you got the whole set?'

'Yes.' It occurs to her that he might be looking for something else to buy her as a present, and before she can stop herself she says, 'I haven't got the babies.'

'Well, perhaps I could get you the otter babies.' She says nothing. She wants the otter babies, but she doesn't want him to get them for her. She watches him look at her awkwardly. She can tell he wants her to like him. He probably feels heavy heavy too, but she can't let herself care. He places his hands on his knees and gets to his feet.

'Well,' he says. 'I hope um . . .'

His eyes are sad, and his nose is on the big side.

'I'll leave you to your playing. I'm so sorry I upset you.'

'That's all right.'

He goes out of the room and it seems suddenly empty.

7

LOOKING OVER A FOUR-LEAFED CLOVER

There were several reasons why Duncan was uncomfortable with the way things were going. First of all, he had been taken by surprise at his feelings of being second best to Reuben. He hadn't expected the man to be so present.

'Why wouldn't you be pleased about her devotion to a former partner?' asked his work associate Lottie Robins. He had ventured to tell her a little about it, since her current partner had been bereaved, and he hoped she could throw some light on things.

'I know. I am. It's just that . . . well, she is *still* devoted to him. It's as if he's still around.'

'It's early days, but I do know what you mean. I told Alex that the photos had to go. If there are children still living there, it's different – and there were for a while in our case – but the bedroom is a complete no-no. Those photos need to go away in a drawer or something, and only be looked at discreetly from time to time. She needs to be telling you you're her number one now.'

He wasn't sure he would be able to say any of this to Freya, but it was good to hear. He had wondered if he was being a bit of a wuss, getting all pathetic and insecure over a dead man, so it was consoling to know that he wasn't alone. And after all, Lottie was a woman and more likely to understand Freya.

'Look, show her that you're here and now and alive. Take her somewhere posh. Have fun. What about the Greenhaven House reception coming up?'

This was a very elegant reception for all the people who had helped or worked with Egmonts, a local firm that had just been awarded a Services to Industry prize, and SwanRobins had designed their new headquarters. Yes, yes, he could take her there, although it wasn't for a while yet. But then there was the other factor, the children factor. They hadn't seemed too keen on him. How could he ever get them to like him? Ridiculous, really, as he had so wanted children. In fact, his online dating profile had made it very clear that he was 'happy to take on existing children'. Perhaps what he had really meant were small children, young enough to start calling him 'Daddy'. But Sophie was small, and he had already made that pretty difficult for both of them.

'And her children hate me. I made her six-year-old daughter scream and run out of the room,' he said gloomily.

'*You* did? How on earth did you manage that?' She said it in such a way as to suggest that he normally had no impact on anyone whatsoever.

He explained the crocodile fiasco, and Lottie started to google crocodile deaths, while at the same time muttering something about otter boats.

'What otter boats?'

'The otter babies are tiny. You need to buy her the otter canal boat as well. Sylvanian Families. Look it up online. I'll help you in a moment. Just a bit busy with crocs. What did you say his name was?'

Duncan hoped he hadn't blown it all with Freya. He had quietly rejoiced at her ordinariness, pleased that he could see something subtle and introspective in her unlikely to thrill other men straight away. Having found women unapproachable most of his life, he was now bored with the artificially inflated string of dates with women who all seemed the same: overly trumpeted careers, the using of bad language with alarming confidence, the shameless enumeration of past lovers and their antics. They made it clear that they 'inhabited their own space' and were not prepared to compromise. They never seemed to ask him about himself, to get below the surface of things. They made him feel a little unnecessary. Most of them wanted children, though, and hid their desperation with varying degrees of success. He had never flattered himself on being able to pick up female signals. He suspected they were looking for alpha males. Most of them never contacted him again for a second date, and he was surprised at how relieved he felt.

All through his childhood and his teens he had suspected that he was deficient in the jolly, fun-loving, easy-talking, Reubenesque skills of the more attractive fellows. At school, he had never put up his hand to answer questions, but when asked he would give the right answer apologetically. He accepted his role as mild freak manfully, laughed at himself whenever possible to avoid being laughed at, and would have been mortified if called upon to dance (as he once was at a spontaneous, end-of-term bash in the classroom). Then his arms had felt like danger-ous, free-floating weapons of self-destruction flopping about his body. In the end he assumed a rigid air-boxing pose, the clumsiness of which made him feel physically sick as he watched the popular boys with their fluid arm movements. He dribbled a football passably, but not well; he ran respectably, but was ashamed of his spidery legs in shorts; he was terrified of rugby scrums. He watched the other boys tell jokes and marvelled at their slick hilarity, and he practised punchlines in front of the mirror at home, imagining an appreciative audience. The smell of wood pleased him, and he liked to make things and design things. He felt a surge of excitement inside the Art room, its odour of poster paints and glue and old cardboard sparking something jubilant in him. His mother had died when he was fourteen, and he was intrigued by the femininity of girls, by every little difference about them. He would borrow crayons just to examine their pencil cases and see the fluffy key rings and intricately drawn names of bands and boyfriends on their bags. He wanted to see inside their bags. He wanted to breathe in their perfume and the smell of their hair. He loved their small hands and their little shoes and their dainty bare feet on the school field in summer. He hardly knew how to speak to them, let alone make them laugh. Once, when he had been in a toilet cubicle at school, he heard three lads come in and talk loudly to each other in that way confident boys did. One of them was explaining something complicated and another one said, 'Watch out, if you get any brainier you'll grow a beak like Swan!' and the other one retorted, 'Eugh! Duncan Swan! He thinks he's *so clever!*' Then he added in a namby-pamby voice: 'Look at me! I'm Duncan Swan. I've got no dick but I'm such a genius!'

'I have it! "MAN EATEN BY CROCODILE." Here you go: "A Gloucestershire charity worker is thought to have been eaten by a crocodile in Kenya on Friday night. According to Chibo Imani, manager of the Maji Bado Wildlife Park Hotel, the father of three, Reuben Gray, ignored warnings not to go near the river at night. 'I told him it was dangerous to go near the edge of the river alone and *never* at night. I saw him leaving his hut after dark and heading for the river and I warned him that the river was high and there were crocodiles you just couldn't see. We found his shoe on the riverside.'" There's a picture of Chibo holding up a shoe. Oooh! And there's a picture of Reuben too. Can't say he's that much to write home about, Dunkers old bean. Definitely a bit of a nascent pot belly and a couple of man boobs going on underneath that T-shirt.'

'Let's see.' He tried to sound nonchalant, but who was he kidding? Lottie knew him too well. She twisted her laptop round to show him. 'Well, he does look a lot better on the wall photos, I must admit.'

'Come on! He's pretty ordinary. Do you think Freya got any life insurance out of that? Pretty hard to prove death from a shoe. Oh my God. It's a Croc as well. The shoe's a Croc!'

'She didn't get any life insurance because he had stopped paying it. She thought it was up to date, but it seems he'd stopped three years beforehand.'

'Sounds a bit of a plonker to me.'

'Not the most reliable of men, no.'

'Not like you. You wouldn't let your life insurance drift.'

'I wouldn't walk by unguarded crocodiles either.'

'And, more importantly, Mr Swan, you would not be seen dead in Crocs.'

'Certainly not.'

'And you're alive. Don't forget that.' She patted his hand and swung her laptop back towards her. 'Reuben isn't here.'

8

GETTING TO KNOW ALL ABOUT YOU

Freya phoned Duncan to say she'd be coming to Cheltenham on Friday and she asked him if he'd like to meet her. She said it was easier to catch the bus than to find a parking space and, anyway, her car didn't do the return journey very well as it wasn't good on hills. Despite his reservations, Duncan couldn't wait for Friday to come round again, and his impatience gathered momentum as the days passed.

He had invited her to his flat with the intention of a relaxing coffee before lunch at a good restaurant around the corner. He even pictured the table they would sit at and imagined their eyes meeting or their feet touching. In fact, when he met her at the bus stop, he felt like a teenager. He could barely form his words.

'I thought . . . Maybe we . . . You look . . .'

She smiled and linked arms with him. He remembered her smell and squeezed her arm. He thought about undressing her.

'What would you like to do?' he said as they walked. 'Go for a . . . ?'

'Show me to your flat!' She said it almost mischievously, in a breathless whisper, like someone coming up for air.

He didn't bother with the coffee in the end. The all-butter Scottish shortbread he'd displayed on a plate sat untouched on the kitchen counter. They didn't bother with the good restaurant either. As soon as they were inside the door, they were pressed against each other, kissing, pushing off coats, pulling at clothes.

The language of their lovemaking was easy, and made the conversation they had later less clumsy. They had a cup of tea in bed and a bowl of pasta on the sofa.

'I like the watercolours,' she said, sitting up in bed. 'Is that . . . ?' She squinted at the adjacent wall. '"D. J. Swan". Is that you?'

'Er . . . yes. I wouldn't normally put up my own work, but I lost most of the good artwork in the divorce.'

'Oh.' She craned her neck to see the one above the bed. '"S.R.R." Is that Serena's?'

'No.' He wondered if she was remembering what hung above her own bed. 'That was my mother before she was married. She used to paint.'

'Runs in the family, then.' She smiled and then bit her lip. Reuben's portrait seemed to have received a small blow. Maybe just a clip around the ear. As if she shared this thought, she put her hand on Duncan's ear and cheek and kissed him gently on the lips.

The following morning he had an urgent call from Freya.

'I wouldn't ask you, but I just don't know what to do. We've got to go to Devon today and my car's packed in. I don't suppose . . . could I . . . if you're not using it . . . I know it's a lot to ask, but I'm insured to—'

'I'll drive you, Freya. I'm free.'

There was a short silence. 'No, really. I have to take the kids to Sylvia and Steve's. They're Reuben's parents. It's Sylvia's birthday and I've made a cake and if we don't go—'

'I'll drive you. I'm not inviting myself to the party, don't worry. I can find plenty to do in Devon.'

She seemed uncomfortable about him driving, although she eventually gave in. She clearly didn't want to introduce him to her in-laws, but she must have known he wasn't nursing a feeling of hurt about this, since he had insisted so vehemently on being the driver.

'Look . . . it's not just Sylvia's birthday. It's Reuben's. It's actually hers tomorrow, but she likes to . . .'

'Don't worry, I'll drive you. Like I say, I can find plenty to do.' And although he was a little curious about Sylvia and Steve, parents to the wunderkind, he had to admit that he would rather explore a bit of Devon on his own than celebrate a dead husband's birthday.

A sea of frothy mist filled the valley as they drove down to the main road. The crowns of beeches and sycamores floated on it like boats, and the ridge of hills in the distance seemed like the promontory of a bay. As the sun rose higher, they left the fairyland behind and approached the motorway.

The journey down was exhilarating and informative. He learnt that none of the children was especially keen to see their grandmother (the grandfather was barely mentioned), that Freya's reproaches on the subject seemed half-hearted, that Will could sing all of the songs of Abba with Jack and Sophie joining in, that Sophie could sing most of the *X Factor* winning songs and that Jack could do a mean imitation of Tom Jones, which provoked a family chorus of 'What's New Pussycat?' Not one of the children said they were bored, which surprised him.

'Mum sings Abba every morning,' said Sophie.

'No she doesn't,' said Jack. 'She sings "*Waking* up is never easy," to get Will out of bed.'

'Hey, there's L-plates in the back here,' said Will.

'Yes. I . . . um . . . they're ancient.'

'Will you teach me to drive? Mum said she'd give me lessons, but she never does.'

'That's because we always end up shouting at each other.'

'No, Mum. *You* shout at *me*. Anyway, will you? Then I can smash your car up instead of ours.'

'Er . . . of course, if you think you can put up with me. If your mum's okay with it, that is.'

Freya agreed, and Jack called his brother a 'jammy bastard'. Duncan was about to say he'd happily give Jack lessons too, when the time came, but realised that would be saying far too much about his intentions. There was a lull, and he asked if they knew the furniture game. They didn't.

'You think of someone and don't tell me who it is . . .'

'Got someone!' shouted Jack.

'Now the rest of us ask questions like: if this person were a piece of furniture, what would they be?'

'A big, uncomfortable chair,' said Jack without hesitation.

'If they were an animal, what animal would they be?'

'Um . . .'

'A horse,' suggested Sophie.

'No, a ferret.'

'You have a go at asking a question, Sophie.' Duncan turned his head slightly and smiled.

'If this person was a . . . bird, what would they be?'

'Um . . . I think perhaps a hawk, or some sort of bird of prey.'

At this point Will, who had been looking listlessly out of the window, said, 'If they were a song, what would they be?'

'The national anthem.'

'Is it the Queen?' asked Sophie.

'No,' said Jack, 'and you can't ask me yet. Ask more questions.'

More questions were asked. The person was a vacuum cleaner, a plate of posh cakes, a white wine, a pair of shiny shoes, a fir tree and a knife.

'Granny Sylvia,' said Will.

'How did you know?'

'Knife. But you should've had "I Did It My Way" for the song.'

'And,' said Sophie, 'a tiger for the animal.'

Jack stood his ground. 'I like ferret.' They all chuckled. Duncan felt he may have crossed a border without a border pass, by sheer fluke. Or perhaps stealth.

Sylvia and Steve were at the front porch of their bungalow to meet the car. There was a look of curiosity on Sylvia's face when the children spilled out on to the gravel drive. She was a lean woman with a corded neck.

'New car?'

'No, Duncan brought us. Our car packed up.'

Then her eyes were on Duncan.

'Hello, I'm Duncan. Friend of Freya's. And I'm not stopping. Just giving a lift.'

'Oh, are you on your way somewhere?'

Freya stepped forward to greet her mother-in-law. 'He has some things to do in Totnes,' she lied. They were nowhere near Totnes, and anyway, when she'd put her bag in the car boot earlier she'd seen an Ordnance Survey map of Devon and Duncan's walking boots. He was probably just going to pootle around locally until they were ready to go home.

A grey-haired man in a tank top and tie shook hands with Duncan. 'Well, it was good of you to help them out in a crisis. Very kind of you. Won't you come in for a drink?'

'No thank—'

'Of *course* you must!' said Sylvia, as if irritated that she hadn't said it first. 'Any friend of Freya's is a friend of ours, and you *have* just driven for two and half hours. Of course you must come in.'

Freya looked at him helplessly.

'Well, maybe for a few minutes.'

Half an hour later he was still there. Jack and Sophie had disappeared into another room and were playing with a dog. Will was stifling a yawn, but stuck with the grown-ups. Fortunately, Sylvia – who seemed to want to know everything about Duncan – had to keep dashing off to the kitchen.

'Can't we offer this young man lunch?' said Steve.

'Oh . . .' Sylvia's moment of hesitation was all it took to have Duncan on his feet. Freya frowned.

'Sylvia . . .'

'No, no, of course he must. It's just that I have cooked for six. Now let me see . . . I could open a tin of—'

'Sylvia!' Freya followed Sylvia into the kitchen and Duncan heard muffled voices. He hovered helplessly, and Will said, 'I should go now, mate, while you still can.'

Perhaps Will resented him being there, standing in his father's shoes? Yes, he should definitely go. He hadn't wanted to come in anyway. 'Tell Freya to ring me ten minutes before you want to set off.' He walked into the hallway and was almost out of the door when Freya grabbed him.

'You can't go now.' She looked upset. 'Please stay.'

Lunch was a quiche and salad. The conversation was about Reuben, or rather, Sylvia introduced him into the conversation at every opportunity. When they had finished, Duncan got up and helped take things into the kitchen. Sylvia grabbed his arm and looked intently in his eyes. 'Duncan, you should know something about Freya.' Her voice was lowered to a hiss. 'She's not over Reuben. She may seem to be, but she isn't. She's not ready for another man in her life – I'm only telling you because I don't want to see you hurt.'

'That's kind of you.'

She looked satisfied. 'No one can replace Reuben, you realise that.'

'Of course.'

'Of course I'm biased.' She laughed, giving a little leeway now she'd made her point. 'But I know Freya feels exactly the same. They were *made* for each other.'

'So it seems.'

'Well, so long as you know.' She gave him a sorrowful look. 'I'd just hate to see you wasting your time, that's all.'

'Much appreciated. Shall I take that in for you?'

9

MY GRIEF IS WORSE THAN YOURS

Will was bored. Dessert was the cake his mum had made, and they all had to sing 'Happy Birthday' like idiots and watch Granny Sylvia blow out the candles. Jack and Sophie had second helpings, then disappeared to watch a DVD that Mum had let them bring. She would die a death if she knew the sort of DVD Will would like to watch.

'So, how do you two know each other?' said Granny S in her most golf-club voice, while Grandad shuffled off to make tea. Will pretended to be interested in the pattern of the tablecloth.

'We met—'

'In a café, actually.'

'Yes, in Cheltenham.' Mum let out a breath of relief, which she tried to hide behind her hand. 'And I really wouldn't have asked Duncan today if I hadn't been desperate.'

'Thanks.' Duncan gave her a wry smile. Everyone relaxed a little.

'So you're not, um, *dating*, then?'

'Of course they're dating,' said Will.

'Will!'

'Well, you could've fooled me.' He didn't see why he should pretend all the time. He knew Duncan was the coat man. He knew Granny S would go ballistic at the thought of her son being replaced, and why not? Who did Duncan think he was, muscling in on their family day out? Not that he would wish Granny S and Grandad on anyone, but he didn't see why he should lie.

Mum looked a bit pissed off. 'Sylvia, we're not an item.'

'I'm sorry. I didn't mean to embarrass you, Freya darling. I know you wouldn't be dating, especially not after such a short time. And, of course, after Reuben.'

Will wanted to read Duncan's face at this point, but he dared not look. Instead he played determinedly with a teaspoon. Granny S would go for him anyhow.

'Are you married, Duncan?'

'No.'

'Duncan's divorced,' supplied Freya, as if she feared this was going to be a long interrogation and she might be able to speed it up.

'*Divorced.* Ah, well. That's so different, isn't it? You're on your own, of course, but it's not the same. My friend Thea – well, she *was* my friend, but I'm not sure I'd call her that now – she's divorced and you'd think the sky had fallen in. I mean, no offence or anything, Duncan, but you simply can't *compare* a divorce to a bereavement, can you?'

'Sylvia—'

'Well, you remember, Freya, how people used to think *you* were divorced – still do no doubt – when they find out you live alone with your children. It's so insulting.' She turned to Duncan. 'It used to upset her so much.'

'Why's that? Is there such a stigma attached to divorce?'

'Oh *no*! No, Duncan, please don't get me wrong, but I mean, people *choose* to divorce, don't they? You don't *choose* to be bereaved.'

'Well . . . only about half of divorcees choose it – I imagine.'

'Well yes, I suppose there's some truth in that. It's usually the man who plays away, as they say, and the woman who asks for the divorce. Did your wife divorce you?'

'Sylvia . . .' Mum was looking really uncomfortable.

Duncan looked cornered. 'As a matter of fact, yes.'

'I've got ginger biscuits and shortbread, whichever people want.' Grandad came in with a tray of tea things. 'Shall I be mum?'

'I suppose you had an affair.'

Go, Granny, go!

Grandad looked up from his pouring, shocked, as though his wife were accusing him of a dalliance in the kitchen.

'Sylvia.' Mum looked desperate. 'Duncan's divorce was amicable.'

'Oh yes, I've heard that phrase. You break the most solemn vows you have ever made, and you give it a nice little name to make it palatable.'

'Actually . . .'

Grandad held the teapot, poised for pouring. All eyes were on Duncan now, including Will's.

'Actually, I didn't have an affair.'

'Oh.' Granny S was momentarily nonplussed. Grandad took the opportunity to hand him tea and offer him milk. Granny S was just warming up. 'So she just didn't find you . . . up to the mark?'

Grandad took in a great breath and opened his mouth to speak, but Mum beat him to it. 'Really, Sylvia, I'm sure Duncan doesn't want to talk about this.'

'No, well he wouldn't. I'm just trying to make my point, that's all. There's no "grief" involved in divorce. If you let your marriage slip because you don't spend enough time together or you don't put in the effort *or* you have an affair, whatever, you can't then go and call it *grief*, when you effectively brought it on yourself.'

There was a startled silence, as people chewed reluctantly on the bitter words and tried to digest them. 'Maybe he's gay,' supplied Will, beginning to back-track on the dating now that things were getting out of hand. Everyone ignored him.

'I'm just *saying*, that's all,' said Granny S, recklessly undeterred. 'People just don't make the effort these days, do they? In my day it was "till death us do part" and that was that. You kept your marriage together through thick and thin, for better or worse – you *worked* at it for the sake of the children. I mean, God knows, there were times with Steve when I might have happily given up . . .' (Grandad looked up from the tea tray, marginally devastated.) '. . . But, I kept going for the children's sake, for Reuben and Ludo, and here we are, still happily married.' (Grandad folded his lips together as if trying to stop something from escaping his mouth.) 'What about your children, Duncan? I suppose you see them once a fortnight for burger and chips, do you? Do you have children?'

Duncan placed his hands on the tablecloth as if he were about to play the piano. Everyone looked at him with different expectations. Will hoped he might land Granny S a punch.

'Actually, no. And yes, you were right earlier. My wife didn't find me up to the mark. That's why she left.'

Granny S looked startled, but mostly vindicated, and sipped some tea. 'Well, there we are. Marriage is no rose garden. It's all about putting in that little bit of effort.'

'We couldn't have children,' said Duncan, ignoring her. 'Well it was my fault: *I* couldn't have children.'

Silence again. The hum of the video in the next room. Barking. *101 Dalmatians.* One hundred and one children. *One hundred and one!* Will thought their silence echoed with 'that little bit of effort'. You could hear Sophie giggling in the lounge, and Jack murmuring something to the television. *It's all about putting in that little bit of effort.* Mum looked horrified, but she was the one who spoke first.

'You mean . . . she left you because you couldn't have children?'

'That's right.'

Granny S almost looked pleased, as though this proved that Mum couldn't possibly be dating Duncan if she didn't know this crucial piece of information about him. In fact, even Will wondered if they were just good friends after all.

'She left you for a man who could give her children?' Granny S seemed to want clarification.

'Well, actually, it turned out she was already pregnant with his child when she told me.'

Mum looked devastated. Granny S looked thwarted, which was not her favourite position.

'Well,' she continued, 'that must've been really upsetting. I can see how you might think it compares to grief . . . But of course you can't possibly compare the two. It's like trying to compare the loss of a spouse to the loss of a son. There is just *no comparison*. I mean, I know Freya's been through hell, but it just doesn't compare to a mother's grief.'

Will looked around at the carnage his grandmother had created. Was still creating. It had been a bit of fun to watch her tear Duncan apart – or at least, he had thought so initially. He didn't like Granny S much, but she always gave them something to talk about. In fact, he had enjoyed not liking her. Now he felt ashamed of his connection with this woman and her dogged determination to be right.

'What about losing a father?' said Mum, suddenly defiant.

'Well, *I've* lost both my parents too, Freya, and I can honestly say that—'

'No, I mean, what about your three grandchildren losing their father? They're not in their fifties or sixties, they're six, eleven and seventeen! Grief isn't a competition, Sylvia.'

'Goodness me! I don't know what's got into you. I was only saying—'

'Duncan.' Will could bear it no longer. 'You promised me a driving lesson. Any chance of having it before it gets dark?'

Duncan stood up gratefully. 'Yes, I did. I think we can fit it in now.'

Will stood up too, and shot his mum a knowing glance. Her eyes said, *thank you*. It made him feel good. He had got something right, and his mother was pleased.

10

UNCONDITIONAL

Freya wanted to apologise for Sylvia on the journey home, but it was awkward with the children in the back. Later that evening, after they had returned to their separate homes, she rang Duncan to apologise properly for her mother-in-law's behaviour.

'Don't worry,' he said. 'I should've listened. You did try to warn me.'

'But she was way out of order. And I just want you to know, when I said we weren't an item, I was simply trying to put her off the scent.'

There was an interesting pause, as though they were each trying to take in the implication of this sentence and savour it. 'I wanted to thank you too. And I don't just mean for taking us down, but for giving Will that driving lesson.'

'Don't thank me. I wasn't insured. I can't believe I took that risk. I will get it insured to teach him.'

'But—'

'There's something I wanted to mention – about Will.'

'Will?'

'Yes. When he was driving, I noticed some marks on his arm. I asked him about them. And he . . . he explained them to me.'

'Oh, that. Yes, he was badly bullied, I'm afraid.'

'Is that over now?'

'I think so.' She felt a little uneasy. It was not like Will
sort of thing so easily. 'Good that he felt he could talk to you. That's
good.'

'What do you think about it all?'

She wasn't sure where he was going with this. She wanted to ask
about his divorce. Maybe he was just steering the conversation away
from that.

'Well, obviously I've been very worried about it. It was terrible, but
I thought it was over now. He certainly seemed to have forgotten about
it. I'll have a word with him.'

There was a silence.

'Duncan, I wanted to . . . I had no idea about . . . I'm so sorry.'

'Serena, you mean?'

'Yes.'

'Does it bother you? That I can't have children?'

'God no! I mean, I adore my children, but three's quite enough. In
fact, if anything, I was slightly worried that you might want me to have
another one . . .' She stopped herself, aware of the implication. Oh,
Lord. Now he would think she was going far too fast. Racing ahead.
'Sorry, that came out all wrong. I just wanted you to know that . . . It
must've been so painful for you, and I'm so, so sorry.'

'It's okay.'

No, she thought, it's not okay. None of this was okay. Not the way
he had been treated by Serena or by Sylvia. And she wished her children could be kinder to him. Duncan would clearly be having second
thoughts about the prospect of a relationship with her now. Sylvia had
not only been downright rude to him, but had made it pretty clear that
there was no room in their collective lives for a new man. Freya tried to
broach the subject again, but Duncan said he was tired and heading for
an early night. He had a 'lot to think about'. So she was already feeling
uneasy when she spotted Jack sobbing quietly in front of the television.

'Whatever's the matter?'

Jack shook his head. She sat down beside him and put her arm around him. He leaned into her and she could feel his shoulders tremble gently from time to time. She waited through a whole episode of *The Simpsons*.

'Anything you can share?'

'Nope.'

'Not even with me?'

'No! Especially not you!'

He leapt up from the sofa and ran to his room. Freya followed him slowly. She waited for some time outside his door, and when she went in he told her to 'go away!' She left him for ten minutes, then tried again. This was how it usually worked with Jack. He usually wanted her to try again.

'I can't tell you because someone else will get into trouble,' he said after much gentle coaxing.

'Is it someone at school?'

He shook his head. 'But it will be soon.'

'Is it Will?'

'I can't say!'

Freya sighed. 'You have to tell me.'

He shook his head, then reluctantly mumbled, 'It's something on the family laptop. I wish I hadn't seen it.'

As she squeezed his shoulder and got up to investigate, he called out weakly, 'Don't watch it, Mum! Promise you won't watch it!'

Ten minutes later Freya sat on the edge of her bed with her hand over her mouth. The video, labelled 'Will S-file', was still playing on the laptop, although it was hard to imagine there was any reason to keep watching. It had started off with Will naked and lying on a bed – *her* bed, actually. She had taken in a deep breath, ready to turn it off after she'd seen enough to establish that her son was making naked tapes of himself, when she realised he was talking to someone. Of course, she had intended to stop the video as soon as she found out who the other participant was. He hadn't mentioned any girls recently, and she was curious. She waited, and a hand moved into view. Oh no, she really couldn't watch this! And then the owner of the hand . . . the owner of the hand moved alongside Will, and she could see another naked body on her bed. She should have stopped the tape then, but she couldn't help imagining Jack's reaction to seeing all this. She needed to know suddenly exactly what her youngest son had been exposed to, and so she continued to watch the tape until she felt there could not possibly be any further ways in which two young men could make love to one another.

She stopped the recording and sat, stunned, for some minutes. Slowly she stood up and took the laptop to Will's room.

'It's a *family* laptop,' she said, in as measured a way as possible. She probably ought to be cross with him. Jack was desperately upset. 'Jack has just watched something he shouldn't have seen.'

The blood drained from Will's face. He bent his head into his hands and groaned as though a death had been announced. Then, tentatively, he turned to look at her.

'Oh God! Oh *God* ! Oh, look at your face! Please tell me you didn't watch it? Promise me you didn't watch it! You did, didn't you? You fuck-ing *did*! This is so humiliating! This is the worst day of my life!'

'Will, I only looked at it because Jack was so upset. How do you think it's affected him? He's only eleven!'

When he caught his breath he said softly, 'I didn't know . . . I'd just got up to go to the bathroom. I didn't know he was going to nick it from my bedroom. I was going to save it on a memory stick, I promise. Jesus! Do you think I wanted him to know?'

'Will, putting it there at all wasn't exactly . . . thoughtful of you!'

She cringed at her own words. She had often wondered if Will was gay, but Reuben had said he'd 'had the chat' and he definitely wasn't.

She was genuinely shaken, and hated herself for not having paid more attention to her son. She had been ready to be angry with him when she'd first pressed 'Play', but now she could see how his most intimate privacy had been invaded – by his own mother – and she was desperately sorry for him.

'Well, whilst we're talking about kindness,' he said, 'you might ask yourself what effect your denial was having on me!'

'What denial?'

'Oh, come on! Over years of knowing I was gay and saying *nothing*. Imagine how that's felt for me, knowing that even my own mother disapproves.'

She felt completely adrift. 'Will, sweetheart, I swear I didn't know. I've *guessed* you might be, but I was waiting for you to tell me. I thought that if you were, you just weren't quite ready to come out.'

'Yeah, right. Come off it, Mum. You always just agreed with everything Dad said and did, and he wasn't having any of it – he was in complete denial and therefore so were you. Dad, yes, Dad I could almost understand, but *you* . . . I always thought you loved me unconditionally. I always . . . thought . . .'

His voice trailed off, partly caught by a constriction in his throat and partly silenced by the look of shock on his mother's face.

'*Dad?* Dad *knew*?'

His mother gazed at him in horror. He was forced, quite suddenly, to reassess his perceptions of events. She wanted information, and so he told her.

He had been fifteen and wildly in love with a boy at school. It wasn't the first time he'd had feelings for another boy, but it was the first time they had been plainly reciprocated. It had become serious quite swiftly, and he found himself walking on air, thinking of no one else but this darkhaired, dark-eyed boy called Rashid. At first, hiding around corners and fumbling under bushes had been exciting, little lies to conceal who they were with and where they were going were thrilling, all their secret rendezvous heightened the romance of the affair; but soon he felt as though his wings were clipped. There was no possibility of ever holding hands in public or kissing each other hello or goodbye. The little ordinary gestures of affection were forbidden to them, and he wanted to scream and shout their love from the rooftops. It was all very well joining the guilty ranks of people having affairs, but all those unfaithful spouses and lovers *chose* their deception. He wasn't a natural liar and he didn't want to live a lie. So it was then, one day when his father came home early from work and asked what he was doing home, that Will had said he was spending some quality time with Rashid. His father stared icily at Rashid and told him to go, and Will became furious.

'What the hell—'

'What do you mean, "quality time"?'

'Well, it may have escaped your notice – because most things concerning me do – but I'm gay.'

'Don't be ridiculous!' Reuben had let out a rather terrifyingly forced guffaw. 'For goodness' sake!'

'I'm serious, Dad. I'm gay, so you'd better get used to it.'

He'd been about to swan off and slam the door behind him when his father grabbed him by the shoulder and told him to sit down. 'Hey, come on, let's talk about this.' His voice became suddenly very controlled. 'I know you may think you're gay, and God knows there are so many pressures on young people these days to decide what they are sexually at an age long before *we* even knew what sex *was*, but . . . the thing is, everyone goes through phases.'

'Dad, this isn't a phase. I love Rashid.'

His father sighed. It wasn't a giving-up sigh but an avuncular, how-can-I-explain sigh. 'The thing is, Will, even *I* had a bit of a crush on a guy in my teens. It's quite normal. You're experimenting with all sorts of longings and desires. It happens to everyone. And then the right girl comes along and *hey presto*!'

'Dad, you're not hearing me. I've known I was gay since I was six. I've *never* fancied a girl.'

Dad was becoming agitated again. 'What about Harriet Holland from over the road? You were mad about her!'

'She had a guinea pig called Silas.'

'*You* had a guinea pig.'

'Yes, but only because I was copying her. I swear I never fancied her. It was Silas I had my eye on.'

He thought his father might laugh, but he didn't. His face flushed. 'Look, Will, you'll just have to take my word for it. This is probably just a phase. There's no need to go round telling everyone. Just give it a year or two and see how you feel then.'

'I don't need to give it a year or two. Let's face it, Dad, it's *you* who needs a year or two to get used to the idea, isn't it?'

'Look, don't go calling me homophobic. I have lots of friends who are gay – good friends.'

'Really? Who?'

'People you don't know. Anyway, I'm fine with homosexuality – I just don't think you're gay. Look, I brought you up. I know you.'

'But that's just it, you don't. There's a bit of me I've had to keep hidden for years because I knew you'd be just like this if I told you. It's textbook stuff. Next you'll be saying, "Where did I go *wrong*?"'

'Well . . . look . . .' His father seemed confused, as if maybe that had been exactly what he intended to ask next. 'Hey, hey . . . listen. Let's suppose you *are* gay – and I'm certain you're not – but let's suppose you *are*. You can't really expect us to be thrilled, can you? I mean, it's not *ideal* is it?'

Will had stared at his father, unsure whether to be intrigued by the sudden inclusion of the word 'us' into the debate, or by the idea that his father thought there was an ideal form of sexuality, from which he, Will, helplessly diverged.

'You just don't want me to be gay, do you? You're ashamed of me!'

'No – but you're *not* gay!'

'I *am*, you hypocritical bigot!'

And that was when Will had stormed out of the room and slammed the door. He had said what he wanted to say and his father wasn't listening. One of the last things he'd called his father before he died (along with 'fascist twat' when he wouldn't let him study Art A-level) was 'hypocritical bigot'. Nobody knew, and when everyone – including him – was praising his father at the funeral, Will looked at the golden eagle in the church and remembered nativity readings. And like Mary in the Bible, he kept all these things and pondered them in his heart.

Rashid never spoke to him again – apart from a text to say it had to end. He was terrified *his* father would find out. The thought that Will's dad might tell him had meant he couldn't sleep for weeks. Will had loved Rashid. He had truly loved him. And then he had moved away to another school, and Will hoped it wasn't because his father *had* found out some-how. He couldn't bear to think of how Rashid would have coped with that.

Now his mother clasped her palm to her forehead and sat down heavily on Will's bed. 'You told *Dad* you were gay? When? *When?*' Her face was the colour of pastry, and she looked haunted, her mouth ajar. There was a sudden silence for several seconds, broken only by her halting breath. 'Oh, Will! I never knew. I mean . . . he never said.' She went over to him and cradled his head in her arms. 'My poor, poor baby. I'm so sorry. You must've felt so alone.'

He could tell she was crying, and he cried too, great whooping sobs that made his cheeks sore and his nose run.

'I'm sorry about the video,' he said at last. 'It was stupid of me.'

'Yes, it was. Hideously stupid.' She kissed his hair and breathed in the wonderful sweaty scent of her firstborn child. 'But I love you.'

11

SECOND BEST

Duncan felt infected by some pathogen taking hold of every part of him. He had thought he had all this under control, but Sylvia had released all sorts of toxins into his system. Or maybe she had just spotted them there already.

He couldn't make comparisons in grief, of course not, and it had never occurred to him to look for them. But he wondered now if it wasn't a lesser-known fact that, in the bloody massacre that marked the end of a long and loving relationship after betrayal, the first stretcher cases were the sweetest creatures of all: the first kisses, first vows, first tumblings on to mattresses on the floors of poky lodgings, fumblings in long grass, longings for trains to arrive, sobbings as they departed. All these innocent victims carried off first from the battlefield, the most seriously injured, dying almost inevitably in the ambulance. A far cry from the carefully dusted framed photos and the oft-told stories of dead lovers. Those tales retold so many times, so lovingly nipped and tucked, snipped of the bits you'd prefer to forget, padded gently with new bits you'd like to have happened, honed and polished into a palatable and enjoyable story, or, as it seemed to be called now – referring to anything from an oil painting to a political manifesto – a 'narrative'. Yes, the *narrative* could be played around with until it pleased everyone concerned: the parents, the children, the lovers, and recounted like a joke with the smoothest punchline in the world. Everything added up. Everything was just so. A sudden death was a clean clout over the head leaving all the memory footage intact, to be enhanced and Photoshopped in any way that pleased. A betrayal swallowed the story whole, and there was nothing lovely to look back on.

The photograph albums were no comfort. Each smile seemed deceitful, each arm around the shoulder a sad mockery. Those albums sat tight on dark bookshelves or in attics, waiting to ambush your tranquillity one day with their ridicule. And then, maybe, far into the future, they might become a mere record of your self-delusion and gullibility, and you could toss them into a skip.

Duncan couldn't sleep. The rain was pelting down outside, hitting the windows like someone drumming their nails on the glass. He had managed to block Serena out of his life – more or less – for a couple of years now. He hadn't expected to be forced to remember her in quite such a giddy, public way. The injustice of it had been bad enough at the time, but having Sylvia put her own discreditable label on his divorce was sickening.

Serena's sheepish look at the moment of her revelation kept popping up in his dreams. But now, quite suddenly, he remembered another look in his ex-wife's sculpted face. It had been determined – indignant almost – her jaw jutting slightly. She hadn't told him first that she was pregnant (that was some relief, at least; she had spared him the dance of joy around the kitchen before the bad news that it wasn't his). She had told him, in the most roundabout way possible, that she was having an affair. She had been standing in the hall with her luggage one evening while he was cooking their evening meal. *I'm afraid I won't be eating with you this evening.* Or ever again, as it happened. And then the long slow shock that she was seeing someone else, the delivery like a paper plane, drifting quietly in an arc to nosedive quickly at the end. That was the sheepish look. He had wanted to know so much, of course, so many missing pieces to this information. She was awkward with her replies. It hadn't been easy between them for a long time (which later became 'unbearable') and Andy had been so easy-going and such *fun*. It was only later, after the questions about sex (he swore he would never ask what anyone else was like in bed, but she seemed to want to tell him anyway, or at least to imply it) that the little chin jut began almost imperceptibly. And then the final swipe: she was pregnant.

So, he said bitterly, she had found someone to impregnate her. Andy was a sperm donor. Oh, she said. *How dare he!* Out came the chin. She hadn't been happy with Duncan. How could he blame her? They had been trying for a baby for years and it had ruined everything between them. It was no wonder she had looked for love elsewhere, but how dare he suggest she had tried to get pregnant. It had just happened. These things *just happened*. It had been the sword swipe to deliver the fatal blow, and it hit home. And when he had said to Sylvia that Serena had been pregnant before she left him, that little chin jut had come back to him, and everything it implied. Don't ever try and blame me. He is a real man. *He gave me what you couldn't.*

For all that this unbidden memory tormented him (together with the idea that he was once again destined to be second best if he ever entertained the idea of following in Reuben's footsteps), it was something else that stopped the comfort of sleep.

He had been grateful to Will for helping him escape Sylvia's vitriol, and had even dared to believe that there might be some perverse common ground to be found there, but something Will had said had given him pause for thought.

They had driven a fairly anodyne circular route of the lanes around the bungalow, and Duncan had been relieved to see that Will was more cautious than he had expected, especially given that he had completely forgotten about the need to insure the car for a learner driver. He would sort that out as soon as he got home. Will's sleeves were ridiculously long, as if he was going for the 'oversized' look that some women adopted. At one point, he pushed them up to get them out of the way, but then swiftly pushed them down again and just rolled the wrists up. In that moment, though, Duncan had spotted the dark pink criss-crossing of lines on his inner arms.

When they stopped on the side of the road to practise a gentle hill start, Will had said suddenly, without looking at him, 'You know I'm gay, don't you?'

Duncan did not know, although the fact itself did not surprise him at all. 'I didn't know,' he said simply, then realised that something else was needed. 'Does it bother you?'

'Does it bother *you*?'

'Of course not. Is there any reason why it should?'

Will sniffed and straightened his arms on the wheel. 'Well, it seems to bother Mum. She's in complete denial about it.'

Duncan frowned. 'Oh. I find that hard to believe. Are you sure?'

'Oh yes. She didn't tell you, then? You see what I mean.'

As they had driven back on to the gravel drive, Freya had appeared at her in-laws' front window and looked out earnestly.

'Are you sure she knows?'

'Oh yes. She's known for over two years.'

He remembered Freya saying that her eldest son had 'issues', but she was so kind when she talked about her children that it didn't make any sense. 'It seems so unlike her.'

'There are lots of things about Mum you don't know, clearly.' He took the key out of the ignition and handed it to Duncan. 'Thanks for the lesson.'

When Will closed the driver's door, he looked over the top of the car and said, 'Do you mean it – about it making no difference?'

'I do.'

This troubled version of Freya now stopped Duncan's eyelids from staying shut. She had phoned him earlier to apologise for her mother-in-law's behaviour. Okay, good. But what did he really know about this woman he had fallen for? He tried to make a list. It might work better than counting sheep. One, she still adored her late husband. (Did he care? Yes.) Two, ergo, he would always be second best. (Was he prepared to put up with that? No.) Three, her family were all hostile to him. (Well, Sylvia in particular, but Sylvia was hideously hostile.) Four, she may not be the person he thought she was. Will had seemed convinced she was practically homophobic. Okay, this last point seemed ridiculous. It was especially ridiculous because he knew that if he told his colleague Lottie honestly how he felt about being second best, she would've suggested the relationship was doomed at One or Two with absolutely no need to go into Four. In conclusion, there was no point going on in this bizarre, masochistic fashion. He was so certain to come a cropper that he might as well give up now. Yes, he decided he would have to call time on this relationship. He would do it sensitively. He imagined telling Freya, and convinced himself he could do this, that he was in control of his feelings. He wouldn't shift his view slightly to see how desolate life would be without her, or to glimpse how helplessly he was already starting to care about them all. He rolled over on to his other side to try to get some sleep.

When he awoke, he felt momentarily elated. There was a recurring dream he woke from with a giddy sense of joy, as he did now. In the few moments between waking and realising that it was not true, he knew something of the enormity of his longing for children. Not a lot happened in the dream. He was standing in a field somewhere, a sloping field with a view. Sometimes he was gazing at a valley with glittering loops of river snaking through the green; sometimes it was a field of sheep with lambs. The weather was always glorious in these dreams. The sun was warming him and, as he gazed ahead, a small hand reached up to his. He could feel the hand precisely: it was soft and pliable, but it *reached* for his hand. Looking down, he saw his small son or daughter (today it was a daughter), aged about two, he had worked out from the height, but the dream child never looked at him, intent also on the view. The little girl today had on a blue dress with white flowers. He could see it from the corner of his eye. There was something in the deliberateness of the reach, in the obvious confidence the child had that Duncan was there, that filled his heart to bursting. It was a feeling he never had in waking life.

Not being able to have children had changed something in Duncan that he didn't care to examine too deeply, but he could not escape the fact that he wanted them. This great hollow inside him. Not up to the mark. Women were reminded of their fertility – or lack of it – every month, but men had no idea until it was tested. His infertility wasn't a problem with Freya. She had her full count of kids and she wasn't – it seemed – looking to have more. But Sylvia's words still hollowed him out. He was wasting his time with her. He wasn't up to the mark. *No one can replace Reuben, you realise that.*

When he went into work on Monday morning, he told Lottie his decision. She laughed. Then when Freya texted to invite him for a meal with her children on Friday evening, *just to get to know them better*, he said he couldn't. Freya didn't beg him. He felt rude. She texted back to say that was a pity, but she understood it was a bit daunting. So he said yes, he'd go.

Lottie's eyes said, Pushover!

12

MAGIC

As it turned out, Friday was a day off for Sophie as well, as the primary school was flooded. Duncan and Freya took Sophie out for a walk in the fields and woods. The grass was damp and shiny underfoot and the palette of autumn colours in the trees was expanding each week. The cuckoos and swifts had already left for more southerly warmth, but a lone swallow swooped across the sky ahead, dipping its wing in farewell as it made its way over the bronze, gold and orange canopies of the glistening trees.

In the afternoon, Freya said she was just popping out for a few things at the shop. He offered to go himself, but she wanted to choose some things for tea. Duncan was very unsure about this. What if Sophie minded being left with him? Freya was adamant that she wouldn't, that she would play quietly on her own, and she, Freya, would only be gone ten minutes.

As soon as she was gone, Duncan went upstairs for the bathroom. There was a toilet under the stairs, but he just wanted to check something. He pushed Freya's bedroom door open a little and closed his eyes on what he saw, letting out a heavy sigh. Reuben was still there. He went downstairs irritated, ashamed at how disappointed he felt.

Sophie was waiting for him. She didn't mind at all being left with him. In fact, she wanted him to join in her game. The hedgehogs' school, under the piano, was flooded, and they didn't know what to do. They would drown if help didn't come soon because none of them could swim. He piled some small whiskered creatures that looked like cats into a slipper and told her the fire brigade was on its way. Sophie enjoyed the racket he made as the slipper sped across the carpet and around the back of the television, but ultimately rejected the rescue attempt. A fire engine in a flood was no good. There was no fire to put out. And anyway, cats couldn't swim. He searched around for a solution, then took off his shoe and threw in some ducks. They went full speed ahead in their rescue boat, making even more noise than the fire engine with their raucous quacking. Sophie seemed pleased. But just as the hedgehogs were all safely placed either in the boat or on a duck's back, there came another threat. Matilda the cruel Barbie doll emerged from a cave behind the sofa and threatened to kill them all. She was certainly ten times the size of any of them and put their rescue in real jeopardy. Two of the small hedgehogs had already fallen out of the boat. Sophie seemed intent on disaster at any cost, or perhaps she just wanted him to show her how to evade it.

'You're not too keen on Matilda, are you?'

'No. She's horrible.'

'Why's that, then? She looks nice enough.'

'She tries to hurt me, though – and the animals, so I have to hurt her first before she can hurt us.'

'I see.'

'Jack usually hangs her.'

Duncan wasn't sure about hanging a doll. Still, he felt Matilda was important, and he didn't want her running loose and getting up to no good.

'Hanging clearly doesn't work. Does she often hurt you?'

'She tries.'

'And how do you stop her?'

'Sometimes the animals gang up on her and sometimes I just hurt myself so she doesn't bother.'

Duncan tried to carry on as if she hadn't said this and he put Matilda inside the piano stool and sat on it. 'Prison. That'll keep her out of harm's way.'

Sophie smiled approvingly. 'The otters are coming to the rescue! This one's called Ottoline. What's yours called?'

'Er . . . Simon.'

'*Hello Simon and Ottoline,* shouted the ducks, *can you help us? Yes,* said Ottoline. *I can dive off a high rock.*' At this point she shoved one of the otters off the sofa. '*What can you do?* they asked Simon.'

'Um . . . *I can do magic.*'

'Magic? . . . No, he doesn't do magic. Something else.'

At a loss to know where he had failed, Duncan said, in an otter voice that was somehow Italian, '*I can sing.*'

'Now the otters rescue the hedgehogs and Mrs Hedgehog asks Simon to sing them to sleep.'

'*O sole mio . . .*'

Sophie tucked them in and made them snore contentedly.

'Dunking . . . ?' she asked without looking up. 'Do you believe in magic?'

It took Duncan a few seconds to realise that this was not part of the game.

He opened his mouth to speak and found himself hesitating. 'Believe in' was a loaded phrase. Perhaps he should be careful.

'Well, there is no such thing as magic in the *real* world, but it's fun to have it in fairy tales and things.'

Sophie eyed him cautiously. 'Well, how do people do things by magic, then?'

'Well, it's all a trick, an illusion. That's why they're called magic "tricks". The magician tricks you into believing something has happened which hasn't really happened. It's clever, but it's not magic.' He picked up a froglet and put it in his left hand, then drew it from behind his right ear. 'You see? A trick.'

He expected her to ask him how he did it, but she looked troubled. 'But what about real magic? When people make bad things happen?'

'Like what?'

'When someone says something bad will happen if you don't keep a secret?'

He felt a rush of panic. 'Sophie, no one can make bad things happen to you by magic. Anyone who says bad things will happen to you if you don't do what they say is threatening you, and that's bad.'

Sophie squished her mouth to one side. They heard Chunkables clatter out through the cat flap, and a blackbird gave an alarm call outside.

He had a feeling in his gut that this was an important conversation. He didn't know if he was up to it, but he tried to sound casual and reassuring at the same time.

'People make threats because they're afraid. You told Jack last week that if he didn't get his hands off your birthday cake he wasn't going to get a crumb of it, but you didn't mean it. You just wanted him to do as you said.'

Sophie stared at the hedgehogs and chewed her lip, scratching her wrist vigorously. 'Are you sure that no one can do magic?'

'Absolutely certain.' He reached out and touched her arm without thinking. 'Has someone been threatening you, Sophie? Is someone saying they'll hurt you if you don't do what they say?'

He asked the question as gently as he could, but still her eyes were shining with tears. She shook her head slowly.

'Because if they are, you must tell someone. No harm can come to you by telling someone.'

'But that's not true!' She looked at him desperately. 'It's not me, it's a friend. She told a secret to her cat and . . .'

He wanted to put his arms around her, but he dared not.

'And what, Sophie?'

'And her . . . someone died!'

He heard, with some relief, the car pull up outside. He knelt in front of her, keeping an elbow on the piano stool to make sure Matilda couldn't escape. 'One thing I can promise you: no one died because she told her cat anything. Cats are interesting creatures, but they can't talk, and they certainly can't do magic.'

She lifted a red, tear-stained face to him. 'How can you be sure?'

'Because there's no such thing.'

'But it wasn't her cat who did it. She only *told* him. What if it was a punishment for telling him?'

'No one can make something bad happen by magic. No one.'

'Are you certain?'

'I am.' He stroked her hand. 'And if she doesn't believe that, tell her to talk to her mum. It always feels better to talk to someone. Then she won't have to be afraid any more.'

'No! No, she can't tell her mummy. Then her mummy might die too!'

He was way out of his depth now. He spoke very gently to her.

'Well . . . maybe tell her to talk to a grown-up she can trust – a teacher, perhaps. Then everything will feel better. There'll be no need to feel afraid.'

He felt the doll under his elbow was laughing at him, and he had no inclination to move in case she leapt out. But he did move. They both turned their heads suddenly to a strange noise, because there, standing at the lounge doorway, arms folded, was Granny Sylvia.

His last words, about there being no need to be afraid, seemed to hang menacingly in the air. He shot his playmate an affectionate and nervous look of complicity and picked up Simon. '*O sole mio, sta 'nfronte a te . . .*'

13

THE ENEMY'S ENEMY

When Jack arrived home from school he could see Duncan out in the back garden fixing some trellis that had fallen down. It was okay if Duncan was useful like this, but he didn't want him getting too cosy. Mum said he was coming to tea today and they all had to make him feel welcome. Jack was just wondering what this might entail when he opened the back door to see Granny Sylvia sitting at the kitchen table with Mum. This was the last thing any of them needed.

He tried to say hello brightly, but what came out was the sort of 'hello' you might give a Jehovah's Witness when you were expecting the postman with a parcel. It was the Hello of Disappointment that he and Will joked about when discussing Granny Sylvia. He smirked a little at the thought of this and turned to the fridge to hide it. He took out a couple of cereal bars and then chose an apple from the fruit bowl.

'Steady on!' said Granny Sylvia. 'You'll spoil your tea.'

'They always have a snack when they come home,' said Mum.

'A *snack*? That's more like a feast! It's no wonder you're getting chubby, Jack.'

'He's not chubby!' said Mum almost fiercely, but he could see from the corner of his eye that she was glaring *meaningfully* at Granny S. This was a waste of time because Granny S was not subtle.

He took his rucksack and snack and left the kitchen, hearing something like: 'Well, I'm only saying . . . he won't have any girlfriends when he's older if he's obese . . .'

Jack sat down carefully and silently on the sofa in the lounge. All the words that Granny Sylvia had just said were now in his head, and he felt that if he moved his head even slightly, then these things might be disturbed and come out. They might ooze out of his nose or ears; they might stream forth from his mouth in a gush of vomit, or else become so disturbed and jiggly that his skull would explode. So he held himself very still. He reached into his rucksack, beside him on the sofa, and felt about in the front pocket for his secret emergency stash. It was a squashed Milky Way with the chocolate coating all cracked – and worse: it was warm. He hated warm chocolate. Still, needs must. He ate it in two mouthfuls. He didn't even enjoy it. That was the worst thing. He was so upset that he would have to go upstairs soon for his usual emergency stash, which was under his Lego in a shoebox under the bed. Mum never looked in his Lego box because he didn't play with it any more, so she never needed to tidy it away. He knew she found his hidden wrappers occasionally because sometimes they disappeared, but she never looked in his Lego box. The thing about a secret stash was that you had to keep it topped up, but the trouble with keeping it topped up was that you knew it was there. It was there, even if you didn't want it, calling to you, promising its sweet consolation.

However, for the time being he was going to stay where he was because he had just heard Granny S dropping her voice and saying, 'You need to watch him, Freya. I'm serious.'

'Sylvia, please . . .'

'I caught him playing with Sophie.'

'Well, what's wrong with that?'

'You know very well what I'm talking about. He was saying there was nothing to be afraid of . . .'

Jack strained to hear now, because he knew they didn't think he was listening.

'I'm sorry, Sylvia. Duncan is my friend, and I think I know him.'

'Oh, that's what they all say!'

Jack was relieved they were not talking about him any more. Even though he didn't want Duncan getting in on everything, he suddenly felt almost protective of him. If Granny Sylvia had it in for him as well, that put Duncan squarely on his side. They were, curiously, allies. And actually, Duncan didn't have any of the spite of Granny Sylvia. In fact, with his short, dead-straight brown hair, which was slightly tufty, he looked a bit like a hedgehog. Come to think of it, there *was* something a bit hedgehoggy about him. The way that hedgehogs shuffled across the lawn almost apologetically, as if they didn't really own the space they lived in . . . Duncan was kind of like that. In fact, there was nothing really threatening about Duncan at all. Apart from the fact that he could turn their family upside down all over again. You had to remember that. Still, you couldn't help feeling a bit sorry for him.

'Believe you me, these men that go trawling the internet for young mothers with small children . . .' Granny Sylvia was still chuntering on.

'Right! I've got to get on with preparing the tea.'

'Oh, don't make anything special for me – I'm on a diet. Unlike *some* people!'

'I'm sorry, Sylvia. I'm not making anything for you. I didn't know you were coming.'

'I always come up to Cheltenham for the last weekend of the Literature Festival to stay with my friend Jenny. I thought you might remember.'

'Well, I'm sorry, I didn't – and I have a guest already.'

'Oh . . . I see.' There was a silence. 'I suppose it's him, is it?' She nodded to the back garden. Mum said nothing. There was a weird silence. All you could hear was Mum clattering a saucepan on the hob very loudly.

'Well . . . I'd better be going then. I'll just go up and say hello and goodbye to Sophie and Will.'

Jack hoped Will wasn't watching porn.

14

SOPHIE'S PIECE OF MIND

Granny S said she would like to give 'that man' a piece of her mind, which was strange. Sophie can't imagine wanting to give anyone a piece of her mind, not only because she doesn't want anyone to see it, but because if she gave some of it away there would be less of it. But then Granny S isn't very good at sums. She's always saying, 'I was *hopeless* at maths', with a laugh, as if it's something to be proud of. She often says she would like to give someone a piece of her mind. Maybe there isn't much of it left now. It is a surprisingly generous offer coming from her. In fact, it is probably just one of those things she pretends she's going to give you to make you excited, like when she promised Sophie a doll's house.

Granny S talked about the doll's house all the time, and used it like a bribe for ages and ages. 'If you eat up all your food, next time I come up I'll bring you a doll's house.' 'If you're a good girl and leave your eyelashes alone, I'll be bringing up that doll's house.' The excitement each time Granny's car crunched into the driveway is something Sophie still remembers, ghosts of the thrill still conjured up whenever she hears a car's tyres on gravel anywhere.

Of course, there was no doll's house. Mummy is still cross about that, because she didn't Follow Through. Sophie heard her on the phone and the words 'doll's house' made her listen. 'I'm sorry, Sylvia, but you can't make promises to children to get them to do things you want, and then not follow through.' It was a stern voice she didn't normally use, and never to Granny Sylvia. Mummy and Will still talk about *the doll's house aga* or something. It means they don't trust Granny to keep her promises.

Sophie doesn't trust Granny S either. She smiles when she isn't pleased and has a madwoman look, which is made even more mad by her drawn-on eyebrows and clown lipstick. She puts the lipstick over the edges of her lips to make them look bigger, but you can see they are thin. Her body is thin too, like there is no softness to her at all, and there are ropy pillars in her neck like a wire structure holding her head up. She wonders what a piece of Granny's mind might look like. Like a piece of chicken breast that Mum cuts up for stew, maybe. Or the gloopy frogspawn on the nature table last year. The funny thing about Granny's mind is that she never seems to offer it to people she likes, so maybe it looks really yucky and she knows it.

Sophie kneels on her bed and looks out of the window. Gloria is grazing in the field beyond the garden. She looks up when she catches Sophie's movement at the window, and Sophie smiles at her, hoping she can see. The window is wet. It is always wet. At the bottom of the pane there is a clammy black line of sooty stuff, and in the corner of the pane there is mould. The metal frames are flecked with black and the paint is peeling. Sophie opens the window to wave at Gloria. The outside stone is dappled in white and yellow splodges like the rash of some weird disease. Jack calls this 'liken', but she doesn't see why because it's not really something you'd like. She calls it 'I-don't-liken', but Jack just laughs. One day they will have new windows with no black mould and the glass will be dry all winter. Gloria is looking at her now and chewing and smiling. One day Gloria will have lambs with trembly tails and carpety heads and she will take one into school and everyone will be amazed. She won't tell Gloria, though, because she doesn't want to give her false hope.

15

FUN MUM SUPPER

The following week, Duncan rang Freya to invite her over on Friday.

'It's still my turn,' she said. The family meal had been a disaster. Will had suddenly remembered an urgent meeting with a friend and Sylvia had dropped him off in town. 'Last week was a bit unfortunate, what with Sophie being home, and then Sylvia arriving.'

'About that . . .'

'What?'

'Sophie. About Sophie. I was going to talk to you about something she said.'

'Oh?' Once again, she felt uneasy. Duncan seemed to be more in touch with her children than she was, these days. Had she taken her eye off the ball with all this dating?

'I'll talk to you when I'm over.'

It had been two weeks since they had been properly alone together. They tumbled on to the sofa and she tried to take him upstairs.

'No,' he said, rather decisively. 'Stay here. I don't want to be overlooked.'

She wondered if he meant by Reuben. She didn't really want to ask and spoil the moment. He seemed very serious. 'Come on,' she said, tugging at his pullover. He wouldn't budge. 'There's a robin eyeing you from the garden. He can see everything.'

'I don't care.'

There was a smile curling at the edge of his mouth that saved the day.

Curled up with him later, Freya felt mean not to have taken the picture down. There had been something in Duncan's initial expression when he'd said he didn't want to be overlooked which had definitely not been playful. It obviously cut deep. She wasn't going to take it down, but she didn't want him feeling excluded by it. She stroked his face.

'It would be good to do more things all together – as a family. Why don't you come for tea tomorrow? Make up for last time?'

'I'd like that.' He kissed the top of her head.

'You were going to talk about Sophie.'

'Yes.' He was quiet for a moment, as if reconsidering this. 'I have to be careful here, I think. She may have told me something important. Something you should know, but if she knows I told you . . . well, she won't trust me again. Does that make sense?'

Freya got up swiftly and urgently on her elbow. 'What do you mean? What's happened?'

'I don't know. It could be nothing. But she said someone had told her a secret, and if she told anyone, something bad could happen. She was afraid you might die.'

'Oh. Oh crumbs.' She felt a little wave of terror. 'What do you think she could mean? Do you think . . . ?

'It may be nothing. But I thought you ought to know. She was a bit tearful.'

'Tearful?'

'Someone might be bullying her, putting harmful pressure on her.'

Freya was choked up with panic. 'Why didn't she tell *me*?'

'I suggested she talk to you, but she was terrified that harm would come to you.'

'I suppose, after her dad dying, she is more susceptible to fears like that.'

'Maybe. But please don't tell her I told you. She's genuinely scared.'

Freya winced at this. It hurt to think of Sophie being any more afraid of life than she clearly already was. 'Could it be some kid messing around?'

'It could be.'

'Okay.' She breathed out deeply. 'Thank you.'

'I didn't want you to worry about it. Just be aware.'

He stroked her hair and she let herself rest on his chest. She would keep a closer eye on Sophie.

'Oh, it's you,' said Will sullenly, when he saw Duncan in the kitchen the next day. Freya, flinching, told Will to go and fetch the others.

She had it in hand. All three children were home and all their tastes would be catered for. It was simple food, and little could go wrong with it. She brought out the pasta with homemade pesto (Jack and Sophie's favourite) as soon as everyone was seated, and made sure the huge salad was well dressed with her homemade dressing (one of Will's favourites). Duncan made awkward conversation about the delights of these humble offerings, and the children, to her dismay, said nothing. Perhaps they were all feeling awkward too.

The barely audible music, which Freya had put on very softly in the background, seemed, by default, to come to the foreground.

'Remember when Dad used to dance around the kitchen?' said Jack.

'Yeah,' laughed Will. 'He used to go mad with his dancing.'

'Yeah, he was great.'

The soft notes of the music did not seem the sort you could go mad to, and Freya could see they were conjuring up an image of their father to challenge Duncan. She pushed her pasta round her plate irritably. No one said anything more for some time.

'How's it going in Art, Will?' she ventured, trying to shoot him a look that implored conversation.

'Fine.'

The silence was so inescapable that you could hear the mastication of pasta and salad as if a pneumatic drill had started up inside their mouths. She gave Will a doleful glance, and he responded with, 'Hey, remember when you said I couldn't do Art for A-level?'

'No, I didn't,' said Freya.

'Yes, you did. You said it was a doss subject and I'd never get a job if I did Art and Photography.'

'Will! I didn't. That was . . .' It was Reuben. Reuben had insisted he not do Art. She hadn't wanted to argue with her husband in front of Will, but she had argued with him in private. Twenty per cent of the economy was held together by the creative industries, she had said. And anyway, their children should follow their passions, not the job market. It wasn't for them to choose Will's future for him. Reuben had been adamant, and she reminded him that having given up on his own degree, he could hardly talk. She put her pasta fork down in remembrance of her indignation. Yes, *she* had given up a degree she loved in Botany to have his child, while *he* had continued with his degree. Then at the last minute he had just given up, because he was 'bored' and it 'wasn't his thing' and never had been really. If her father hadn't given him a job in his printing company, he would never have got anywhere. How dare he say that Will couldn't pursue a career he was passionate about.

'Actually, that was your father.'

'No, you agreed with him.'

'Well, you're doing Art now, aren't you? So obviously I backed you.'

Will stuffed a great wodge of salad into his mouth while he thought about this, giving Jack the opportunity to make Mum-enhancing conversation too.

'Hey, Mum, remember that time you killed Alan Lewis?'

'I didn't kill him. He fell.'

Duncan looked confused.

'Alan Lewis was our guinea pig,' supplied Sophie, entering into the spirit of things, 'and Mummy killed him.'

'I *didn't* kill him. He fell off the top step of the slide.'

'You dropped him,' said Jack, grinning.

Freya sighed. It had been Jack's idea to put Alan Lewis down the slide, and she had only been trying to oblige and keep the poor animal safe. She had been planning to hold him all the way down, something that Jack would certainly not have done, but he had simply walked off the top step.

'I didn't realise I was friends with a murderer,' said Duncan, grinning.

'I didn't realise the lemming-like tendencies of our guinea pig.' She sounded like Jovial Mum. 'Any more parmesan for anyone?'

This was a terrible mistake. Why had she imagined her children would act normally, would be the strange, quirky, loveable, chatty beings they usually were at mealtimes?

'Mum' – Sophie looked like she might be going to say something endearing – 'do you remember when it was Jack's birthday and all the mums brought their children to Cattle Country and you'd booked the wrong day?'

'Yes,' said Jack with delight, 'and you'd left all the goody-bags at home, so there wasn't even *that* to cheer people up.'

So this was it. They weren't going to big their mother up to her new man, just in case he got too fond of her. No, they were going to edit out anything half-decent she had ever done and play the Crap Mum video for him. *This is what our life has been like. See how she dictates our choices, see how she cocks everything up.*

'Hey, Mum . . .'

Why didn't they remember the nights she read to each one of them in turn, and the special nights since Reuben's death when they all piled into her bed and she read them some picture book, sharing the silly voices with Will? Why didn't they remember the time she queued for three hours with Will to see some God-awful rock star at a music shop in London? Or the parties she had let Will have, staining their poor carpet and burning holes in it? Or the time she stayed up all night for a week in hospital when Sophie was ill? Or when she had made a parrot out of scraps when Jack had desperately wanted to be Long John Silver for a school Book Day? Or the cat costume she made for Sophie's minor part in a school production? Or the hours she had made wicked Matilda speak in Sophie's games? Or the lamb she had made for Jack that he still took to bed with him? Or anything, really. Anything normal or good out of the years she had mothered them, supported them, wept for them, taken their part and believed in them. Was there nothing they remembered? Would they wheel out these grim memories of dead pets and disastrous birthdays to their children and grandchildren? *Granny Freya, what a disaster she was!*

'So,' said Duncan. 'Where did you go on holiday this summer?'

There was a short – only slightly uncomfortable – silence.

'Devon,' said Will, coming to the rescue. In fact, they had been to stay at Sylvia and Steve's house because they couldn't afford to go away. 'And we went to the beach as well.' This was true. They had gone on day trips from the house to the beach as often as possible.

'And on the way back we went to Glastonbury,' added Jack. 'It was great! You could see for miles from the top of the tor!'

'One day we're going to go to Italy, aren't we?' said Sophie. 'Mummy wants to go to Italy one day.'

'Who wants apple pie and ice cream?'

Fortunately, no one said they wanted anything different. There was no reminiscing of collapsed soufflés or sludgy stews. It was as if they were satisfied with their performance and could now happily knuckle down to the job of eating peacefully. Duncan commented on how glorious the pie was – a torte, really – and it was true that it was one of her best. Sophie had helped her, she said. She bit her tongue, waiting for some new comment to blacken her name, but none came. Duncan even ventured to ask Jack what his favourite food was, and to compliment Sophie for helping to arrange the apple slices so well.

'Duncan . . . ?' Sophie looked at Duncan with curiosity. 'Have you got a disease?'

This was out of the blue. Now what?

'No . . . no, I don't think so. Why do you ask?'

Sophie licked her spoon thoughtfully. 'It's just that Granny Sylvia said I mustn't let you touch me.'

The music had stopped. The silence seemed to stop everyone's spoon from moving and to freeze every part of their bodies except their eyes, which darted this way and that, looking for reactions. Freya could hear the blood pumping through her temples. *Remember that paedo you went out with, Mum?*

Gloria bleated from somewhere in the next field.

Sophie waited, spoon poised mid-air, for an explanation.

'She didn't mean *touch* you,' said Will, trying not to grin.

'Yeah,' said Jack, smirking. 'She meant *touch you up*, in private places. Like a kiddy fiddler.'

Sophie was crestfallen. It was clear that she really had been confused, and perhaps still was. She looked mortified.

'That woman!' Freya couldn't help herself. 'Sophie, sweetheart, it's not your fault. She simply doesn't speak plainly (although she can when she wants to). Please don't worry about it. Duncan isn't that sort of man.' She made a mental note to explain what that meant later.

Poor Duncan seemed shell-shocked. He gazed at the remains of his glorious apple torte and then at her, not quite sure what to do. There was a silence as people awaited his reaction. It seemed to last forever.

'Your mum's right, Sophie. I'm not that sort of man, but I'm sure your granny was only thinking of you. There are some nasty men around. You can't be too careful.'

'But I don't think you're a nasty man, Dunk,' said Sophie, almost tearfully. 'I think you look sad, and sad people are never nasty.'

Freya waited for one of the boys to come back with a contradictory comment, but no one said anything. Duncan's sadness, and the general agreement about its existence, lay thickly in the air.

Remember that sad guy Duncan that Mum went out with?

16

EAU PLEASE!

If it weren't for Art, Will would have happily left school by now. He no longer dreaded the journey in because he had Jack to talk to on the bus and earphones to cut out anyone else as he made his way in to the school grounds. But everything else was a nightmare.

Just today there had been a prefects' meeting. He didn't know why he was a prefect, but suspected it was because there was a lack of pupils who could put two words together coherently and could therefore be a credit to the school. The Head Boy was Ashley Carter. With his broad shoulders, wide neck and record-breaking performances on the sports field he was a classic alpha male and a 'team player', not to mention a 'good all-rounder' and a 'people person'. The Head liked People People. Will wasn't one, apparently, although people fascinated him and he liked most of them. Not Ashley Carter's sidekick, though. Donovan Southgate. 'Donno' was a bell-end, and took great pleasure in baiting Will at every opportunity. Such as the prefects' meeting.

The meeting was about end-of-term entertainment. There was to be a comic review on-stage at sixth-form assembly, and the same review at main-school assembly. Then there was to be some playground entertainment for the lower school at break time on the last day of term. The performers for the review seemed to have already been chosen before the meeting – or else they chose themselves. Volunteers were now required for the playground entertainment.

'Come on! Anyone ever fancied themselves as a clown?' Ashley looked around amiably, displaying his casually moussed hairdo as he turned. 'Anyone up for some unicycling or custard-pie-throwing?'

There was hardly anyone left who wasn't already in the review. Just Will and a few other losers. Donno caught his eye, and Will looked swiftly away.

'Will's a born clown!' shouted Donno. 'Yay, come on. Gay Gray's your man, Ash. Stick him down as in charge.'

'Why me?' asked Will, knowing it was a bad idea to question Donno.

'You're a born entertainer. You've got the gay swagger. You've got the moves. Just get a team together and be your usual gay self. Put him down, Ash. That's sorted.'

And to his horror, Will was duly allocated 'playground entertainment' for the last day of term. There were eight other sad prefects for him to rally, four of whom weren't there, so he would have to find them and break the news of their golden opportunity. He wouldn't have minded so much, but there were less than six weeks to go.

It followed him everywhere, this prospect of entertaining, of making a fool of himself. He knew that's what Donno was hoping for. He tried to picture himself foxing Donno completely by juggling, somersaulting and fire-eating expertly next to the tennis courts with a crowd of cheering onlookers. If only. Will wished he had a father to ask for advice. What would Dad say? Oh, it was stupid. Dad had been a 'people person' – he would never have been landed with the playground entertainment in the first place. He would have said, 'Why don't you stand up to them? Tell them you want to be in the review. Just tell them.' But then again, if he had ever been saddled with such a crass task, he would have found a way to make it fun. He would have taken it in his stride. He would have made people laugh.

Will winced. He remembered a time when his dad had come into school to talk about providing clean water for developing countries. He had no idea whether the Head had specifically invited him because he had chosen this as the school's charity that year, or whether it had been his dad's own initiative, but there he was one day in assembly, Will's dad on-stage and all set to embarrass him.

For starters, he had been wearing a pink T-shirt with the words '*Eau Please!*' emblazoned across it. And he had matched it with a pair of what he called 'smart casual' trousers, which had a crease in them. It was not a cool look.

There was a slide show with music as Will's dad bounced jovially across the stage, talking about securing sustainable water sources and connecting them to villages in need. He explained how women and children had to walk miles each day to bring home filthy water that led to waterborne diseases and diarrhoea. Then the music had dramatically stopped and he waited until you could hear a pin drop before he asked, 'How would *you* feel if you had to walk miles each day just to get hold of clean water? If you had to find the nearest natural source of water to where you live now? If you had to miss school every day because you had to make that journey?' His face was deadly serious, and he had his fingers pointed on his chin as if pondering this question himself. Will could hear people in his row saying 'great' at the missing school question, and he couldn't help thinking he'd prefer to haul water than come to this place, but he closed his eyes, mortified. He didn't even have Jack at school with him then to share in his shame.

Then there had been another slide show to demonstrate how this charity, *Eau Please!*, could provide clean water, sanitation and healthcare education to one person in Africa for as little as one pound per year. Yes, one pound per year! Think what little difference that would make to their pocket money! (Well, it would make no difference to Will's because Dad didn't believe in giving him pocket money. He might remind him later.) And then there was the excruciating explanation of each slide. 'Here's me with some very grateful villagers in Kenya. Here's a little boy getting water from a tap connected to a well we've created. Here's the school thriving now that the children are free to learn instead of hauling water – and here's me with them. And here's a group of women by a well I've just had installed – and that's me.'

'Here's *me* by a well!' the kids had said to him afterwards. 'Well, well, well! If it isn't Gay Gray!' Even then Donno had had it in for him. It didn't take much.

Still, the school had raised £1,150 for *Eau Please!* And Will should have been proud of him, according to Mum. He knew she was right. He just wished . . . He wished so many things. He wished he had someone to help him now. He wanted to believe that Dad being there would help him sort things out, but a little voice that he tried to silence said that if Dad were here now, he might just be making things worse.

17

DREADFUL MOTHER

When Freya arrived at his flat the next Friday, she apologised more profusely for Sylvia's remarks to Sophie, and Duncan said it was fine. It really didn't matter – Sylvia was just looking out for them. Forget it. She also told him how Will had come out as gay at last, and how she should have known all along. He was relieved. Not only because it was not a secret he had wanted to keep, but because it vindicated her. He listened. He nodded. He said he was pleased for Will, and she smiled.

Still, something was wrong between them, and he could see that she knew it too and it made him feel weak and uncomfortable, as though someone had taken all the muscles out of his body and all the air out of his lungs. He tried to reply naturally to her questions, but his answers came out clipped and closed. He noticed that her knee was shaking at his coffee table, and he wondered if he mattered to her more than he had realised up until that point.

He sensed that she wanted him to take her to bed, but he kept offering her tea, and then music, and then books to read. When at last they lay down together she stroked his face and asked, 'Why don't we make love in my bed more often?'

Duncan took some time to reply, aware that this could be danger-ous territory. He could so easily sound petty. Still, there needed to be some honesty here. Why did it feel so much as though there were a real bull, writhing and powerful, with real horns, and he was taking hold of them in his hands?

He tried to explain about Reuben looking at them from above the bed. She was silent for some time.

'The thing is, Duncan, I still love him. You have to understand that. Just because he died, it doesn't mean I stopped loving him.'

'Of course not.' One of the bull's horns gored him in the gut. But he had to keep going. He looked up at the ceiling for what to say next. 'Let's say I had a giant photo of Serena here, above the bed. And let's suppose you asked me why it was there, given how things ended. And let's suppose I said, "But the thing is, I still *love* her. Just because she betrayed me, it doesn't mean I stopped loving her." How would that make you feel?'

She took in a deep breath and frowned. 'You don't, do you? Still love her?' He shook his head. 'Well . . .' She didn't take long to consider. 'I think I'd respect your feelings.'

'Oh, come on! You wouldn't be wanting to make love under it!'

She propped herself up on one elbow. 'Maybe not. Maybe you're right. But this is about loyalty. I have a loyalty to Reuben. If I took his photograph down, it would be disloyal.'

He wanted to say, 'He's dead. He has no feelings. But I'm alive, and I *do* have feelings.'

Instead he said, 'Do you believe he's looking down on you from some afterlife?'

'*No!* Not at all. I'm an atheist.'

'Well then, disloyal to whom?'

'Disloyal to his memory.'

His memory? How could you be disloyal to a memory? 'What does that mean, exactly?'

He could feel the energy of the bull as it jerked him round, threatening to toss him out of the ring.

She thought for a while and sighed impatiently. 'Well, okay, disloyal to the memories the children have of him – that *we* have of him.'

How did that work? How could you be loyal to anyone's *memory*? 'Do you mean that you want to keep memories of him alive for the children?'

'Yes!'

'And a photo of him over your bed – as opposed to any other room where they might see it – is best-placed to do the trick?'

He would be gored to death for certain. He braced himself. She turned away from him.

'You're asking me to take down a photo of Reuben.'

He wondered if all women were this illogical.

'No. I'm not asking you to take it down. I'm merely observing that you haven't.'

'But you want me to take it down.'

'No, not at all. That's not it. I'd like you to *want* to take it down. And the fact that you haven't lets me know that you're not ready to move on.'

'Move on! Move on! I wish I had a pound for every time someone told me to do that! Well, it's not that easy, you know.'

He did know, but the bull was charging. He reached over and took her face in his hands and said, 'I love you, Freya. I love you so much, but I think, perhaps . . . it's a bit too one-sided.'

'No. No it isn't.' And as if to prove the point, she climbed on top of him and removed her jumper. Then she removed everything else they were wearing and made love to him.

They slept for over an hour until she woke up aching from her leg being clamped under one of his, her nose in his armpit. How thrilling it had been, how exhilarating. And yet so close to sadness.

She would not feel guilty about Reuben. She would not. Of course she still loved him. Of course she did, and Duncan simply couldn't understand that it wasn't something she could just put away.

Reuben had been a good man. She had sometimes felt his goodness as a great weight that she and each of her children had been forced to carry around with them on their backs, like a rucksack heavy with the plight of sub-Saharan Africa. Whenever she had suggested that Will or Jack might benefit from pocket money in order to fit in with their peer group, she had listened with a hanging head to how many children could live for how long on the water that amount of money would buy. A hanging head and a broiling frustration at his moral high ground.

She turned her head towards the bedside clock. Didn't she deserve some pleasure? The clock said two thirty. Two *thirty*? It was later than she'd expected, but she wasn't yet late. She could still shower and dress and be there to pick up Sophie.

Sophie, with her little bald eyelids. Who could tell what was going through Sophie's young mind? What torments made her pluck at her own eyelashes with such dogged determination to inflict pain on herself? And what had she, Freya, ever done about it? Her daughter was, this very minute, sitting in a schoolroom on a red plastic chair, confused and anxious, terrified of something Freya had not even bothered to explore. Even now some snotty-faced kid was probably taunting her. *Baldy.* They probably all did. Her eyes were most likely welled up and pink and she was bursting with the pressure of unspoken pain, and where, oh where, was her mother? In bed with a lover!

And poor Jack, with his secrets and his quiet sobbing into her neck. He'd tried to protect his brother but hadn't been able to, and now it was probably all over Facebook and he was being taunted about his gay brother. No, don't be daft. Kids didn't do that these days. It was cool to be gay. But not cool to be chubby. You're not chubby, sweetheart, not chubby. No, no, you're not. Don't listen to them. She'd recently found him all sweaty doing squats in his room and following a workout video. And his little face. His little imploring, mortified face!

And Will. She remembered holding him for the first time and being dumbfounded that she was allowed to take him home, to be responsible for his little jelly-soft limbs all by herself. To think that all these years . . . all . . . these . . . years! God in heaven. How could she have been so blind? And Reuben had *known*? Surely not. Anyway, *she* should have known. She was his mother, wasn't she? There he had been as a fifteen-year-old trying to keep his secret safe, all those furtive longings and looks and kisses, all the obligatory lies that were *her* fault, her fault for not noticing and reassuring him and being there for him.

And here she was, exhausted from sex herself, exhausted from her own pleasure. Here she was *enjoying* herself while her children suffered! She saw the montage of her motherhood: a newspaper spinning round on the screen, slowing to the headlines, *Dreadful Mother*. A feeling between guilt, sorrow and homesickness had her by the throat. Something was making a noise, a loud, uneven noise. It was her breathing. She leapt out of bed, flung her clothes on and left.

'What is it?' murmured Duncan. He put out his arm and there was nothing but warm cotton sheet.

18

DON'T CHANGE A THING

Jack had things to think about. His image, for one. He was 'liking' things on Facebook that cool people liked, and it was exhausting keeping up with it all. But his own Facebook page was a disaster. He had worked hard on his new photograph, because up until now he had had a picture of a fox, and Warren Gifford commented, 'What loser puts an animal as their Facebook image?' and Danny Logan said, 'One whose own face is too ugly. Nice try, Chubbers.'

It seemed to Jack that all his dreams had turned to fat. He had spent some time using Will's Photoshop to create a slimmer, less flawed version of himself from a selfie. He had got rid of all the animal posters behind him, slightly elongated his face and given himself the faintest hint of a tan. Nothing orange, or anything. And he wasn't smiling. He looked thoughtful. Yes, he had a *brooding* look, really. He was pleased with it when he put it up.

'What dick photoshops a picture of himself to put on Facebook?' Danny Logan posted. 'A knobhead with a knob for a head,' wrote Warren Gifford. This was a blow. Jack lay on his bed and felt helpless.

Thinking about being uncool made him think of Duncan for some reason. Duncan seemed to like animals. Last time he was round, Duncan had got up to go and discovered that his scarf was on the kitchen floor and had two large holes in it. He picked it up and frowned. Chunkables had, over a period of years, eaten his way through several pairs of socks, a teddy bear, a shirt and a pair of knickers. He had a preference for cotton, but wool would do. Usually he didn't ingest the entire article, but merely ate holes in it. But instead of being angry at the state of his nibbled scarf, Duncan had knelt down beside Chunkables and looked concerned. 'He could get a blockage in his gut. Perhaps you should try him on some dry food? Does he have plenty of toys?' The next time he came he brought a large catnip-stuffed toy banana.

To be honest, he hadn't given Mum's new man much thought. So long as Duncan didn't go trying to befriend him or something, or make embarrassing conversation with him about school or girls, so long as he didn't go *changing* everything . . . But now that he thought about it, now that he felt sick and unhappy about everything, maybe this Duncan guy was more of a threat than he thought. If he kept on coming round, and if Mum kept on going out, things weren't going to be the same, were they? It was bad enough after Dad died, but they had sort of got used to things now. Dad not being around had made things sort of . . . well, easier, really.

Mum wasn't someone who shouted, at least not in an angry way. She used to cry a lot when it first happened, and that was awkward, because you never knew when she was going to do it, like in shops or in front of people. They were with her when a parking warden gave them a fine once and Mum just crouched down on the pavement and sobbed. Jack had pretended not to be with her and examined the bark of a nearby beech tree, and then Sophie cried too and Will called him a prick for wandering off. And Mum started crying a lot at parents' evenings and school concerts and documentaries about baby elephants. But lately she'd been okay, and Duncan seemed to have fixed the shower and made her happy and smiley and quite a cool dresser for once, but then maybe they should be wary. Maybe this man would move in, like Granny Sylvia said. Maybe he would start to use their bathroom and tell them that they were watching too much television and what time to go to bed and limit how long they spent on the internet. This feeling of uncertainty seemed to mix around with his wobbliness about his image and he began to feel sick and sad.

Liking animals wasn't cool. But he had always liked animals, and it wasn't any old fox, it was Merlin Nettles. Sophie had thought up the name because he seemed to just emerge from the nettles at the bottom of the garden and sit there looking at you. He was magic. Sophie thought he was a magician because he could appear and disappear without you seeing it happen. He was a wonderful fox, even if he did turn out to be a vixen when two little cubs appeared, frolicking in the lavender. Glorious, stealthy, clever, elegant creatures. But not cool, it seemed. *Although* . . . Ellie Chapman clearly did like animals. Her Facebook page was stuffed with photos of horses and lambs and rabbits. She even had a deer that she claimed to have photographed herself, but he knew this wasn't true because he'd found the same picture in an old *National Geographic* and had it on his wall. Still, you could forgive someone like Ellie the odd fib. That's what it was when you didn't mind it: a fib. If you did mind it – not being told the truth, that is – then it was a lie. Most of the time he hated being deceived. He hated it when Dad told him lies to get him to do stuff, like 'If you practise your piano I'll give you a hundred pounds' (he never did), or 'If you eat up all your broccoli I'll take you to see Man United' (he never did that either), or, when he bought him some dirt-cheap replica trainers, 'All the cool kids are wearing these this summer!'

He hated it that he couldn't remember his dad properly. Of course there were photographs in every room, but he couldn't remember Dad ever looking like any of them. He wasn't sure he could really remember ever looking Dad straight in the face. He must've kissed him goodnight or read to him sometimes, but his only memory of that was one time with the whole family and Dad and Will doing the voices of some picture book. He couldn't even remember which one now. And he couldn't remember Dad's voice. In fact, despite all the talk of him, Jack wasn't even sure if his dad was around that much. Either that or he was a ter-rible son who never had the time of day to notice him. They didn't have any videos of him, because none of them'd had smartphones at the time, and Mum certainly didn't have a video camera. Granny S had some footage that she'd promised to dig out sometime and copy for them. Maybe there was some clip somewhere with Dad's voice on it. Maybe he sounded like Grandad, or maybe not. He squeezed his eyes tight shut and tried to remember. He thought he could hear it when Mum and Dad were arguing and he was sitting at the top of the stairs. 'That boy's getting fat. He needs to eat less!' But he couldn't hear an accent. *Fat.* He couldn't hear now if it was deep or high. *Eat less.* He couldn't make out the timbre of the paternal voice, or any warmth in it.

Something was making his cheek sting. It was a fat tear that had rolled across it and down on to the duvet. He turned over and reached underneath the bed, where he knew there were five Milky Ways.

When Jack went into the kitchen he felt miserable. Mum was making shepherd's pie and he wouldn't be able to enjoy it because he'd eaten too much. He was just contemplating using the end of her hairbrush again to make himself throw up, while she was busy in the kitchen, when the doorbell went.

Oh God, it was him again. No one had said anything about him coming over, and clearly even Mum was surprised. In fact, as Duncan came into the kitchen, it wasn't even clear that Mum was especially pleased to see him.

'I wasn't expecting to see you,' she said. 'You must stay for tea, of course, now you're here.'

This would mean less shepherd's pie to go round. Jack was ready to implode, when he heard Duncan say that he wasn't staying, just drop-ping something off.

'I'm actually going running, believe it or not. Thought it was time to trim down a bit and get fit.'

'Oh,' said Mum. 'Well you look perfectly trim to me.' Jack sensed that Mum was relieved he wasn't staying. 'What's that?'

Duncan was carrying a large package wrapped up in pink paper with dolphins on it. 'Is Sophie here?'

As if by magic, Sophie appeared at the kitchen door. She was eyeing up the package already, as if she knew it must be for her, but hardly dared believe it.

'This is an alternative birthday present for you, Sophie – only about five weeks late.'

Sophie simply beamed. She rushed over to the table where he had placed it and looked up at Mum to see if she could open it.

'Go on, then,' said Mum. 'Duncan, you really shouldn't have. It was an honest mistake. There's absolutely no need . . .'

Sophie unwrapped a long box with a picture of a canal boat on it. 'It's the otter boat!' She was beside herself. Opening it, she squeaked and marvelled at all the little knick-knacks inside. 'There's a sink – and an oven. And a fold-down bed, and . . .' Jack went over to help her explore the intricacies of the boat.

'There are a couple of people steering the boat too,' said Duncan, looking pleased with himself.

'It's the otter babies!' Sophie was ecstatic. She was practically jumping up and down. She caught Mum's eye and could see that she had to thank Duncan. She rushed over and grabbed him round the waist. 'Thank you, Dunking! Thank you!'

Jack was feeling even more sick than before. He was about to retreat when Duncan made a move to the back door himself.

'Actually, since I'm here, I thought I'd go for a quick run nearby. At least that way nobody I know will see me.' He grinned at Jack, as if they were mates. Jack tried to move his mouth into a smile, but it got stuck halfway. 'Know any good places I could go?'

'You could just run over the field out the back,' said Mum. She seemed to be more enthusiastic now. 'And if you want to go further, there's the field beyond that one. They both have a public footpath. Jack, why don't you show Duncan how to get to it?'

'I've got homework.'

'*Jack.*'

'Don't worry,' said Duncan.

Jack knew Duncan was trying really hard to be their friend, so he was unlikely to push it.

'I don't suppose you'd do me a favour, though, if I help you with your homework? Would you come with me? I always feel a bit of a prat running on my own. And actually, I'll probably walk most of it, because I'll be out of breath after fifty yards.'

Oh God. This was just the pits. Mum was widening her eyes at him as if to say, *You dare say no.* He sighed heavily and said he had no decent trainers. Mum just widened her eyes again, so he went to put them on.

He led Duncan to the footpath that ran down the side of their house to the field. Duncan started to jog, and Jack joined in. By the time they had covered one side of the field, Jack was almost out of breath. He couldn't even hear what Duncan was saying. But then Duncan slowed to a walk.

'I like to run then walk,' he said. 'It's the only way I can stand it. Get too out of breath otherwise.' They walked on vigorously together, and Jack showed him the stile into the next field. Duncan kept on walking fast. 'I'm hopeless at running long distance.'

Jack said nothing, but felt relieved. He was only just beginning to get his breath back. They got into stride together, then Duncan said, 'I suppose we should try running again. How about to the end of this field?'

They ran, then walked, then ran. The grass was wet and he could feel it through the soles of his old trainers, and the cool of it was good. It was beginning to get dark. Inside the house the lights would be on now, but out here you could still see the pale blue-green ribbon of the sky behind the trees, and it looked like something wonderful waiting for him over the horizon. They said little, but their panting started to get into a common rhythm, and the lack of conversation seemed okay. As they made their way back on to the home straight, a dark figure ran at them and nearly knocked them over.

'Gloria! Fucksake!' said Jack. They laughed, but kept on running. Gloria trotted alongside them, mocking their speed. A rabbit tail bobbed away into a hedge, followed by two or three more.

'Did you know,' said Jack suddenly, 'that rabbits are mostly nocturnal because they have so many daytime predators?'

'I didn't,' said Duncan. 'Who are their predators?'

'Ah . . .' Jack took in a deep breath. 'You've got hawks and buzzards and . . . daytime foxes round here, and . . . weasels and stoats and snakes, of course,' he gasped, forgetting that he was running now. 'And a badger will take a rabbit, though usually at night.'

'You know a lot about rabbits.'

Jack panted happily. 'And did you know . . . that rabbits eat eighty per cent . . . of their poo?'

'I had no idea. Why's that?'

'It helps them use their food more efficiently. But . . . they mostly eat grasses and . . . clover, so it's okay.'

They stood outside the kitchen door, bent over double, heaving together.

'You okay?' asked Duncan.

'Yeah. My feet are sopping wet.'

'What size trainer are you?'

'Five.'

'I think I have a brand-new pair that size. My nephew's feet had grown when I bought them and I forgot to take them back. You could try them if you like.'

'Okay.'

'What's your homework?'

'It's okay. I can do it myself.'

'Right, well, I'll be off.'

By the time Mum opened the back door, Duncan was already in his car, waving at her from the drive.

Jack wouldn't bother with the hairbrush. He was feeling a lot better, and the shepherd's pie smelt good.

19

THE MATING GAME

They are sitting on the carpet, and Miss Dowling asks Dillon to tell everyone his news.

'Our kittens are going to new homes on Saturday, and there are four of them, two black and one tabby and one tortie.'

'How lovely!'

'And when they were born, she licked them all over and they went to suck milk from her tummy.'

'That's—'

'*And* we saw her mating. When she mated in the summer, this big black tom cat came and climbed on her back.'

Now Sophie is intensely interested. As soon as the bell rings for break she goes to sit next to Dillon, and asks him about the kittens. He says his mum might bring them in after school, and she can hold one if she wants. Sophie does want. She is already imagining a little ball of soft fur held close to her chest. She asks him as casually as she can to tell her more about the mating, and Dillon says that the tom cat got right on top of her and bit her neck.

'Like this.' He bites into his sleeve.

'Why did he do that?'

Dillon shrugs. 'Dunno. Maybe to stop her moving.'

'Doesn't she like it, then?'

Archie, who is sitting on the other side of her and has now finished peeling his satsuma, says that biting is normal in sex. 'My sister's boyfriend bites her on her neck. She has loads of marks there and she calls them "love bites". My mum doesn't like them and she gets cross.'

Sophie is disturbed, but she doesn't want to show her ignorance. 'Is it like tupping, then?'

'Tupping?'

'Yeah. When the sheep in our fields mate the ram gets up on their backs and it's called tupping. He leaves a big patch of red dye on their backs to show he's done it. He tups them, so they can have babies.'

Archie laughs. 'I never heard it called that before, but it's all the same. It's so he can put his willy in her. Humans do it too. That's what sex is.'

'Yeah, but humans don't get on each other's backs,' says Dillon, laughing now too.

'Yes they do,' says Archie. Archie knows they do. He's seen it. His brother has shown him sex videos, and the man gets on the woman's back. He tries to demonstrate on Dillon, but Dillon pushes him away.

Now Sophie is very anxious. 'Do they have their clothes on?'

'Course they don't!' sneers Dillon.

'Sometimes they have some little tiny clothes on. And high-heeled shoes.' Clearly, Archie is the expert and he will not be deposed. 'But mostly they are naked.'

Sophie is suddenly very dizzy. The fish made of water bottles on the walls seem to swim towards her, and the curvy yellow edging paper on the class points board is waving at her.

'So,' says Dillon, determined to be the most expert, 'that's how humans make babies too.'

'Yes, but they don't *just* do it to make babies,' says Archie. 'They do it because they like it.'

'Why would they like it?' Sophie doesn't want to show her ignorance, but it slips out before she can stop herself. 'Doesn't it hurt?'

Archie scratches his head. He isn't sure about this one. 'The women make a lot of groaning noises sometimes, so I'm not sure.' He doesn't want Dillon to see him uncertain. 'The men like it, though.'

There is a gap while they munch into apples or drink water.

'I don't think my parents did that to make me,' says Dillon decisively. 'There must be other ways to make babies.'

'There are,' says Archie.

Sophie is only a little relieved. Something that was a mystery to her up until today has now been revealed. She is not sure she wanted it revealed after all. Her apple is feeling hard to swallow, and she places it back in her lunchbox with a sticky mouth-sized crater in it. A bad memory has come back to her as a series of bright pictures. She wants them to go away. They have always been there, but now they are vibrant and everywhere inside her head. She wants to think about the kitten she will hold later and the softness of its fur, but there is no space for anything but human tupping.

20

THE INVISIBLE MAN

Duncan felt he had a purpose, but he wasn't entirely clear what it was. Freya's children made him feel necessary, even if they didn't really want him around. The photo discussion with Freya had been tricky, but at least he had explained things, and she had assured him – quite emphatically – that she was ready to move on. That was something. He knew she felt a huge responsibility for her children, and he had been on the point of talking a bit more about Sophie when Freya fled after their last lovemaking. He had imagined a bit of relaxed post-coital chat over a cup of tea in bed. But he hadn't even had time to put the kettle on.

He lifted the lid on the box of trainers he had bought specially for Jack and eyed them with a premature pleasure. He could picture Jack's face when he saw them, tried them on, stood in front of the mirror secretly admiring himself in them. He had asked the shop assistant for *the* most popular trainer. Then he had had to debate whether to go top-end or really extravagant, and had decided not to embarrass Freya by the latter. Still, they were perfect, and they were a generous size five, he was assured, so had a bit of room for growth as well.

He had also bought a small make-up bag for Sophie with a few toy make-up products in it. This was Lottie's idea. He had found something online that helped to promote lash growth, and it was applied just like a mascara. Lottie thought it could only be given as part of a 'make-up' set, or Sophie might think it drew too much attention to her problem. He would never have thought of something like that, but Lottie always seemed to have good ideas. More sensitive ideas. He really was a great big clod when it came to tact.

He often wondered how people saw him, and it made him shudder. All the worst blunders he'd ever made came back to him as though they were strung out in front of him on a washing line. Blunder after blunder stretching back in time. On and on went the washing line, over hill and dale. Whenever anyone pointed something out to him, like Lottie, he saw it immediately as a sign that he had made a far greater faux pas than they were letting on. A subtle mistake, after all, would not be worth a mention. No, he was a serial bungler, a clumsy oaf. And when he picked up the scent of his insensitivity, he was hurtled back to the loneliness of adolescence, when he had tried so hard to look cool by untucking his shirt on the way into school, as if it made up for his greasy hair and doing well in Maths. His mother was a stickler for 'making do', and his blazer always seemed massively too big or hideously too short. He had tried to agree with the In-Crowd, but sometimes it hurt to say such drivel about bands he didn't know, and it was like homework keeping up with them. Even when he spat his chewing gum out on the way home, like they did, it would take a defiant trajectory and stick to his shoe or something, so that he had to do a little dance to get it off, and they would bellow with laughter and girls would join in. He would laugh too, because it hurt less that way.

He was beginning to care a lot about her family, but it was Freya above all that he wanted to woo. He may not be the coolest guy in town, but he could help her. Not that she was incapable, but things were tough for her. He saw her struggling, and he wanted to be the one to come to her rescue. He had sourced some replacement double-glazed windows for her house and told her they were part of a 'showcase' offer if she agreed to have them photographed before and after. A friend of his was prepared to do them free of charge. This wasn't true. He had a good friend in the business who did a lot of houses for SwanRobins, but he was expensive, and had agreed to do them at half-price for Duncan. But new windows would make such a difference to that house. The mould spores would disappear and the rooms would be cosier. He hoped this would not be a blunder. After all, she need never find out.

So, he had something for Jack, something for Sophie and something for the whole family, things he hoped would please them – or Freya – but which might go horribly wrong. And for Will he had the occasional driving lesson – and an idea. He would suggest a trip to the Ashmolean Museum in Oxford to show Will some artists he had expressed an interest in. And he could take the whole family – they could visit the University Museum and see the dinosaur skeletons. He had a surprising suspicion – as he pictured their pleasure at the museums – that he wasn't just doing this to woo Freya. Looking forward to the delight he might bring to each of the children was now, quite unexpectedly, something that preoccupied him.

Will needed to feel comfortable in his own skin and accepted by everyone. Jack needed a boost to his self-esteem. And Sophie, poor little Sophie, she needed to grow her eyelashes back, but he was determined to get to the bottom of why she needed to hurt herself in the first place. And there was something else. With all his own uncertainty about himself, she was one person who made him feel useful and accepted. He could see the careful cocoon she had spun around herself and he knew, with an intuition he rarely felt so sure of, that she wanted him to unravel it. That she was waiting for him, waiting for a grown-up to make things safe so she could come out.

If he was perfectly honest with himself, he would probably never make it with Freya. He found the extremes of joy and hurt he felt around her almost too much to bear. If anyone could supplant that superman she still loved, he was the least likely candidate. And now, it seemed, Granny Sylvia had found some old videotape and had it copied to DVD, so Freya and the children were able to admire him at leisure in their own living room. He was now a moving, speaking Reuben. He just kept on becoming more alive, instead of more dead.

He remembered how it had felt when his own father remarried after two and a half years. There were two main concerns. First, Duncan had not realised until then how much he had got used to the new motherless setup. He hadn't appreciated just how much he enjoyed the responsibility of being asked an opinion on various household matters by his father, how much more easily his father entrusted him with information than before. Suddenly, at the age of fourteen, he had been promoted to the status of adult, and while he thought he resented it at the time, as soon as the role came under threat from Shelagh, his dad's new woman, it became a role to be cherished, and one that he was reluctant to relinquish. The second concern was one of guilt. He knew that Shelagh made his father happy. Both he and his brother, Alistair, could see that Dad was a changed man: smiling more, joking more, curious about the world around him and more interested in his sons than he had been for some time. And yet, whenever they spent time with Shelagh, whenever they were pleasant to her or accepted a meal from her, they both felt they were betraying their late mother in some inexplicable way.

Shelagh had tried hard with Duncan and Alistair. She had made herself scarce sometimes to let them have time alone with their dad; she had suggested they simply call her 'Shelagh' as that, she said, was her name; she had been respectful of their privacy and did not intrude into their teenage bedrooms, but clean sheets and pillowcases appeared on the beds at regular intervals and smelt reassuringly and deliciously fresh. And then, as Duncan showed an increasing interest in Art at school, she had started taking him to galleries. She knew a lot more than his mum would have known, and together they made day trips to visit exhibitions which she knew would inspire him. So he came to see Shelagh as someone different, someone his father loved, but not a replacement wife or mother. And once that process had begun, he stopped feeling he was betraying his mother by liking Shelagh, or at least he felt it less.

So he knew it was hard for Will and for Jack. He understood exactly how they might resent him and feel guilty even as they appreciated aspects of him. Sophie probably remembered her father less and, being a girl, was less likely to feel threatened by another male presence. But it was Freya whose guilt seemed the most firmly entrenched. Her sense of betrayal of her late husband was so keen that Duncan could not imagine how she could possibly call herself 'ready' for someone new. His memory – or whatever it was she needed to be loyal to – seemed to be alive and kicking. He could be conjured up at any moment. He was as alive in their household as if he had just been out at work for the day. There was a point where Duncan felt he was simply banging his head against an unyielding wall, and he knew that only fools did that repeatedly. Already, his head ached, and so did his heart.

21

PRESENTS FOR EVERYONE

Ever since their special chummy supper for Duncan, Mum'd had a crumpled look to her. Duncan seemed to be around less often lately. At first Will didn't care. Keeping them all safe from a new man was important, and even maybe keeping Mum safe from herself. He didn't feel good about this. He had, for the first time in ages, seen her look all bright and cheerful, but now she was even more weary-looking and defeated than she had been before Duncan. It was strange; Duncan not being around so much didn't seem to take them back to where they were before as a family.

It wasn't easy to watch the video footage of Dad. Will almost resented Granny Sylvia for bringing the DVD one Saturday. Of course, she'd had to pretend she had driven all the way up from Devon to give it to them. This wasn't true. She'd been staying a few nights at her friend's house in Cheltenham to go Christmas shopping. She had only called in on the way back, and if she hadn't cared so much about driving in the dark, she would've hijacked their family supper (which she sort of hijacked anyway, because Mum was upset about having had to take her to task when she'd implied things about Duncan to Sophie).

In the home movie, Dad looks like someone from a clothes catalogue, posing by a tree. Then he is posing by the slide as he pushes Jack down it, always looking at the camera. This seems to be some sort of family barbecue, and he can remember it now. Will is shocked to see himself, aged thirteen, scowling from a deck-chair. His eyes are circled with Goth eyeliner and his hair is dyed black. Dad is joshing with people now, and there is laughter. He was always able to make people laugh, as neatly as a puppeteer. He reaches out for Jack and hangs him upside down. Jack is surprisingly skinny, screaming and yelping as his long, rangy legs are gripped by Dad at the ankles. He does that thing that some dads do, swinging him and threatening to let go, to throw him over the hedge. There is something in the way he does this that is so slick, so easy, that Will feels he is not made of the same ingredients as his dad. It is like watching a trapeze artist swing effortlessly through the air, knowing, with all the awe it inspires, that you will never achieve this trick yourself.

Mum must be taking the footage, because when Sophie toddles across the screen Grandad says, 'Here, let me,' and then Mum is beckoning her forward. Dad grabs Mum and pulls her towards him. 'My gorgeous wife,' he says to the camera. Granny Sylvia moves in front of the camera and smiles directly at it. She takes hold of Sophie and turns to the camera again. (Another model in the clothes catalogue.) Then Dad's voice is heard, loud and jovial, 'Come on, Dracula, let's see you score a goal against your dad!' and the camera shifts to Will, still scowling in his deck-chair, but even more mortified than before. Dad leans over the back of the chair and smiles cheekily at the lens. The screen goes blank blue because there is no more.

Mum was crying now. Jack went and put his arm round her and, because he was sitting at her feet, Will patted her knee. Sophie wanted to go back to the bit where she was toddling. It was a strange, spooky feeling, seeing Dad come to life like that. Will could tell they all felt it a bit, although he had no way of gauging quite how it affected them individually. He thought – or wanted to believe – that Mum disapproved slightly of Dad calling him 'Dracula' like that, even though, looking back, he did look a bit ridiculous. He wasn't going to be showing this to any of his friends.

He obliged Sophie by showing her the bit with her toddling again, and she was pleased with the small version of herself, but thought that Daddy looked a bit different to how she'd remembered him. Will wanted to say that this was because all they had were these giant photographs of him, captured just so, at one arbitrary moment, smiling from his best side. Now they would see him swinging Jack by the legs, telling Mum she was gorgeous, making people laugh and grinning from behind Dracula's chair, over and over, over and over, for the rest of their lives. Because that was all they had. He thought he preferred the memories.

The video was still playing for the third or fourth time when Duncan turned up. He looked awkward when he caught sight of it, and Will was relieved to have an excuse to turn it off. He wasn't sure he wanted Duncan to see it anyway, because maybe it didn't show Dad in the right light, whatever that was.

'Ah, it's Duncan!' said Will, a little too sarcastically, perhaps.

Duncan discreetly handed Jack a box, and Jack looked thrilled and scampered off to his room. This was a turn-up for the books. Jack couldn't stand Duncan the last time he spoke to Will about him. He hoped Duncan wasn't 'buying them off'. And if he was, where was his gift, then?

'I'm not stopping,' said Duncan.

'Good.' This was not quite as under his breath as Will had intended.

'Please do,' said Mum, looking a bit rumpled. 'I'm just about to make tea.'

'No, please. I'm only going for a run again. Hope you don't mind me popping by.'

The look Mum gave him was a bit pitiful really, like she was imploring him to stay, like she was apologising for the heartless cruelty of her family – mother-in-law and children alike. Duncan really didn't have a clue. He stood there like a big friendly giant who'd tried hard to be scary and failed. He opened his mouth to speak and nothing came out.

'Could we talk?' said Mum, and ushered him into the kitchen.

Will hung about near the kitchen door, trying to catch what they were saying. Duncan, weirdly, was giving her what looked like a make-up bag, and they were talking in hushed tones, which became a little urgent. Duncan said something about needing to talk about Sophie. Then Jack breezed past him into the kitchen with these brand-new trainers on.

'You sure I can have these?' he heard Jack ask.

'They're going begging. My nephew's a size six and he's not getting any smaller.'

He heard Mum say Jack could keep them, so Will swung the door open and asked for a look. Jack pranced up and down in them. They were pretty cool.

'Fancy trying them out?' Duncan had a hopeful look on his face.

'Could do, I guess.'

And before you could say 'Jack Robinson', Jack was out of the back door and away over the fields with Duncan.

'Well,' said Mum, scooping up the make-up bag. 'Who'd've thought?'

22

MY GORGEOUS WIFE

Freya considered it an inspired idea of Duncan's to buy Sophie some eyelash growth promoter. And the make-up bag was a sensitive addition. His idea – to encourage Sophie to think positively about her eyelashes by coating them with clear 'mascara' twice a day – seemed to make sense. He said the make-up bag filled with toy make-up products was Lottie's idea (Lottie Robins, who made her feel a little stab of insecurity), but even so, she pictured him looking up Sophie's problem on the internet at home, studying it for hours, then sourcing the best products and sending off for them. All this time she had been finding him a little cool with her, he had been quietly doing these things, and waiting impatiently for the little packages to arrive.

When Duncan and Jack came back from their run, Duncan had shot straight off home again. He had given her a cheerful enough wave, so there was no indication that he was in a bad mood with her. She wondered how she looked to him, waving through the kitchen window. Did he see her wrapped up tightly in her grief, remembering her frantic departure from his bed last week? Or did he see her face raw with expectation, desperate to hold its contours in place?

Maybe he had been more than just fishing when he said he didn't think she was over Reuben. Maybe he really did think things were just too difficult. She wished he could grasp the fact that Reuben couldn't simply evaporate overnight. But seeing him wave at her now and go straight to his car, she knew she had hurt him with the photo debacle. On these occasions when he called by to do something helpful, she felt such a wave of tenderness for him. All she wanted was to run after him and tell him it was okay, she would take all the photos down, throw out every reminder of Reuben. She didn't know why she held back, and thought it was partly because of the children. She couldn't be seen to be binning their father. But there was something else, something about the finality of it, the gesture itself and her responsibility for it. It was almost as if she had been dishonest in saying she was ready to move on.

Still, she watched Duncan check his wing mirrors as he reversed on the gravel, and she felt some fat, sturdy buds pushing up through her old resolve. She longed to wrap her arms around him and deliver the news that was bound to come in a giant bloom: I am ready. I am, I am, I am.

And two years was nothing, let's face it. She still had to stop herself checking the mirrors and the fridge door for little notes from Reuben saying, 'I love you, Freya', 'Missing you already' and 'You're my girl, and I love watching you move'. She could still feel his arms around her, and still felt a little alarm from time to time when she woke up in the night and thought he hadn't returned from somewhere or other. She still occasionally had to stop herself reaching for the fifth knife and fork, even though the table was now so much easier to set for four. This grief was a given, and she expected Duncan to understand.

Even so, now that Duncan had questioned her, she once more had an uneasy feeling that her grief was a coat that had become a little too comfortable to wear. She had a foreboding that maybe, underneath it, there might be some very surprising outfit that she was concealing. It struck her sometimes, for example, that the chaos of her life had been curiously reduced by Reuben's passing. Something to do with all his last-minute changes of plan, his over-generosity with charities, his constant and unpredictable travel arrangements, his lateness for meals, the requirement to support him in ventures that seemed daft or doomed. All this surplus energy she had been able to redirect to her children. There was something almost like relief in regaining control of the calendar and the bank balance. Although of course not relief. That was not the word. That was not the scary hint of colour peeping out from underneath the coat that she now wrapped more tightly around herself.

She was concerned about Duncan, though. And if she was irritated by his lack of sensitivity about grief, she was also worried that she was not an attractive enough prospect, with all her clutter of daily life and debris of widowhood, for him to want to see this through. Perhaps he really had had enough. But then he had only yesterday rung her about a friend who could do their replacement windows for free, as part of some deal or other, and had asked her if he could put it in place.

Sophie used the lash promoter straight away. As soon as she heard that Duncan had left her another present, she couldn't wait to take everything out of the little bag and try it out. At bedtime, Freya stood her in front of the bathroom mirror and showed her how to do it properly, like a grown-up woman. 'This will actually help your eyelashes grow, if you use it every day.' She said nothing about pulling them out, just left the positive idea in the air. Sophie gazed at herself in the mirror, and Freya thought she caught the slightest hint of approval, but she may have been imagining it.

She and Reuben had been the happiest couple anyone knew. They celebrated their anniversaries, no matter what the circumstances, and he brought her gifts however penniless they were. She had been a treasured wife, and she knew it. And so did everybody else. Freya remembered the eulogy at his memorial service. 'A most loving husband, a truly attentive father, a man who went the extra mile to help others . . .' He had been all those things. She deserved her spell of greedy grief.

Freya's sister, Rachel, had been the one person who disapproved of Reuben. Right from the very beginning she had urged Freya to get an abortion. Having a baby as a student would ruin her life, Rachel said. Then, of course, she'd relented when Will was born and he'd turned into such a beautiful little nephew.

Rachel, of all people, knew that Freya's love life had been pretty unremarkable. Unlike her younger sister, Freya had gone through the sixth form without a single date, and none the sadder for it. She had been happy studying plants and animals, and going for long walks with her sketchbook. Her first taste of romance had been with a student in freshers' week at university. There had been a 'fun dating' event, which entailed being matched with another fresher based on fairly random criteria. She, for example, had been paired up with an Engineering student called Dev, and they both had to dress in green from head to toe and meet in the union bar with one foot in a bucket. He turned out to be fairly pleasant, and after ten minutes of conversation they discovered that the only thing they had both put down in common on their 'dating' form was that green was their favourite colour. Still, he was trying hard, she thought, and her face was aching from smiling. She felt a little sorry for him. In fact, she quite liked him. And, since he kept buying her drinks and told her she had 'beautiful eyes', she could tell that he liked her too. If he asked to see her again, she wouldn't turn him down. He wasn't good-looking in any traditional sense, but she felt they had a few things in common, in addition to the colour green.

On her way back from the ladies' toilets towards the end of the evening, she heard his voice around a corner where the noticeboards were. She made her way towards it and then heard the friend he was talking to: 'You're too nice, mate. What are we going to do with you?'

'Please,' she heard Dev say, 'find some excuse to get me away. She's just so fucking *boring*!'

She had slunk backwards towards the toilets she had come from and shut herself in a cubicle.

Maybe that first hurt had something to do with why, looking back, she had made some fairly wild decisions. She had started going out with Reuben in her first year at university. He had been studying Economics, and he took her for rides out into the countryside on his old puttering moped, letting her search for plant samples and laying her down in meadows with a flagon of cider. It had been a zealous and exciting romance. She felt that there was nothing he wouldn't do for her. As if to prove it, he climbed up to her room on the second floor of her student block one morning to wake her with a kiss and a small box of chocolates. Someone had taken a photograph of him hanging on to a downpipe, and it was the talk of the campus. She remembered his easy hilarity. He was a risk-taker, and she was cautious. He was a socialiser, and she had a few close friends. Everyone knew his antics, and she was known only in relation to him. *Reuben's girl.* It was what she wanted to be, and she studiously sought to please him like an over-earnest job applicant trying for a desirable post. All of it went against the grain. She had to pretend skills she did not have, do things she had no inclination for (like attending late-night parties, trying drugs, demonstrating in fancy dress for things she didn't care about, waving her hands about at pop concerts for bands that bothered her eardrums, and being spontaneous.) And, like a job applicant, it was only when she got the job that her shrill optimism quietened down and she questioned whether it was really going to deliver on her expectations. In fact, it clearly didn't, because she dumped Reuben at the end of the spring term. That's right, now she remembered. They didn't often mention that.

She had fallen in love with a shy biologist called Daniel. She had first noticed him because he smiled at her every morning on her way across the campus, and then one day they had found themselves at the same table in the library and he had smiled some more. They soon found themselves choosing to sit in the same seats at the same time every day, and he showed her how to find a research article she wanted to read from the archives. And then she had met his friends, and they were subtle people with a passion for dry humour and quiet evenings in. Their lovemaking had been a revelation to her. She had never known such tenderness or such electricity. Gazing into each other's eyes was enough to spark her off. She felt she had come home.

She often wondered if they would have married. No, in truth, she knew they would have. But what happened next scuppered all of that. If only she had had the capacity to pretend then, but those fake days were gone. She could never allow Daniel to bring up another man's child. But Rachel was right: she could have dealt with it without Reuben even knowing. In fact, that was why she had gone to see him, to tell him she would deal with it. She hadn't bargained on his sudden zest for parenthood. Was it jealousy? Did he see it as a way of getting her back? Whatever his reasoning, he wanted that baby. No woman was going to deprive him of that. He suddenly developed a set of pro-life morals that would have staggered even the student Christian Union. She would have been unable to keep it from Daniel then, even if she had decided to.

And so she gave up her degree. She planned that her mother would look after the baby while she went back to complete the remaining years. But then, with the unexpected death of her mother, Freya wrapped herself up in Will and gave no more thought to a future career of her own. And soon afterwards Reuben decided, on a whim, it seemed, to give up his degree just as finals were approaching. Rachel had tried to hold her tongue as she watched their father provide him with a job, but could never resist, at Christmases after a few glasses of wine, commenting on 'that dickhead who cocked up your life'.

But then, as Freya told her, love grows. Children change everything. And they did. Nothing could have prepared her for the onslaught of love she felt for Will, and again for Jack, and then again for Sophie. Sometimes Reuben made her laugh, and whenever she was fighting disappointment, he seemed to spot it and turn up with a surprise: a bunch of flowers or a piece of jewellery they could not afford. Like the solid-gold chain with the four-leafed clover that he'd had made especially. She knew it had cost a fortune because of the money withdrawn from their account. He always paid for things in cash, so she could never be sure, but a lot had been taken out that month and it stretched their finances, although she was so touched she couldn't bring herself to show disapproval. Domestic life was a pleasure and a chore, full of makeshift happiness and disappointments, emotions that he appeared able to expand and shrink like elastic. But he never stopped loving her. He had won her back from a rival; he had stepped up to the mark. That was the one thing that kept her going: a certainty in his colourful commitment to her. And he was always so kind, and kind to other people too. His charity work was renowned. Locally, what he had done for African villages without water was legendary. He was, really, something of a hero, and she would just have to accept that he was the one who had made a career for himself and not her. That had been her decision, and she had no right to resent him for it. She was quite sure that if she'd finished her degree she would have done nothing so worthwhile as her husband. She would probably have married Daniel and had children anyway. That was something else she tried not to think about, because imagining children with Daniel would have meant unimagining her own lovely children. She winced at the thought.

Besides, her love for Daniel was not real love in any sense. It could never be tested, stretched to its limit, pummelled, worn down or wounded. It would always pull through, as fantasy love always did. Its invulnerability was both attractive and ridiculous.

All these thoughts of alternative life paths she had long buried, because they were not helpful in any way, but for years Rachel would bring them up, and cause her to brush against them from time to time. Not in a malicious way, but only if Freya happened to say, by mistake, that she would only understand something or other if she had children herself. Rachel had never married or had children. There was still time, at thirty-five, but Freya was never clear whether Rachel wanted this or not. They had always been close as children, and Freya suspected that much of her hostility to Reuben was born out of the fact that he had taken Freya away from her so soon.

In fact, the two sisters had continued to be close, until one day not long before Will was born. Rachel was helping them decorate a room for the baby. All of a sudden, it seemed, there was a coldness between them, not long after the washing of the paintbrushes. She had rarely come to stay again once she left for university herself, mostly appearing for day visits on the children's birthdays. It hurt Freya that she couldn't work out where she had gone wrong. There had been tears in her sister's eyes as she'd hugged Freya goodbye, but Freya couldn't think for the life of her what she had said or done to hurt her, and on the occasions she'd asked, Rachel had swiftly changed the subject. To be fair, Rachel had been very good to Freya when Reuben died. She visited more often now and offered her support.

The video had been a strange experience, and it continued to be an experience because after the children went to bed she watched it over again, several times, watching Sylvia put herself into the frame so many times that she wanted to break the DVD in two. She knew what everyone said off by heart now, even the voices off ('Stephen, your burgers are burning!' from Sylvia and 'Daddy, look at me!' from Jack), and the tears provoked by certain phrases had all dried up now. An onlooker might think it had lost its power to move her, but that was not true. There was indeed something different, but if anything, it was a different set of feelings, not a lack of them. These sprang from a whole new toolkit of emotions, like a row of strange-flavoured ice creams: quite pronounced, but subtly different from anything she had known before. At least, they were not feelings she could place. They made her stay up, watching and listening over and over. The most prevalent was a great adrenaline-inspired emotion, somewhere between fury and spite and heartbreak, with a great chocolate flake of indignation wodged into its core.

She started shaking and, imagining she must be cold, went on up to bed. She looked in the mirror as she brushed her teeth far too vigorously, and her mascara had smudged all around her eyes. *Come on, Dracula. Come on, Dracula.* The thought of that sullen thirteen-year-old scowl, and all the pain that lay behind it, the lie he was having to live but trying so hard to tell, made Freya slam down her toothbrush. She applied make-up remover with trembling hands, held some cotton wool under the tap, then wiped away the tears and the grime as carefully as she could. She looked at her naked face. *My gorgeous wife. My gorgeous wife.*

23

BULLIED MEN CLUB

Will was writing his university entrance personal statement. He re-read it with a sinking heart. It was dull. 'I am passionate about illustration, and I particularly admire the works of . . .' Why would anyone believe he was passionate? What evidence was he giving of that? And what about animation? He quite fancied that, really. 'I am passionate about animation, and am very keen to find out more.' What? Why hadn't he found out more, then? He should have written this months ago. He did try, but came up against this same barrier: his own lack of confidence. And what was more, he had to choose five universities, and he hadn't visited any of them except Gloucestershire. He liked that one, but he really would like to get away. He was thinking of Bristol UWE, Falmouth, Southampton and Bournemouth for the others, but he'd only seen them on the websites.

'You should visit as many choices as possible,' Duncan advised. 'I'll take you, if you like.'

Mum must've been hovering because she popped up all grateful and keen. 'That's really kind of you, Duncan. Isn't that kind of Duncan, Will?' It was embarrassing to see her fawning like that, but he didn't really want to be indebted to Duncan. He knew Duncan's game; he was just trying to ingratiate himself with them all and slither into their lives without them noticing. Soon he would be indispensable for lifts and stuff, and then they wouldn't be able to do without him or get rid of him. So, no, Duncan. No thanks, mate.

However, it would be useful to see some of these places. This was, after all, his future. Some of them had open days, but he'd missed three of them already. Duncan said it didn't matter. He could take him for a look round anyway, and ring the departments in advance to see if he could chat to someone. He said the important thing was to have a good portfolio and an interesting personal statement. Will showed him what he'd written. He was reluctant, but nowhere near as reluctant as he was about sending off what he'd got so far.

Well, it was like some sort of miracle. Duncan sat down with him and went through it paragraph by paragraph. He asked Will why he really wanted to do illustration.

'All I've ever really wanted to do since I was a child is draw.'

'Well that's the most honest start, then. "All I've ever really wanted to do since I was a child is draw." That's a good opening sentence. We know who you are.' And off he went, asking questions and nipping and tucking until the profile read like a dream. It was seamless, it was easy to read, it made him sound as passionate as he was without using the word 'passionate' once. It was good. Duncan told him it could take a while to find your own voice. He didn't find his until he was at university. Will wondered where his might be hiding: up a tree, maybe, or under a bush. He imagined a small, scurrying creature that scampered away when he approached.

Duncan reminded him that he didn't have long to meet the January deadline, and he really should know what these courses involved. Will closed his eyes at the thought of all the difficult tasks he had to complete before January, including the dreaded 'playground entertainment' that Donno had forced on him for the end of term. And so he accepted Duncan's offer, and spent the next few Saturdays visiting universities. Falmouth was such a long trip that they all went down together and stayed for a night in a Cornish hotel. (All paid for by Duncan – God, he was so transparent. Good of him, though.) In the evening, they had all stood on the shore eating chips, and watched a giant cloud of starlings swoop and twirl like a piece of black chiffon caught in a gentle breeze. He did the others with Duncan alone, and the trips involved long hours in the car, which Will dealt with by listening to his music, effectively cutting out any 'man-talk' that Duncan might wish to engage in.

After they'd visited the department at Bristol, Duncan took him to see the Aardman Animations studios, where he had a friend. Will loved it. He loved everything about it, from the animators he met to the little caricatures of all the people who worked there on the wall. He loved the atmosphere and the smell of the place, and he was just a tiny bit impressed that Duncan knew people like this. Duncan introduced him as 'an animator of the future', which was mortifying. And ever so slightly pleasing.

The rain was tipping down and Bristol seemed clogged with Christmas shoppers. They went for lunch at a café on Park Street, so Will had to have a conversation with Duncan. It wasn't too bad. They talked a lot about favourite illustrators, and Duncan admitted to a private passion for painting watercolours himself. Then he said:

'Those scars on your arms, does your mum know?'

'Oh God, no! Please don't say anything. They're . . . ancient.'

Duncan nodded slowly. 'Were you bullied?'

'What? For being gay?'

'There doesn't need to be a reason, in my experience.'

In his *experience*? 'Were you bullied, then?'

'Yes.'

'*Why?*'

'Well, I'm still trying to work that one out. Just not a cool guy, I suppose.'

Will nodded, then wished he hadn't. They ate in silence for a while; then he made Duncan promise not to tell his mum about the cuts. 'You know how she is. She'll get herself all wound up. She's got enough to worry about. And they're ancient.'

Somehow, the thought that Duncan had been bullied intrigued Will. He was, after all, a very gentle man. He never spoke loudly to anyone, and when he did speak it was after thoughtful consideration of what to say. He didn't shoot from the hip. He looked at you with his sad donkey eyes and delivered something useful. Mum could do worse. Although she was better with no one at all. Then again, all these visits to universities brought it home to him that he would not be around for much longer. This time next year – if he didn't go to Gloucestershire University – he would be living away. Without Will's protection, Mum would need someone. Someone like Duncan might be the best bet.

The windows of the café were steamed up with the damp from people's wet coats and umbrellas, but you could see the sun beginning to break through outside at last.

24

MEMORIES IN THE ATTIC

During the three or four weeks that he visited universities with Will, Duncan experienced a new sense of well-being in the Gray household. Will seemed focused. Jack and Sophie seemed excited about the run-up to Christmas, and Freya was more affectionate and laid-back than he'd known her. She made him suppers, sewed on his buttons, bought him watercolour paper, surprised him sometimes with a cake at home on her other day off, and made him sing to her.

On the first Saturday in December he was measuring window frames for the new aluminium windows, and went around the house with his tape measure. In Freya's room he noticed something different immediately. Hanging on the picture hook above her bed was the four-leafed clover on its gold chain. He stood and looked at it, and smiled. A halfway house, perhaps, but a deliberate change. His chest swelled. He began to whistle.

Sophie's room was pink. All along the bedhead and down the side of the bed were neat rows of fluffy animals: teddy bears, cats, seals, penguins, ponies, foxes and sheep. The only things they had in common were their softness and their unthreatening faces. Duncan felt encouraged by them as he measured the mouldy window space. The windowsill was covered in little coloured blocks, each with a bendy stalk sticking up from it with a clip gripping a dog-eared photograph. Mostly they were of Chunkables or Sophie holding lambs. It moved him that her treasures were so simple. He imagined her in this small room at night, huddled up with her animals, blanketed in kindly furry smiles. And he pictured her kneeling in front of her long mirror, pulling out the lashes, tears welling as she inflicted pain on herself. Around the mirror were strings of plastic beads and a long boa of pink down. On the floor were an array of crayons and drawings, a sparkly wand and a discarded fairy dress with wings. The windowpane was covered in condensation, and through it he could see Gloria standing in the garden, looking up at him as if in hope of seeing Sophie.

The world was a complicated place, but this room seemed to simplify everything. He wanted to flop back on the bed and drift off somewhere safe on its softness. Freya said she had tried to persuade Sophie to choose a different colour for her room, but she had doggedly chosen pink. It was as if she had woken up one morning at the age of three and shouted, 'I'm a girl! I'm a girl! Give me pink!' and no attempt to stop gender stereotyping was going to stand in her way. Duncan lay down on the bed and pondered on this, fascinated. He was amazed at the implacable advance of femininity. He loved it. He missed it. By way of explanation he had told Freya that it was probably because his own mother had died when he was fourteen and he had no sisters, only a brother.

He picked up the sparkly wand in his hand and gazed at it wistfully.

'Sorry it's a mess.' Freya stood at the bedroom door, looking at the wand in his hand. 'Thinking of doing some magic?'

He laughed and tried to sound nonchalant. 'Well, let's hope the new windows will feel like magic.'

She sat down on the bed next to him. 'Tell me about your mum.' She looked at him gently, but he couldn't help the feeling that this was a trick question. His sense of panic and mild nausea must have shown, because she added hastily, 'I'm sorry. Don't worry if you'd rather not,' and she gave his hand a squeeze.

'No, no – it's fine.' It wasn't. He took a breath in, and focused ahead of him like someone about to jump a small ravine. 'She . . . she was . . . sweet-natured and kind; calm – always calm; she liked Turkish delight and sugared almonds – and she was a great cat lover; she loved ironing and hated washing up and vacuuming; she, um, was a good listener, she would just listen sometimes and not try to solve things, and somehow that solved things; and she loved walking – but only in good weather, and she used to grow roses in the garden and tend them like children; she loved children and making party cakes, and if she had survived she would have been disappointed that I couldn't have children – I think – it would have broken her heart, but she wouldn't have said; and actually, apart from cakes, she was a truly atrocious cook, but a very enthusiastic one; um she liked to read trashy novels about handsome surgeons and scatty virginal nurses; she loved all the old Cary Grant films and she wanted to go on a romantic holiday to Rome one day. One day . . . that was what she wanted to do—' He broke off abruptly, because he could feel his voice losing control of the wheel. Freya was very quiet. When he ventured a glance, she had tears in her eyes.

'You loved her,' she said, as if it was the most surprising thing in the world. 'You loved her very much.'

He nodded. He had cleared the ravine successfully, but he wasn't quite sure where he was. There was something mysterious about this little episode that made him fairly certain there was more to it than he could see.

Duncan ordered a small skip for them, and work began the following week, as it was the only space his friend Graham had before Christmas. Freya had found a whole roll of curtain material in the attic that she had intended to use years ago, and she had made new curtains for five of the windows to replace the faded old red velvet ones. She watched with awe as the window frames came out and were disposed of, collapsed and mould-speckled, into the skip.

Having checked with Graham that there would be some spare space left in the skip, she had started her own clear-out of the attic. Duncan helped her down with box after box of things she wanted to throw out. Then, sitting at each box for ages, she would become entranced by some small child-drawing of a donkey, or a picture book, or an old exercise book. 'Oh, I can't throw this away,' she would say every few minutes, so the progress through the boxes was slow. He tried to help by bundling the definite 'throw out' piles into bin bags and lugging them out to the skip. He also shredded unwanted paperwork by hand before he disposed of it.

And that was how he came across 'Reuben Gray Curriculum Vitae'. He was on the point of tearing it in half, along with everything else, when he spotted the enticing title. Thinking it a chance to learn something, he stuffed it into his pocket to look at later.

In a box of books to clear out he found an Italian phrasebook. His Italian was quite good, but he picked it out anyway to see if it could be of use. He pictured Freya learning Italian at an evening class and then, clearly, giving it up. There was a page corner turned over at a chapter called '*Dov'è* . . . *?*'. She hadn't got very far.

'There's an Italian phrasebook up here. I didn't know you'd learnt Italian!' he called down the stairs.

'Oh, that old thing,' said Freya, coming up the stairs. 'We had some pipe dream of going to Italy one day, and were going to have evening classes.'

'You started learning, then?'

'Oh, that's Reuben. I only got to one class. *Sono inglese* . . . It didn't work out with the babysitting. So . . . chuck it out, unless you want it.' She opened the bin-liner she had in her hands so that he could throw it in.

Duncan put the book to his mouth and thought. 'Well, I'm not going to throw it out, as it happens. I think you might find it comes in handy sooner than you think, *signora*.'

She raised her eyebrows and he smiled at her. She returned the smile quizzically, as though she hardly dared to take this in.

'You were planning to go to Italy one day, then?' he said.

'Not really. Not *realistically*, I should say.'

'You don't think Reuben was going to surprise you one day and whisk you away?'

She gave a short laugh and leaned against the landing wall. 'No, 'fraid not. Not for one moment. We were pretty hard up. We never went anywhere.'

'What about Africa? Didn't he ever suggest taking you on one of his charity trips?'

'Same thing applies. No money. And anyway, even if he had taken a notion to invite me to Africa or Italy, what would I have done with the children? Even Will was only fifteen when he died, and Sophie was still three, coming up to four.'

'Sorry – of course. I didn't think.'

'It's so sad, really, when I think of it. He was due to come home the very next day – after he died, I mean. Well, he died on the Friday, and he was due to catch his flight on Saturday and be home later that day. And the thing is, the children had made this big banner saying "WELCOME HOME DAD", and we'd already put it up in the front window when I got the call. You know, the call saying he had died. It was the hardest thing, telling them, when I could hardly take it in myself. And then taking down that wretched banner with Will. It was heartbreaking.'

'I'm so sorry.' They were talking about Reuben, and it was okay.

Will emerged and asked if he could help. He and Duncan started shifting things from inside the back door out to the skip.

'Gosh, these bring back memories,' said Duncan, holding the bundle of old red velvet curtains. 'When I was a student we did a Red Arrows display wearing red curtains like these for rag week.'

'How did that work?'

'We all dressed up in a red curtain cape and ran around in formation to the music of *The Dam Busters*. It was ridiculous. But everyone loved it.'

'Give them here,' said Will, setting them aside. Then he disappeared to his room and came back down with the laptop. He brought up the tune to *The Dam Busters*. 'Show me.'

Duncan felt a bit reticent to start with but, anxious to please Will, he draped a red curtain across his shoulders. 'I'll need some assistants. You can't do a formation on your own.'

Sophie and Jack were willing volunteers, and the four of them trooped outside. Will turned up the music and Duncan shouted commands at them, demonstrating a spread-wings position and a running speed. He found he was in his stride as all the old moves came back to him. They had rehearsed it all so carefully when he was a student and he was surprised to realise that he remembered everything. When he had them all peeling off like dancers stripping the willow in a folk dance as they completed their first formation, he looked up to see Freya doubled up with laughter at the back door.

'What on earth?'

'We're the Red Arrows,' said Duncan. 'And actually, we need an odd number for the arrow formation. Won't you join us?'

'Of course.'

Duncan was about to explain when Will chipped in. 'It's going to be my "playground entertainment" for the last day of school. Thank God! And thank you, Duncan, for the idea.'

'I'm not doing this in front of people,' said Jack.

'Fear not. I have all my pilots lined up. I just need to learn the synchronised moves from Duncan.'

'Right,' said Duncan, feeling a huge surge of warmth for Will. 'Move number two . . .'

25

CONNECTIONS

There was a box of old sketchbooks in the attic. Each one contained scores of plants and animals, drawn throughout Freya's childhood and teens. Freya leafed through them with the aim of throwing them out, but the children paused over each one and examined them for some time before awarding them a reprieve. There was even a tiny, stapled-together homemade booklet about sheep, something she had written and illustrated when she was not much older than Sophie. Sophie laughed at the crazy drawings and giggled at the bad spelling, and Freya laughed too.

Will was fascinated by the nature drawings she'd done in her teens. There was a careful crayon drawing of a skylark, underneath which she had written in spidery writing, 'With no bright plumage, it is with the tenacity and stamina required to maintain long song flights that the male skylark impresses its mate.'

'Hey, these are amazing,' he said, incredulous. 'I didn't know you could draw!' It was as if he'd discovered a link between the two of them he hadn't known existed. The fact that she'd brought him up and sung him to sleep and fed him and taken him to school was as nothing to those sketchbooks, which announced to him more solidly than anything that there was a connection to this strange woman, his mother. Jack was the quietest of all. He turned the pages slowly and thoughtfully, with an almost pained look. Freya herself was surprised to see the sheer numbers of hedgehogs and robins and blackbirds and butterflies and field mice that she had once taken meticulous care to draw, filling the pages of these cheap sketchbooks. And she was maybe a little startled, as she imagined Jack to be, by the stark similarity in their mutual love of these things. He was thinking, probably, with a stab of excitement and panic, that she too had been a Nature Nerd. That she was just like him, and he hadn't known it.

She remembered once when her grandmother, her mother's mother – a quiet, stoical woman – had told her a story about her childhood. She rarely spoke of her youth, and never told stories, so Freya had treasured this one. Her grandmother had been about ten years old when some prisoners of war were stationed nearby. Her mother had told her on no account to speak to any of them, as they were German and the enemy and not to be trusted. But she had seen some of them working in the field at the back of their house and had struck up a conversation with one of them, a young man called Franz, over the wall. He had held out an injured hedgehog, and asked if she might be able to keep it warm until it was better. He explained that she would need a cardboard box and a hot-water bottle wrapped in a towel (not too hot, and never allowed to go completely cold) and some screwed-up newspaper. She was to feed it hard-boiled egg (or mixed powdered egg) and water, but no milk. As he explained all this to her, he held the hedgehog so tenderly in the palm of his hand that she knew he was a kind man. His eyes were most earnest, she said, and she had never seen a grown man care as much as he did about small creatures before. Her mother had caught her talking to him and had rushed outside and told him to clear off, but not before the German had handed over the creature to be hidden inside her cardigan. And when Freya heard her grandmother tell this story, she had felt a huge jolt of tenderness for this strangely nervous yet defiant ten-year-old version of her grandmother. In the story, she suddenly caught a glimpse of the timelessness of kindness, the invisible ligaments that connected some people to others. And she suspected now, when Jack took some of her sketchbooks up to his room, that he too had seen these connections, and was moved by a jittery exhilaration somewhere between alarm and delight.

The house felt different now, as if it had sweated out some of its past. With the windows finished too, Freya sat up in bed reading and reflected on how much warmer and cleaner her house seemed. Duncan was looking after her family. Outside the rain was pelting down. *Pit putter pit.* You could hear the water pouring out of the guttering and splashing loudly on to the paving outside the back door. But the windows were dry, and the new wooden windowsills smelt of the Danish oil she and Duncan had applied at the weekend. It had been a good feeling, working alongside him. It had been satisfying spring cleaning together too. He had helped her clean up the attic and she had helped him sort out some space in his wardrobes. They had taken five full bin bags from her house and two from his to the Red Cross shop in town. He'd laughed at her help, though, as she'd tried to save everything of his that caught her eye.

'You can't throw out this jacket! What do you want to throw this out for?'

'I haven't worn it for ten years.'

'*I'll* have it. Let me try it on.'

And she had twirled about in front of his bedroom mirror, and he had conceded that his old blue jacket looked a lot better on her than it did on him. Then he had put his hands on her shoulders and said, 'You seem to be making a habit of keeping my clothes. I rather like it.'

That had been two days ago. Now she took her bookmark from the bedside table. It was a photograph, and she had found it yesterday in the inside pocket of that old jacket, along with another photograph.

She looked at it closely, as she had done many times since yesterday. She handled it carefully, guiltily, certain she was trespassing on some very private ground. In it, a woman was sitting on a rock, her naked legs towards the camera and her head tilted slightly back. She was wearing a large white shirt, and her long blonde hair was swept over one shoulder. There was something playful in her smile. She was flirting. She was Serena. She must have been.

Freya had examined this photograph in such detail that she could conjure it up without even looking at it. She could reproduce those grin-creased blue eyes, the perfect teeth, the slight tilt of the head: back and a little to the side. She could see the exact shine on the polished, tanned legs, the shins disappearing into the edge of the picture, and catch the glint of the ring on one of the hands that supported her on the flat rock. The left hand. She could see the untanned inside of one of her arms, flawless and youthful, and a gold pendant around her neck, whose clasp had worked its way round to the front and sat only inches from the pendant, which was golden and straight and pointing towards a gleaming and fulsome cleavage.

She was shocked by the complicated mixture of curiosity and pain she felt each time she looked at Serena. So this was how it felt for Duncan, when he saw the photographs of Reuben. Hard to assert that there was no sense of seeing a rival, however wrong that was. Serena was gone. Serena didn't love him. She had hurt him so badly that he no longer displayed pictures of her. He certainly no longer loved her, as she loved Reuben. And yet, and yet.

She placed the photograph reverently inside her book and picked up the second picture. This one showed Serena being given a piggyback ride. The photographer – or perhaps it had been taken on a timer – had cut off the top of her head, and the face that caught your attention was that of a young man, in his late twenties, perhaps, peering at the camera with a look of joy and hopefulness. Perhaps he had waited too long for the camera to click, perhaps the girl on his shoulders was wriggling, or giggling, or shrieking. He seemed happy, if a little anxious. Again, Freya had studied the picture so intently that she knew it by heart: the short brown hair, the thick eyebrows, the loping smile and the large nose. The dark-haired chest, the navy-blue vest, the taut biceps and washed-out denim jeans. It had taken her a few moments when she first saw it, to recognise Duncan. Now he was unmistakably Duncan.

She kissed his face, then sighed at her stupidity and slipped him into the back of her book. This changed something, but she wasn't sure what.

She kept seeing those eyes, and when she saw them, they were looking at her, that intense look he gave her when they were lying together, the look that climbed inside her head. She tried to remember. Daniel, the shy biologist. *That* look. It occurred to Freya suddenly that there was only one reason she could possibly be feeling so . . . reckless. And it was true. Ever since she and Duncan had been rubbing Danish oil into the windowsills together, there had been a sense of inevitability about things. A great wave carrying her along and she didn't care. She *liked* it. It could take her anywhere and it would be okay. It was that leap-off-a-cliff feeling, that don't-show-me-his-flaws feeling, that I-don't-care-what-else-I-find-out-this-is-too-wonderful-to-stop feeling. The give-it-to-me-now, I'll-take-the-job-lot, devil-may-care, I-can-do-anything feeling. This was 'in love', as sure as eggs were eggs, and she had never thought to feel it again.

26

MAKING BABIES AND KEEPING SECRETS

Miss Dowling has taken Sophie aside at lunch-time because she thinks that something is upsetting her. Sophie can't understand how Miss Dowling can possibly know this, and she finds it a bit scary. She has been trying hard not to cry, it's true, since Dillon approached her again about men having sex with women like cats. He wanted to make it clear that he knew as much as Archie. He saw it, he said, on the internet, and he smiled at her as if she might be pleased. She has managed to blink away some tears, but no one normal would see it, and she has the troubling feeling that Miss Dowling can read her mind. Now they are sitting by the coat pegs in an eerie silence. She hasn't answered any of the questions because it is making her head explode.

'Has someone said something to upset you?'

She says it so kindly that Sophie feels inclined to please her with an answer, and thinking about what did upset her, it did sort of start with what someone said.

'When sheep mate they have babies, don't they?'

'Usually – I believe so.'

Sophie sucks the nose of the sheep on her sheep pencil case.

'So, when people mate, they have babies too, don't they?'

Miss Dowling folds her lips together, then draws in a careful breath. 'Not always. No. Sometimes.'

Sophie finds that her lip is making strange movements on its own, and her eyes are filling up with tears. Miss Dowling rubs her arm gently. This is all going badly wrong.

'Hey, Sophie, you know you can talk to me. You can tell me anything, anything at all.'

Sophie strokes the fleece of her pencil case.

'Sophie?'

'I can't. I can't tell anyone.'

'And why's that?'

'I can't. It's a secret.'

Now Miss Dowling's hand stops its gentle rubbing. She takes it away and looks all alert.

'You don't have to keep a secret, Sophie. Can you remember what we said about secrets?'

Sophie vaguely recalls someone coming to talk to them a year ago in assembly, but it was so long ago that it's all a bit patchy. It makes her think of birthday cakes, and she feels suddenly hungry for the chicken sandwich in her lunchbox.

'Birthdays?' she tries.

'The only secrets that are okay are surprises,' says Miss Dowling. 'So, yes, keeping a secret about a birthday present so that it will be a nice surprise, that's okay. But . . .' Blah, blah, blah, blah. On she goes, and Sophie is too scrambled in her head to listen. It's all too much. Chicken sandwich, chicken sandwich.

'Sophie?'

'But bad things will happen if I tell anyone.'

'What bad things?'

'I don't know. But very bad things. Dying.'

There is a long pause. Miss Dowling is picking bits of imaginary fluff off her cardigan, which is red. 'If you can't tell me, can you talk about it to Mummy? She's a very kind person, and I'm sure she'd understand.'

'NO! Mummy mustn't know! Promise you won't tell Mummy anything!'

Sophie is feeling suddenly dizzy. Why is she telling Miss Dowling anything? What has she told her exactly? She wants to stand up and get her lunchbox, which she can see sitting underneath her hanging coat, but tears are spilling down her cheeks now, and she is breathing heavily. She wants Miss Dowling to go away and mind her own business. And she wants to tell her everything. She longs to tell someone who will make it all go away.

Now Miss Dowling has moved in closer and put her arm around her.

'Sometimes it's good to just talk, you know. To someone you can trust.'

'That's what Dunking says.'

'Dunking?'

'Mummy's new boyfriend.'

There is a pause, as if this is important.

'Do you like him?'

'He's all right. When he plays with me. He gave me an otter boat. It's brilliant. It has a fold-down bed and little pots and pans.'

'Mmm-hmm. Does he often give you presents?'

'He gave me otter babies as well – they're what I really, really wanted. That was because I didn't like his first present, but I don't want to talk about that. He gave me make-up too. Can I have my lunch now?'

Miss Dowling lets her go, and smiles a little too brightly and suddenly. She is not acting normal. She is being odd. Still, Sophie is too hungry to care. She collects her smiling kitten lunchbox and takes it to the classroom.

27

CHEAP AS CHIPS

The Greenhaven House do was spectacular, although it had been delayed because of flood damage. Duncan was glad that Lottie had suggested it. He was proud to have Freya with him, and she seemed impressed by the circles he worked in. He was pleased when people he wouldn't normally care about came up and thanked him for this or that, and especially when the director of Egmonts clapped his big hands around his hand and treated him like a long-lost friend.

'Aha! The man himself! I can't tell you how much we're enjoying the new space!' He turned a beaming face to Freya. 'A masterful designer you have here!'

'Oh, let me introduce you! This is my . . . girlfriend, Freya,' – he tried to catch her eye to see if this was all right by her, but she was all smiles – 'and Freya, this is James Egmont.'

James and Freya were chatting amicably when another man and woman approached and tapped Freya on the shoulder.

'Peter!' said Freya, turning in surprise. 'Eloise! Oh, James, Duncan, this is my late husband's boss, Peter Ferguson, and his colleague, Eloise.'

'*Peter*, old chap!' said James Egmont, clearly familiar with him already, and they began to chat with each other and with Freya like old friends.

Duncan was feeling that Reuben had somehow usurped him once again, when he noticed that Eloise (the 'colleague') was also at a bit of a loss.

'So, you know Freya too?'

'Not too well,' said Eloise, adjusting her shoulder bag awkwardly. She had a very distinctive long black plait going down her back. 'I worked with her husband, though. Late husband, I should say. Did you know him?'

'Er, no. I only met Freya fairly recently.'

'It's good to see her with someone.'

She smiled at him, and it was clear that they were both grateful to each other for the company. It was beginning to become crowded, and the thought of standing around like a spare part, prey to anyone who might clap you on the shoulder, seemed to be as much her fear as his. Of course, what he longed to ask her was stuck somewhere in his throat.

'I hear he was quite . . . quite a character – Reuben.'

'Oh. Yes. You could say that.'

He waited. She folded her lips together, as if to stop anything more coming out.

'You wouldn't, then?'

'Oh. Well. He was gregarious. *Very* good-looking. I suppose he was fun. Until he got the sack, anyway.'

Duncan tried to assimilate all this new information, but as soon as he tried to grapple with the '*very*' of good-looking, he had to deal with 'fun', and just as he began to kick it into the long grass before it hurt him, he had 'the sack' come and slap him like a friend telling him to wake out of a dream.

'The sack?'

Eloise looked awkward.

'Oh. I don't suppose Freya told you. Actually, he may not even have told her. He seemed to disappear off to Africa pretty sharpish.'

'You mean . . . that wasn't part of his job? Setting up new sources of clean water?'

'Not at all. No. He had been raising money for it. Maybe that's why his eye wasn't on the job. He got a bit too slack with the finances. Don't tell Freya I said that. I'd hate to upset her needlessly. I mean, she must've had a lot to put up with, what with the death and everything.'

'Canapés?'

Someone with a foreign accent was holding bite-sized what-nots between them.

'*Cannabis?* Good grief!' said Duncan, who had misheard for a moment. 'They don't do things by halves, do they? I'd better not, I'm driving.'

Eloise laughed, so much that she spilt some wine on her hand and Freya turned round for a second to observe them. Duncan was pleased, and he was just beginning to feel exceptionally mellow when something quite extraordinary caught his eye.

As Eloise went to open her bag for a tissue, he noticed an unusual key ring dangling from its zipper. For a moment he was speechless. He glanced over at Freya – she was still talking with the men. He tried to turn so that his back blocked them out; then he looked anxiously at Eloise.

'That's an unusual key ring. Where did you get it?'

'Oh, this?' She lifted it up indifferently. 'It's not a real four-leafed clover. We had them made for the patrons of Children First. Just a little knick-knack to go in their goody-bags, you know? They're quite realistic, aren't they? Just a fake paper leaf under clear plastic. Cheap as chips.'

Duncan could feel a rush of adrenaline. 'Not gold, then?'

She laughed again, and he tried to chuckle with her.

'What? The chain? I wish. Twenty-two-carat brass, I'm afraid. That's my kind of accessory!'

Duncan was terrified that Freya would see it. He tried to compute everything as fast as he could, and his greatest priority now, it seemed, was to prevent Freya from making any eye contact with the trinket dangling from the handbag. With this in mind, he turned and smiled at his girlfriend and she, as soon as she saw him, smiled back. James Egmont immediately included him in the conversation.

'Ah, here he is! This, Peter, is the best architect in Gloucestershire! Duncan Swan!'

He saw Freya glowing on his behalf and, in his peripheral vision, he saw Eloise being collared by someone else. Although he would have liked to question Peter about the man he had sacked, it was with some relief that he saw him accosted by a tall, colourful woman with a pretentiously arty trilby. He took Freya's arm fondly, and perhaps a little possessively, and he felt her warm to his gesture, sinking in to him slightly. They mingled for another half-hour, and then went back to his flat where he made love to her earnestly, as if he could keep her safe by covering every inch of her. He knew she had enjoyed seeing him in a professional context. He should have felt flattered, but instead what he felt was an exquisite and overpowering protectiveness for her. He suddenly knew with absolute certainty that he loved her more than any woman he had ever met, and that he wanted to spend the rest of his life with her. That he *was* going to, no matter what.

'I love you,' he said, unable to stop himself.

She beamed. 'I love you too.'

There had been a lot to take in, and he wasn't quite sure what to make of it.

After Freya left, Duncan rifled in the pocket of his other jacket and unfolded the papers he'd found in Freya's attic.

Reuben had had a pretty varied career. A reasonable set of A-levels (although nowhere near as good as his own); two years of a degree in Economics; two years as 'executive' at Barnes' Printworks; one year in the marketing department of a bank; two years in the marketing department of a DIY company; eighteen months for a cheese-spread manufacturer; eighteen months self-employed in marketing; one year part-time for a lottery fund; three years for a charity called Old Age Gracefully; two and a half for Food for Famine, and then nothing. Attached was an application letter for Children First, and a lot of stuff about how he was a 'people person' and how innovative and committed he was.

Duncan breathed in and out heavily. So . . . a man with itchy feet. A man who couldn't hold down a job for very long. A man who didn't *want* to hold down a job, perhaps. He tried to think what he had learnt. Something. Maybe nothing useful. The second and third sheets were not part of the biography, but were bank statements. A lot of their monthly income seemed to go out to a charity. He felt terrible snooping. What did this matter now? He should have torn the papers up and stuffed them into the skip. He folded them and slipped them back in his pocket.

On second reading, and after the Egmont's event, the curriculum vitae took on a more troubling appearance. He took it into work the following day and showed it to Lottie, along with the bank statements.

'Oh, tut, tut,' she said. '*Snooping* now. This is serious. You are seriously obsessed with this man, aren't you?'

He was disappointed. He had been convinced that Lottie would be horrified, especially when he told her about the cheap-as-chips four-leafed clover.

'Well, he was a wanker. That's all it is. He had a nerve, I'll give him that. But he was basically just a wanker. Stop worrying about him.'

'But *she* doesn't know it!'

'Why is that important? Do you want to be the person who disabuses her of the thought that her late husband was a good man? Who loved her so much that he bought her a priceless piece of bespoke jewellery? Hmm?'

Duncan sighed and looked back at his work. Lottie relented.

'Oh, Dunky! Dunkety Dunk. Listen. I do understand, actually. If you want to know – just for your own interest – if he's a real charlatan, why don't you look up *Eau Please!* in the Charity Commission records?'

Duncan brightened up. 'I will!'

He didn't want to get involved in a full-scale investigation of Freya's late husband, though. Whatever would she think of him if she found out? What could he do with the information if he found out something dodgy?

Lottie smiled at him. 'Why don't you do a trip to Africa yourself? You could do with a holiday. Do some digging.'

'No! Anyway, I'm planning on taking them all away at Easter, if things are still going well. Those kids have never been abroad. Except for Will, who did a day trip to Boulogne with his French class.' He leaned back in his chair. 'I'm going to take them all to Italy. I want to give them the best holiday ever.'

A few moments later Lottie looked up from her desk. 'Oh pull-ease! Sorry mate. I beat you to it. Curiosity – couldn't help it.'

It seemed that there was no record of *Eau Please!* at the Charity Commission.

28

DUNCAN HELD RESPONSIBLE

Duncan had been insistent that this Red Arrows thing would do the trick. Everyone, he said, would enjoy it. They would enjoy being teased that something far more grand was going to happen, and they would find the display so completely bonkers that they would be too tickled to care. Will was full of gratitude to Duncan for the idea, but he had invested so much in this display that he knew he would hold Duncan fully responsible if it went wrong. Nonetheless, he had begun to savour the fun of it all. He couldn't wait to see Donno's face when he came up with something so totally unexpected. He had even had some flyers made saying:

> ### DON'T MISS THE FUN:
> ### RED ARROWS DISPLAY
> #### FORMATION FLYING AT ITS BEST
> ### FRIDAY 10:45 AM
> ### THE PLAYGROUND
> #### (BROUGHT TO YOU BY WILL GRAY ASSOCIATES)

As soon as Donno saw the flyers, he was scathing. He came up to Will and scoffed at him. 'What you up to then? You think you can get a few buzzy little drones in the air to impress people? Don't make me laugh. Ash is relying on you. You'd better not cock this up, Gay Boy. Because you know what'll happen if you do, don't you?'

As he uttered this last sentence, his mouth became contorted with such spite that Will had to look away. His knees felt suddenly crumbly. There was so much riding on this display. God, he hoped it went okay.

He left nothing to chance. The eight other sad prefects agreed to meet in the house of one of them, Bradley, who lived nearby. There were six boys and two girls. They all met there at lunch-times and practised the display moves in the garden. It was cold outside, and the sky was a dull, oppressive white. Bradley's garden was spattered with soggy dead leaves and the grass was damp. When they came inside, they wiped their feet respectfully and Will gave them all a pep talk about how important it was to get this right. This was going to give them new respect in the school. This was going to make people laugh, but not 'at' them so much as 'with' them. They were going to show the alpha males and females and the likes of Donno (who pissed off all nine of them) that they were a force to be reckoned with.

Bradley was a hefty great beast with a friend called Louis who was equally tall and broad. They should have been prop forwards, but neither of them had any interest in sport. They were both computer geeks and each of them would apply to top universities and would probably get in. Bradley spent most of his time with a sugary lolly in his mouth and was very generous in his distribution of sweet lunch-time snacks.

'How about me and Louis pick you up on our shoulders at the end, and we do a sort of display pyramid?'

'A pyramid? Steady the fuck on!' said Louis, who wasn't sure he could hold up seven other people.

'No, I mean just Will. We lift up Will, and then the others sort of stand or kneel and we make a triangle shape.'

Will, who was perplexed at the thought of getting on top of anyone's shoulders at first, began to warm to the idea, and before that lunch break was over they had hatched a plan. When the last day of term arrived, there was far more interest than anyone had imagined in the mysterious Red Arrows display. Most of the staff had come out of their staff-room burrow to take a butcher's at this tantalising promise of aerobatics. Not least because Will Gray, that rather quiet, arty boy from Year Thirteen, was allegedly organising it.

Jack tried to make himself scarce for his brother's Red Arrows display. He was sickened by the general excitement about it, and especially tormented by Warren Gifford's pre-emptive contempt. 'It's clearly gonna be crap, but let's face it, I wouldn't miss it for the world. A chance to see Plumper's brother make a twat of himself. I am *so* gonna take some photos and post them everywhere!'

Jack pretended he didn't hear any of this. He stared at his phone and scrolled down his list of contacts as if there was some urgent and interesting message he was reading. There wasn't. He lingered over Will's name and pretended to answer an important message. He typed 'Good luck, bruv'. And then, because there was still time to kill, and he still wanted to be invisible, he carried on: 'Hope it all goes well for you!' and added a smiley face and a sheep. Then he recklessly pressed 'Send'. Oh well. It wasn't as if he didn't *hope* it all went off okay for Will; it was just that he was weighed down with the shame of it all.

The banter didn't stop. Ellie Chapman was in earshot and he could see her, in his peripheral vision, making her way outside with her girlfriends. Reluctantly he followed. He was going to have to watch his brother humiliate himself – and, by association, him – in front of the whole school, so he might as well witness the true extent of the damage. On his way outside he went to the toilets. He shut the cubicle door and ate a cheap brand bar of chocolate. It tasted disgusting. So disgusting that he took out the second one he had bought and ate that too. He might as well get rid of it, since it was so revolting. Now he felt sick, but he wasn't sure if it was the inferior chocolate or the thought of his brother's imminent humiliation. He concentrated on puzzling this one out to distract himself from being sick. Now was not the time. After tea, he would make himself sick with the hairbrush handle, although the chocolate and all its calories would be way ahead by then.

Outside, he took his place with the rest of his year group, who were lining the exterior fence of the tennis courts. There was a group of prefects in a huddle nearby, alpha males with the Head Boy and that bell-end Donno. Jack looked studiously down at his shoes. They used to be Will's. They weren't in very good nick now, because Jack had scuffed them a lot. He'd told his mum that if he got new shoes, just for himself, he wouldn't scuff them, because then he would have some pride in them. Oh God, Donno had spotted him.

'Oh look, here's the brother of the Gay Gray!' he shouted, and everyone in his year group heard it. 'You ready to watch your brother make a total tit of himself?'

Before Warren Gifford could join in, Ellie Chapman suddenly piped up, 'You being homophobic or what? You should be ashamed of yourself, you should!'

'Oooooh! Hark at the tart!' said Donno, clearly awkward at having been taken down a peg or two. But this didn't end it. Warren Gifford, to Jack's amazement, came out in manly defence of Ellie.

'Who are you calling a fucking tart?'

'You mean who am I fucking calling a tart?'

'You heard!'

Oh God oh God oh God. Please stop. This was *his* job. This was Jack's fantasy, to come to the rescue of Ellie Chapman, and now Gifford had pulled the rug from under his feet. No. *No!* He should've be the one to say that she was no tart. *He* should've be the one. And she had defended his brother. In the midst of his inner rage he found a warm wave of gratitude towards Ellie. She was okay with his brother being gay. She was more than okay. She might even have thought it cool. He was certain that she thought it cool. When he looked up to catch her eye and to give her a meaningful – and possibly smouldering – exchange of eye contact, what he saw was his brother peeping out from the door to the science block. Please God, may this not be too shit.

The pupils lined the edge of the tennis courts and the science block, mostly wearing tinsel and stuffing themselves with the chocolates and toffees they had brought in for each other as Christmas gifts. They were a rowdy bunch. Will and his Arrows took a peek at them from behind the science block doors and were daunted. Mr Fry, the Music teacher, had set up some speakers in front of the tennis courts and looked over to them. Will gave him the thumbs up and Mr Fry turned on *The Dam Busters* music.

'Right,' said Will. 'Here we go! Smile!'

They filed out on to the playground with little running steps and their arms spread out like wings under the red curtains, and the whole school seemed to erupt with laughter. They scattered to their positions with the same steps, smiling now because of the wonderful reception. Will was taking nothing for granted. He allowed himself a sense of relief as they ran into their first pattern and completed a strip-the-willow. Everyone was still hooting with laughter, and he wondered if something had gone terribly wrong. Were they scoffing? Did he have egg on his face or something? Had Donno smeared something on his outfit? But he didn't have time to think too much. The next move was more complicated: they had to weave up and down, up and down, in a sort of waves-of-tory move. People were clapping! People were whistling!

He hardly dared to look at his audience, but when he looked up, he saw the six boys and two girls who were in this with him trooping around in perfect formation, a formation he had taught them himself, and he felt an unexpected surge of pride and camaraderie. As the display began to reach its climax, Will could feel his breathing become more laboured. This would make it or break it. It would make him or break him. What folly to take this risk! What had he been thinking?

He saw Bradley and Louis go down on one knee just beyond the vaulting horse that Mr Fry had positioned for him. Will approached it now with his practised running step. He leapt on to the horse, glanced down at the broad shoulders of his friends, and placed one foot on each shoulder. Their hands came up and grabbed his calves, and as they did, both boys rose up to a standing position. The horse was swiftly taken away by one of the others and all the Red Arrows arranged themselves around him, standing or kneeling accordingly, for the final bars of the music.

The spectators were in uproar. They cheered and whistled and shouted, and now that the music had stopped the sheer volume of their applause could be appreciated. Will saw their audience fully for the first time. His Art teacher, Mrs Scriven, was clapping and hollering like a madwoman, and he caught sight of Evan Trinder, a boy he had a crush on from Year Twelve, leaning against the science block wall with what seemed to be a wry smile on his face. Will looked away, and then he looked back at him. Evan was definitely smiling, and he was definitely looking at him. Quite intently.

Will's stomach flipped. His lungs seemed too full of air to breathe in any more. People were still shouting, and now they were chanting for more. Louis and Bradley tapped him on the shins and he dismounted, leaping forward on to the soft mat that they had laid earlier. Instead of an encore they circled the playground with their red curtain wings held out proudly, and at the end of the lap of honour Will peeled off and led them back into the changing rooms. They all heaved great sighs. Will gave them all high fives. Clearly some of them had never done a high five before.

They were heroes.

29

BOXING DAY MORNING

Sometimes Jack had the strangest feeling, and he couldn't quite put it into words. It was something to do with what was hidden and what was revealed. It was as though they were all playing a game, everyone in the family. Mum was the unofficial organiser of the game, and they all followed. She knew the rules and they didn't, but they quickly got the hang of it.

He was thinking about this now as he looked at the large framed photograph of his dad on the dresser. Dad was wearing a warm red pullover, a sort of russet-red with a shawl collar (knitted by Granny Sylvia). His teeth, in the slightly soft-focus gaze of the camera, looked perfect, although in real life they were not. At least, not as far as Jack could remember. Also, he hadn't looked quite so much of a film star as he did in this picture. Mum talked about the eczema on his chin, which was always a little pink. Not so here – he seemed tanned, which would be unlikely in a winter pullover. Unless, of course, he had just come back from Africa. But Dad didn't often take a tan. And then there was the question of the smile itself: so easy and relaxed, so warm and full of bonhomie. Yes, yes, part of that was true. But this was not a smile for him, for Jack. It wasn't a smile for Sophie or for Will either. This was a smile like the one over Dracula's deck-chair. This was for that elusive everyman: the camera.

He wondered if Will and Sophie felt this too. He was so handsome, their dad, so clever, so funny, so witty, so healthy, so wise, so polite, so generous, so likeable, so perfect. So dead. Memory was all that held him in place, like the cardboard stand at the back of the photo frame. Mum said, 'He was so proud of you, Jack, so proud,' and he wanted so badly to remember Dad saying that, but he couldn't. He studied his father's wide smile when no one else was around, watching it for clues. Jack was feeling a pain in his head. It was a sharp constriction in his forehead, like two banister posts pressing against it. He was craning hard, desperate to catch what his father was saying. And there it was. He could hear it above all else. *That boy's getting fat.*

It had been a strange Christmas this year: a nice one, actually. For the first time in ages they hadn't been to Devon. They had stayed at home and Granny Sylvia and Grandad Steve just visited once a few days before. The only person there on Christmas Day was Aunty Rachel, and she was in a good mood. They had seen quite a lot more of Aunty Rachel since Dad died, but never like this. She brought them all presents and dressed up as Father Christmas and made Mum laugh – a lot. In fact, Mum seemed pretty laid-back altogether lately. Aunty Rachel said it was because she was all 'loved-up' over Duncan and that Duncan was good for her. Duncan had had to go to Scotland to visit his brother, Alistair, and his nephews the week before Christmas, and then he spent Christmas with his father in Stroud, so they hadn't seen him at all. Jack felt that if Aunty Rachel hadn't been there, they might have almost missed Duncan. In fact, in some ways . . .

Hang on. There was a horse looking in through the kitchen window. Jack was so excited that he didn't notice for a moment that there was also a rider sitting on the horse: a woman. He called to everyone to come and take a look. The woman was giggling and apologising for her horse, who was no respecter of private property. The woman was pretty, with short blonde hair and a wide smile. She was smiling now at a man who had driven up. They could hear the car door slam and it was Duncan's voice. Duncan knew the woman. He seemed to be with her in some way. Mum looked a little fragile, but she was managing a smile.

'I'm so sorry!' said the woman as Freya opened the back door. 'Biscuit can be quite naughty when he's excited.'

All of them went out and stroked the naughty, snorting horse. The lady dismounted and grinned at Duncan.

'Freya, this is Lottie,' said Duncan, walking up to Lottie and giving her a squeeze. 'Lottie Robins, my partner in crime.'

He was all smiles as he explained that Lottie's horse was stabled nearby, and he'd given her a lift up from Cheltenham so she could have a ride. He had been coming up anyway to bring the children some presents and Lottie thought it might be fun to show them all her horse. Jack was thrilled. The horse's nose felt like velvet, and he was letting Jack stroke him.

'Want to give him some treats?' said Lottie, rummaging in her pocket. 'Here.'

There was no stopping Biscuit now. He loved Jack. Jack loved him. He was a beautiful toffee-coloured horse with a thick cream mane and tail. Sophie liked him too, but she was holding back a little because of the steamy breath and the nodding head.

'Would you like to sit on him?' asked Lottie. Sophie shook her head. She wasn't ready.

'I'll sit on him!' Jack was more than ready. He was eager. He didn't want anyone else to take this chance from him. Lottie helped him up and there he was! He had his feet in the stirrups and he felt like a king. 'Take a photo, Mum! Take a photo!'

But Aunty Rachel was on it. She took loads of photos. She took photos of Jack on his own, mounted proudly on Biscuit, and she took photos of Jack with Sophie and Will standing beside the horse. Everyone was beaming, although Mum's smile was a bit wooden. Jack wondered if Mum was unhappy about Duncan being friends with this pretty woman, but he couldn't think about that now. This was just too important. This was one amazing moment. It was him on a horse. It was going to go global. Eat your heart out, Warren Gifford.

'Come on,' said Aunty Rachel. 'Let me take one of all of you.' Mum obeyed and came to stand next to her children. 'Come on, Duncan! You as well!' said Aunty Rachel, and Duncan went to stand next to Mum. Jack was glad when he put his arm around her. They all looked at Rachel, and she told them to smile. 'Come on, Biscuit! You as well! Why the long face?' And they all laughed. That's when she clicked the button. She was cool.

'Um. Would you like to come in, Lottie? And Duncan? For a coffee or something?'

'That's so kind of you, but I've got to get Biscuit back to his stables, and I'm meeting my wife at the pub for lunch.'

'Your wife?' Sophie was interested. Will was really interested.

'Yes. We only married last year, so we're newlyweds. Known each other for ages, though. Would any of you like to join us? There's going to be a mummers' play on at two, outside the pub.'

'I'll come!' said Will eagerly. 'I'd like to meet your wife.'

'Me too,' said Aunty Rachel.

Jack was forlorn. He didn't want this moment to end.

'Would you like to ride Biscuit back to the stables?' Lottie asked suddenly. 'I can lead you. He seems very happy with you.'

'Yes! Yes please!'

Sophie examined Biscuit's face with her head on one side, and Jack knew she was wondering how Lottie could tell that Biscuit was happy, because he probably wasn't smiling any more than he was before. He hoped she didn't say this. He also hoped she didn't want to come too, because then Mum would say no. But Sophie now had her eye on a colourful parcel that Duncan had brought out of the car.

Mum looked bewildered. Maybe she was relieved that Lottie was married to a woman, but she wasn't freaking out about him going off on a horse and going on to the pub. Also, Duncan said that he wasn't going with Lottie because it was really her that he'd come to see. This distracted her. Good. He hoped Lottie would be on for taking some photos of him actually riding her horse – and some more of him looking cool over a pint. Or something that looked like a pint. Eat your knee-caps, Warren Gifford.

30

O SOLE MIO

Sophie is intrigued. Inside the kitchen Duncan explains that he just called by because he has some presents for the children and he hopes Mummy doesn't mind. Of course she doesn't mind! She has been all soppy about him lately, and she thinks they haven't noticed. Anyway, why should anyone mind? He has brought them presents.

Sophie watches and waits patiently as Mummy makes him a cup of tea and offers him a mince pie. The parcel he has brought in from the car has mauve paper with reindeer on it. It's quite big. It must have presents for all of them inside. She won't say anything because that would be rude, but she likes the fact that Duncan has thought about them, and she likes the way his sellotaping is not very neat. She pictures him wrapping it up at home on his own, with no one to hold the paper in place. She imagines the paper not doing what he wants, like when she tried to wrap some chocolate bars for Will and Jack before Christmas, and a picture she had drawn for Mummy, and when she imagines him doing this for them all on his own, she feels a great tingly surge of cuddliness for him.

Now Duncan is rubbing the crumbs off his hands and he says he will just get some things from the car. When he comes back in, there are four more packages. He sits down again and says he must explain things about the presents for Jack and Will, and he will quite understand if they are not a good idea. What he has brought them are two laptops. They are from his work and they are less than three years old, but they always update every three years, and these belonged to him and the lady with the horse, and they have been 'reconditioned'. They are welcome to have them, but he will quite understand if . . .

Sophie tries to stay patient. She traces a picture of a sheep on the table with her finger, and then a picture of a lamb. Then she pulls the wax from around the candle. Duncan has given Mummy some of her favourite perfume and she is kissing him. Now, at last, he looks at Sophie and says he's made her wait long enough. He says he expects she'd like to wait until the boys are back before she opens her present, and she is about to feel upset when she sees that he is teasing. The big present is for her, and there is another, smaller one for her too.

When she tears off the paper, she can see straight away a picture on the side of the box: it's the Sylvanian log cabin! She is so excited she can barely breathe. But she remembers to say 'thank you' to Duncan, even if it comes out all jagged and funny. She gets down from her chair and goes to give him a hug. Mummy looks radiant. This hug has pleased Mummy, and that makes Sophie feel proud.

The log cabin is for her animals, and she thinks the beavers might like it especially, but the sheep will also be invited. There is a little ladder going up to the loft, two hammocks, a veranda and lots of space for entertaining and adventures. But there is the other parcel, and when she opens it she sees that Duncan has already thought of what the animals will need: a sofa, an oven, a sink and a rocking chair. Sophie is so happy that she has a funny feeling all over. She suddenly thinks she might cry or something. All these years she has waited for a doll's house from Granny Sylvia and now Duncan has given her this. Far better than a doll's house, and he has thought of everything. And he has never said he might get it – he hasn't said a word. He has just thought about what she would like and he has tried to please her. She looks at Duncan's gentle donkey face and she knows he cares about her, and for some reason it makes her feel as if her throat is being twisted. She goes to hug him again, and asks if he will come and play.

The others are still not back and the sun is sinking outside. Mummy puts the light on in Sophie's bedroom and asks Duncan if he would like another cup of tea. He nods, but he is playing a very important game with Sophie and she knows he won't desert her until the otters have arrived at the log cabin and sung for their supper. Right now, they are fighting against a massive storm under the bed. Duncan says he'll come down in a bit and go and fetch the boys from the pub if Mummy likes, but there is the sound of a car outside on the gravel, and Sophie is pleased.

The otters manage to get in their boat and make their way by river to the meadow where the log cabin is.

'Simon has been invited to sing for the beavers,' she tells him. 'And they've prepared a great feast in his honour.' At this point she plonks a half-eaten mince pie inside the log cabin. 'He can't wait to eat it.'

Duncan obliges by making Simon jump up and down in excitement. He drools with hunger and says how hungry he is in an Italian accent. Sophie is pleased that he remembers Simon's character.

'Did your friend manage to have a chat with her teacher?' he asks suddenly.

Sophie frowns. She doesn't want to talk about this now, but she knows Duncan is only being kind. 'She did try. She said she tried, but it didn't really work. Her teacher didn't really . . . understand or anything. Will you make him sing?'

'Yes. But just remember to tell her, she really will feel better if she talks to someone. Maybe, tell her to talk to her mum. Nothing bad will happen. I promise.'

'I can't tell Mummy,' she blurts. 'Please don't ask me to do that. I won't tell Mummy!'

Someone gives a little cough, and for a horrible second Sophie thinks Mummy is standing in the doorway. But it isn't Mummy. It's Granny Sylvia. She is standing there with her arms folded like she has caught them doing something they need to explain and she is waiting for the explanation.

'*Che bella cosa . . .*' sings Duncan, sticking the otter's face into the mince pie, "*na jurnata 'e sole . . .*'

Sophie wonders if Granny Sylvia heard her say she won't tell Mummy something, but she is pretty certain that Granny S would not miss the opportunity to interrogate her if she had. Perhaps it's okay. Why did *she* have to come and spoil everything? She hopes Duncan won't stop playing because of her.

In fact, Duncan looks up and nods at Granny Sylvia, then he continues in the loudest and most exciting voice Simon has ever used:

'. . . *O sole mio*
Sta 'nfronte a te!
O sole, o sole mio
Sta 'nfronte a te
STA . . . 'NFRONTE . . . A TE!'

31

THE MISTAKE

It took some time to persuade Sylvia to go. She was adamant that she deserved to see her grandchildren on Boxing Day. After all, she hadn't been allowed to have them down for Christmas Day, as usual. Freya explained wearily, as she had already done on the phone some weeks before, that she wanted a Christmas with her own family for once, in her own house, and with her sister, who was coming down from London specially for a few days. Sylvia didn't see why this precluded her *real* family – the children's real family. Aunty Rachel, said Freya, was their real family too. Ah, said Sylvia, but the children weren't her *sole contact* with her dead son. Freya could simply *not* imagine what that was like. Instead, she was foolishly letting some *complete stranger* into her house, and by the way she needed to talk to Freya about this Dougal chap. Duncan. His name was Duncan. Okay, whoever. She needed to know just how dangerous it was to let him into her house and play *alone* with Sophie, because you heard about these men, these men who preyed on women with children and pretended to be interested in them when actually, *actually*, they weren't remotely interested in an adult relationship at all. They were just using the poor single mother as a *way in* to her children. Oh, don't give me that he's-suffered-too stuff. They all have a sob story. Oh yes. You really need to smarten up, Freya. I'm sorry to say this, but you can be very *gullible*. And I don't mean that in a bad way. You always have been far too trusting. Of course, it's not exactly an *attribute*, but it's not your fault. Well, I'm just going to wait here until he's gone, and until the children get back.

'They're not coming back.' Freya didn't know what she was going to say next. The sun had pretty much set and there was just a glow on the horizon. They might turn up at any moment. They would hear the footsteps on the gravel when they did. She listened, alert, but there was nothing yet. 'They've gone out for the day. With . . . some friends.'

'Well, in that case, I'll just stay here until Dougal's gone.'

'Duncan.'

Freya filled up the kettle and dumped it on to its base. She said she would just text the children to see when they would be home, but instead texted Duncan upstairs to beg him to go to the pub and keep them there until she had got rid of Sylvia. She also asked him to pretend he was going but didn't explain why.

A few moments later he came tripping down the stairs and smiling into the kitchen, saying how good it was to see Sylvia again, but sadly he was off to visit his father. He gave Freya a hug, and went out of the back door. Sophie, who was halfway down the stairs, was still begging him to stay and play when the door closed. It occurred to Freya that she had wanted to ask Duncan something before he went. It was what she'd heard Sophie saying to him. She had been halfway up the stairs herself when Sylvia had interrupted his playing with Sophie. She had heard, 'I won't tell Mummy!' or something. She would quite like to know what they'd been talking about. Still, she knew he'd tell her. He had talked to her before about Sophie's fears, and he knew it was important to her.

Granny Sylvia did not let up. Despite her insistence that she deserved some time with her grandchildren, she totally ignored Sophie who, having looked briefly into the kitchen, went back upstairs to prepare a beaver–otter soirée in the log cabin.

Half an hour later, Sylvia was still there, and holding forth on what Reuben would have thought of Duncan.

'It's getting dark. You know you hate driving in the dark,' said Freya.

'Well, it's going to be dark anyway, so I might as well stay. I'm sure you can find somewhere to put me up.'

Words would not come to Freya. She was cornered. No! She felt a fury rising in her chest.

'I'm sorry, Sylvia. That's not possible. We have a house full. You can't just pop by with no notice and ask to stay, and for everyone to be free. I'm sorry. And I can look after Duncan myself, thank you.'

There was an uncomfortable silence. Sylvia flared her nostrils.

'Well. You may be able to look after Duncan, but you don't seem to want to look after your daughter!'

Oh joy! Oh relief! Sylvia had made it easy for her.

'I'd like you to go now, please.'

After a dramatic exit and door slamming (the back door didn't really do a slam – more of a rattle), Freya was left alone in the kitchen with a curiously exciting sense of triumph. And at that moment her phone bleeped. A text from her sister:

> *Just to say, Duncan is absolutely GORGEOUS! If you don't mind some advice from your little sister: Don't you dare let him go! Let yourself be happy, for God's sake!*

Freya smiled. She quickly texted Duncan to give him the all clear. It was so reassuring that Rachel liked Duncan. After years of understated disapproval, she had this new warmth and affection. She typed a quick reply to her sister, and found herself saying something quite reckless. It felt cathartic.

She bit her lip at how dangerously she was behaving.

After a few seconds a horrible thought swept over her. God, no!

She grabbed her phone. Oh, no. Oh no, no, no, no, no! She had sent the message intended for Rachel to Duncan. She doubled up and then lay down on the kitchen floor, her hands over her eyes.

32

HAPPINESS CREEPS IN

It was not a long walk to the pub, but Duncan obediently took his car out of the drive, edged past Sylvia's car, and parked it around the corner nearer the village. All the way along Stonely High Street he could hear music – fiddle-playing and concertina – but when he reached the King's Arms it had turned into predominantly very loud singing with harmonising. There were two bars. He put his head into the crowded public bar and looked around. It was so packed he could see no sign of Will or Jack. He went to the lounge, which was a little quieter.

'You look a bit lost,' said a woman on a bar-stool. She was middle-aged, with the tanned and grooved face of someone who worked outdoors. She had a strong Gloucestershire accent.

'I'm looking for . . . um . . . three women with two young lads – about seventeen and eleven? Their mum wants them back home.'

'Oh, Jack and Will. They're in there, having a good old sing-song.'

He looked over the counter and through into the other bar to where the woman nodded her head, and now he could see Jack and Will, sandwiched between Alex and Lottie, singing at the top of their voices. 'Amazing Grace'. They were both smiling and seemed to be having a whale of a time. He was reluctant to break things up.

'You must be Freya's new man?' the woman continued, raising her voice above the din. She held out her hand. 'Hilary. I run the farm up behind her house.'

'Ah! Good to meet you, Hilary. You must be Gloria's owner. Yes, I'm um . . . Freya's um . . .'

'So *you're* the fella!' shouted the barman, his attention suddenly piqued. 'We were wondering when you'd come in here. I'm Pete, by the way. AKA "the Poet".'

It seemed Pete wrote poetry, snippets of which he left on the pub tables on pieces of folded cream card. They were changed on a daily basis, if Duncan was interested, because he was quite prolific. He didn't get writers' block or anything. He couldn't understand writers who did. Poetry just came into Pete's head every day, and he had to write it down. He also liked baking, following a popular television show, and gave out free samples of his tray bakes if you were lucky. He offered Duncan a raspberry and almond slice.

It occurred to Duncan with sudden force that he had missed a trick. Of all the places he could have done some easy research into Reuben, the village pub had not even crossed his mind. He primed himself to ask a key question, but nothing came to mind. He felt he was in an interview and had reached the last dreaded question: *Is there anything you'd like to ask us?*

'Thank you. I'm Duncan. I . . . I haven't, um, explored much yet, I'm afraid. Great pub.'

'Well, you must be doing a good job with those boys,' said Hilary. 'Haven't seen them so happy in years.'

'Ah, yes. It must've been hard for them, what with . . . their father . . . um.'

'Oh, him!' said the barman, leaning on his elbow now, as if for a chat. 'He's some act to follow and no mistake!'

Duncan felt very small and stupid. He wished he hadn't come.

'Yes. I hear he was quite something.' He cringed at his own lack of subtlety. Clunk, clunk. Please tell me something. Anything. Crumbs of information eagerly awaited. But nothing I don't want to hear. In fact, nothing.

Pete changed leaning arms, as if he were in for a long conversation.

'If he were in here now, he'd be going round with his collecting tin, getting cash out of everyone. He wouldn't miss a trick, he wouldn't.'

'Yes. I hear he was good with charities.'

'Good with his *own* charity, he was.' Duncan was about to ask him to elaborate when Pete continued: 'And what's more, if he was in here now, he'd be stood there in the middle of that crowd singing lead vocal, like it was his do or something.'

'And he'd buy everyone a drink, wouldn't he?' supplied Hilary.

'Oh yeah. He'd put 'em all on tab and then forget his wallet. Oh yeah. Generous fucker, he was.'

Duncan was shocked at what he was hearing. He wanted to be pleased. He felt guilty that he had provoked the revelation of a stream of flaws in Reuben. He hoped there might be a few cracks in his guilt for the pleasure to seep in, but it didn't seem to be happening. Instead, he felt a moment of panic. Everything was turned on its head. It was like the moment he discovered that the key ring was a fake: his first impulse was a desperate need to protect Freya. And now he felt a great protectiveness for her children too. And he felt indignation as well. How dare Reuben have enjoyed the privilege of being Freya's husband all those years. How dare he have been even a tiny fraction not good enough for her. He found he was suddenly gritting his teeth at the injustice of it.

'I'm glad you're with Freya,' said Hilary. 'She's had a hard time.'

'Yeah, she *has* had a hard time,' said Pete. 'You look after her, mind.'

Duncan said he would, and at that moment he spotted Rachel coming out of a large oak door marked 'Toilets'. He made his way over and she beamed.

'Duncan! Have you come to join the fun?'

He explained that Sylvia had arrived unexpectedly, and they were not to go back until the coast was clear. She laughed at the mention of Sylvia and called her 'a piece of work'. He offered to buy them all a drink, but she declined, saying they had all gone non-alcoholic for the sake of the boys, and they were on water and crisps at the moment, of which they had plenty. They were suddenly hemmed in against the window by a group emerging from the other bar. Duncan saw that Rachel had the same big front teeth as Freya and the same elegant neck and large, heavy-lidded eyes. Her brown hair, unlike Freya's, was cut short and gave her a gamine look. He didn't know which way to turn, so he smiled.

'Are you staying to eat with us?' she asked.

'I'm afraid not. I'm spending this evening with my dad in Stroud.'

'That's good of you.'

'That's the kind of sad bastard I am.'

She put her head on one side and considered him. 'Hm. You do look a little sad at times, but you're no bastard.'

'But women seem to like bastards. You mean I'm not sexy.'

'I definitely don't mean that.'

He didn't know what to do with this compliment. It was so unexpected that he wasn't sure if it *was* a compliment – or a mistake. Or was she flirting with him? Impossible. Women didn't flirt with him. He stood frozen, looking at a tree through the window, like a deer waiting and listening for a rustle in the undergrowth. When he brought himself to look at her, she was smiling a wide, generous smile.

'You're good for my sister.'

'Am I?'

'Yes. You are.'

Good for her. He wasn't sure about that. It made him feel a bit like a bottle of vitamins.

He could see she was about to make her way back to the other bar to join her nephews, and that he would have to go too, when it occurred to him that this was another unique opportunity. He tried to summon the courage to ask her. Tell me about Reuben. What was Reuben like? I mean, what was he really like? Did she love him so helplessly that I'm wasting my time? I may be good for her, but can she ever really love me as much?

Someone jostled them accidentally, and she made as if to go. He pounced clumsily with his question: 'Rachel, is there something I should know . . . about Reuben?'

She turned and hesitated. 'Yes,' she said.

'What?'

She came in close to his ear: 'He's dead. As a door-nail.'

Then she was smiling again. What did she mean?

'Sometimes . . . it doesn't feel as though he is.'

She nodded knowingly. 'She'll get there. Believe me, he hadn't really been around much for years. Not in any real sense. At least now he's properly gone – although it was hard not having a body to bury, so it may take a little longer.'

'Of course. I hadn't taken that into account.'

They were making their way to join the others now. She sat down next to Lottie and chatted for a bit, then texted someone. Lottie and Will pored over a piece of cream card that read: *The earth tilts me towards the dark, and I have to wait till dawn now for the lark.* Will was trying to work out with Lottie how to make this scan effectively, and Duncan tried explaining to Will about Granny Sylvia's arrival, when he felt his phone vibrate in his pocket. It was Freya to say the coast was clear. He told Will he was just heading for the toilets and then they had better make their way.

Just as he reached the gents' toilets, his phone buzzed. It was Freya again:

> *Glad you think he's gorgeous. So do I! Of course I don't mind some sisterly advice. Actually, I think I may have met the man I'd like to spend the rest of my life with!*

He stared at his phone incredulously. It took a while to sink in. Then he felt a rush of empathy for Freya. He closed his eyes as he imagined her torment on discovering what she'd done. He tried to think how he could help her out of this faux pas and keep her dignity intact. But there were definitely some little cracks in his sympathy for the pleasure to seep in, and this time he let it in. A trickle at first, and then a flood.

When the children were dropped back home, Duncan didn't stay. He met Freya's eyes briefly: a quick, curious glance, as if to verify what he had read. She couldn't look at him, and he went to his car in the lane as Will and Jack regaled her and Sophie with stories of horses and rides and men in coloured rags and gay marriage. Both Jack and Will seemed radiant. He knew she had longed to see them both this happy and he wished she could feel radiant too.

He texted her from the car:

> *Hi Alistair, of course I don't mind a bit of brotherly interest. Actually, I think I may have met the woman I'd like to spend the rest of my life with. She's simply wonderful.*

33

OUT OF HARM'S WAY

Will thought things were pretty wonderful for the rest of the holidays. Aunty Rachel rang Mum regularly and that made her happy. Once she spoke to Will on the phone and said to tell Mum that Duncan was 'a keeper', and that if she didn't already have a boyfriend she would be going for him herself, so she'd better watch out. She emailed them all the photos she'd taken, and Freya gazed lovingly at the five of them: her and Duncan, Sophie, Will and Jack with Biscuit the horse. 'You even look like a family,' Rachel had put on the email. And they did. A very happy one.

On New Year's Eve Duncan made them all a great lasagne and served it up speaking Italian. He taught them Italian phrases and promised to take them all to Italy sometime. Even Sophie learnt *Buon appetito!* and *Prego*. Afterwards they went out to watch the low-budget fireworks in a field by the pub. When they'd got back and Sophie was in bed, Duncan mentioned the photo of the five of them he'd spotted above Mum's bed. He really liked it. He stayed over that night. It seemed like the natural thing to do. Nobody minded, least of all Will.

What Will hadn't been able to tell his mother – or anyone – was how angry he was with his father. It wasn't just because of the refusal to accept his sexuality (although that really was the pinnacle of his fury); it was also because his father died before he could prove anything to him or make him proud. He could not, *could not*, forgive Dad for not being there when he got an A* for his Art GCSE, and an A* for Photography as well. Put that in your pipe and smoke it! Oh ye of little faith! He had *needed* to see his dad's reaction to that. Dad who did so many good deeds, Dad who was always right about everything, Dad who just *knew* Will would grow out of his gayness and fall in love with a girl, Dad who thought Art was a waste of space: that Dad. He wanted to see that Dad's face when he saw Will's success. He wanted his dad to happen upon his work, displayed all along the school corridors, on parents' evening. He wanted him to be there when he received the Art Prize at prize-giving, and he wanted him to hear what Mrs Scriven had said about him. ('And now for the artist whose paintings this year have blown me away, an artist you are all going to hear more about, so just remember you heard it here first . . . Will Gray!') After all that crap from Dad, and just when he needed him, just when he could've made him proud, he goes and buggers off and sodding well dies! Well, that wasn't something you could calm down about easily.

And although this wasn't something to be proud of, he would've liked Dad to catch a glimpse just once – and just a quick flash – of the cuts on his arms. He would've liked his dad to wonder if he'd seen it properly. Surely not? His son? Cutting himself? Although, when Will ran this one past in his mind, he knew there was a strong possibility that it would not have evoked anything like sympathy or regret in his father. Probably just irritation and more denial. ('Am I supposed to think you're a *victim* or something? There are people starving in the world, Will, people with no clean water to drink, and you think it's clever to copy a load of sad people who are "self-harming". Well, let me tell you . . .')

The cutting had all started when his dad had come home and discovered him with Rashid. It had never been done with any wish to be discovered, even if he did fantasise now about his father discovering it. He couldn't say why he had done it. A form of control over things, perhaps, when he felt he was going to implode with frantic emotions he couldn't stop. And maybe even some self-punishment and self-loathing after his dad's reaction to his sexuality. And somehow it did make him feel better. It seemed to calm the chaos of his exploding emotions by creating a dramatic diversion. He really couldn't say for certain why it was almost pleasant, but, after the horror that wouldn't go away, it was.

He stopped doing it for a while, but then it started up again last year when Donno and some of his mates roughed him up on the bus on the way home from school. They grabbed him when he came up the stairs to the top deck and pushed him down the gangway to the back of the bus. They shoved him hard again and he fell heavily sideways and hit his cheek on the floor. He'd chipped a tooth and cut his tongue, and his knuckles were scuffed and bleeding. The next time they did it they kicked him, and he was scared he would be left for dead on the top deck, discovered at the end of the shift by the driver or someone cleaning for the bus company. In fact, he hadn't been too badly hurt, and the bruises could all be hidden by clothes. But that was when they first called him 'the Gay Gray', and he knew he must always, always hide that side of himself, or it would never stop. In fact, it stopped this term when Jack started secondary school and began catching the bus with him. They obviously picked on loners. He didn't know what Jack had heard about him, but lucky for Will that Jack was no cool guy either, and he seemed happy to stick with him on the bus.

He didn't want his mum to see the scars. He didn't want her to be upset, and he knew she would be. She'd had enough upset recently, so he hid them as best he could. It was bizarre how much of your flesh you could hide from the world. But now, when he looked at the scars, he couldn't really grasp why he'd done it. He felt no desire, any more, to increase their number, and he wished they would melt away.

Today, on the first day back after the Christmas holidays, he and Jack were both cool guys. They went to sit upstairs defiantly. Other kids smiled at the famous 'Red Arrows' leader. He smiled back. Jack was happy because he'd gained some mileage from being a horseman on Facebook, and the girls all wanted to know about his horse. He may have been losing a bit of puppy fat too. But above all, Will had met Lottie and Alex, a gay couple who were happily married, and he knew that everything was going to be all right. One day he would be like them. He would find someone to love and make it public and nobody would mind. They could celebrate in style. And Donno would have to make do with any idiot who'd have him, some poor girl who'd end up wishing she'd never married him. But that was her lookout.

34

QUESTIONING SOPHIE

Sophie is wobbly about being back at school. At first, she liked telling everyone about her Christmas presents and hearing about other people's. But now she is sitting in a room at school she has never sat in until now. It is something to do with the grown-ups, although not necessarily the teachers, because she has never seen these two women before. Miss Dowling is there with her, but there is a thin woman with very short grey hair – almost like a man's – and another one with plump hands and big rings. One ring is red and glassy and Sophie thinks it looks like a sweet you could suck. The grey woman introduces herself as Sheila, and the ring woman says she is called Erica. Erica smiles a lot and Sheila doesn't, but she seems gentle.

There's lots of chit-chat, asking Sophie stuff about her cat and what she likes doing in her spare time. 'I play with my Sylvanians,' she says, and Erica clearly knows what these are as she asks her about her favourite animals. 'I did like the ducks, but now my favourites are the otters. Duncan bought me the otter boat, and the otter babies, so now there's lots for them to do.'

The women exchange glances.

'Who's Duncan, Sophie?'

'My mum's, sort of, boyfriend.'

'And what's he like?'

Sophie squishes her mouth over to one side. She has never been asked to say what Duncan is like before, and it's not easy.

'He's . . . a bit like a donkey,' she says at last. This feels like a very difficult game – harder than the furniture game. She sighs heavily with the weight of her decision. 'And a cello . . .'

There is a pause before one of them asks, 'In what way is he like a donkey and a cello?'

'He's got . . . a very big nose, and big sad eyes and . . . he's very gentle. His voice is deep.'

'Uh-huh,' says Sheila, writing something down. 'And does Duncan play with you?'

'Sometimes. He makes Simon, one of the otters, sing *Oh-so-lay-miaow*.'

'And does Mummy join in?'

'Not when Duncan's there. She's usually doing something else.'

Another pause. And now a creepy smile.

'And does Duncan often give you presents?'

'He bought me a green crocodile, but that made me cry so he bought me the otter boat and the babies, and then he bought me some make-up in a special make-up bag.'

Erica looks concerned and starts to fondle her fruity red ring, and Sheila scribbles something quickly in her notes. Sophie looks at Miss Dowling for some guidance, but Miss Dowling gives her an anxious smile.

'Does Mummy know about the make-up?'

'Oh yes. He gave it to her to give to me.'

'And when do you put it on?'

'Oh, it's not real. Well, the mascara is real – sort of – but the rest is only pretend, really.'

Sheila nods slowly. 'Do you often pretend to do grown-up things?'

This feels like a trick question. Erica doesn't look like she thinks this is a good question, because she is frowning a little at Sheila. Sophie looks at the red stone in Erica's ring, and it looks like something strawberry-flavoured. She imagines how it would taste in her mouth.

'I'm hungry. Can I have my banana now?'

35

TAKEN IN

A chilly January Friday to spend together. Freya arrived at Duncan's flat mid-morning, cold cheeks ablaze.

'I'm going to take you out to lunch,' he said, slipping the Italian phrasebook into his pocket. 'And I'm going to teach you some Italian. But first, *carissima*, I need to take you into this room here . . .'

They made love in his bed. It was leisurely and intense, and when she lay for some time afterwards with his head on her chest, the expression 'loved-up' came to mind. She felt entirely loved-up, as Rachel would say. Loved up and down. Loved through and through. Things were about as perfect as she dared believe they might be. And it was a shame, really, that events had to happen as they did, right then, on that particular morning.

They had moved into the lounge and were holding mugs of coffee, planning their little trip out, still flushed and feeble from loving, when the doorbell rang. Duncan went to the window and looked down. There seemed to be two women standing by the door. They could have been Jehovah's Witnesses, but he couldn't really tell whether they were dressed smartly enough from the view he had.

'Let's ignore it,' he said.

'Might be important,' said Freya. 'Might be a parcel?'

'Two women?' He moved over to the entry phone anyway and picked it up. 'Hello? . . . Yes . . . Well, I'm a little busy. What do you want? . . . Yes, that's me . . . What? I think you've got the wrong Mr Swan . . .' He heaved an exasperated sigh and pressed the buzzer to let them in. 'I think they've got the wrong flat. They'll soon realise.'

Footsteps could be heard on the stairs and by the time he'd pulled on his shirt and opened the door, two women stood there, one with a deep fur collar and the other wearing a flimsy scarf. 'Can we come in? This won't take long.'

Freya frowned. She was snuggled comfortably on the sofa in Duncan's pullover and didn't want to be interrupted on this precious free Friday. She wanted Duncan to deny them entry, but they were in now, and looking for somewhere to sit. Freya did not move. There was another, smaller sofa and the two women sat on it without waiting to be asked.

'I'm sorry, who are you exactly?' asked Duncan.

'I'm Cheryl and this is Anne. We're from the Police Child Protection Services,' said the woman with the fur collar, smiling.

'So you said, but I think you've got the wrong flat.'

'You *are* Duncan Swan, from SwanRobins?'

'Yes.' Duncan rubbed his forehead and swallowed hard.

The fur-collared woman stroked an A4 folder on her knees and turned her head towards Freya. 'And you are . . . ?'

Freya was speechless with indignation. She must have looked as if she would say something angry, because Duncan said, 'She's my girl-friend, Freya.'

'Ah,' said the woman, exchanging looks with her partner.

What did she mean, 'Ah'?

'Look,' said Duncan, sounding clearly irritated himself now, 'you've caught us at a difficult time and we really are extremely busy. So if you could just get to the point of your visit, we'd be very grateful.'

'You might like to talk to us on your own.'

'No, I wouldn't. Freya is here as my guest. I don't want her to go.'

Freya felt a sense of relief. It was good to hear Duncan stand up to this woman. But she looked at Freya now with something like pity and breathed out a long breath as she turned back to Duncan.

'There's been an allegation against you.'

'An allegation? By whom? What sort of allegation?'

'Child abuse.'

'*What?*'

'Child sexual abuse.'

'But I—' He gasped and looked at Freya for help. She was aghast. He paced over to the window and back again. 'But I don't . . . work with children. I'm an architect.'

'We know. We went to your firm first, and they told us it was your day off.'

'Look, who's made this allegation?'

'We're not at liberty to say.'

'What do you mean, you're not at liberty to . . . ? What . . . ? I . . .'

'What child?' asked Freya, finding a voice at last, but only a very small one.

Now both women looked uncomfortable. Once more they consulted each other's eyes and the furry one said, 'I'm afraid we're not at liberty to say.'

'I'm sorry,' said Duncan, angry now, 'you come in here – into my home – and tell me I've sexually abused a child, but you can't tell me which one or who says I did?'

'We are not accusing you of abusing anyone. If you'd like to come with us, we could give you more details about the child concerned.' She glanced at Freya. 'But I'm afraid we can't do so in front of a third party.'

'Oh, now I have to go with you? And if I do, do I get to hear who made this ridiculous allegation?'

'I'm afraid we won't be able to divulge that.'

'Oh, so not the child in question, then?'

The woman rose and so did her partner. 'Is that your laptop?'

Duncan didn't reply. He put his hands to his head in horror.

'Is that your laptop, Mr Swan?'

'Yes! Yes, it is my laptop. And you can search it all you like, but there's no child porn on there, if that's what you're hoping for!'

'Mr Swan, please try to stay calm. As I said, we're not accusing you of anything. We're simply investigating a claim at this point. Of course, it could be totally false, and we hope it is. You are not under arrest.'

'But you want to search my laptop.'

'If you have nothing to hide—'

'Take it! Search it – please!'

'Thank you for being so cooperative. You are being very helpful.'

And that was how the pleasant morning ended. At first Freya took herself out and walked around town, imagining that Duncan would soon be returned and they could go for lunch, as if they could even salvage something of the day. She looked listlessly at the January sales in the shops, her pulse pounding, stroking clothes on their hangers but not registering them at all. Something was happening. Her stomach felt empty and she was taking fast, deep breaths. It was only when she went for a coffee and was unable to drink it, when the smell of croissants and Danish pastries from the counter made her feel nauseous, that she realised, with sudden certainty, that there would be no rest of the day. This was not going to go away. A great fault line had opened up, and from now on, events would be referred to as before and after this happened.

She picked up her phone in terror and checked for messages, but there were none. She thought of phoning Sophie's school, but knew that no one would be able to tell her anything. Surely if Sophie were involved then she would have been informed? No . . . no . . . She tried to remember her training. If the child's family was suspected of being involved, then there was no requirement to inform the mother in advance of questioning a child. She thought that was it. She couldn't be certain. What if they suspected *her*? No, more likely they were afraid she would collude with Duncan to protect him. Oh, come on! Duncan? Sex abuse? With Sophie? Sophie adored Duncan. She didn't get agitated when he came around. She hadn't started wetting the bed or . . . washing her hands or . . . refusing food. No. It was ridiculous. Although . . . What if it had only *just* started? What if he had been grooming her? He might well have waited until the moment that Sophie trusted and adored him and then . . . *pounce*! Think about it. He had told her he needed to talk about Sophie, that he suspected someone might be threatening her or making her promise stuff. He had, maybe, implied abuse. What if all that had just been a lulling tactic? Maybe he had been trying to put her off the scent by playing the caring friend? Oh God. What if those gift laptops had been scrubbed because they'd contained . . . ?

What was she thinking? She loved Duncan. She *knew* Duncan. But wasn't that the thing with paedophiles? Their wives always thought they knew them. They stood by them in court, they sent the newspaper reporters packing, they held their spouses' hands in public because they knew. They knew the fabric of their husbands. They were utterly certain of their innocence. They brushed aside stray thoughts of enticing treats, of hands stroking, of veiled threats and vile acts of . . . oh, oh – they shoved those rogue thoughts away. And then the verdicts came through: either guilty or not enough evidence. Some still smiled at the cameras and held tightly on to the spousal hands. Others avoided the prying lens. And you could imagine all of them, all of those tortured wives, having a moment of suspicion: *What if he did . . . ? What if he was . . . ?* And then rallying, preferring denial, preferring loyalty to a lifetime of memories than to any new evidence. Loyalty to memories . . . Where had she heard that? You can't be loyal to a memory. It has no feelings. Or something like that.

36

STILL QUESTIONING SOPHIE

'Now, Sophie, do you remember we asked you if you liked pretending to do grown-up things?'

Sophie breathes out heavily and nods. It is making collages after break and she is missing it.

Miss Dowling leans forward and says, 'Sophie, do you remember when we were talking about sheep, and you said you knew about "tupping" in humans too?' She waits for Sophie to nod warily. 'And you were anxious because someone was making you keep a secret. Was that Duncan?'

Sophie is horrified. She takes in a sudden breath and doesn't know, momentarily, how to let it out. 'No!' she exhales. 'No! That was—'

Silence. Glances. Anxious faces.

'Who, Sophie?'

'I can't say. I told you! I can't say.'

'You were afraid something bad would happen if you said, but nothing bad will happen. I promise.'

More exchanged looks. Was this a *real* promise, or a Granny Sylvia promise? But Sophie is feeling heavy heavy. More than anything she wants to believe them. She wants to tell. And didn't Duncan tell her she would feel better if she told someone? And Duncan seems to know stuff.

'Just, you mustn't tell Mummy.'

There is a hesitation amongst the women.

'I can promise you nothing bad will happen to your mummy if you tell us. Who has told you it will?'

Silence. She wants to tell.

'One of your brothers?'

'*No!* It was Daddy. Daddy said if I told anyone, bad things would happen. And I didn't tell anyone except Chunkables, but as soon as I did, Daddy died. So you see, bad things can happen if you break a secret.'

There is a quiet kerfuffle amongst the women. The bell rings outside in a corridor. Miss Dowling whispers something about 'dead' and 'two years ago' and Sophie knows who they are talking about.

'Who's Chunkables?'

'Our cat.'

The next question is very gentle. 'Did he touch you, Sophie?'

'Chunkables just sort of brushes past you.'

'No, your daddy. Did he touch you?'

'Daddy? How do you mean?'

'Did he touch you anywhere that made you uncomfortable?'

Oh no! Sophie is fed up with all this now. This was meant to make her feel better, but now they're asking more questions, and she's hungry.

'I'm hungry,' she says.

'Sophie,' says Miss Dowling. 'When we spoke you were worried about someone having babies. Was that you?'

37

BUBBLES IN THE AIR

Her coffee had gone cold and Freya pushed it to the far side of the café table. She fidgeted and fought to keep her hands away from the phone. She waited until it was school break time, then picked it up and rang Emily Dowling, Sophie's teacher. It went straight to voicemail. She texted her:

Hi Emily, sorry to bother you. Is Sophie okay?

Some time went by. The waitress cleared her coffee away and Freya felt like an impostor at the table with nothing in front of her, so she ordered a cup of peppermint tea. When the phone bleeped at last, it was Emily to say that all was fine as far as she knew. *As far as she knew.* What did that mean? Freya began to wonder if there was something being hidden from her. What if Sophie had been questioned? She'd seemed fine yesterday. In fact, she'd seemed fine all week. Or had she? Had Freya failed to spot something? What if she was being questioned right now? What if poor little Sophie was being asked grotesque questions about . . . dreadful things? She grabbed her phone again. Emily was a friend as well as a colleague. She wouldn't keep anything from her. But then again, if Sophie had been questioned and they had decided not to tell Freya, Emily would be put in a difficult position by Freya demanding to know what was going on. To hell with it. She texted Emily again:

Hi Emily. Is something going on with Sophie?

There was no reply. Of course not. Emily would be in lessons. Emily would be teaching now and the children would be sitting cross-legged on the carpet as she showed them something new and answered their waving arms. Or else Emily didn't want to answer because it would involve telling her a lie . . . Maybe Freya should simply march into the school and bring Sophie home. Ask Sophie herself. Oh, Lord. What would she say? Has Duncan ever . . . ?

Then a recent memory thumped her in the stomach. She had gone upstairs to rescue Duncan from Sylvia, and she'd heard Sophie saying to Duncan, 'I won't tell Mummy!' And Sylvia had heard it too. Oh God. Maybe Sylvia had been right all along.

She started to walk fast down the Regent Arcade. Suddenly a wheel in the massive ornamental clock started spinning, a mouse peeped out of a flap, a serpent rose up, bubbles started floating around her and the tune of 'I'm Forever Blowing Bubbles' rang out like a barrel organ. Small children danced about her trying to touch the bubbles.

The phone bleeped. It was Duncan:

I'm so sorry, Freya. This is taking longer than I thought. I'm waiting for a solicitor now. I can't believe it. I even have to show them this communication! At least no charges have been made, but I'm taking no chances. I think we'll have to abandon our plans for today. Please don't wait for me. XXXXX

Well, that was it. Why would he have to show them the communication if Sophie wasn't in some way involved? Especially as he hadn't been arrested. Oh God. Oh God. She was going straight to the school as soon as it was home time. She would know. She would know from Sophie's face.

Duncan sat for two and a half hours in the police station waiting room before he was 'booked in'. Anger did not seem a helpful reaction, so he tried to remain as affable as possible. After half an hour, he asked at the desk if he should have a solicitor, and then decided that he would like one anyway. His own solicitor, it transpired, was away in Mauritius, so he agreed to any other solicitor in the practice. No one would be free until after lunch, he was told. Looking at his watch, he felt pretty certain that it would make no difference. Everything was taking an age. While he waited, information about the allegations was passed on to the staff sergeant within earshot of everyone else in the waiting area. He hoped there was no one he knew there. He looked steadfastly at his shoes. They looked calmly back at him. Who would want to be in his shoes now?

38

AND STILL QUESTIONING SOPHIE

'Sophie,' says Miss Dowling. 'When we spoke, you were worried about someone having babies. Was that you?'

Whatever is she talking about? Sophie wiggles in her chair. She knows she is going to have to make herself remember what she doesn't want to remember, but maybe that is the only way to stop all this. To stop the heaviness, to tell someone, to get out of here and these women looking at her.

She remembers that she was ill, but she can't remember now what she had because it was so long ago. Before Daddy even died. She must have been very ill because she was in bed and Mummy came up and gave her some Calpol and told her she could stay in bed and not go into school. Mummy was going out but Daddy was able to work from home, so he would be downstairs if she needed anything. She was very tired and she probably slept. All that is a bit of a blur, but she does remember feeling better later and wanting to do some dressing up. She crept out to the dressing-up box – which was a big ottoman on the landing – and rummaged through it to find the cat costume. The cat costume was the best thing Mummy ever made. Jack said the best thing was his parrot, but that's not true. It was definitely Sophie's cat costume. Mummy made it for a playschool production called . . . Sophie can't remember what it was called now, but she was a cat. It wasn't a big role at all. All she had to say (once) was 'Miaow!', but Mummy made it the best role of all by making the best costume. It was made of black fur material from head to toe, with a big oval of white fur on the tummy. The whole thing zipped up at the back. There was a hat thing that did up under the chin, also in black fur, with big triangular black ears. There were furry paw mittens, which you could take off so you could scratch your nose or something. Mummy had drawn big whiskers on her face with eyeliner stuff on the day itself. But the best thing of all was the tail, which was long and Mummy put wire inside it so that it turned up at the back and didn't drag on the ground. Everyone had loved the tail. Children stroked her. She'd looked like a real cat.

She found the main bit of the costume and put it on, although she couldn't do it up at the back. She found the mittens, and the tail still looked good, although it had a bit of a kink in it. She didn't know how to do the whiskers. She went into Mummy and Daddy's bedroom and looked in the long mirror. You could tell she was a cat anyway, and Daddy would be surprised and amazed. She couldn't find the hat, so she put a pair of Daddy's pants on her head, because that's what Jack used to do when he was pretending to be a bishop or a judge. She thought she looked pretty funny, and she knew Daddy would laugh, so she crept downstairs very, very softly to surprise him. Ta-da!

He wasn't in the kitchen, where he normally did his work if he was at home. She went to the living room and there were some people in it. That's what she remembers thinking: there were strange people in the living room. One was a lady who was wearing no clothes at all. She had her elbows on the sofa and her knees on the floor. She looked like she had lost her clothes down the back of the sofa. The other person was a man and he wasn't wearing clothes either! He was kneeling down behind the woman and nudging his hips into her bottom. Sophie stood there trying to work it out. She isn't sure quite when she realised the man was Daddy, because she wasn't really expecting to see him like that, and because it wasn't until he stopped and turned to look at her that she really noticed his face.

'Ta-da!'

She said it a bit half-heartedly, but, well, he didn't seem to think her outfit was funny. In fact, he looked quite pissed off. He asked her what the hell she was doing and she thought he meant with his pants on her head so she said, 'Sorry'. He was zipping up his trousers when he calmed down suddenly.

'Sophie, sweetheart . . .'

'Who's that?'

'This . . .' He turned to indicate the panic-stricken woman covering herself with a cushion. 'This is . . . Matilda. Tilly. We were. Just. Um. Look. Go upstairs and get out of that gear, and I'll come and chat to you. You shouldn't be out of bed.'

They were just um. Sophie was confused, and she has been confused ever since, except when Archie and Dillon told her about human tupping. But even if she can't remember enough to know if it was exactly what Archie described, she does remember very clearly some of the words that Daddy said when he came up to her bedroom.

She didn't get back into bed because she didn't feel like sleeping. She sat on the bed by the pillow and waited for Daddy to come in. He said lots of things that she can't remember any more, but he also said, 'Don't tell Mummy. Okay?' And when she asked why, he said because *bad* things would happen if she did. She wanted to know what bad things, and he said really, really bad things, and she said, 'To Mummy?' and he said, 'Yes. Quite possibly to Mummy. To all of us.' And he made her promise, so she crossed her heart and hoped to die. And she must never say anything *at all* to Mummy, *ever*.

'Sophie?' asks Miss Dowling again. 'Was that you?'

Sophie has forgotten the question, but suddenly remembers about the having babies thing.

'*No!* That was her!'

'Mummy?'

'*No!* The woman he was . . . with.'

Everyone seems to breathe out at the same time, and Sheila asks if she will just tell them what she can remember, and then she can have something to eat.

'I came downstairs. I was ill at home. I came downstairs and there they were. Daddy and a woman. Matilda. And she was sort of kneeling over the sofa and he was . . . tupping . . . Can I have my banana now?'

'Yes, of course.'

'And you won't tell Mummy?'

'I don't think Mummy needs to know any of this.'

'No. You have to *promise*!'

The other two women are frowning at Erica, but she writes something down and they read it swiftly, then nod. 'You needn't worry about that.'

Sophie is starving. She wants to grab Erica's hand and eat the red stone. She doesn't want the end-of-lunch bell to go before she has her banana because it will go all black and slimy. This has been a weird meeting, and it has made her feel weird too. But Duncan was right. She does feel better having told someone. And knowing that Mummy won't be told is a relief, and hearing yet another adult say that no harm will come to Mummy is the best thing ever.

And now Sophie remembers something else, which is why she dressed up in the cat costume to surprise Daddy. On the Saturday of the actual performance at the village hall she had been so excited (Mummy said she'd had ants in her pants) that she'd asked Mummy and Daddy to get there early so they could be in the front row. Daddy had been held up by something, but she could see Mummy in the second row, because she had lots of time to look over at her. Just before her big 'Miaow!' she looked over at Mummy and there was an empty chair next to her. (Mummy said later that Daddy had just popped out for a bit but he had seen her big moment. In fact, later, Daddy said she was 'fabulous'.)

Sophie wanted to believe this so much that she somehow did, but actually there had been something in her throat stopping the grand miaow, and it had come out as a little sobby mewl. And she couldn't help thinking that Mummy had said he was there to be kind, because she was all watery-eyed when she said it and, like Sophie, she had so badly wanted it to be true that she nearly believed it too. But now that Sophie remembers the empty chair it occurs to her that it is a bit like wanting to believe in Father Christmas or the Tooth Fairy, something you see in your head because it makes you feel good. But he was the daddy who wasn't there. Otherwise, why had she thought the cat costume would surprise Daddy? It was because, deep down, she knew that he hadn't seen her in the cat costume ever before.

But this doesn't make Sophie sad any more. She is happy because Mummy is safe. She feels light and a bit giddy.

Miss Dowling takes her to the door and Sophie says 'Goodbye' to the two women. Then she turns and adds, 'Um . . . you know *Dunking*?' All three look at Sophie as Miss Dowling holds the door back with her hand. Sophie puts her head on one side, thoughtfully: 'He's not a kiddy fiddler. Just so you know.'

39

AFTERMATH

Sophie was quite chipper when Freya picked her up from school.

'You okay?' asked Freya, crouching down and studying her daughter's dear face.

'I'm very happy.' She gave her mother a huge squeeze. 'I love you, Mummy. You're the best mummy in the world. And I'm very, very, VERY happy. I don't think I've ever been happier! What's for tea?'

There was nothing in for tea, so they called at the village Co-op and bought the ingredients for a cottage pie. On the way home, there was a definite skip in Sophie's step. She was bouncing up and down and taking Freya's shopping arm with her.

As soon as they were home, Freya peeled potatoes and set them in a pan to boil. Then she went off to her room to ring Sophie's teacher.

'Emily, has something happened today? Has Sophie been questioned, by any chance?'

There was a short silence. 'Well, I don't think I'm supposed to say, but they're going to contact you anyway, so you didn't hear it from me. Yes, some social workers came.'

Freya closed her eyes in horror. 'Why? Has Sophie said something?'

'Um. Well . . . there was a phone call, and the Head had to act on it. Seems the woman had already phoned the police, so . . .'

'The woman?' Oh God. Sylvia. It had to be Sylvia.

'She said she'd seen Duncan stroking Sophie in her bedroom, and Sophie was crying and saying, "I won't tell Mummy!"'

Stroking Sophie. Freya's pulse started to quicken. 'And . . . And so . . .'

'Well I'd had a word with Sophie at one point, and she did seem upset about something, but then when the social workers questioned her, it was nothing at all. Well, nothing to do with Duncan.'

'What do you mean? Who was it to do with?'

'Oh, no one. I mean, there had been a bit of a misunderstanding. I think they'll explain . . . um . . .'

'So what was she upset about – when she talked to you?'

'Oh, that. I think she was just a bit worried about "tupping" . . .'

'Ah! That'd be our sheep, Gloria. She so wants her to have a lamb. She knows all about tupping.'

'Yes. That's good.'

There was another silence.

'Was she upset about being questioned? Did they ask her things that upset her?'

'She was fine. She was mostly worried about missing break and getting to eat her banana.'

Freya attempted a laugh. How many people knew? What if all the staff knew?

How could she limit the damage?

'So . . . there was no truth in any of it, of course?' She tried to sound nonchalant.

'Oh no. It was all just . . . you know. A misunderstanding. They'll be in contact, I'm sure. But I haven't said any of this, okay?'

'Okay. Thanks, Emily. I'm sorry you've had all this hassle. Okay. See you soon.'

'Freya . . .'

'Mm?'

'He sounds a good man. Duncan.'

'Yep. Thanks.'

She sat on the side of her bed and stared at the new aluminium window frame. She looked at the beautifully oiled windowsill. Yes. Duncan was a good man. He was. He hadn't stroked Sophie. He hadn't done anything like that. He wouldn't. He was a good man. A good man. Absolutely.

Interesting. Sylvia rang every Thursday, after her bridge afternoon. She hadn't rung yesterday. Freya clenched her teeth and went to fry some minced meat. She muttered as she chopped up a slithery onion as if it were Sylvia's eyeball and threw the mince in the pan. Then she relented and wondered when anyone had last stroked Sylvia.

40

QUESTIONING DUNCAN

At three o'clock he sat with a solicitor he had never met before and was told that an allegation had been made against him. His solicitor was a smart woman in a camel coat who smelt of some jasmine-like perfume that Serena used to wear. The interviewer was a plump man in his fifties with a wide, egg-shaped head. Did he know Sophie Gray? What exactly was his relationship with Sophie Gray? Had he ever touched her inappropriately? Had he had any physical contact with her that might be misconstrued? He answered everything honestly. His mouth was parched and tasted sour. He hadn't eaten anything since breakfast, and had drunk only a cup of tea that tasted of plastic kettle and which had burnt his tongue.

Duncan wondered if this would go on record, if he would have some history of child abuse allegation, but his solicitor assured him that he had not been charged with anything. The word 'yet' crept into his head, and once there, would not go away. Notes were made. There were a lot of breathings in and out from the egg-head man, and several interruptions from people putting their heads around the door.

At about three-thirty a short man in uniform came into the room and handed a piece of paper to his interviewer.

'Okay . . . You're free to go.'

'What?'

'You're free to go. Questioning by social workers has established that an error has been made. I'm sorry for your inconvenience. Thank you for your time.'

Before he left, he thanked the solicitor and asked what would happen about fees. She smiled and said she would be in touch. He winced at the thought of how much time she had spent with him. He was about to follow her out of the door when he remembered his laptop. Apparently he would have to wait while someone went to see if it had been sent off or not. If it had already been sent off, then he would have to wait up to six weeks to get it back. And so he waited. And he waited.

He put his hands in his pockets and found the Italian phrasebook. He was leafing through it with little enthusiasm when something fell out on to the floor. He unfolded what was a sheet of A4, and studied it, expecting to find some clue to Freya's former self. It took him a while to register what he had found. He clapped his hand to his head as though a strong wind had just swept his hat off. His heart was knocking at his chest now. Maybe he should just digest this for a bit. He would give himself some time to reflect. Things would become clearer with a bit of thinking time. One thing was certain: he couldn't possibly tell Freya.

Carefully, with hands that no longer seemed to belong to him, he leafed through the phrasebook to see if anything else fell out. There was nothing.

Time passed and his laptop still didn't appear. He was reassured only by one thought. If Sophie had spoken to a responsible adult, she had clearly caused enough concern for things to go further. She had obviously raised his name, and now, just as obviously, had cleared it, or else he wouldn't be going home with his laptop. But what *had* happened to her? None of this changed the fact that something terrible had happened to Sophie, something which had made her pull her eyelashes out. Had that been winkled out of her at last? And was it something to do with Reuben? He thought about what he had found in the Italian phrasebook. The man was a mystery.

A bubble-wrapped laptop was brought out to the front counter, but after unwrapping it, they found it wasn't his. The process was repeated, and in the late afternoon he was able to walk away from the police station with his own laptop, still wearing the partly unbuttoned shirt that Freya had peeled off him earlier that day.

When he got home, Duncan checked his text messages, hoping to find something from Freya. But there was nothing. He had two messages from his mobile phone provider and one from Lottie asking if he was okay. He threw the phone aside and put his head in his hands. His hands were shaking. His heels seemed unable to stay flat on the ground and his knees were wobbling too. A wave of emotion crept up from his stomach, growing until it reached his eyes. And then the tears came. Tears the like of which he had not shed since he was fourteen when his mother died, great hot things dripping on to the carpet and making his nose run too. He let them come. He cried for his helplessness, and for Freya, and for the hopelessness of their loving. He cried for Will and his yearning to be accepted, for Jack and his longing to be noticed, and for little Sophie and her deep, deep hurt, and the way she smiled through her pain, and for all the children who *were* abused and carried the burden alone on their little shoulders. And most of all he cried because he could not stop their hurt, or the hurt they had to come.

41

DIGGING

Duncan knew that Freya would have been devastated by the false accusation, and was furious with her mother-in-law for making it. He assumed it was Sylvia. He'd had several hours to work it out. He was shell-shocked by all the different emotions that had exploded in and around him in the last twenty-four hours.

When he went into work the next morning, a Saturday, to do a client review with Lottie, he opened his laptop and sighed heavily. Lottie was sitting next to him today and placed a hand on his arm. He had rung her the previous evening and she had dropped everything and come over to his flat. He had told her all about the accusation. She knew better now than to quiz him about how he was feeling.

He unfolded the familiar piece of A4 paper, which he had taken from his pocket again. He stared at it.

'What's that?'

'Nothing. Just a receipt I found in a book . . .' He took in a great breath and refolded the paper. It was an email receipt to Reuben for two airline tickets, that was all. Two flight itineraries from Nairobi to Rome, for which you had to change at Dubai.

'Come on. Spill the beans.'

He took in a deep breath. 'I think Reuben was having an affair.'

'Oh God, is that all? Look, the guy was a liar and a fraud. You already know that. So he was a player too. It's hardly surprising.'

'It just seems so . . . chilling, somehow.'

'Look, he's dead. What does it matter now?'

'I feel like I'm betraying Freya by not telling her. By knowing something she doesn't know.'

'No, no, no, no, no. Duncan, he's dead. Leave well alone.'

He was quiet for a while, tapping away on his laptop. Lottie looked over, clearly exasperated.

'What are you doing? "Man Eaten By Crocodile"? Stop it right now.'

He closed the window and sighed. 'The night of Friday, July the ninth. It just doesn't add up.' He unfolded the ticket receipts and showed them to her. 'The flights were booked for the very day after Reuben died.'

'So what? So he died before he could have his little fling. And she will never know, because you're not going to tell her.'

'But she was expecting him back. If you were going to have a fling you'd build it into the time you had away, wouldn't you? That's what I'd do.'

'Would you now? Look, he had a meeting in Rome on the way home. People do. Stop being obsessed.'

Surely he was right to be suspicious. He felt in his bones that something was wrong. What were the chances of a man booking two plane tickets – *two* – to a destination his wife seemed to have had no idea about, the very day after he 'died'? But then, he didn't know for certain – because he couldn't ask Freya directly – whether Reuben was expected to fly out to Italy from Nairobi. But she had said he was due to come home the next day. Why then would he have planned to stop off in Rome? With someone else? For a few hours? And without telling her? That welcoming banner would have waited there with cheerful cruelty for some time even if he hadn't died. Good grief, who *was* this man?

'But what *if* . . . ?'

'No. Don't even go there. If he was alive he'd be in South America by now.'

His face ached. All he cared about now was Freya contacting him.

'But why would—?'

'Who knows? Who cares? We will never know. You've had enough stress to last a lifetime, and so has Freya. Give yourselves a break.'

Of course Lottie was right. But even as he thought this, he knew he couldn't stop now. He slipped the paper back into his pocket, where it felt like a hand grenade.

His phone rang. It was Freya.

42

NO SMOKE

The aftermath of the false accusation (because an accusation is what Freya considered it to be) was difficult for all of them. It took her until the following day to reconnect with Duncan, a delay which made her feel shabby, but she couldn't bring herself to call until then. Coming down from such a peak of suspicion and fear was not an easy thing to do. She was disorientated, dizzy. And then she had to find a way of excusing those terrible thoughts, because Duncan must have known where her thoughts would have led her. And somehow trying on the outfit of gullible single mother had left its mark, as if a tight zip had ripped her skin or an itchy tag had sparked an allergic reaction. It would fade in time.

He came round as soon as she rang, not wanting to talk on the phone. She met him by the back door and wrapped her arms around him. They held each other in silence for some time.

'I'm so . . . so . . . sorry, Duncan. I just . . . I don't know what to say.'

'It's okay. Do you know what happened?'

She shook her head. 'Social Services rang me. You're off the hook, obviously' – she looked at him guiltily when she said this – 'but they've recommended counselling for Sophie.'

'That's good, isn't it?'

'Yes, but they said there were some "other issues" that needed addressing concerning her "self-harm".' (Freya had wanted to ask

'What self-harm?' when they said this, and had realised with a shudder that that was indeed what pulling out one's eyelashes amounted to.) 'I agreed, of course, but apparently there's an eight to ten week waiting list!'

'Oh dear. Well, there's a plan, though. That will help. What can we do to help her now? Has she got any friends she can have over? Can we arrange some trips out?'

'I'm just going to try and normalise things for her. I have encouraged her to invite friends round, and she says she'd like her friend Nadine to come and play.' Her lips were wobbling. 'I haven't been paying attention, have I? I've been a crap mum and a crap lover. I'm so sorry. So sorry, Duncan . . .'

He pulled her in close again. 'You're a wonderful mum, Freya. This isn't your fault. We'll get to the bottom of it, don't worry.' He rested his chin on her head. 'And you're a wonderful lover as well. I'm going to make you a cup of tea, and then we're going to make some plans for something fun to do in the Easter holidays.'

'All of us together?'

'If you're okay with that?'

'I'd like that more than anything.'

On Monday, Sylvia came up for an unannounced visit to 'apologise', and not taking into account that Freya worked that day, she had arrived to pick Sophie up from school. So Freya and Sophie emerged at the end of the school day to see Sylvia in the playground with the other mums. The sun was already low and Freya didn't have the heart to tell Sylvia to drive back to Devon, so the whole family was on edge as she had an evening meal with them and read Sophie a bedtime story. Once the children had gone to bed, Freya had made up the sofa for herself so that Sylvia could sleep in her room. It was then, at the last minute, that Sylvia did manage the apology, but every sentence was countered with a 'but . . .' so that in the end, it had felt more like a justification for her behaviour than contrition.

Sylvia had never been known to apologise for anything, and since Freya had always believed, with her own children, in reinforcing good behaviour by praising it, she found herself thanking Sylvia for the clumsy apology. Even so, she was seething that Sylvia had put Sophie through so much – and Duncan – and that her motive had almost certainly been malicious.

On the way to pick Sophie up the next Friday, Freya popped into the local Red Cross shop to see if she could find anything for the girls to play with when Nadine came round. There were two charity shops and a Co-op in Stonely. The charity shops had once been a post office and a pharmacy, but the post office was an early victim of post office closures and the pharmacist had struggled to make ends meet for years. There were some new children's books on the bookshelf in the Red Cross shop, but they were mostly Young Adult. There were some picture books in a plastic rummage box on a lower shelf, but they were far too young. There were two very sparkly dresses that would be great for dressing up. Sophie still liked dressing up. Freya looked at the tags but she couldn't afford nearly seven pounds each for them, so she went to the baskets beside the counter, where there were usually some miniature toys to be found, cheap jewellery and other knick-knacks. She found two Disney figurines almost straight away. They were a bit bashed about but they would do: fifty pence each. And she was about to pay, when something caught her eye. It was as though her whole body were being swept out at that instant. A whoosh of blood as powerful as a toilet flush went crashing through her. She could feel prickles on her skin. She forgot to breathe for a moment. She looked down at the adjacent basket and dipped in her hand, moving it around in the knick-knacks. There were several items the same. She pulled one out and examined it with a trembling hand.

'They're lovely, aren't they?' said the elderly shop assistant, Mrs Morse.

Freya couldn't speak. She proffered the Disney characters and waited while Mrs Morse put her items through the till.

'Yes!' said Freya at last. 'Where did they come from?'

'Ooh, someone brought them in from Cheltenham, I think. Could've come from the Cheltenham branch, but I couldn't rightly say. They do that sometimes when they have a lot of the same thing. Lovely, though.'

Freya paid, and then went to examine some pullovers, but she had no idea what she was looking at. It seemed suddenly important not to leave this shop. If she did, anything might happen. Nothing now was quite the same as when she had come through its door. She felt as she had when she'd spent ages on a friend's trampoline with Sophie and Jack. She had stepped off on to a magnetic lawn that sucked her down into it as though she were a cast-iron weight. And now the floor of the shop – its cheap fake-wood lino – would not let go of her. She turned and moved slowly back to the basket. She put in her hand and selected all seven of the identical knick-knacks.

'How much for all of them?'

'All of them? Well, they're fifty pence each, so that's . . . Well, I tell you what, love. If you're having all of them, let's say two pounds.'

Freya gave her the money and asked for a bag. Then she found her feet were free-moving again and she left the shop. As soon as she passed the waste bin by the Co-op, she dropped the bag in and carried on towards the school.

Nadine and Sophie emerged together. Nadine rushed over to her mother, Fiona, and asked excitedly if she could go and play at Sophie's.

'It's okay,' said Freya, smiling and moving into Fiona's orbit of friends. 'I told Sophie it was okay. It can be any day to suit you. Today if you like.'

'Oh,' said Nadine's mother. 'Oh that's great! Um . . .'

Fiona wore big beads that matched her earrings and a mauve suit and shoes. She looked like a woman who spent some time on colour coordination in the mornings. Sophie and Nadine were giggling about something silly, and it warmed Freya's heart to hear them. 'How about Sophie comes to us?' said Fiona. 'Say, Thursday? Next Thursday?'

'Oh, but that's *ages* away!' Nadine objected.

'But, Nadine, darling, I can only do Thursdays and Fridays,' Fiona said. 'You know that.'

Freya assumed that today was too short notice for this busy woman, but she was confused. 'Well, why not just come to us? We can do any day you like. Honestly, it's no trouble.'

'Oh, but . . . I think Nadine went to you last time. It's my turn. Really. I insist.'

Freya was about to object again when she had the feeling that there was no point. Something about this woman's determination made her feel helpless, as though she were trying to climb a barbed wire fence. Her silence must've perturbed Fiona, because she suddenly said, 'I was sorry to hear that Sophie's had a bad time of it.'

A little jolt of recognition. A slither of dread.

'Really? Oh, she's fine! Where did you hear that?'

'Oh, you know. Word gets about. I heard about the trouble with um . . .'

'With?'

'Oh, look, I'm sorry. Please don't blame me. You'd be the same, I'm sure. I mean, I'm not one of those people who thinks there's no smoke without fire or anything – really, I'm not—'

'Where did you hear this?' Freya saw with relief that the two girls were stroking a cat at the side of the playground. 'Please, Fiona. *Where?*'

They both now focused on their daughters and the stumpy ginger longhair that was rubbing up against them by the side of a low stone wall.

Fiona played with the clasp of her leather bag. 'I think she was your mother. She was waiting in the playground for Sophie.'

'Sylvia?'

'I didn't get her name.'

'My mother-in-law. She makes things up. You mustn't listen to a word she says.'

'But Nadine says there were some women in to talk to Sophie, and—'

'Yes. But it was all a misunderstanding. Duncan is a good man.'

Fiona smiled while her eyes still frowned. 'I'm sure he is.'

The girls came running over.

'Well?' asked Nadine, dramatically.

'Well?' asked Sophie in exactly the same voice, making the two girls giggle again.

'Well . . .' Fiona turned to Freya. 'Will your . . . Will he be . . . ?'

Freya glared back, aghast.

'Look, I'll think about,' said Fiona with an awkward briskness, and grabbed an unwilling Nadine by the hand to walk her over to their car.

Freya rang Emily as soon as she got home, and Sophie's form teacher said she would deal with it, that she would have a quiet word in someone's ear.

'Oh, no!' said Freya. 'Please don't say anything to Nadine's mum. I don't think she'll listen. It might make things worse.'

'Don't worry. It wasn't her I was thinking of. I'll just casually mention what a lovely man Duncan is to Jocasta's mum, and how easily mistakes can occur, and how idle gossip can ruin lives. She likes to think she's an authority on things.'

'Do you mean Estelle what's-her-face?'

'Exactly. Leader of the A-Team. She'll be pontificating to the mums-that-matter within hours. Wait and see.'

Emily was a star. Nadine's mum rang two days later and said that she couldn't bear Nadine's nagging any longer, and would it be okay for her to come and play with Sophie on Monday?

43

MORE DIGGING

Lottie offered Duncan a hot chocolate, but he shook his head.

He reached into his pocket and took out the unsettling piece of A4 paper again, which he unfolded carefully. He stroked his mouth. 'How do you get hold of a list of Italian charities?'

She looked at him, puzzled. 'What are you up to?'

'Nothing . . . Just I think Reuben may have another fake charity, that's all.'

One thing was certain, he wasn't going to tell Lottie about what he was planning. No siree. He would keep that to himself for now. She might tell him to do something sensible. Or, more likely, she would tell him not to do anything stupid, but he might find he wanted to do just that.

She rolled her eyes. 'Try googling "List of Italian Charities"?'

'I tried that.'

'Let me see . . . Maybe you have to register.' She watched him thoughtfully. 'What are you really up to?'

'Nothing. Just . . .'

Christ! If he found out that Reuben had intended to go off with someone without telling Freya, or that he *had* gone off with someone, if he was still alive, then he would have to tell her. Or would he? Of course he would. It was this dilemma that had kept him from digging as soon as he found this wretched piece of paper. That and a mountain of work to catch up with from the last week or so. Well, he would cross that bridge when he came to it. First, he had to establish the facts. Reuben may simply have died before he took these flights. That was the most likely scenario. His fingers were shaking as he sat typing various combinations of searches into his computer.

Eventually Lottie placed a mug of coffee next to him with a biscuit. 'Try "Italia non profit".' He did. There were a lot of organisations. He whittled it down by city, and tried Rome first. Would he find an Aqua Per Favore? Surely not. No. Reuben wouldn't be that obvious. But there was an Emergenza Acqua, set up over two years ago. There was a website. An email. A contact telephone number. An address.

He sat staring at this page. There were no names on it. Should he email? Would someone smell a rat if he had an English email address? Was his Italian up to a phone call? Could he go there when they were in Italy?

Right. To hell with this. He cobbled together enough coherent Italian in written form to attempt one of the phone numbers in Italy. He braced himself for the call, preparing for the possibility of Reuben's voice.

In fact, a woman answered, and she talked so fast that he couldn't quite make out what she said. He repeated his prepared piece.

'*È inglese?*' she said at last. 'This camponay 'ave move. Eh . . .'

'*Può darmi l'indirizzo?*' he tried, safe in the knowledge that this woman was nothing to do with Reuben.

'*Sì. Aspetti . . . un momento . . . ecco!*'

She read out an address in Rome and gave the name of the boss. *Roberto Gallo.* (R. G. – Reuben Gray?) He copied the address and googled it. It was a street about a mile from the historic city centre. He zoomed in very close on the map. It didn't show anything more, but he felt he was getting closer to his target, whether that target was dead or alive. Right, Reuben Gray, here I come! Possibly.

Then he realised he had nothing else for this new place. No email, no phone number. Just an address.

He closed his laptop and took stock. As he saw it, there were four possibilities. Only two possible actions, but four possible consequences. One: Reuben was still alive and Duncan did nothing. Consequence: he might marry Freya one day and turn her into a bigamist. But then again, Reuben might never be discovered. Two: Reuben was still alive and Duncan tracked him down. Consequence: Freya would be heartbroken by his actions. She would shoot the messenger. The children would be devastated at his leaving them. They would never get over the sense of betrayal. And Freya might even take Reuben back. Three: Reuben was dead as a dodo (more likely) and Duncan cocked everything up by telling Freya that he had evidence to the contrary. Consequence: Freya would never trust him again. Four: Reuben was dead and he did nothing to prove or disprove this. Consequence: life could continue as normal, if Freya could ever get over the false accusation over Sophie.

It was ridiculous. Reuben may have been a dodgy character, but why would he leave three lovely children, even if he had fallen out of love with Freya for some bewildering reason? This was madness. Reuben was so obviously dead.

Okay, no matter. He would go to Rome. He was going to sort this out once and for all. If he found an unsuspecting Italian called Roberto Gallo, so be it. He would feel a little stupid, nothing more. He had no idea what he would do if he found Reuben Gray. But if he did, the *very* good-looking, wonderful, fun, simply gorgeous man had better watch out. Team Leader to Red Arrows: assume attack formation. Duncan was going to root him out.

44

LAMBING

Hilary has told Sophie that Gloria is two years old and is expecting a lamb. The vet's scanner has shown she has one lamb, although a lot of the other sheep are having two or even three. She has told Sophie's mum that she will phone up as soon as there is news.

Nadine comes to play with Sophie quite a lot now, and sometimes Sophie goes to her house. Sophie likes going to Nadine's house because it is different. Everything is neat, and she has loads of toys in labelled boxes – far more than Sophie because she has two older cousins nearby who have passed on their old toys as well. Her cousins are called Giorgia and Calypso, which sound far more exotic than Will and Jack. Still, Nadine says she wishes she had a brother and her cousins are a waste of space. Calypso, the older one, is the worst. She calls Nadine a fuckwit. She is a pain in the bum. Nadine's house always smells fresh and sweet, and the toilet smells of flowers. Sophie's own house seems cluttered and chaotic and smelly in comparison, but Nadine says she prefers it. She likes the fact that they can eat biscuits on the sofa and no one cares about crumbs, and that they have a cat called Chunkables and a sort of pet sheep who charges in through the kitchen door whenever she can. Most of all, she tells Sophie, she likes the stories they make up together with the Sylvanians. 'Giorgia doesn't do making-up stories like you.

She just wants to do pop stars and karaoke. It's okay sometimes, but I prefer this.'

Sophie loves this about Nadine. She knows Mummy isn't like Nadine's mummy. Nadine's mummy wears big necklaces and bracelets and has a special room called 'the snug' where they watch television; she offers them posh lemonade and digestive biscuits as a snack at the kitchen table, and they have to take their shoes off in the hall. Their cat, Penelope, is not allowed in the house at all, and they are not allowed in the living room. Nadine once sneaked Sophie into her mother's bedroom and showed her shelves and shelves of beautiful shoes: all different colours with heels of different heights – some even great tall things like celebrities wear. Her own mum's shoes are all flat and piled in the bottom of the wardrobe with her trainers.

Sometimes Sophie is embarrassed about these differences, like when they have cut-up apple and homemade flapjacks for a snack, with just water to drink, or when Nadine looks at the walls and sees pictures that Sophie has done Blu-tacked all over the place, or when Mummy points out something on the dresser and it is covered in crap: crumbling clay models, balls of string, empty glue sticks and old classroom paintings curling round the edges. But Nadine still says she prefers this house, and keeps finding more things to like about it. She likes that she doesn't have to take her shoes off and that Sophie's mum has stacks and stacks of dressing-up clothes, doesn't mind them making a mess, and even fills up some water pistols for them to use in the garden when the weather's good.

When Nadine says she likes things here, Sophie is proud. She is especially proud today, a Saturday, because while they are playing, the phone rings, and Mummy comes in to say that Gloria is starting to lamb, and Hilary has invited them up to see it.

They could walk across the fields, but then they might miss it. So they pile into the car – Jack and Duncan as well – so that they can be at the farm in no time. Sophie explains to Nadine that Gloria is two years old and that's when they start having lambs. Gloria missed out last year, she says, and that must've made her very sad.

The lambs that are already a week or two old are out in a distant field with their ewes. Gloria is in the nearest barn with the other one-lambers. The barn smells of fresh hay and a musky sheep smell that Sophie thinks is lovely. Hilary and another woman helping her are wearing big rubber gloves. She takes them over to a little pen where Gloria is lying down, her woolly fleece juddering backwards and forwards with her fast breathing. She is licking her lips a lot. Mummy says that's in preparation for what's to come. She will need to do a lot of licking soon. Sophie can't think why, but she says nothing, in case it will make her look stupid in front of Nadine.

'It's all right, Gloria,' she whispers, and Nadine joins in solemnly with, 'Don't worry, Gloria.'

Then Gloria is on her feet, and as she turns they can see something gloopy drooping from her bottom, and also a big blob, which is in the shape of a lamb's head. The head is covered in something like a pair of tights, so they can't really see it. And there's something else beside the head, which Duncan says are little hooves. Gloria is making funny noises now. There are tiny lamb bleats from the other pens, but Gloria's lamb is not making any noise. It is still just a blob. It must be hard for Gloria, hearing these other lambs already born. She is breathing heavily now, and her head is trembling. She's still licking her lips and moving her head.

Sophie is worried. She knows Gloria, and this isn't like her. This isn't like her at all. Something is wrong. 'Is it hurting her? Shall we get Hilary?'

Hilary is with another sheep, and so is her helper.

'Mummy? Shall we get Hilary?'

Mummy says it's okay, she just needs a bit of time. They settle themselves on some hay-bales and watch intently.

Now Gloria sinks back to the ground and flops on to her side. Her fleece is still juddering with her jagged breathing. She lifts one back leg a little, and they can see that the thing coming out of her is stretching her a lot. It's getting bigger. They can see hoof tips more clearly now, and it is definitely a head but the eyes are closed, and Sophie hopes it isn't dead. Poor Gloria. She wants to go and hug her, but all she can manage is a tiny, scared, 'Don't worry, Gloria. Everything will be all right,' although she is not sure if this is true, or if the words even come out.

Then Gloria is on her feet again. Her head goes back. The skin holding in the lamb stretches back like a pullover neck and the thing begins to come out, suddenly slithering to the ground. No sooner has it hit the hay than Gloria is on it, licking its face, licking this strange sack of skin that Mummy says is its 'caul'. She even seems to gobble it right up, and soon the lamb is bleating, and they are all smiling. Sophie finds there are tears running down her face, and Nadine takes her hand and squeezes it. This makes Sophie's tears come even more. She doesn't know which thing has made her more happy.

After a minute or two Hilary comes over and lifts the lamb out. She hands it to Sophie and Sophie is glad to bury her face in the carpety coat of the little creature and let it mop up her tears. It smells so sweet and earthy. It is warm and fragile in her arms. She loves the lamb so much. So much.

'Can Nadine have a go?'

Nadine is thrilled, and Sophie is so, so proud. And she is proud later when Mummy shows them photos of each of them holding the lamb, proud when one is sent to Nadine's mother, and proudest of all of Gloria, who has got what she wanted most in all the world.

45

A DREAM COMING TRUE

Jack was happy. He'd had loads of 'likes' on social media after the pictures of him astride Biscuit. All the girls wanted to know whose horse it was, if he rode it often, how many hands high it was, where it was stabled. Some of them even wanted to come and see it. Even Ellie Chapman was interested. He had simply basked in new-found popularity lately, and he just didn't care when the boys called him Chubbers any more, or when they called him a girl for liking horses. Nope. He didn't give a toss.

For three weeks now he had been going to help muck out Biscuit's stable on Saturdays. This had been Lottie's suggestion. She was paying a local girl, Danielle, to do it, but she knew that Danielle was under pressure from her parents to study more at the weekends, so she wasn't sure how much longer she would do it. Jack hoped she'd give up soon, and then he could earn the money himself. Still, it was useful learning the ropes from Danielle.

Unfortunately, he didn't fancy Danielle. She was a very plain girl with brown hair tied back tightly in a ponytail, and she wore glasses. She was quite skinny, but he couldn't really see her shape because she wore big, thick jumpers. He couldn't see her tits or anything. He wondered if he'd see more of her shape in the summer, if she still came to see the horses in the summer.

When he first went, she had shown him how to tie the horses up outside (there was another horse called Toffee); then she showed him how to put the wheelbarrow across the door and throw the clean bedding at the wall with a pitchfork so that the damp bedding and droppings left below could be removed and chucked in the barrow. The cleaner straw was tossed about the floor and new straw was laid down, and then packed in a ridge around the walls to protect the horses from draughts and knocks. She told him to hold up his pitchfork and drop it prong first. He did so. 'That's good,' she said, smiling. 'It didn't hit the concrete so we've laid enough straw.' He liked that she said 'we'. He felt accepted.

Today she was showing him how to groom the horses. This was the longest task, and he didn't really feel up to it, but he said nothing. She gave him a hoof pick to clean out the hooves and he did his best, copying her as she worked on the other horse. They moved on to brushing with a dandy-brush and then massaging with a plastic curry-comb. He liked this bit, but was nervous when they later moved on to the face, mane and tail. The tail in particular bothered him. He tried to stand to the side but the horse kept kicking. Danielle did it all so smoothly.

'I'm just more practised,' she said when she saw him pull back. 'You'll get the hang of it.'

After they'd finished, she usually had a little ride on Toffee, her parents' friend's horse. Today she saddled up Biscuit too, and showed him how to mount and walk, and a little later how to trot. Jack loved it. He just loved it. He felt like a king all over again, trotting around the meadow. Afterwards she said, 'You know my parents don't want me to do this any more because it takes up the whole of my Saturday morning?'

'I sort of heard . . .'

'Well, why don't we share it?'

'Alternate weeks?' Jack was pleased, but daunted. He wasn't sure he'd quite mastered the grooming.

'Yes. We could do that. Or we could do it together. That way I could still teach you stuff, but the cleaning would take half the time. Share the money?'

Now she was talking. His Saturday mornings stretched out before him like glorious holidays: horses and riding, endless photo opportunities for social media. Girls would like him forever. He'd have to make sure Danielle was out of all the pictures, though, or they'd think he'd found himself a nerdy girlfriend.

Duncan started staying over quite a lot. It wasn't as bad as Jack had feared. In fact, it didn't make much difference. Then one of the boys in Jack's class had asked if he'd heard them having sex. Jack was appalled, but managed to shrug and say, 'Not yet.'

'Well, you will do soon, mate!'

This seemed unlikely. Mum was far too old for sex, and Duncan, well, he just wasn't the type. Imagine! Yuk! Nonetheless, he started listening out for noises. After they came to bed, he would creep out and listen at the bedroom door on the pretext of going to the bathroom. He never heard anything except mumbled conversation, and he was relieved. He felt stupid that he'd even taken his friend seriously. Imagine Mum and Duncan doing it. It was ridiculous. Some things you just knew.

In late January it was Jack's birthday and Mum and Duncan gave him a pair of binoculars. They were better than anything Mum could normally afford, and he knew he had Duncan to thank for this.

They went for a walk to try them out. Soon it became a thing. They all started to go walking together on Sundays: Mum, Duncan, him and Sophie – and even Will came with them. February was relentlessly cold. Sometimes the sun wasn't strong enough to reach the margins of the fields, which kept their frost for days in a row. The birds were struggling to survive, and robins and sparrows puffed out their feathers for warmth. He could see them up close with his new binoculars. High in a beech tree a mistle thrush's song competed with the wind's blustery noise and the croaks of a ragged band of crows. Underfoot the green prongs of snowdrops were beginning to push through the damp earth, and it was clear that the world was waking up. Gloria's lamb joined a field full of lambs. And as the sap rose and the first spikes of dog's mercury appeared through the dead leaves, as the spring advanced and announced itself with the swelling buds of hawthorn and their stealthy creep of green, the five of them strode into March through the damp grass of the field paths and the mulchy leaves of the woodland like a family that had always been together.

It was on one of these early walks that Duncan asked them all if they'd like to go to Italy some time over Easter. He was dead serious. They could hardly believe it. Will cast a bit of doubt on things by saying he had to revise (as if!), but when Duncan said it would only be for five or six days, he perked up. 'Can we go to the Uffizi in Florence? Can we go to Verona? Or Siena?'

'We could do a little tour, if you like. We might even manage a day trip to Rome. Let's look online when we get back and see what everyone wants. We could book the hotels now.'

'*Hotels?*' Sophie was all excited and wide-eyed.

Jack took a while to digest this information. They would be going abroad, all of them together. Mum had always wanted to go to Italy, and Duncan had remembered this. He had remembered this longing of their mother's and he had thought about it and how he could make her dream come true. She deserved this. He watched Duncan's face as they chattered excitedly, a face almost startled by happiness.

46

PLANNING

This was a happy time for all of them. Walking together became a habit. He didn't have to ask them to come; they just tagged along. Sophie, who had always been quite agile, faked weakness at stiles and stream-crossings so that Duncan would lift her up. Jack said she was putting it on. He didn't mind, though, because it seemed to make Sophie happy. She chattered away to Duncan, and Jack kept up a running commentary about birds he could see through his binoculars. Will sometimes talked to him about art and about university courses, and Freya just seemed to bumble along in a smiley daydream. These walks were always the same: they were circular, they lasted about two hours, and Duncan always found somewhere nearby they could go for tea and cake afterwards. And somehow, this tea and cake was nothing more than they deserved. They were usually numb with cold, pleasantly exhausted, and felt it well earned to thaw out gently in a steamy tea-shop.

The walks carried on each Sunday throughout March. The hazel catkins swung on the branches as did a few dried-up old leaves still on the beeches. Then out came the yellow stars of celandine, the snowy blossom of cherry in the woody hedges, followed by blackthorn blossom. The snowdrops still nodded under the trees in great drifts, along with the emerald flowers of dog's mercury and bright green arrows of wild arum leaves, all silently opening on the woodland floor and colouring up the drab ground of a receding winter. Above them, the swaying branches were covered in densely packed buds, biding their time for the great awakening. And sometimes, out over a fallow field, a solitary skylark rose, practising its faltering song for a future mate.

Duncan enjoyed organising the trip to Italy with Freya. He enjoyed it when she called her children over to the laptop to admire the hotels they would be staying at. He basked in their excitement. He had all the details worked out, and most particularly, he was planning a little train trip to Rome from Florence.

It was all very fluid, but he intended, during the day trip, to slip off for a moment on some pretext, while they were all having lunch at some nearby trattoria, and pay a visit to the offices of Emergenza Acqua a few doors down. If there was any connection to Reuben at all, he would, if he played his cards right, manage to get some contact details. He had vague ideas about saying to an assistant that he wanted to donate a sizeable sum to Emergenza Acqua, and would arrange for a meeting to discuss this with Roberto/Reuben and . . . hey presto! This seemed a bit implausible, and horrific, but he toyed with the idea. And that particular scenario was the last thing he wanted. He had to think of the children. He really wasn't quite sure how he could protect them, although that was his first priority. He knew he was playing with fire, but felt in control. And if he'd got it all wrong? No matter. At least he would have given Freya the family holiday she had dreamed of. That was really the most important thing.

He certainly wasn't scheming or anything. He had wanted to take Freya to Italy long before he found the receipt – since he had found out at the supper table that she had always wanted to go there. He knew way back then that he would take her. And Rome had always been on his list. No, he absolutely wasn't scheming. And yet this absurd coincidence made him feel something of a fraud. Perhaps it wasn't a coincidence at all. Perhaps Freya's wish to go to Italy dated from her husband's evening classes in Italian. The two things had, almost certainly, been inextricably linked. And so he couldn't help it if his research into Reuben and his desire to give Freya and her family a dream holiday just happened to take the same trajectory.

He still wasn't entirely certain what he would do if he found Reuben there. At the moment it felt improbable, but an itch that he had to scratch. Surely, though, discovering Reuben's worst treachery – if indeed it existed – was in everyone's interest. Living a lie was holding all of them back. Especially Sophie. Freya too. It could only help if she knew the truth. With any luck, he could swing it so that he was not the messenger, so that Reuben unveiled the truth himself.

Life was sweet. He barely wanted to change it, but he was nervous and excited about the changes that would have to come, whatever they might be. He knew he would be carrying a hand grenade to Italy in his pocket.

PART TWO

PART TWO

47

CITY OF DREAMS

They caught a flight to Pisa airport, and they marvelled at the tower as they circled over it. Sophie couldn't understand how it could stay standing, and Jack took pictures on his phone to send to friends. Duncan had booked a hire car, and after a sweaty wait in a chaotic queue, they stuffed all their luggage into the boot of a Fiat and set off for Florence. All the while he stood in that queue for the hire car Duncan felt jittery and unresolved. The hand grenade still seemed to be in his pocket. As soon as he started driving, he relaxed. He hadn't taken the pin out of the weapon. It was safe for now. He still had choices.

They reached the old city on a mellow April evening and the sun bathed the peeling stucco of the buildings in gold and ochre. Will couldn't get enough of it. It was a different world; even the air was different, still and heavy and aglow. Duncan knew Florence quite well and took them on a circuitous route which passed through a little of the old city, then up into the hills to Fiesole, where he had booked a hotel.

'If the rooms aren't great, it's only for three nights,' he said, when they erupted from the car into the still blue air above the city. But the rooms were spectacular. Will and Jack shared a twin room with a balcony, and leapt around exploring the minibar and the en suite bathroom with a freestanding bath on four ancient-looking claws. Duncan and Freya had a large double bedroom with a single bed made up in the corner for Sophie. She was happy to share with them, and didn't want to be in a strange place without Freya close at hand. Their room had a long balcony that overlooked the city, and the sun, which was beginning to set, trailed a deep pink ribbon across the horizon. Sophie could only just see above the balustrade, and she stood between them and declared that she had never seen anything more beautiful. *A fairy tale.* Freya smiled at Duncan and leaned her head on his shoulder, and he indulged in a moment of self-congratulation – or perhaps relief – at the way things had turned out so far. He wanted to give this family the holiday of a lifetime. He wanted Will to be excited about the architecture (which he was already) and Jack to marvel at the history, and he wanted all of them to relish the casually delicious cuisine. Above all he wanted Freya to relax. He wanted to pamper her. He wanted so many good things for her and her quirky family. They were treating him like a bit of a hero really, but he had never been anyone's hero before, and they were all so pleased, so grateful, that he allowed himself to bask a little in the warmth of his success with them. He enjoyed Will's obvious delight. He was moved by every smile that curved on Sophie's lips, by Freya squeezing his hand and by the wild shrieks of Jack rushing in behind them and throwing himself on to the queen-sized bed. *Ciao! Ciao amore! Che bello!* They had been practising in the car.

'*Avete fame?*' asked Duncan, making eating signs with his hands.

'*Sì!*' they chorused, which was just as well, as he had booked a table for five in the dining room downstairs for the first evening. They looked out over the sunset, and they ate and drank and nibbled and tasted until the sky turned to pale green on the horizon and the first stars appeared.

48

LETTING GO

The following day they took a bus into Florence and walked in the early sunshine. Freya was surprised by how relaxed she felt. As if for the first time in many years she did not have to neurotically count her ducklings. Now she had Duncan to keep an eye out as well. How she loved this gentle and competent man. She could put her trust in him completely. And Will too, how grown-up he had become lately. She sighed in the sunshine, happily letting go of the maternal reins, with just a single antenna functioning on half-charge for Jack and Sophie. An American passer-by obliged her by taking photos of them standing all together on the Ponte Vecchio. Duncan bought Sophie a little silver bracelet, and commented coyly on the rings to Freya. She almost willed herself to try one on, but she didn't. She would need certainty from him, not hints.

Later they went to see the copy of the statue of David in Piazza della Signoria, took more photos and bought warm dripping squares of pizza from a street stall. In the afternoon they visited the gardens of Boboli, and sat in the shade with enormous slices of watermelon. Freya kicked off her sandals (she was wearing sandals!) and stretched her bare legs out in front of her on the warm grass. She pictured Serena's legs in the secret photo she had of Duncan's ex-wife. What a far cry she was from Serena. She wondered if he ever compared them, Serena of the gleaming legs and Freya, middle-aged woman of the pasty flesh and arms it was better to cover up these days. Then she reminded herself how he had wooed her. He had beaten his way single-handedly through the thick ivy to the top of her tower, and managed to pass the three armed guards of her children, in order to claim her. He had overcome all the obstacles. He was here now, with his arm propped behind her as they sat on the grass. She breathed him in and felt sixteen again. She loved the smell of him, the subtle smile of him, and the helpless smile that cracked his face into hundreds of creases and made his shining eyes disappear. She loved the apologetic way he told jokes, the lolloping way he walked, the way he held a pencil: cautiously, then firmly and with great purpose, producing a confident sketch or diagram. She loved his politeness to strangers, his respectfulness, his strength, the way he held her with his eyes when they made love, the purposefulness of his lovemaking, and his powerful, raw, unexpected desire.

On their way from Pisa airport to Florence the previous day, Duncan had made a mistake with parking. They had stopped off to look at a village and because Sophie wanted the toilet. He had failed to read a small Italian notice correctly, and had simply understood that it was a two-hour-stay parking area and not, as it turned out, for residents only. A rather irate man had told him off, probably less angrily than it sounded. There was something hugely poignant about a competent man making a mistake, and Freya had felt choked with emotion for him. Her instinct was to support him, to back him up, to say it should have been clearer or some such excuse. But she had sensed that Duncan would not want this, and would feel patronised by it. And even as she thought these things, she was struck in the stomach by all the times she had defended Reuben in this way, and how he had lapped it up. All his mistakes had been someone else's fault, and he had liked his wife to corroborate this.

They lay back in the shade, sticky with watermelon, until it was cool enough to make their way round the streets again. And as she watched her unfamiliar naked toes move on the pavement, Freya thought again how much she loved this man, and how strange that felt. How sweet and safe and dangerous; how wonderfully out of her control.

49

WILL IS AMAZED

Will had some news he wanted to tell everyone, but he wanted to wait until just the right moment to do it. Just before they'd left, he'd had an email giving him an unconditional offer at the University of the West of England in Bristol. He didn't want to say anything yet. Mum probably wanted him to stay local to save money. He knew she'd like him to stay at home, and he'd had a pretty good offer from the local university. But really, he'd like to go to Bristol, and although he knew Mum would back him, whatever his decision, he'd rather tell her at the end of the holiday. He planned to break the news on their last night. Duncan would probably make a toast to his success. He was glad Mum had met him. He made everything easier. Aunty Rachel was right: Duncan was a keeper.

The second day was devoted to the Uffizi Gallery. At first Will let out a groan when he saw the queues, but Duncan had, magically, pre-booked and they walked straight to the head of a queue and were in within minutes. Then Will just took off. He couldn't help exclaiming at everything. He kept coming back to them, saying they had to come and see this, not believing they just didn't share his excitement. Of course, Sophie found it all too much. After a few rooms of great masters she was wheedling Duncan into giving her a piggyback, and he crouched for her to clamber up. They walked around together, limiting themselves to a few seconds at each painting, and passing by others completely. Will was always a few paintings behind, and he could feel his mouth permanently ajar. He shook his head in disbelief. This place was just amazing.

After a while Duncan seemed to think that Sophie and Jack had had enough of the Renaissance, and suggested they go down to the gift shop with Mum to purchase some cards, and maybe have a coffee. Once he'd taken them down and found them seats, he came back up to find Will, and talked him through some more of the paintings. What a feast! It seemed wrong that there should be so many in one place. It would be fairer to share them out a bit around the world. For the first time in ages, Will felt that he was truly happy. Life seemed full of promise.

Eventually, after he had bought a few posters, they walked lazily through the streets to a little trattoria that Duncan knew. During the meal Duncan encouraged Mum to take up her degree again. This was a brilliant idea. She needed something more in her life than them. Take the pressure off a bit. Especially now he was going, he didn't want her to be a door-mat.

No one had mentioned finishing her degree since before Sophie was born, and she made the same excuses she had made then: she'd forgotten it all, her first year wouldn't count any more, she had to earn a living, she'd be older than everyone else. Duncan countered them all gently. He mentioned Environmental Sciences and how she could do a part-time degree. He made it all sound possible. It moved Will that he had looked into it.

'You should, Mum,' he said. 'Good call, Duncan. You persuade her!'

They clinked glasses to new beginnings, to Firenze and their holiday.

50

THIS IS IT

Panic was rolling in towards him. The more he thought about it, the more uneasy he became, and the more ridiculous it seemed to go to Rome. This charity, Emergenza Acqua, was legally registered, and therefore it was unlikely to be Reuben's. That was not his style at all. He hadn't registered *Eau Please!* because it was fake. Nope. The whole thing was a wild goose chase. He would abandon his plan for a day trip to Rome. He would take them somewhere else. Why waste a whole day on some stupid hunch? He could just tell Freya. He could casually show her the piece of paper he'd found in the phrasebook. Let Reuben damn himself. He could even let the receipt accidentally slip out of the book and 'find' it for the first time in front of her. *Yes.* He would tell them Rome was a bit of a slog after all. It wasn't a long train journey to the sea instead. How about Argentario? They could perhaps hire a boat and have lunch in the sunshine. Yes. They would like that.

They loved the seaside at Argentario. Duncan couldn't yet bring himself to put the receipt back in the phrasebook, ready for its discovery. It was too soon. Freya was so happy. Unless some perfect opportunity offered itself – if all the children were engrossed in the Arena in Verona or something – then he would leave it as late as possible. But it would have to happen in Italy, or the phrasebook idea wouldn't work.

It was a three-hour drive from Florence to Verona, so they meandered through Modena and Mantua en route. Three nights in Verona lay ahead, followed by the drive back down to Pisa and the plane home. In Verona, Sophie would share a room with the boys, and he and Freya would be alone.

Freya had kicked her sandals off and had her feet up on the dashboard. He couldn't help remembering Serena sitting next to him once, her feet up on the dash-board in the same way. But he also couldn't help remembering the look on her face for the last year of their marriage. It seemed to him that for the whole of that time she wore a look that was vulnerable and superior, turning his infertility into a moral weakness on his part rather than an accident of nature.

Freya was a different matter. There was a glorious tension between them as they drove. Sometimes she brushed his arm or placed a hand on his knee, and he was shot through with a shock of lust. He loved her. He loved the way she managed her family life so tenderly, how she worked patiently at its puzzles like someone with a combination lock. He loved her excitement at simple pleasures and he loved watching her lose her words in a giggle. She was like a calf set free in a field of new grass, and he liked to think that he had opened the gate. He wanted to make her forever this light-hearted. He wanted her always by his side, just as she was now, surprised by her own newly painted toes on the dash-board, singing to Abba, and smiling hopefully at the edge of her future.

They visited San Zeno and studied the magnificent bronze panels on the porch door. Sophie was bored by the interior, so he took them to Castelvecchio and showed them the statue of Cangrande sitting on his horse. Sophie loved Cangrande because he was smiling, and because his horse appeared to be wearing fat leggings. They had lunch in a trattoria down a side street, and sat on the pavement watching people go by. In the afternoon, they went to Juliet's balcony. Duncan told them he was going to write his name under the arch with Freya's. In fact, he imagined scrawling 'Marry me!' underneath it, and felt such a rush of love for her that he decided to do just that, if he could hold his nerve. But since he'd last been here some years ago, there seemed to be a small gang of women guards whose job it was to stop lovers doing anything of the sort. So the graffitied archway, heavy with the scrawl of lovers' vows, overlaid with more lovers' vows, was never to see Duncan and Freya entwined in an artistic little motif of his own design, or any sort of proposal. However, he was so fired up. Stuff it, he was going to do it anyway. But as he fingered the felt-tipped pen in his pocket, sliding it out only a fraction, a heavily made-up woman in a uniform pounced on him, wagging her finger and firing her voice like a machine gun: '*No, no, no, no, no!*'

Will and Jack fondled Juliet's 'lucky breast' on her bronze statue, and Freya climbed up to the balcony with Sophie while Duncan took photographs of them singly and together. Then Will turned to him. 'Go on then. You go up and I'll take a picture of you and Mum. Lovebirds on the balcony.' Duncan could have hugged him.

It was pretty busy, but they found a few seconds on the balcony alone. He saw Will wait for a tourist in the background to move aside before snapping them three or four times. Duncan leaned in close for an embrace and Will snapped them again.

'I love you. I've never loved you more,' he whispered into Freya's ear. Then they were joined by a group of Chinese tourists.

They started to make their way down the stairs, and it was suddenly very noisy. He tried to stay close to her, and watched a smile playing on her lips.

'Might you be prepared . . . ?' he shouted above the din. A very sweaty man, gabbling at his friend, barged between them and became sandwiched as the crowd grew thicker. They would soon be down the stairs and outside with the children again. Duncan had to raise his voice above the babble, and he had to finish his sentence quickly: '. . . to spend the rest of your life with me?'

He lost sight of her face completely for a while, and when he saw it again, outside in the courtyard, she turned to him and grinned. A little later, as they moved back out into the street, she said, 'I might!'

The following day they must have looked doe-eyed over breakfast, but no one noticed. The children chattered excitedly about the day ahead and practised their Italian on an obliging waiter. Duncan was excited too, and not just at Freya's response to his question. He felt all the nervy energy of someone on an unstoppable trajectory towards the truth. Because even though he was still undecided as to an exact course of action, whether to take things to the limit and tell her everything he knew (the four-leafed clover he'd spotted on a handbag, the fake charity) or to just let the pennies drop, things did now feel unstoppable. The receipt was now back in the phrasebook. He had loosened the pin of the grenade even if he hadn't yet lobbed it. He hoped that all it exploded was the myth of Reuben Gray.

Later that morning they visited the Arena, and were bowled over by it. Jack, in particular, could imagine some poor wretches having to fight lions, and was struck by the similarity of the rows of seats to a football stadium. He stood for a long time contemplating the space, and Duncan took pictures of him standing alone on the stone seats. They had to drag him away. If only they had lingered a little longer . . .

51

PAYING

Duncan knew that if Lottie had had the slightest inkling about his plan to check out the possible offices of Reuben Gray in Rome she would have roundly disapproved. *Leave well alone,* she would've said. Lottie was his barometer, and he was pleased he had cancelled that plan and consequently gained her imaginary approval. Then again, he knew she wouldn't approve of his phrasebook idea either. *Why create unnecessary misery?* It was a compromise, though. It was nothing to do with wanting to shaft Reuben. It was about Freya deserving the truth. He imagined telling Lottie that but found he didn't want to hear her reply.

It seemed obvious, with hindsight, that something was bound to go wrong.

Everyone wanted to eat in the grand Piazza Brà, outside the Arena, but Duncan explained that it was a tourist trap. He knew of a little trattoria where they could eat outside, and it was only a fifteen-minute walk away. He checked the map on his phone.

Strolling in the spring sunshine, they stopped to admire street performers and to look at shop windows. Freya tried on some very chic sandals, and was tempted. They all trooped into the shoe shop and Freya tried on a pair in her own size.

'I'll buy them for you,' said Duncan, reaching for his wallet. But Freya didn't want them. Why was that? Why could Freya never treat herself?

'How d'you say "I'll take them"?' Will was pulling the phrasebook out of Duncan's pocket before Duncan could stop him. 'No, don't tell me . . . Shopping . . .' Will flicked through the pages. Duncan swallowed. 'Here we go . . . *Vorrei prenderle per favore.*'

The receipt stayed resolutely and invisibly in place. Duncan held his breath.

'It's okay,' said Freya. 'Really, Will. They're very glamorous, but I'd never wear them.'

'Come on, Mum. Live a bit.'

'You would like them?' said the shop assistant, bolstered by Will's Italian.

'No, really.' Freya looked awkward and shook her head.

Will, exasperated, held the phrasebook by one cover, letting it drop open dramatically. 'Whoops!' And he was bending down, picking up the folded paper from the polished floor. 'Sorry, Duncan.' He put the paper carefully back in the book, which he returned to Duncan's pocket. Simple as that, as if it were an ordinary, harmless piece of paper.

'Your loss, Mum. You look great in them.'

'You do,' said Sophie, who had completed a circuit of the little shop, fingering all the sparkly shoes.

Duncan knew he should have added his weight to this argument. He should have said how lovely they looked on her, but even as he opened his mouth, all he could think about was how Freya had seen the piece of paper. If he didn't remark on it now, he could never be surprised by it in future.

'I don't know what—'

'Let's find somewhere to eat,' said Freya. 'It's really kind of you, but I think everyone's getting a bit peckish.'

A little further up the street they spilled out into the Piazza delle Erbe. The frescoed walls were bathed in sunshine and the market stalls were covered in giant sunshades. The dappled sunlight and shade was startling. The smells of the stalls were enticing, and they all started to get very hungry. Duncan's planned trattoria was quite a bit further on, and hidden from view, and he urged them onwards, sick with torment. Maybe he could still swing it, but it would have to be today. Maybe if they reached the trattoria before it filled up they could sit out on the pavement, and he could find some way to get Freya to practise her Italian with the phrasebook, and he could say, 'Yes, what *is* that piece of paper?'

Just a bit further now. Not too far. But Sophie wanted the toilet. How urgently did Sophie need the toilet? Now.

They went into a café-bar on the square itself. The pavement tables were full, so they ventured into the cool interior. It was noisy inside. They found a small table and crammed five chairs around it. 'We'll just have a cool drink here,' said Duncan, 'then we'll make our way.' Everyone agreed that they didn't want to stay. Freya returned from the toilet with Sophie just as some mineral water was served up on a tray, and Will went off to the toilet in turn.

On his way back Will got chatted up by a waiter at the bar. Duncan could tell by the look in his eyes that the young Italian was doing more than practising his English. The two of them were laughing and smiling at practically everything. He was gladdened to see Will enjoying himself so much. Maybe he should just ditch the whole plan. *Why cause unnecessary misery?* Everyone was so happy.

When he returned to the table, Will seemed excited. 'Hey, Mum, there's a man round the corner who looks just like Dad – only with a beard!'

Freya smiled and shrugged. Duncan was uneasy. He could see she didn't want to start talking about Reuben on holiday, so much so that she began to talk about what they could eat for lunch.

'We need to drink up fast,' said Duncan, his pulse going at full pelt. 'Tables start to fill up fast at the trattoria I'm thinking of. If we leave now—'

'No, but I mean he *really* looked like Dad. I'm not kidding.'

'Let me go and see.' Jack started to get up from the table, but Freya held his sleeve.

'No. We're off in a minute. Please don't start being silly.'

Jack looked disgruntled. He turned to his brother. 'Did he see you?'

'Course not,' said Will. 'He doesn't know he's a lookalike, does he?'

Even as he finished this sentence, Will, who was facing the back of the café-bar, grabbed Jack's sleeve and stood up, his face suddenly bloodless.

'*Dad?*'

A man walked by and turned briefly.

'Dad!' shouted Jack. 'It *is* Dad!'

The man bolted towards the door.

Chairs scraped and banged as Will and Jack together ran at the man. He almost reached the open glass door, but Will practically rugby tackled him, and the man fell. As he scrambled back on his feet, a woman with slinky blonde hair ran up to him, saying, 'Rubi? Rubes? You okay?'

'Shut up, Tilly!'

Freya rose to her feet as if she had a book balanced on her head. She stared at the door. The man's face was turned away, but she was shaking. Duncan had barely time to notice the extent to which the burgundy-coloured serviette was trembling in her hand when Sophie ducked past him and ran to look for herself.

'Daddy?'

The man turned at the voice. 'Soph . . . ?' The word had slipped out, unbidden, and he must have known there was no hiding now. He took in Sophie, and Duncan, who had followed and was resting his hands gently on her shoulders.

Sophie frowned at the man, as if trying to work him out. He turned to the open glass door and pelted through it. Jack and Will and Duncan were now in pursuit through the terrace tables, and then the young waiter came rushing out too and proved nimbler than all of them as he grabbed the hem of the man's jacket just as he was darting between the stalls in the piazza. He fell back on an array of fruit, and as the stall collapsed to the ground, shiny strawberries, grapes, split watermelons and freshly made fruit cups went flying in all directions over the hot medieval stone slabs. The stall-holder started shrieking. Duncan caught up just as the waiter (whose name he later learnt was Lorenzo) twisted the man's arm behind his back. Duncan took his other arm. Will and Jack were panting in disbelief. Sophie ran over too.

'Is it you, Daddy? Is it you?' Sophie, unlike her brothers, had not seen her father for a third of her life, and it was hard to imagine what must have been going through her head at that moment.

The woman who was with him was now at his side, having screeched and whimpered a little. 'He doesn't have any children. You've made a mistake! This is just a terrible mistake!'

Freya was standing with Sophie now too, and the dread that had spread over the ruins of her happy face would be a hard picture to forget. Her neck was corded. One jittery hand was over her mouth, and the other clutched her daughter to her. Sophie tried to look up at her. 'If it's Daddy, why's he with her and not with us, Mummy?'

Will, who clearly had no doubt whatsoever that this was his father, beard or no beard, was shouting at him now, demanding to know what the fuck was going on. Reuben struggled to get free, but kept his mouth firmly shut. Surprised at his own strength, Duncan held him fast.

'I think you owe this family an explanation,' said Duncan, as calmly as he could, but he knew he sounded angry. Angry enough to clamp this man's other arm behind his back, but he'd only ever seen it done on cop dramas. For a while he seemed to be holding his hand. It was not a slick move.

'Who the hell are you?' said Reuben, unable to keep quiet any longer, and Jack stared at him in recognition, as if he knew that voice for certain.

'That's a question I think we'll be asking you, Reuben!' said Duncan, at the same time feeling all his dreams collapse like Freya's face.

A small crowd had gathered and the stall-holder was explaining what had happened to everyone who would listen. The words *inglesi* and *polizia* and *tutto rovinato* were mentioned a lot, and he hit his fore-head with the inside of his wrist. Freya and her children all watched the newborn truth slither out and lie motionless in front of them, but no one said a thing. They watched it as they had watched Gloria's still lamb, waiting for someone – for Freya – to lick some life into it. But in the end, it was Will who nudged it to its feet.

'Dad, what the fucking fuck . . . ?' he said.

'Yeah, Dad, what the fuck . . . ?' said Jack.

'Look,' said Reuben, almost amiably. 'This is not what you think.'

Freya, at last, exhaled a voiceless, sarcastic laugh. 'Not what we think? And what would you *like* us to think this is? A *resurrection*?'

Reuben smiled and shook his head. (The gall of the man was incredible.) A crushed strawberry fell out of his hair. 'The thing is, I've no idea *what* happened to me. One minute I was taking a walk by the river in a game reserve, and the next thing I came to with a head injury in shock somewhere – in a remote village. I lost my memory!'

'But you remember the game reserve,' said Duncan calmly, sud-denly remembering a piano stool and a trapped doll.

'I . . . Who *are* you?'

'And you just happened to bump into your lover, Tilly. Or is that Matilda? In this remote village? In Africa?'

'No!' Tilly looked panicky. 'No, I'd never met him before!'

A sloppy piece of nectarine slithered from Reuben's shoulder on to the ground, leaving a snail's trail of pulpy juice down his leather jacket. And it was at that moment that some penny dropped for Sophie, for at that precise instant she chose to look Tilly squarely in the face and say: '*Matilda!*'

It came out like a reprimand, as though she didn't believe Matilda was telling the truth, rather than a simple acknowledgement of some distant recognition.

'You two knew each other before?' said Freya, incredulous.

'No! No, of course not!' said Reuben. 'I'd never seen Tilly in my life – before the accident.'

'*Daddy!*' And that was all Sophie said – somewhat firmly – and Reuben's head sunk into his chest.

'You faked your own death!' said Jack.

There was a pause that was so potent even the fruit-seller and his colleagues stopped gabbling and looked across. Reuben did not, or could not, look up.

'You *did*, didn't you? You bloody well did!'

'Fuck you, Dad!' Will put his arm round Jack. Lorenzo temporarily released a hand and put it comfortingly on Will's shoulder. Sophie swallowed hard, attentive, alert.

'I'm not going to explain any more until I see a lawyer.'

'*What?*' said Will. 'You can't speak to your children without a *lawyer*? Fuck you!'

Sophie was crying now, and clinging on to her mother. Hearing her brothers swear so openly must have shocked her. Then, quite suddenly, she turned her head back to her father and said, in the most pitiful sob: 'I didn't tell Mummy, I *promise*! I *didn't!*'

'What?' Freya was bending down to her, aghast. '*What* didn't you tell me?'

'*Scusate, signori,*' said the head waiter, who had run out to join them with an air of restrained panic. '*Non avete pagato!*'

Duncan reassured him they would be paying. Don't worry, they would all be paying.

52

HANDCUFFED AND GUILTY

It was a peculiar kind of torture sitting in an Italian police station with your devastated children, opposite this Matilda woman. And nobody saying a thing, but each finding the polished floor worth looking at. All around them were effusive Italian voices, filling what would have been the most unbearable of silences: a policeman at the counter jabbering down a phone, a trio of women sitting a few seats away, and a giant of a man reeking of aftershave who seemed to be the subject of their wrath.

It wasn't so much that Matilda was pretty – although she was. She was young and slim with long blonde hair, now tied up in a hasty but elegant topknot. She wore khaki shorts that exposed perfectly tanned and shapely legs in a perfectly casual way. No, it wasn't any of that. In fact, Freya felt almost sorry for her, obliged as she was to sit diagonally opposite the family she had helped to betray, and who held her under their constant scrutiny. (Not that they all stared at her together. There seemed to be an unwritten rule that only one or two of them at a time would glance over at the opposition, and then look down at their own feet to digest any new observations.) No, what Freya found the most humiliating about this ordeal was the pungent smell of pity exuding from her family and from Duncan. She thought it was overwhelming (although she may have been confusing it with the aftershave). There was something this girl had. She knew they had all seen it. None of them mentioned it, except for Sophie, who pointed it out by whispering in her ear. It was impossible to miss the four-leafed clover key ring dangling from her bag strap, impossible to convey to Duncan that she knew already about her false treasure, that she had thrown away half a dozen of them. She trembled with shame. It oozed out of her like sweat, or maybe *with* her sweat, because it was inordinately hot and the air-conditioning seemed to be on the blink. She was damp under the arms. She winced as she remembered a stupid past version of herself telling Duncan how unique and precious this gift was, how she wouldn't take it off even when she and Duncan made love. How hurt he had been. She wanted to lean over, tap the girl on the knee and say, 'It's fake. It's not real gold. He didn't have it made specially. He gave me one too, and I found a load of them dirt-cheap in a charity shop. He's conning you too. Don't waste your time with him. He's not worth it.'

But she didn't. She sat and sweated out her degradation until they were seen by the police, and then they were dealt with fairly swiftly, with the help of Lorenzo, who stayed to explain something to a policeman with Duncan for a while after Freya had sat down again. Then Lorenzo (or 'Renzo', as Will was already calling him) came back from the police desk and, giving Will the glad eye, said they should all come now to his uncle's restaurant nearby and eat. Will smiled back – his own eye pretty gladdened. Renzo was inviting them.

Sophie wanted to visit the toilets first, and Renzo found out where they were so that Freya could take her.

She stood against some gleaming cream-coloured tiles while Sophie went into a cubicle. The tiles were cool, and Freya pressed her back and hands against them, as if they might helpfully open a secret door to another world and swallow her up.

As Sophie was washing her hands, Freya asked, 'So . . . do you . . . ? Do you know Matilda, then?'

Sophie put her hands under the dryer and the noise was hideous. Then she dashed at Freya and sank into her waist, arms wrapped around her.

'I only met her once. When I was little. I *think* it was her. She was called Matilda, anyway.'

A coldness rushed through Freya.

'You met her? Where?'

'In the house. When I was ill. When they were tupping.'

'Tupping . . . ?' She stared at Sophie, for a moment hoping that her daughter didn't know what this word meant, but its truth landed into a perfect slot. 'Oh, sweetheart! Oh, my darling little Soph!' She tried to mask her heavy breaths with kisses. 'Why didn't you tell me?'

Even as she asked this, she had a dread of the answer.

'He told me not to tell you.'

'Daddy?'

Sophie nodded. 'He said bad things would happen – and they did! He died! Only . . . he didn't, did he?'

Freya was crouching in front of her daughter now. 'Oh, sweetheart!' She tried to look at Sophie, but Sophie buried her head in Freya's neck.

'I'm sorry, Mummy!' she sobbed. 'I know I should've told you. I know that now. Duncan said I should tell you.'

'*Duncan?*' She drew back, holding Sophie gently by the shoulders. '*Duncan* said that?'

Sophie's face was blotchy and sad. 'He was right, wasn't he? I'm sorry.'

She started to cry again, and Freya held her close, stroking her hair to soothe her but kissing her frantically.

A woman with a very deep tan came in, and Freya got to her feet. She wanted to check her face, but didn't dare glance in the mirror because she couldn't bear to see the idiot who would look back at her.

When they returned to the waiting room, Renzo was ready to escort them all to his uncle's restaurant. Things had been sorted at the police desk. Reuben had to stay in custody, but only because of some details that Duncan had provided. (That Duncan should have provided any details struck Freya as bewildering, and then shocking.) Faking your own death, it seemed, was not a crime. Carrying a fake passport was. As was raising money for a charity that didn't exist.

53

HOW LONG HAVE YOU KNOWN?

Back at their hotel, the coolness of the elegant air-conditioned rooms seemed to ridicule them. Freya consoled the children as best she could and made sure that Sophie was asleep in the boys' room before she returned to her own room and took a shower.

When she came out, she saw Duncan sitting on the bed and ignored him. She wrapped the huge white hotel towel tightly around her and combed her wet hair. She did it with jerky, angry strokes. She could see in the mirror that her mouth was set hard, and she looked grim.

Duncan opened his mouth to speak, but seemed to think the better of it. He came and put his hands on her shoulders from behind and she shook him off, rounding on him suddenly.

'Don't! Don't even *think* about it!'

Duncan lifted his hands away, high, as if her shoulders had been hot irons. 'Freya—'

'How long have you known? Hm? How long?'

She threw the comb across the floor and faced him, a sodden animal with nostrils flared and no idea what she might do next. She felt feral, not responsible for her actions. She had never thrown anything to intentionally break it, but she wanted to now. There was nothing to hand in the minimalist room. She flung open the shutters. The glorious medieval view seemed hideous. The glowing sun was an insult.

'Freya, I swear, I didn't know he would be in that café.'

'But you knew he was alive!'

'No, I just suspected he might be.'

'Why? What made you think that?'

'There was a tickets receipt. I found it in the phrasebook we found when we were clearing stuff out of your house. Two tickets to Italy, for the day after he died. Here.'

She opened her mouth in disbelief and rolled her eyes, sighing dramatically. 'I don't believe it!' She walked over to the window, gazing at the piece of paper he'd given her. She stood quietly with her back to him for a while, trying to take in what she saw, remembering the day they cleared the attic together. Then she turned. 'And you've known since *then*? Since we . . . since . . . ?'

'No – not quite—'

'All this time you've known – okay, "suspected" – and you didn't think to tell *me*! And you *knew* his charity was fake, and you didn't tell me that either!'

'I was going to, but . . . how could I? It would've destroyed you.'

'And I'm not destroyed now?'

He sighed and slumped down on the bed. 'I got it wrong. I'm so sorry. I got it wrong. I didn't know what to do. I was going to investigate an address in Rome, just to be certain he wasn't alive—'

'Rome? And you were going to take us there! You were going to expose the children to that possibility!'

'But I didn't, though! I was torn. I didn't *want* to find out he was alive. But then I wondered if I was doing the right thing ignoring it, hoping it would go away. And I thought, what if one day you found out you were a bigamist or something?'

'*A bigamist?* Don't flatter yourself, Duncan Swan! You think I'd marry a man who has put my children through what you just have? Hm?'

'I didn't put them through anything – *he* did! He was the one who lied. He was the one who walked away from his lovely wife and children and faked his own death!'

Her towel dropped off her, and she picked it up and thwacked him with it as hard as she could.

'Ow.'

'And how long have you known what he did to Sophie?'

'What?'

'Don't look all innocent with me! She told you she'd seen them having sex together!'

'Oh, no! Oh God, I swear I didn't—'

'She told me! And *you* told her to tell me! So don't try and tell me you didn't know! How much more have you hidden from me?'

'Oh God! Oh . . .' He put his hands over his face.

She was breathing deeply, taking in great gulps of air. 'And you just thought you'd take us all to Italy! What a kind gesture! And I really thought you were doing it for *us*. I really did.'

'But I did. It was only afterwards that I got the idea—'

'Oh, and don't tell me you didn't enjoy *investigating* him behind my back. Don't deny that. Don't deny you wanted to prove him a bastard—'

'Freya, he *is* a bastard. He had sex in front of your daughter. Your *little* girl. Now at least we can know what's hurt her. Now we can start to help her properly.'

'*We? We* won't be doing anything. I'm getting the next plane back with my children.'

'Freya—'

'You can help me change the flights tomorrow.'

She opened a wardrobe door. The hanging dresses she had carefully selected for the holiday were listening and had the nerve to look indifferent. She grabbed them off their hangers with a great clatter and slapped them on top of her open suitcase. Then she swept into bed and turned her back on him, covering herself carefully with the sheet. She stayed like this as long as she could, until her back ached and she had to turn. Duncan was curled away from her. She thought she could hear faltering breathing, and maybe a sniffle, but she couldn't be sure.

Where were the clues, then? There were always good things to remember when someone died, and the good things seemed to line up and ask to be counted. Quick! Before we slip out of your memory forever. Think us through carefully. Dwell on us. Celebrate us. Weep for us. She felt as though the protective layer of widowhood had been rudely removed, like cling film, leaving her exposed and open to anything.

She lay in the luxuriously cool cotton sheets next to Duncan, unable to drift off to sleep, unable to touch him. The most telling memories were stacking up like cars in a traffic jam and she knew she would have to release them if she was to stand any chance of getting rid of the buzzing engines clogging her head.

It had been a party. Of course it had been a party. Someone like Freya never met anyone like Reuben in the normal course of events. Sober, he would probably never even have remarked on her. But this was a Halloween party, so it would have been barely halfway through the first term. 'Tarty Witches and Wizards' or, as one of her housemates had drily remarked, 'Wizards and Tarty Witches'. There had been no need for the male students to dress up – apart from the obligatory pointed hat, (although one or two hopefuls had gone off-theme with some quite racy S&M costumes). The witches, on the other hand, were mostly in short skirts and wearing suspenders and very low-cut necklines and push-up bras. Freya had been wearing a black dress and a witch's hat and felt out of place the moment she walked through the door of the Students' Union. There was no chance of conversation, since the music was so loud you had to shout. She bought herself a cider with her friends – who soon wandered off – and stood in a corner, inspecting a noticeboard that she couldn't read in the gloom.

Some long time passed. It was hard to remember quite how it happened: their versions differed. Reuben remembered seeing her across a crowded room and being 'awe-struck'; she remembered someone pushing him (a girl?) and him falling into her so hard that he spilt her drink down her front. The next thing – they both agreed – he was apologising and patting her front with his hand, as if that would somehow soak up the liquid. He offered to buy her another drink, but she said she was heading off anyway, so would just go back and change.

'Oh, but you can't go yet!'

'*What?*' (The music really was very loud.)

'You can't go yet! I've only just found you!'

He shouted it with such a smile on his face that she warmed to him. Still, she felt wet and miserable and his face was too close to hers and she could smell how much he had been drinking. She smiled back and made her way to the door.

She was already on the path back to her student accommodation – a little purpose-built 'house' on three floors – when she realised he was behind her.

'You know, a woman should not be left to walk on her own at night. Allow me to accompany you.' He held out his arm for her, and when she didn't take it, he took hers, and she let him. 'There, you see: I don't bite.'

When they arrived at her house, he went in through the front door with her and into the dark communal kitchen.

'You can go now,' she said.

He stood very close to her and put his hand on her chest. 'We must do something about this.' He pulled at her neckline, and then his hand was inside it.

Freya had never been touched quite like this before. It was, she felt, very different to the groping she had been subjected to at a nightclub once. And she was about to push his hand away, when the other one came up behind her neck and pulled her in close. His lips were on hers, and she felt a warm, tugging sensation in her insides. This was Reuben Gray. All the girls loved Reuben. He was smart (apparently), he had long eyelashes and a brother called Ludo and his family took skiing holidays. Maybe it was time. All her housemates told her it was high time she got it out of the way, although not one of them had any good stories to recommend the first time. It would hurt; she would bleed. They hadn't really sold it to her. But she couldn't stay intact forever and besides . . . besides . . . this was . . . quite . . . nice . . . wonderful!

He had followed her up to her room anyway. She doubted she would have been able to shake him off, as he pushed his way in as soon as she opened her door. She made her excuses and left for the bathroom. Here, she panicked. She had some condoms in her bag for this very occasion. Guys never checked to see if you were taking precautions, her friends said. But how could she possibly ask him to use one? Mercifully, she had her bag with her. She checked her make-up and rummaged in the zipped pocket to locate the condoms. Right.

When she opened the door to her room, Reuben was sprawled across her bed, snoring loudly. She wondered if it would be too forward to take off her clothes and try to slip in beside him, but her sticky dress made up her mind. She took off everything, and eyed her embarrassing, worn pyjamas that were clamped under the pillow. She pulled them out gingerly and stuffed them into the bottom of her wardrobe, then selected a lumberjack shirt, turned off the light and edged on to the bed next to him. There were barely six inches for her to lie on, and not enough to curl up on and fall asleep. She spent the night shivering and wondering about what would happen in the morning.

She must've slept a little, because she woke with the sun beginning to turn her stiff orange curtains into a blaze of golden light. She took her dressing gown to the bathroom, showered, and then went down to the communal kitchen to clean out two stained mugs and make tea.

His eyes opened when she placed the tea on the bedside table. He pulled her towards him. She could smell his sour alcohol breath as he opened her dressing gown and slipped his hands inside. She could feel his erection pushed up hard against her. He was telling her that she was special, that he had been watching her for some time, that he liked the fact that she didn't seem interested in him.

'But you are, aren't you?' he murmured, his breath overwhelming her.

'What?'

'Interested.'

'How do you mean?'

'In this . . .'

He was touching her now in ways she had never been touched before. So confidently, so full of self-assurance.

'I'm not . . . I haven't . . .'

She could barely think straight. He was melting her. She didn't care how much it would hurt; this was it. This was her time. She began to stroke him too. She kissed his chest, and made her way down to his erection, which was a source of considerable interest to her. She had never seen one like this: up close and personal.

'I'm not on the pill.'

He hesitated, then lay back and stroked her arms. 'That's okay,' he whispered reassuringly.

'Are you sure?'

'Of course.'

She hadn't imagined he would be this understanding. People could surprise you. She was about to reach into her bag for the condom when he really did surprise her. Of course, she thinks as she conjures up his face now, she could let this memory fall through the cracks so easily, if she let it go.

She thought of Sophie now and wept. She tried to do it quietly but she was out of control. She snorted and snivelled and moaned. Duncan reached out and put a hand on her shoulder and kissed her gently on the back. She pushed him away violently.

They couldn't get five seats on the same flight the following day, or even four. There were just three available, and only two of those were together. Duncan tried to persuade her to wait another day and they could all go back together, but she was in no mood to agree with him about anything. Against her own better judgement, she took the three flight seats and returned with Jack and Sophie, leaving Will – since he didn't seem to mind – to come back with Duncan on the original flight.

54

BACK HOME

It is so obviously her fault. Sophie has hated every moment since they saw Daddy in the café. Except he didn't seem like Daddy. He seemed like a random man. It was just that *one* moment when he said her name: 'Soph . . .' and then he seemed a bit like Daddy, but there is something she isn't telling them.

The last time she didn't say something it all went very wrong. She knows now, she should've told Mummy. When Daddy said, 'Don't tell Mummy, okay?' she *should've* told Mummy. Then Mummy would've known about the woman, about Matilda, and then she would've known he was a cheating fucking bastard. She knows that now, because Mummy is telling Granny Sylvia he is a cheating fucking bastard, and it's making Granny Sylvia very cross. Mummy doesn't know they're listening, but they are all sitting on the landing: her, Jack and Will, and for once, Will doesn't send her to her room. He's letting her and Jack listen to the grown-up talk, because they all want to know what's going on and no one – not even Mummy – is telling them.

'There's bound to be a simple explanation, Freya, so please stop jumping to conclusions.'

'Jumping to—?'

'He told me he wandered about for weeks, not knowing who he was or what he was doing in Africa. He was completely stunned. Someone had clearly hit him over the head and robbed him of everything. He had no wallet and no means of identification on him, and—'

'God, you really are the limit, Sylvia! He lost his memory in Africa and suddenly found himself with a woman he used to work with? A woman Sophie saw him having sex with before he went missing?' (Will and Jack raise their eyebrows and stare at Sophie.) '*Yes!* I've learnt a few things this holiday. Don't look so shocked, Sylvia! Your son is a cheating fucking bastard, and he'd even stopped paying for his life insurance, and do you know why? Because he knew the insurers would investigate if they had to pay out a large sum of money!'

'Oh no you don't! No son of mine would've left his family with nothing *deliberately*! Can't you see, it's proof that he didn't intend to disappear?'

'And the police here have found that *Eau Please!* was a complete fake! And his passport was fake! He's going to be done for fraud if nothing else! He made over a thousand pounds out of innocent kids at Will and Jack's school! He siphoned off hundreds each month from our family account to fund his new life with *Matilda*! What a creep! What a pathetic fraud!'

Sophie doesn't know what fraud means, but Will and Jack are frowning at each other now, and don't look at all pleased.

'I think you're jumping to conclusions about her. Reuben says he only bumped into her in Italy, and—'

'Didn't you hear what I said? Sophie *saw* them together. Your irresponsible *dick* of a son had sex in front of her and made her promise not to tell. *That's* what she didn't want to tell me! Nothing to do with Duncan! It's *your son*, Sylvia, who abused Sophie! *Your son* emotionally abused his own daughter – my little girl!'

Mummy is sobbing so much that Will gets up and goes downstairs, and Jack punches the air when they hear him say, 'Granny Sylvia, you have to go now. If you really can't accept what Dad has done, you're no help to any of us.'

'Well! He's not the first husband to stray!'

Sophie wonders what Grandad Steve is doing. She pictures him rocking back and forth on his feet downstairs, pretending it's nothing to do with him. Although she feels sorry for Grandad Steve, this evening it irritates her that he isn't doing something to help.

'Please go now,' they hear Will say.

'If a man isn't getting what he should, if his wife isn't doing her duty by him, then—'

'Fuck off! *Fuck off!*' It is strange because Mummy normally never swears. But this evening she uses lots of swear words. It's exciting, but also scary. It's a bit like stopping after you've been twirling around and things keep moving.

'Come on,' says Grandad Steve. 'Come on, Sylvia.'

'Stop it! I'll come when I'm ready. I haven't finished. I—'

'You'll come *now*!'

Oooh. Grandad never speaks like that. Grandad Steve is really cross, and Granny S must be really shocked, because the back door rattles loudly, so they know she's left. Sophie and Jack both go downstairs as well then, and they all cuddle Mummy. Her face is very red and snotty, but they don't mind.

What upsets Sophie most is that Mummy and Duncan don't seem to be talking to each other any more. Sophie hasn't seen him since Italy. And that doesn't seem to be making Mummy happy either. But still, there is something Sophie hasn't told them. Everyone seems to be talking about her and how she has been badly treated and stuff, and Mum outlines what happened to Sophie because Will and Jack keep asking, but what Sophie really wants to say might land her in more trouble, and it's making her feel bad. Really heavy heavy. The thing is, she doesn't really feel bad about Daddy. She hasn't really missed him. She's heard Jack and Will say they don't want him to go to prison. They're really, really angry with him, but they can't totally hate him because he's still Dad. But, if Jack and Will hadn't recognised him, she definitely wouldn't have. And it was only when he looked at her and said, 'Soph . . .' that she thought he probably was Daddy. She is not glad they've found him. She doesn't want him to come back.

55

A MOTHER'S WARNING

Somehow Sylvia seems to bring Reuben right back into their living space. Freya is exhausted now, and lies on her bed running over the early footage of her memories of him that should have helped her unravel him sooner.

She was back with his hands in her dressing gown, back with her kisses on his chest, her close-up of his erection.

'I'm not on the pill.'

She remembers how he hesitated, then lay back and stroked her arms. How he whispered so reassuringly, 'That's okay.'

'Are you sure?'

'Of course.'

And he had put his hand around the back of her neck. She had heard of 'withdrawal'. It wasn't safe. She hoped he wouldn't suggest that, but she didn't want this to stop. She was on fire. She made to reach for her bag, but the hand clutched at her neck and pushed her down, down on to his erection. She thought to kiss it, perhaps, but he was pushing her so hard once her mouth was on it that she could barely breathe. She made a sound, but his hand clamped her down on him and he moved beneath her. In and out, in and out until he groaned and shuddered and her mouth was full of the saltiness of him. Then he lay back as if nothing had happened.

The ache was still deep inside her, but he seemed to fall asleep again. She sipped her tea, watching him carefully, tears welling in her eyes. Then she drank his tea as well. She went down to the kitchen so that she wouldn't have to see him when he woke up.

When she had refused a date after their first sexual encounter, Reuben had been fired up. Unavailability, she learnt too late, was just the sort of thing to get him going. Hard to say now whether or not he knew straight away where he'd gone wrong, or whether something in her frostiness, her dull refusal, had made him realise. But woo her he did, with apologies in spades and heaps of promises.

'Oh God, I'm so sorry! I was so drunk. I must've behaved really badly. I was totally out of order. I'll make it up to you. Please, let me make it up to you!' and so on.

Freya's lack of interest could not have provoked him more. He fussed around her and flirted openly – that was the time he climbed up to her room to deliver chocolates through a second-floor window – and she had to laugh. And, in fairness, he did seem to pull out all the stops for a while, but as soon as they were an item, he became casual, as if he deserved his reprieve, as if he had earned it and forgotten it. So, she lost her virginity to him, and he indulged her once or twice, but thereafter it seemed to be all about him, and he didn't seem to feel any awkwardness that his 'lovemaking' served his needs alone. Of course, she should have said something, but he was her first – and what did she know? It wasn't until she locked eyes with Daniel in the library that she knew there might be more to it, and it wasn't until they locked legs that she knew she could have expected more from Reuben all long. She doubted, though, that Reuben had it in him to give what Daniel gave her. Something she had tried to forget all through her marriage.

She had once accused Reuben, when Will awoke screaming at night because Reuben had come in late from somewhere and tripped noisily over the table leg, of only asking her to marry him to win her back from Daniel, of only insisting on her having the baby for that reason. She said it because Reuben was thumping the wall and asking why the baby couldn't shut up for once, and she felt suddenly aggrieved at the unfairness of it all. If she followed a logical pathway in her thoughts, she knew she would come out where she didn't want to be, so she had blocked up that path, built a wall in front of it, and truly believed every Post-it note that said 'Where would I be without my lovely wife?' or 'Can't wait to get home to you!'

And now that wall had been kicked right over. The path ahead was in full view. She knew that the anger she felt was really with herself, but it didn't stop a deep humiliation and resentment. All those little lies of Reuben's, those sly signs she had thought so trivial because she hadn't wanted to see them. Looking back, how well she had always stuffed them away like dirty clothes lying around, bundled them out of sight – from her own sight most of all. And yet, come to think of it, there had always been something of the truth visible, like the tip of a sock peeping out from a closed drawer.

She remembered sitting at the table with her mother and sister. They had eaten a whole punnet of cherries between them after school, and Rachel was counting out her cherry stones: 'Tinker, tailor, soldier, sailor, rich man, poor man, beggar man, thief. I don't want to marry a thief! I don't want to marry any of these men!' and she had set about making her own list of careers for potential partners: doctor, artist, engineer, lawyer, architect . . . What else? There had been a farmer and a documentary film-maker in there somewhere, and they had laughed about it when Mum's cherry stones said she would marry a politician. They had been in their mid-teens, and their relationship with their mother had only a few more years to go, although they didn't know it then. She remembered the sun slanting in through the window and the sense of well-being as the three of them giggled together. And she remembered a rare piece of advice from their mother, who was not prone to look too far into her daughters' future love lives.

'Whatever you do,' she said, 'look very carefully at the relationship your man has with his mother. If he is kind to her, he will be kind to you; if he lies to her, he will lie to you; if he blames her for everything that's wrong in his life, he will blame you.'

Rachel had questioned this, saying surely all men did not see their wives as mothers, but Mum had said simply, 'No, I don't suppose they do. And I may be wrong. But it is something I have always observed.'

They laughed then, and pointed out how their father always rolled his eyes at his mother's knitted pullovers, and she said that's why she never knitted anything. But Freya did remember that her father was always kind to his mother, and he was always kind to hers too. She thought now about Sylvia, and Reuben's relationship with her. There had been contempt. He'd blamed her readily when things went wrong, and he'd insisted on not telling her things he didn't think she would approve of. He'd often lied to her – even in front of the children – and yet he had always been delightful to her face: the best mum in the world. Reuben had explained once – in a more tender moment – that his mother had been beaten by a violent father, and had shown some rare sympathy for her. Freya had been relieved that Sylvia had a back story, that she wasn't just some cardboard cut-out of a vile mother-in-law, but now she didn't care. She was glad Sylvia had a back story to help excuse her, but it didn't stop her from being one of the most selfish and unkind people she had ever met.

56

DUNCAN SWAN THINKS HE'S SO CLEVER

It was clear to Duncan that everything he had feared about himself was true. He had observed Freya and her three fragile children and he had found a new self with this family; it had seemed to come naturally to him. But he wasn't made for heroics. He hadn't been able to pull that off. He should've stuck with being the solid, dull Duncan that he was.

He stood in his flat, the remains of a sandwich curling in the sun, and he wondered what he was going to do now. Now, tomorrow and the day after tomorrow, and all the tomorrows stretching into his old age. Lottie had joked by saying that all the money he'd secretly spent on the new windows for Freya would benefit Reuben when the house was divided for the divorce. Duncan couldn't give a toss, but now all the things he'd done, those windows, fixing the guttering and the garden, taking Will to interviews, going running with Jack and taking them all on a grand holiday, all of these things had something a little desperate about them.

They had been back home for five days. During that time Freya had not wanted Duncan to be around. Time dragged. He had texted her repeatedly, and she had answered him once, but only to say that she was 'dealing with Sylvia and Steve' and it was best that she came to terms with things on her own. At one point, Will had texted him with 'Please come. Mum is a mess.' He'd turned up only to be sent away again by

Freya, sobbing, 'This is my mess. Can't you see? I'm married! I'm still married! Back off, Duncan.' And then, when he was by the back door, she had rounded on him, 'You've got your own way!' He had stared at her, nonplussed. 'You *knew* he had committed fraud,' she hissed. 'You'd been checking up on him behind my back! You *wanted* me to stop loving him, and now I have! Satisfied? Please, just leave me alone.'

Duncan fetched Mr Simpkins a fresh bowl of water, with little enthusiasm. He cleaned the kitchen worktops. While she had loved him, Freya's acceptance of him and her trust in him seemed to buoy him up. He floated, he felt empowered. Everything he did had a purpose. His very existence mattered to the world. Now her contempt would grow with each passing day, and his life would become one long, unbroken routine. He would work hard and reap the financial rewards of it, he would buy a new car when the current one had done fifty thousand miles, he would update the lighting system in his flat, he would replace the sofa when it became too saggy, Mr Simpkins would need feeding twice a day, then one day this companion would die and be replaced by another cat with another name and the same mixture of need and indifference that cats managed to perfect.

57

LOVE DON'T COME EASY

The end of April was perfect. The firm new leaves plumped out every tree and hedgerow and the dreamy sunsets bathed their tatty house in gold and bronze. Blackcaps and dunnocks trilled their hearts out along the hedgerows. The blackbirds tumbled about the garden in a frenzy of lovemaking, trumpeting their triumphs with the sweetest songs. Every morning was a chorus of smug territorial rights, and every evening the saddest and most poignant line-up of feathery love songs.

It seemed to her natural that she should fail. It was as if she had been waiting for this all her life, expecting it. Rachel had been right about Reuben. Of course she had. Goddammit, *she* had been right about Reuben: those first instinctive thoughts to get him out of her student bedroom, never to see him again. She must take a full burden of responsibility for all this trauma brought to bear on her and her children. She had made bad choices.

Rachel had taken time off work to come to see her for a few days. The Rachel recently was the old Rachel, the younger sister she remembered growing up with. Now she took charge, distracting the children with takeaways and walks out to see the lambs, and in the evenings, she had long chats with Freya, letting her offload.

'Do you think I was a bad wife? I mean, being so involved with the children that I neglected him, or something?'

'Neglected Reuben? Oh Lord, Freya. Never was a man more spoilt. He had plenty of your attention, don't worry. More than he deserved.'

'Why do you say that? I must've done something wrong. I mean, this woman must've had something that I didn't.'

Rachel pressed her lips together. Freya knew that look. She knew that Rachel had something to say that she didn't want to say. She watched her sister tap out an unknown rhythm on the arm of the sofa, biding her time. The sun had gone down, but suddenly a blackbird pitched in with a stunning solo performance. Their eyes met.

'What?'

'Well, I wasn't going to tell you. Ever. It seemed best not to, what with . . . the children and everything. But he made a play for me once.'

'A play?'

'He grabbed my bottom in the kitchen – when you were still pregnant with Will.'

'He grabbed your bottom.'

'Yes.'

There was more, of course. Freya could see that Rachel was brimming over with unspoken history, and she wanted to hear it. He had grabbed her bottom when Freya was out baby-shopping with her mother, and Reuben and Rachel were decorating the small room. He had tried to take her to bed. He had been *very* insistent. He had even pushed her on to the bed so that, after a struggle, Rachel had left her paintbrush unwashed and dripping and gone out for a long walk, until its bristles hardened into peaks. She had already advised Freya to get rid of the baby and finish her degree, but this was when she told Freya she was making a big mistake in marrying him. It was too late then to get rid of the baby, but not too late to call off the wedding. Freya had never really forgiven her.

'I'm sorry, Freya.'

Freya closed her eyes. 'You were right to tell me . . . Thank you. Oh, Rachel, I'm the one who should be saying sorry to you. I *am* sorry. I'm so sorry.'

But Rachel had more to say. At each of the children's birthday parties he had tried it on with some mum or other, and it all fell into place now. The mothers who stopped coming round, the friends Sophie and Jack suddenly lost. A woman from her book club. Rachel's friend Candice who came up with her one Easter. And early on their father had caught Reuben in flagrante with one of his office staff. Over the desk. He hadn't sacked him, but he'd wanted to. He didn't want Freya to suffer her husband being unemployed. 'Dad was in a terrible state. He didn't know whether to tell you and break your heart, and break up your family, or let you find out yourself further down the line, so your heart could be broken later. Of course, Reuben insisted it was a one-off. He made a great act of total contrition. It was impressive, apparently.'

And it didn't stop there. Rachel had seen him, just a few years ago, in the British Museum. He had been in the restaurant with a girl – a woman. She had very long dark hair in a single plait down her back. Quite distinctive, quite striking. They had kissed over a light lunch, and walked away arm in arm.

Freya's head sank into her shoulders, as if avoiding a rainstorm of pennies dropping. But somehow, they didn't hurt her – they were going to help her make sense of things. It was a strangely welcome shower, and she tilted her face up to it now. There was too much there for it not to be true. So it wasn't just something with Matilda. It was a pattern.

'But Matilda must've lasted a good two years if Sophie had seen her before he . . . "died". At least he'd showed *some* fidelity, if not to me.'

She tried not to see the pity in her sister's eyes. She looked stead-fastly at an apple core one of the children had left on the arm of a chair. *A goodly apple rotten at the heart. O, what a goodly outside falsehood hath!* Rachel said that if she was the Matilda she had once caught him flirting with in the pub – and she matched the description – then she was the daughter of a very wealthy local businessman. Very wealthy. She said the last words slowly, as though that explained things. And, Freya was beginning to see, it probably did.

'You know, Freya, not all men are the same. Duncan is a good man.'

'Hmm . . . Well . . . I don't know if I'm officially married now. I'll have to see a solicitor and see if the marriage is void or if I need a divorce. But I'm way past having another man in my life. I don't think I can do it again now.'

'Well, you know what Mum said?'

'What?

'You can't hurry love.'

'That was The Supremes.'

'No. Well, they may have said it too. No, it was Mum. Just probably didn't say it to you. You never seemed in any hurry. And then suddenly it was too late.'

The blackbird was singing again, trilling away to itself in the dark. It seemed all wrong that her world, and the world of her children, should be folding in on itself, just as the world outside was blooming, opening itself up to the spring skies. She had wanted to hide away and lick her wounds, but now these wounds were far more extensive than she'd thought, and no plan seemed sufficient. She was probably inoperable. She knew she was supposed to leave the past behind now and 'move on', but what she wanted to do more than anything was to prise it open and examine it first.

'I wish I'd listened to you. I could've stopped all this pain that my children are going through. I could've—'

'Freya, I'm glad you didn't listen to me. Just think, if you had, Will would never have been born. Nor Jack, nor Sophie.'

Freya groaned. It was a deep, bear-like growl from somewhere within her. What a fucking conundrum. She couldn't even wish she'd never set eyes on him. She couldn't even wish that.

58

JACK GETS PHYSICAL

Before term started again, Jack got a visit from Danielle. She arrived on their doorstep with a spare riding hat. 'It used to be Mum's, but she says you can have it – if it fits.'

He invited her in. Mum was immediately embarrassing in that way that she was whenever their friends came round. She started fussing about feeding them or offering them something, or else she said something cringeworthy and had no idea that she had. Now she was at it in full flood.

'Danielle! We've heard so much about you from Jack! Have a sit-down – sorry about the mess. Can I get you a cup of tea? Or would you like a hot chocolate?'

Jack was determined to get her out of the kitchen and shook his head at Mum, but Danielle went and said, 'Ooh, a hot chocolate would be lovely! Thank you, Mrs Gray.'

'Nothing for you, then, Jack?'

He flared his nostrils, then resigned himself. 'Okay. Same.'

They sat at the kitchen table while Mum boiled some milk. She plied Danielle with questions about Biscuit, and Danielle was eager to tell her all about him and how he'd been getting on while Jack had been away. He'd wanted to ask her about Biscuit himself. He felt cheated.

When the drinks were ready, Mum sat with them for a while and chuntered on for a bit, saying things like, 'Jack's always loved animals, but I would never have taken him for a horse-rider, and he talks about little else these days. You seem to have transformed him!' Then she caught his glowering eye and said, 'Why don't you take Danielle out and show her your wrens' nest?'

So he did. He didn't really know why he minded so much, because it wasn't like he fancied Danielle or anything, and he'd made that very clear to everyone since he'd started at the stables to avoid teasing from Will. Still, she was looking quite nice today. Her hair was loose and had a pleasant swing to it as she crouched down next to him by the front hedge. He pulled the leaves aside and said, 'It's quite hard to see now. All the leaves have come out, and the wrens are enjoying the cover.'

'I can hear them,' she said, putting her hand next to his to hold back the foliage. He liked her slim brown wrist. He could smell her hair, right next to him, and it had the scent of peaches or something fruity.

'Look!' he whispered. To her delight, they could make out three yellow diamond shapes, which were open beaks, squeaking in alarm or hunger.

'Oh, aren't they cute!' she whispered back to him. 'Their beaks are huge compared to them. I've never seen babies this close before.'

He felt proud. He continued to hold the scratchy bit of hedge back so that she could see them and take out her phone to get a picture. He looked down at her feet. They were so neat and small in her open sandals, and it gave him a strangely protective feeling to see that they were smaller than his, even though Danielle was a bit taller than him. Her hand, he noticed, was smaller than his too, and the little nails were so clean and well kept, the fingers so delicate. He was enthralled. Usually she was wearing big rubber gloves and wellington boots.

As they crouched there, his bare arm brushed up against her hair. It was electrifying. He was intrigued. This was Danielle, after all. He tried not to read anything into it. But there it was again. This time she was leaning slightly and tipping her loose hair against his arm.

There was a sound of car wheels on the gravel, and he looked up. It was a police car. He and Danielle got up and stared. It was pulling up next to the house.

'This Mrs Gray's house?' asked a policeman politely as he got out. A policewoman got out of the passenger side.

'Yes. She's in there.'

Jack led the way and Danielle and the two police officers followed.

Mum suggested he take Danielle up to his room to show her his binoculars. Honestly, as if he needed to be told what to do – he wasn't ten! Still, he knew she was only saying this to get him out of the way. Danielle seemed keen to see his room, so he hoped to Jesus he hadn't left his pants on the floor.

Phew. All clear-ish. Only a few socks lying around and his pyjamas stuffed in a corner by the pillow. He took out his binoculars and knelt on the bed in order to lean on the windowsill. Danielle followed. He focused the glasses and showed her a blue tit hanging upside down under the leafy branches, looking for insects. 'Here,' he said, handing them to her. 'Look in the apple tree. Just there . . .'

As she looked, he watched her face to see if she'd seen it. Her lips were full and soft. He hadn't noticed that before. He hadn't ever seen her in a T-shirt before either, and he saw that she had small mounds at her chest. He wondered if she was wearing a bra. Ellie Chapman wore one – he could see the blue clasp through her blouse when she was sitting in front of him in History. But Danielle's T-shirt was giving nothing away. Her bare arm was brushing against his now. Oh mercy! He breathed her in again and thought he might be falling in love with her. But he couldn't be. This was just Danielle.

'I see it!' she said, and handed him back the binoculars. 'What do you think the police are here for?'

'Haven't you heard? Something horrible happened when we were in Italy.'

Danielle looked full of sympathy. 'Well, I had heard a rumour. What happened?'

He told her how they had bumped into their dead father, and how he had run away but they caught him.

'Oh, Jack!' She whispered this almost passionately, and for a moment he thought she was going to put her arm around him. He tried to squeeze out a tear so that she would, but he just couldn't do it with her looking.

Instead he looked tragically down at the bedcover and said, 'It's been terrible. It's Mum I feel most sorry for.' Seeing her face tilt to one side in empathy, he added, 'She's falling apart. I wish there was something I could do to help her.' He did mean this. It wasn't just put on, but it did seem to make her melt in an interesting way.

'Oh, Jack!' said her lips again. Then she added, 'Perhaps we could both do something to help her.' She looked thoughtful for a moment. Jack couldn't imagine anything they could do to help. She climbed down off the bed (pity) and said, 'Why don't we offer to make them all a cup of tea?'

In the kitchen, they filled the kettle. Jack fetched some biscuits from the cupboard. Before they drowned the kitchen in water-boiling sounds, something made them both stop and listen. Jack put his finger up to his lips, taking control.

'It's very likely that he will receive bail when he gets back.'

'*Back?* I didn't know he was coming back!'

'Well, it actually isn't a crime to fake your own death, but he certainly did fake his passport. He also appears to have committed fraud by setting up a fake charity, and that was here in Britain. He'll be travelling back next week, I believe.'

'*Coming back?*' Mum sounded as if she was going to lose it. '*Here?*'

'I understand your distress, but can you tell us if he will use this as his home address for the purposes of a bail hearing?' The policeman's voice was loud and boomed into every part of the kitchen. It covered the kettle and the row of hanging mugs with the threat of Dad's return. Dad would soon look at the potted parsley and the basil and the fridge magnets and lidded jar of biscuits and he would *own* them. He would come back and fill Mum's bedroom with his things, he would pat Sophie on the head, he would patronise Will and he'd ruffle Jack's hair and make fun of him. He'd spread his fun-dad jollity throughout the house, and every room would be filled with the scent of his lies.

'But he can't come back here! I don't *want* him back!'

'At this point, then, I would suggest you seek the advice of a solicitor. You may be able to have some sort of exclusion order. A solicitor will be able to make you fully aware of your rights with regard to a husband who has been "dead", so to speak, for more than two years.'

'He really can't stay here! Absolutely not!'

Jack looked at Danielle and she was watching him. Now she reached out her hand and gave his a squeeze. The room was his friend. This tatty kitchen with its peeling paint and cluttered windowsills and crusty cat bowl, this was the most romantic room in the world. He held his breath.

'We'll be asking you to come to the station to make a statement soon.'

'A statement?'

'Yes. You're saying you didn't stand to gain in any way from your husband's apparent death.'

'Not at all. He'd stopped paying his life insurance for us, but I had no idea until after he died . . . seemed to die.'

'And you had no idea that his charity, *Eau Please!*, was fake?'

'No. As I've explained. It wasn't until . . .'

Fucksake. Did he really want Danielle to know the extent of his father's criminality? But Danielle saw his pain. She squeezed his hand some more, and before he had time to think, he put his other hand on top and pressed down on hers too. They looked into each other's eyes . . .

'And I would advise you not to talk to the press. I can't stop you, but that's my advice. Tricky buggers. They ask you if your husband's life was insured and you say "no", next thing you've got a suggestive headline saying, "WIFE DENIES CLAIMING LIFE ASSURANCE AFTER HUSBAND'S FAKE DEATH". That sort of thing.'

'But he abandoned his children! Why would I . . . ?'

Another squeeze from Danielle, and an anguished gaze.

'Mrs Gray, I'm just saying keep them at bay. They'll be on the doorstep soon. You should give them nothing. That's just my advice.'

Not long after that they left. Mum showed them out through the front door, so Jack and Danielle didn't see the police officers again, and Mum didn't get to see their hastily withdrawn hands. Under any other circumstances, Jack knew he would be questioning Mum for more details about the fake charity and stuff, and shooting upstairs to his room and the comfort of his secret stash. Actually, he didn't have anything in his most secret stash any more, only a KitKat in his rucksack, and that had been there for weeks. No, Danielle had saved him.

To be honest, he hadn't really given Biscuit a thought while he'd been away in Italy, but he found he had a suddenly renewed interest in him.

59

LARKING ABOUT

Freya decided to brave a walk down the lane into the village to the shop before picking up Sophie. They were out of milk and bread and anything to eat this evening. It was the second day of term, and she had sent the children off to school. She had telephoned the boys' head teacher a couple of days ago to explain it all, and he had kindly offered to mention it in assembly on the first day back, and to get the Head of Sixth Form to mention it to Will's peer group, to warn pupils against mentioning it in school. He said that of course the worst of any bullying would be online, and that was out of his territory. 'I could imply that the police have asked Will and Jack to make no comment, and that I would take a very poor view of anyone who tried to introduce the subject online.'

'But the police have simply suggested they don't talk to the press.'

'I could *imply* that it's *sub judice* – if it would help. These things can get out of control very fast. It's up to you.'

'Thank you. Thank you.'

The Head's kindness had made her feel wobbly with gratitude. What must he think, having invited the Good Reuben Gray into his school to talk to the pupils about drought? And where had all that goodness sprouted from? At university, when she'd met Reuben, he'd been an outrageous flirt. All the girls liked him, but his good deeds to others, as far as she could remember, amounted to zero. And yet he had made the transformation from charming, self-indulgent bad boy to charming, evangelical do-gooder in one imperceptible move. A swift sidestep, as if nothing untoward had happened. What fool of a wife would not question it?

The Head was a kind man, but she was still worried. She had asked the boys to keep away from social media for a few days, but she knew they hadn't listened. It was everywhere already. Last night it had even made the ten o'clock news on the BBC with a weirdly old photograph of the family (in which Freya was still pregnant with Sophie), and this morning there had been cameramen outside the house – fortunately the wrong house, and by the time they'd found the correct one, the boys had left and she had taken Sophie to school (the front entrance and not the playground, to avoid the mums).

Now she stopped at a wooden five-bar gate and leaned on it for succour before entering the village itself. Her phone bleeped: yet another text from Duncan. She ignored it. The gate was warm in the sunshine, and the view was spectacular. Ahead was the quiet harmony of rolling fields with a fringe of beeches in almost-full leaf in the distance. Beside the gate the lichen-encrusted Cotswold stone wall was warming gently, and a yellowhammer was perched on a top stone further along, unaware of its colour coordination with the golden lichen. At the base of the wall was a cluster of yellow primroses, whilst underneath a nearby ash tree some ice-white wood anemones swayed in the gentlest of late April breezes. In this new, adrenaline-fuelled world, everything seemed brighter and more hard-edged than before. High above her a silver plane scratched a cruel white line across the sky in silence. How dare it! How dare something so distant and remote split their perfect dome of blue in half! Reuben, bloody Reuben Gray. She wondered she hadn't found a portrait of him in the attic all evil and wrinkly.

And then, from nowhere, a skylark. She watched its complicated song-flight as it spiralled sharply upwards high above the meadow. There it hovered on fluttering wings, trilling its high-pitched love song. Larking about, she thought. Showing off while the female has built the nest and is busy tending it. She had studied the lark as a girl, drawing its long crown feathers, dark eyes and short beak with the longer upper mandible like an overbite, the stocky legs with the long rear toe. You would be lucky to see it on the ground, where it foraged stealthily, and your main chance was to catch the male like this, flaunting himself in flight. In flight . . . while the female built the cup of a nest from hair and grass, hidden away, hidden away. That fine singing was meant to strengthen the pair bond. She watched the male flutter his wings in a frenzy to stay in place, singing his intricate song for long minutes as if he owned the sky. Then he spiralled swiftly downward and dropped like a stone out of sight. Show-off, she thought callously. *Men.* She turned her face to the sun and closed her eyes.

'Hello, my dear.'

She looked around, and leaning next to her on the gate was an elderly gentleman whom she vaguely recognised from village fetes and local fundraising events. Colonel Spears. She had a feeling that he'd actually had nothing to do with military combat, but that he was a colonel in the same way that Captain Mainwaring was a captain. He was a bit of a bigwig, but bent over now and frail.

'I'm sorry to hear about all your trouble.'

She felt slightly nauseous and could tell that her pulse was speeding up. 'Oh. Yes.'

Bad news spread like grass pollen. It was everywhere. It had started the minute they got back – long before the BBC news. It had arrived on a breeze, from nowhere distinguishable, and passed to the Co-op, to the primary school, to the mothers, to the pub, the fathers, the farmers, the press. It seemed buoyed up on an invisible thermal all of its own.

'You must be feeling quite lost. In need of a shoulder, my dear.'

At this, Colonel Spears put a hand on the small of her back. She tried not to pull away. He was old, his eyes were sad and rheumy and he looked at her kindly.

'Thank you. I'm okay.'

The hand stayed there, and then began an upward and a downward route, gently caressing her back and then the top of her buttocks, backwards and forwards, higher then lower, until she pulled away abruptly. She opened her mouth to say something, but still he stood there, old and decrepit, engaging her sympathy. And then suddenly she felt enraged. What made him feel he could touch her? He was just like Reuben, going around trying it on with every woman he could lay hands on. He was an elderly Reuben. What made him feel so entitled? She was furious. But seeing his teary eyes and his tumble-down face, she didn't have the heart to say anything. How weak she was! She turned away and continued briskly down the lane, mumbling something like a goodbye.

She strode angrily, her pace lengthening as her fury grew. She picked up a stick that some walker must have abandoned and thwacked it against the hedgerow. A blackbird flew out and flapped noisily as it gave its rattling alarm call. High in the crowns of the beeches the rooks screamed and bickered, whilst the starlings wheezed out their courtship calls in the lower branches. She thwacked the undergrowth again and again. The grassy verge was spangled with spring flowers, full of themselves. Why were they there? Didn't they know it was inappropriate dress for this mood? This dark, dark mood. The lane darkened then as the trees formed a canopy above it, and the sun broke through the green, dappling the stony ground. She could hear her breathing lengthen and deepen, hear the gravelly chink, chink of her pulse inside her head. Her jaw hurt from clenching. She could do someone an injury. She had never felt rage like it. That he should have damaged their daughter so. The counselling for her self-harm had not even kicked off yet, and who knew what *this* experience would do to her? She might need counselling for the rest of her life. That he should have damaged Will so, that he should have denied their son's sexuality and not even *told* her! And Jack, that Reuben should have been cross enough about him needing new clothes once to raise his voice and say, 'That boy's getting fat!' loud enough for Jack to overhear. Couldn't he *see*? What was his problem? These were his children, his own children whose childhood he had so casually abandoned. And childhood lasted a lifetime. He'd let them all grieve for him. He'd put them through that. She was so angry that she snorted. She actually heard herself snort. And now she would have to brave an entire community who knew how gullible she had been. What a sad, gullible, hopeless and unprotecting mother she had been.

In the Co-op she was relieved to see that it was Paris on the check-out. Paris was a cheerful girl she had known as a toddler. She had nothing to fear from Paris. Freya edged her way around the tall displays like a spy, ducking back behind breads and cakes when she saw a school mother. At last she had pretty much all she needed except washing-up liquid, but she wasn't going to risk the household goods aisle now that she had made it to the check-out.

'Hello, Mrs Gray! How you doin'? Sorry to hear your bad news.'

'Yes. Well . . .'

'Ooh. When I say bad news . . . Perhaps it's good . . . ? Or bad? I mean, I'm so sorry. Maybe you're glad your husband is alive. Oh God, I'm sorry. I didn't think. Me and my big mouth.'

'No, really . . . don't worry.'

Paris put all her goods into Freya's bag for her, apologising again.

'Well, um. I hope it all turns out well for you, Mrs Gray.'

'Thank you. Thank you.'

She made her way to the school gates. She could've gone in the front entrance, as a teaching assistant, but she knew the school secretary took a dim view of anyone using the front entrance if they didn't need to because it dragged her away from her desk to check their identity and let them in. There was nothing else for it. She would have to brave the mums sooner or later, and it might as well be now. People in Stonely appreciated a bit of bad news. You couldn't blame them. Nothing much ever happened there, and they all wanted to feel the thrill of it, just as much as they were appalled by it.

She hovered just inside the gates. Clearly, they all knew. No one looked at her. Even though they all knew her and she knew all their children, no one so much as glanced her way, or, if they did, they did so from the corner of their eyes like cartoon spies. She was completely invisible. She had left it until the last minute anyway, and now she longed for the bell to go. There it was. A loud hum followed from inside the classrooms, a scraping of chairs, muffled yelps.

Then suddenly a woman from a group of mothers next to her turned to look at her. It was Nadine's mum, Fiona, from the A-Team. She placed her hand on Freya's arm.

'Oh, Freya, how are you? You must be going through hell.'

Freya wasn't sure if she nodded or not. She couldn't even be sure of the expression on her own face. But Fiona looked at her kindly.

'Why doesn't Sophie come over for tea? It would give her a bit of distraction. Give you a bit of time. I haven't got anything much in, but kids don't mind, do they? How about it?'

She was stroking Freya's arm. Freya suspected that this show of empathy was for the benefit of the other mothers in the group, who were all beaming at her now, clearly impressed by Fiona's top handling of the situation. But it was the stroking of her arm that got to Freya. Her throat was full of stone. Fiona had touched her. She was touched.

Sophie beamed at the idea, and Freya made her way back home through the village alone, wondering if she could go and get the washing-up liquid now. She decided she would. She went straight to the check-out with it and smiled at Paris.

'*Bad* news. Just for the record. It's bad news that he's still alive – not good.'

Paris nodded. She clearly thought so too.

She was just heading back down the lane when she decided to check her phone. Three texts from Duncan. She sighed. The last one caught her eye.

> URGENT, for info: I called by earlier and as I was leaving the press were gathering outside your house. I said you weren't in. If you get this in time, tell the boys to stay put in town. They can come and stay at mine tonight. They can come for tea. Tell them not to go home. I know you're cross with me, but you and Sophie can come too if you like.

She texted the boys straight away. They were just waiting for the bus and sounded almost relieved to be told to go to Duncan's flat. She heard the press people around the corner of the lane and turned tail. She went to Fiona's house and apologised. The girls were upstairs playing noisily in Nadine's bedroom. The squeals made it safe to explain about the press. And then when Fiona insisted on sitting her down and making her a cup of tea, she found herself spilling all her beans to this disturbingly confident and frighteningly competent woman.

'I can't believe I've been so stupid. So *gullible*! And it looks like everyone knew. Everyone knew what he was like except me . . .'

'You haven't been gullible, Freya. You've been trusting. That's a good thing. And believe me you needn't feel stupid. I've been there. I found out my husband had been cheating on me for ten years when we split up. Nadine was only two and we were trying for another child. That's why Nadine's an only child. I'd have liked another.'

'You're on your own?'

'Yes. Don't imagine I do this dreadful PR job for pleasure. I'd love to spend more time with Nadine. I'd have had to sell the house, though. Get something smaller. And I know we don't *need* three bedrooms, but I do tend to invite more friends and family now it's just Nadine and me. So this is the only way I could stop him taking half my house. I bought it, you see.'

Freya looked at her as she spoke. Fiona seemed to mutate into someone far softer, someone with a hard outer shell with which she protected herself. A good egg.

'You know what got to me most?' Fiona continued. 'It was all those years I'd wasted loving him, supporting him, bigging him up in everything he did. Years he was seeing other women and I could've been meeting someone else. Now look at me. Figure like Winnie-the-Pooh. Haven't got time to buy a decent tea for my daughter's friends let alone have dates with fiery lovers. It was the time he *stole* from me that I resent him for most. Liars are thieves. All of that time was *stolen*.'

Freya opened her mouth and began to speak, but what came out were wobbly words that shook all over the place like jelly, and she realised that her face was running with hot tears. Her shoulders began to shake and she bent forward into Fiona's arms. Fiona pulled her towards her and stroked her hair. 'It's okay Freya. It's okay.'

When Freya had stopped crying, Fiona said that if she was sure she didn't want to join Duncan, she was welcome to stay in the guest bedroom, and Sophie could have a sleep-over with Nadine. They could defrost some ready meals.

60

FINDING A VOICE

The night at Duncan's flat was a relief. It was a really cool flat: neat, elegant, sort of minimalist. Duncan cooked them a great meal and they all watched *Starship Troopers*, which was old but amazing. There was something about Duncan that radiated calm. He never seemed to get wound up, and he always had good ideas. He was *reflective*, that was the word. Will would like to be reflective. He was going to work at it.

Will lay in the spare room with Jack and talked about 'the press'. Duncan said they shouldn't speak to them, just say they had no comment, but Jack said imagine if they were on TV, imagine all the attention they'd get on Facebook if they appeared on the news. Will told Jack this was not about being popular; this was their whole life in the balance. What if it all went horribly wrong? What if Dad became the most reviled man ever to fake his own death, and that whenever there was news footage of him there they were, Jack and Will and Mum and Sophie, forever linked with him and his shady dealings? They didn't know the half of it yet. He might have a luxury apartment in Panama built on drug money or something – they just didn't know. Nothing would surprise him, because it seemed his dad had been siphoning off money from the family account for years. It wasn't just that he had made up a charity; he had also stolen from *them*. Will thought of all the new pairs of shoes and the phones and the holidays they had never had, because he had siphoned them off for his own new life. He thought up all the things he would say to his father if he ever saw him again. He exhausted himself running through these heated imaginary dialogues. He would shout at him, make him squirm. He wanted answers.

And one day, he would show his father what he had made of himself. How his own choice to pursue an artistic path had been the right one. Or rather, his father would just have to find out through social media or something, because Will wasn't going to stay in touch with him.

He still hadn't had a chance to make the big announcement about his unconditional offer from the University of the West of England. The last night in Italy had been a disaster. He'd been intending to tell them all together when they got back, but Duncan hadn't been with them yet, so he was going to save it for the next time they all met. He wanted Duncan to be there because he was even less sure now how Mum would feel about it. He knew she wanted him to stay local, because it would save money, but he knew he had to get away. He could take out a loan. He needed to spread his wings. Duncan knew that. Mum probably knew it too, but this wasn't an easy time for her. He'd rather Duncan was with her to help her come to terms with it. He knew he'd miss her – he'd miss all of them – but it was a complex trade-off and one he was eager to make. He was going to make his own way in the world, and he'd won a place to do it. He could hardly wait to tell everyone, but he didn't want it drowned out by other miseries. With all the things going on at the moment, shaking them all up, it felt like a wonderful piece of hopefulness. It made the future something to look forward to instead of dread. He felt sorry for the others that they didn't have it, this tantalising light just up ahead.

Now Duncan was driving them back home after the following day at school. It was nearly six o'clock because he'd had to work while they did their homework at the offices of SwanRobins. Lottie was there and it was cool.

As they went up the lane near their house, Will knew that in some way, this would always be his home. He felt rooted here. He would always want to come back and see the carpet of May bluebells and the snowy white garlic and hear the distant bleat of lambs. He opened the car window and breathed in the scent of his territory and felt suddenly proud and nostalgic. But the thought of their house and the curling Goth posters in the corner of his room, the threadbare carpets, his earliest attempts at drawing proudly framed by Mum on the living room walls, the sofa scratched bald by Chunkables, the rattling back door, and the tatty fridge plastered in grinning photos of them all made him feel an affection grazed by guilt, like smiling with an old school friend whose jokes you had outgrown.

Duncan suggested dropping them off around the corner so that they wouldn't get trapped in the car by any photographers. Jack clearly thought this was fun. At least that's what he thought until they actually walked around the corner and saw a swarm of journalists and cameramen around the drive. As Will and Jack approached, they homed in on them like mosquitoes. Jack was frightened. Will put his arm around him and tried to push through the mass of people. They stood still, trapped.

'Did you know your father was alive?'

'Did you have any idea he was running a fake charity?'

'Is it true he came into your school and cheated children out of their pocket money?'

'Did you know your mother was in on this with your father all along?'

Will could feel his blood thudding. He wanted to answer these questions. He wanted to put them right. He could hear so much noise, and above it all a horrible heaving sound, which he came to realise was his own breath.

The door clattered. Fuck, they had broken in the back door. But he twisted his head and there was Mum coming up the drive. Sophie had run out after her and was trying to cling on to her. There was a movement in the ranks and he reached out and grabbed Sophie. Now he stood with his arms around Mum on one side and Sophie on the other. Jack also held on to Sophie. The questions continued, jabbing at them like the points of knives.

'How does it feel to know your father never provided a single well of clean water to any African village?'

'Mrs Gray, how have you spent the life insurance money?'

'Mrs Gray, how long have you known your husband was alive?'

Will tried to let his own heavy breathing block out the noise. Then he caught a movement off to the side and thought he saw a creature cowering under the hedge. Perhaps it was a bird giving an alarm call, but Will imagined it was his voice, the one he hadn't found yet. In his mind it came towards him, tentatively at first, but then growing bigger and bolder with each hop. It came right up to him, tall and strong, and reached around behind him. Will knew that it was unclipping his wings for him, and as it did it disappeared. A flicker, a flap, out they spread, glorious and wild:

'Please leave my family alone – they've suffered enough. Can't you see there are children involved? We're all going through our own private hell. Please leave us alone. We have nothing more to say.'

'Is it true that—'

'Is that why—'

Will felt his giant wings spread wide. He fluttered them mightily and puffed out his chest like an eagle. 'WE HAVE NOTHING MORE TO SAY!'

He took them all inside, and within fifteen minutes there wasn't a trace of any of the journalists or cameramen, only an empty sandwich wrapper and a squashed cola can.

61

IT'S NOT FAIR

In the stillness of the afternoon, the house telephone rang. It would be someone from the press, or Sylvia or Duncan wondering why she wasn't answering their texts. Then again, it could be the school. Or Fiona. Freya approached the loudly trilling machine, half expecting it to fly away like a crow.

'Look, I've got ten minutes, so please don't hang up.'

'Reuben?'

'Freya, listen. We need to talk. Mum says you're talking about a divorce. Is that true?'

Freya opened her mouth to speak. This disembodied voice from Italy seemed so irrelevant to her life now, and yet she knew its owner could change everything – had already turned her world on its head. She was tired of good behaviour and her own miserable politeness.

'Did you seriously think I would want to carry on being married to you? *Really?*'

There was a short silence. 'Look, you know I've always loved you and the children.' For the briefest of moments, he was letting her believe in him again. 'By the way, you looked stunning in Italy. I could hardly keep my eyes off you.' A familiar feeling lulled her insides.

She began to shake.

'Freya? You can't say I haven't been a good father and a good husband. You can't say that, Freya.' He didn't pause for a reaction; he talked as though on a timer. 'You know I lost my memory, and Mum says you don't believe it, but it's true. But if you insist on a divorce – I mean, if you really insist on one and that's what you really want – you should know that you wouldn't be able to keep the house. I would be entitled to half of it.'

'But it's my family's house! It's where your children live—'

'And, of course, they would probably be allowed to stay in it until Sophie left home at eighteen, but then it would have to be sold . . . Freya? Are you still there?'

'They would *probably be allowed*? You mean, you wouldn't *want* them to stay there? You mean, if it were up to you their lives would be churned up all over again so that you could have half the house? Don't you think you've put them through enough? They've mourned your death, for God's sake!'

'Look, I've had to talk to a lawyer. That's just lawyer-speak.'

'Well, tell your lawyer I inherited all your worldly goods when you died.'

'Well, I'm not dead.'

'But you wanted to be dead to us.'

'That's not fair.'

'Not *fair*?' She closed her eyes. This was like talking to Sylvia. Why had she never seen the similarity before? 'Reuben, you can do what you like, but leave my family alone. Leave our house alone. Our home.'

'So what do *I* get?'

Freya gazed out of the window. A song thrush was sitting on the hedge and singing its heart out. Mating. Territory. That was all it was about. And she had thought life so complicated.

'You get to take your children to McDonald's once a fortnight and tell them I've poisoned their minds against you.'

She hung up, shaking. She looked out for the thrush, but it had flown away.

She was glad that all three of her children were away in their rooms or watching television. She had barely replaced the receiver when the crunching sound of a car on the drive came through the open window. It was Steve and Sylvia's car. She sighed heavily, but then saw that only Steve got out.

'Don't panic,' he said as he hovered by the open back door. 'Sylvia's still in town. She needed to talk to an old friend – at length, I believe – so someone's receiving the full treatment!' He gave a watery smile, but his heart wasn't in it. 'Although, I warn you, she is going to be dropped off here later. I think we've got at least an hour, though, so I thought I'd make myself useful. The grass could do with a cut. Would you mind? I'll keep out of your way.'

Freya looked at the grass. Gloria hadn't been around to nibble it lately, and Duncan had taken to cutting it for her, but it hadn't been cut since before the trip to Italy. She had meant to do it, but it stood there, lush and green and warm, begging for a trim. She smiled. 'Thank you.'

She showed him to the shed where the mower was kept. It may have been the sight of the dilapidated shed in need of repair, with great gaps between its crooked slats, or it may have been the opportunity of being alone with Freya, but he turned then, with the look of someone whose dog has run through a children's picnic.

'Freya, I apologise for my son.'

Freya wanted to hug him. 'It's not your fault,' she said.

She watched Steve pushing the mower up and down from the kitchen window. He looked taller, somehow, without Sylvia near him. More solid and substantial. Even the way he moved was different. The way he bent down to empty the grass collector, the way he walked over to the garden waste bin and threw it in decisively. She wondered if he knew how much Sylvia diminished him.

When Sylvia's friend dropped her off, the children slunk away quickly upstairs to their rooms. That, at least, was some small relief, given what followed.

'I'm sorry to disturb you, Freya darling, but I wanted to apologise.' Sylvia gave an awkward sidelong glance at her husband. 'I was out of order the other day. I'm sorry.'

Freya sensed how much willpower this had taken for Sylvia. It was not in her nature to be humble. It smacked of defeat. It smacked of not being right. 'Thank you, Sylvia. I appreciate that.'

They all smiled a little falsely, as if each of them was trying to behave within boundaries that none of them were sure of, ones which kept shifting at an alarming rate. Freya looked at her watch and Steve yawned, both of them signalling that the mission had been accomplished. That was that. They could go home now.

'But what I *would* say, is that nothing happens without a reason.'

Steve looked weary rather than panic-stricken, as if he had known it was all too good to be true.

'Now I'm not saying you're to blame, Freya. Please don't think that. But I would say that men don't leave for no reason. There's always something that makes them go. Something that isn't right in the marriage.'

62

GET LOST

Sophie is sitting at the top of the stairs again. Will and Jack are listening too, and they don't send her off to her room. They all know it's important to be quiet. This is the only way they can find out anything these days. They have to be quiet as mice. And listen.

'Well, obviously,' says Mummy, 'there was something wrong with the marriage. Your son was screwing around. But I'm afraid I was too stupid to see it.'

This can't be right. Mummy is not stupid. She looks at Will and Jack for a reaction, but they are craning their necks to listen.

'Now look, I know you're upset, Freya, but you really do have the wrong end of the stick here. Just because he appears to be with another woman, doesn't mean he's been a philanderer.'

'Sylvia, you've kindly apologised for being out of order. Please don't go there again.'

'Yes, darling,' says Grandad. 'Leave it, Sylvia. Just leave it there. We all know what you're trying to say.'

'*Trying* to say? I don't need to try and say anything. I won't have Reuben portrayed as some sort of womaniser!'

There is a muffled sound, and they have to strain even more to hear, but one thing comes over very clearly. Mummy thinks Daddy is a Nutter Bastard, but Granny S doesn't agree.

'I had a phone call from your dead son earlier,' says Mummy. 'It seems he wants half the house from his widow. Oh! He concedes he might have to wait for Sophie to reach the age of eighteen first, but he says it's his.'

'Well, it just sounds to me like he's taken some legal advice.'

'It just sounds to me like he's an utter bastard.'

'Now that's enough!'

'Sylvia—'

'You shut up, Stephen. I'm not having her talk about our son like that. If she'd been a bit more wifely, instead of—'

'*Wifely?*'

'Well, Freya, let's face it. You didn't have much time for him, did you? I mean, having Sophie was just the limit. That really was a mistake. As if you hadn't tricked him into marriage in the first place, you have to go and have a *third* child. And after another six-year gap. Anyone would think it was deliberate. So, after he's waited so long to have you back after Jack, suddenly it's all Sophie this and Sophie that. He *told* me he didn't want another child. It's as if you didn't want any time with him. Don't you see? Men need some undivided attention from their wives.'

'Do they?' says Grandad unexpectedly. Jack and Will exchange smirks, but Sophie isn't smiling. She is thinking about being a big mistake. What does that mean?

'So that explains why Sophie had to witness her father having sex with another woman does it? That lets him off the hook?'

'Well, God only knows what you were doing leaving Sophie in the house alone on that day.'

'She wasn't alone!'

'Well, if she was ill, she shouldn't have come downstairs, should she? My children would've done what I'd told them to do.'

'You really are the limit! Are you trying to blame me or Sophie now? If she hadn't seen something it would've meant it hadn't happened, is that it?'

'And if you hadn't been so selfish – if Sophie hadn't been born – none of this would've happened! Mark my words. I know a thing or two about lasting marriages.'

'Right, that's it,' says Mummy, her voice getting louder now. 'Please leave. *NOW!*'

Will starts to go downstairs at this point, and Jack turns to Sophie in delight. She tries to smile too, but the truth has now come out. None of this would have happened if she hadn't been born. It is, as she had suspected all along, all her fault.

When they have tea, she wants to ask Mummy what a Nutter Bastard is, but Mummy looks like she might start crying again. She is not her usual self, and bangs things a bit heavily on the table, and then apologises. Will and Jack are giving each other sidelong glances, and Sophie wants one of them to say something, to ask Mummy to explain stuff, but they don't, so she asks, 'Why doesn't Dunking come over any more?'

Mummy looks away at the edge of the table. 'It's difficult. It's a difficult thing to explain.'

Sophie hates it when grown-ups think these sorts of answers are enough. She wants the Difficult Thing (which she sees vaguely as something like Thing One or Thing Two from *The Cat in the Hat*) to be invited into their home, to be put on the kitchen table and made to feel welcome. She wants it to be stroked and spoken to kindly. She wants it to be opened up, unzipped, examined and understood. Tying laces can be difficult. Sums can be difficult. When they get a difficult sum, Miss Dowling always says give it a try because sometimes you can solve it if you just keep trying. And also, if you show your working, she gives you a tick. And she always shows you how to do them in the end, and you see that they were easy all along. So things that seem difficult can be easy. She wonders if she should tell Mummy this. 'I miss him,' she says instead. 'I miss Dunking.'

Mummy folds her lips together and her eyes start to glisten again. She kisses Sophie on the top of her head, and Sophie goes up to her room, where she lies on her bed for a moment, plotting. She has been thinking about this for days, so she knows what she has to do. She had thought of asking Nadine, now that Nadine is her friend, but that would be no good now. This is obviously when she has to do it. It must be tonight. She gets quietly off the bed and fetches her rucksack from underneath it. Then she packs her favourite mauve jeans, her flowery T-shirt and a pink jumper. She puts on her long-sleeved pink hoodie with the kitten on it. She chooses red socks and her trainers. She has to squeeze her feet into them because she can't do up laces easily. She opens the door gently and stands for a moment on the landing. She can hear Mummy crying quietly in her room and is tempted to go and give her a hug, but that would be silly. She tiptoes downstairs, trying to avoid the creaky bits. She knows that she can't go out of the back door because of the clatter, but she makes her way into the kitchen to get some provisions. In the tray at the bottom of the fridge she finds a packet of cereal bars. She takes two. Then she closes the fridge door and listens. There is just the sound of birdsong. She takes a single banana from the fruit bowl. There are only three and if she takes two it will show straight away. Very slowly, she pads towards the front door. She closes it behind her with such stealth that she feels momentarily pleased with herself.

It has been a bright day, but breezy. The warm sun is only very gently slipping towards the horizon of an almost-clear blue sky and the few clouds now are cream and grey and stretched thinly above the darkening distant ridge of the hill. She realises that she hasn't taken her coat, but it is nearly summer, so not likely to get that cold anyway. The thing about mistakes is that you can correct them. She can't use a white pen for this, but she might be able to make things right for Mummy and everyone.

The trouble is, even as she sets off down the lane towards the trees and the so-softly sinking sun, she has a funny feeling that what she really wants most is for someone to love her enough to come and find her. But they will only be able to show they love her enough if she gets really, really very lost indeed.

63

THE LONGER VIEW

The boys staying the night at his flat to avoid the press had seemed like a step forward, but Freya had insisted on picking them up from school herself yesterday, a Friday. Duncan felt bereft. Pacing the flat, he knew he had to get out, so he drove to the edge of town and went for a walk.

He knew he had cocked up, but what else could he have done? His hunch had been right, hadn't it? What would've been a good way to deal with it? Those children and Freya were going to be hurt, one way or another. He'd managed to put his big clumsy foot into the middle of it.

The footpath was dark and enclosed by scrubby blackthorn. A little further along, the path opened up to some beech trees, underneath which was a white-spangled carpet of flowering garlic. He barely noticed his surroundings, didn't stop to admire the lovely violets or the wood sorrel crouching in the humid shade of ash and beech. The sound of a cuckoo made him stop and look up. He could see nothing but a fat wood pigeon in the branches above. There it was again. He turned over a coin in his pocket, as his mother used to do on hearing the first cuckoo of spring, and wondered what she would have made of everything. The migrant birds were returning, and with them the heart-rendingly sweet singing of early summer evenings. He reached the foot of the hill and marvelled at the greenness of the ancient ridged field sweeping up to the golden stone ramparts high above him. He started to climb. It was steep and gravelly and he began to sweat. One foot in front of another. That's all you could do. One step at a time. His breath grew more laboured and he started to enjoy the strain. It was a small punishment to keep him alert, like a tap from a horse whip or a cut on an arm. He wouldn't let himself stop until he reached the top. Nearly a thousand feet above the River Severn, he sat on a ridge and looked across the wide valley, panting out his shame and his disappointment, then lying back on the sun-warmed grass and gazing at the cloudless sky.

Will had said his mum was a mess. He had been imploring Duncan to go round since they'd come back from Italy. But earlier this week, after Duncan had given the two boys a takeaway in front of the television, carefully not mentioning their mother or father or anything that had happened, Will had followed him out to the kitchen and said, 'It's like this. She thinks you were checking up on Dad's past. That's what's got to her. Just go and tell her you weren't. You didn't.'

He could feel the cool of the earth seeping through the grass now, and he sat up to watch the sun on the bright yellow gorse which illuminated the hillocks and humps beneath him. He stood at the very top of the escarpment, looking across the Severn Valley. The hawthorn blossom was out, puffing up the hedgerows, announcing the advent of summer. In the distance, the Black Mountains, a faint line way ahead, the Malvern Hills to his right. Clouds slipped across the landscape, leaving sun-drenched fields behind them. A buzzard wheeled across the sky, letting out a high-pitched mewl that could easily have been his own.

What had he done? She was right. He had been snooping around about Reuben's past. And, let's face it, after the first hint of something not quite right, he had hoped to find something to discredit him, even if he never intended to use it. And he wouldn't have looked up *Eau Please!* and discovered that it didn't exist if he hadn't been snooping through Reuben's bank statements and found something odd. And if he hadn't done that, he wouldn't have been able to tell the Italian police that Reuben had been guilty of fraud. Except that, of course, the fake passport, he now realised, would have been enough to keep him in custody. Duncan should not have mentioned his charity fraud. Freya had a right to know, of course, and Jack and Will had a right to know, but he, Duncan, should never have been the bearer of that particular news. *Duncan Swan. He thinks he's* so *clever!*

But Duncan knew. He knew that if Freya blamed him for snooping, she would always blame him. And she was right. He had behaved like a jealous teenager. He and Freya could have had a future together, and the children could have been happy. For Chrissake! *Why* couldn't their prat of a father have even faked his death properly?

Sorrow and panic held him by the throat. Tears he had held back for so long now spilt over and ran hotly down his cheeks. He let the breeze dry them and sting his face. He stood, gazing out on the scene until the shadows became so long that the sun would soon be swallowed up by the horizon. A man came up behind him and said, 'I like to think you get the bigger picture up here,' or something. Duncan said, 'I liked the smaller picture.' Only he may not have said it. He may have just thought it, because there were tears in his eyes and words felt stuck in his throat.

A swallow swooped across the valley. And another. The sound of the buzzard again, high above, made him look up. Then another sound confused him: lower-pitched, more urgent. It was his phone. He scrabbled in his pockets for it. Will. He almost didn't answer it.

'Duncan. Don't hang up – this isn't about Mum. Please come urgently. You must come. Sophie's gone missing.'

PART THREE

64

CONSEQUENCES

Freya was already feeling tightly sprung when she noticed it. Sylvia had surpassed herself, and tea with the children was tense after she'd left.

She didn't notice anything when she cleared away the tea things. Her mind was re-running the altercation with her mother-in-law and she thought of other things she could have said. She replayed the conversation with Reuben too, making him say things she could respond to decisively and cleverly, trouncing him at every turn. She closed the cabinet doors with unusual force. She was harsh with the crockery.

Even when she called upstairs for Sophie to clean her teeth, she did not suspect anything from the silence. She thought Sophie was probably sulking or upset. It wasn't until she went up to reassure her that she knew something was wrong. When Sophie wasn't in the bathroom, Freya expected to see her bent over her otters and hedgehogs, making up little conversations between them, chuntering away to herself. But there was no Sophie, just a silence that seemed to expand and fill the room like gas.

'Sophie?' She looked under the bed, opened the little wardrobe. 'Sophie?'

She called to Jack and heard him reply, 'What?' in the sullen voice that suggested he was on his laptop. She flung open his door. 'What . . . ?'

'Have you seen Sophie?' She could hear a breathlessness in her voice now.

'Nope.'

She ran to Will's room and knew, before she opened the door, that Sophie wouldn't be there. She tore down the stairs, shouting Sophie's name louder and louder, checking each room. She made a dash for the back door as though she were in a house fire or a sinking ship. She scoured the garden, clawing at the rosemary bushes, opening the dilapidated shed and raking through the garden utensils as though Sophie might have curled herself up into the size of a football. Even as she trawled through everything in her wake, she knew Sophie was not there. She darted down the side of the house to the driveway and out on to the lane. She looked up the lane. She looked down it. She called. Sophie wouldn't have come out here. She hated walking on the lane because there was no pavement. She was an anxious child.

She ran back inside the house, half expecting Sophie to appear from one of the rooms and look at her, bewildered. *What's the matter, Mummy? I was only in the* . . . But there was no Sophie, only Jack and Will looking worried. Freya held on to her hair and abandoned herself to a screech: 'SO-PHIE!'

'Perhaps she's gone to find Gloria,' offered Will, 'across the fields.' But he looked worried.

Pam, pam, pam. Her heart hammered in her chest. *Pum, pum, pum* in her head, and she knew now, from the concern on both her boys' faces, that this was not some hysteria of her own. Sophie had gone. Disappeared. This was real. *Pum, pum, pum, pum.*

More suggestions from the boys about ringing Nadine, trying the farm. There was no time, no direction. Will sat her down at the kitchen table. Perhaps she was overreacting. His presence of mind gave her hope. The sink, the Pingu mugs on the drainer, the wellingtons by the door, the haphazard fridge magnets of otters and Clangers and Spider-Man, all looked at her with insolence. Their calm, their stillness, appalled her. She ran upstairs again, thumping urgently on each step.

In Sophie's bedroom, she looked for clues. Her meerkat pyjamas were still on her pillow; her toys were on the floor. She opened the little wardrobe again and stared at the shoes thrown in the bottom. The rucksack was missing. Was it? Her mauve jeans were missing. She had packed! Freya threw shoes and clothes behind her like a creature burrowing in the ground, throwing up earth. The rucksack was definitely missing.

She reported her findings, gasping for breath, as she came downstairs.

'She's probably just gone out to see Gloria or something,' suggested Will again.

'Why? *Why* without saying? Why after tea-time? Sophie wouldn't *do* this. Her rucksack's gone. She's taken her rucksack!'

'She was a bit upset,' said Jack.

'Upset? What do you mean, upset?'

Jack shrugged. 'Well, we all are. Our dead father's come back to life, we're living in hiding and . . . well . . . Granny Sylvia didn't exactly keep her voice down, did she?'

'That *woman*!'

'Or you. What did you mean about Sophie seeing Dad having sex?'

'Sweet Jesus!' She started to shake visibly and to hyperventilate. She was trying to stay calm, but she just couldn't.

'I'll search the barns,' said Will, taking control. 'Mum, you ring Nadine's mum and see if she's there. Jack, you search the garden and around the house. If none of us find her, we'll ring the police. Second thoughts, maybe we should do that now.'

Jack sat her down at the table again, like some seasoned paramedic urging her to stay calm. Will was on the phone. He had dialled 999. So it was, it *was* an emergency. A brief, triumphant sense of validation was suffocated by dread. It held her by the throat and she thought she might pass out. Sophie was missing. She was a missing child.

65

CRAZY WOMAN

Will was trying to hold everything together. No one had seen Sophie since tea-time. It took them a while to realise she was nowhere to be found in the house. Mum paced the house looking for clues. Sophie's pyjamas were still in her bed, and her coat was still on its hook. This suggested an unintentional departure, or a very spontaneous one. No sooner had Mum scoured the bedroom than she flew downstairs to trawl through the kitchen, the living room and the playroom. Will and Jack, who had hoped to finish playing a video game at least, were now caught up in her panic.

It was unbearable. They all seemed to be darting around like flies, and there was no plan. Will rang Duncan. That would make things better. If Duncan could get there quickly, then somehow some sort of order would be restored. Because they had only found out that Sophie was missing when she was called to brush her teeth after tea, and tea was normally about five thirty but was a bit later tonight because of all the rowing with Granny S, and they had only a rough idea when she even left: after half past six? Six fifteen, at the earliest. At some point when they were all doing something else, she must have slipped out of the house. They didn't even know if it was the front door or the back door. All they knew now was that she had taken her rucksack with her, so it looked like she went of her own accord after all. No one abducted her.

Will rang 999 anyway. Mum was like a crazy woman, wailing and heavy breathing everywhere. It *was* scary, as it turned out, because now they had searched all the cupboards in the house, they had rung Nadine's mum and the school and the pub and even the farm. No one had seen her. No one had any idea where she might have gone.

He'd never seen his mum like this. She had completely lost it. They thought she was losing it after the Dad thing, but that was nothing compared to this. The last two hours had been surreal. Thank God the police gave her a list of things to do when they spoke on the phone. That focused her a tiny bit, but not for long. He was the one who had to download the most recent photos: two in Verona and the one of them all with the horse on Boxing Day. The Boxing Day one was important because in it she is wearing the clothes she probably left the house in. They couldn't be certain, because Mum was spinning round in circles trying to work it out. The police wanted her name, date of birth, weight, height, mobile phone number if she had one – all sorts of things that Mum was frustrated about giving, as though the police were just wasting valuable time. They wanted to know where she had searched already, and he could tell she was thinking that she should be spending her time combing the fields and lanes and not telling them Sophie's weight. Then they turned up at the house about an hour later, and asked to see her bedroom and take some clothing recently worn. Sophie only had an old second-hand mobile which she used as a toy. It wasn't charged up. Sophie never charged it up. Then they found it in her Sylvanian family boat being used as a tabletop.

Now Will was in the pub, and three local guys were making a plan of action. He picked up the landlord's latest poem and idly read it: *An idea on its own can't do much, can it? / But acting together we might even save the planet.* He sighed. Pete the Poet was ringing people, and more locals were arriving. There was a tatty map open on the bar, and men were dividing up the area. Will put a recent photo on the bar too. They all knew who Sophie was, but it showed her in her mauve jeans and her T-shirt. Pete wondered if people would like to sample his lemon drizzle cake.

Will was worried now because it seemed like she really was missing. He had been left out of the rescue delegation, and he was pissed off and anxious. He wanted to be in on it. He was, after all, the man of the house at the moment. He was the one who had been taking all the flak from his mum's batty madwoman behaviour lately. He still hadn't told her that he had an unconditional offer from Bristol. It was going to have been his big piece of news to tell everyone today, since Duncan didn't seem to be coming around any time soon; and then he'd planned to wait until tomorrow when Mum had calmed down a bit after the Granny Sylvia episode had ruined the moment for an announcement at tea-time. And now the news would be completely swallowed up. But the thing was, this all made the future a bit clearer. He would be leaving home in September, and that was really only a few months away. And then Mum would be on her own: no Dad, no Duncan, no Will. Just her and two children. Oh God! Maybe just her and Jack, if something had happened to Sophie. And this sudden picture of a radically different family life made Will realise that his mother needed someone around. He couldn't have her ringing him up in Bristol all the time. She'd need someone like Duncan to take the strain.

66

A MAN WITH A MISSION

It took Duncan far too long – at least fifteen minutes – to rush back down the hill to his car. In the process, he slipped on the stony path and grazed his backside quite badly, although he would only discover this later when he went to bed and saw in the mirror that his behind looked like two small pizzas. For now, he felt no pain, only an urgency like no other. His despair, and its even more painful sister, hope, had been churning around for so long that they had nothing new to feed on. Now everything had changed. Now all he could see was Sophie's dear face: its delight at the statue of short-legged Cangrande on his horse in Verona, its tenderness and adoration as she held the new lamb, its confusion and hurt as she said, 'Is it you, Daddy?' to the man who had just run away from them. He remembered those little eyes, with their bald eyelids, welling up when he had first known her, and the new, happy eyes that had smiled on them all since Christmas. He hardly dared to think what had made her 'go missing'. That was all the information that he had. Sophie was missing.

He made the trip to Stonely in eight minutes (it usually took him twelve) and he nearly collided with a four-by-four as he overtook a tractor on a hill. On arrival, he found only Jack in the house.

'I've been told I have to stay here in case Sophie comes back, but I want to go out looking. What if she's been kidnapped?'

He could see that Jack was both disgruntled and terrified, and that being left in the house alone was difficult for him. He asked for all the details, and discovered that Will was at the pub and Freya had gone out to question Sophie's friend Nadine.

'I know it's tough, Jack, but you do need to stay here. It's actually the most likely place she'll come back to, and if she can't get in, or if no one's here, she might panic and go off again.' Jack looked miserable. 'Hey, why not ring that girl you muck out the horses with? She's local, isn't she? Maybe she could come round and help you search the house and garden again and keep you company.'

'The police say I must let no one go in her room as it's a possible crime scene,' he said importantly.

'You and she could ring around people you know together. Put it out on social media and stuff?'

Jack brightened up a little. 'Okay. Maybe.'

The pub was busier than usual. Freya had joined Will there now. Duncan went straight up to her and put his arms around her, and for the briefest of moments, she let him, before pushing him away and saying breathlessly, 'We've got to find her. We've got to find her! The police can't send a search helicopter out because it's already busy looking for some escaped prisoner in Gloucester! She may have been gone two hours already!'

Whatever she said, her look and the shove away said to him clearly, *See what you've done! See what your meddling has done!* He asked them both for details, and it seemed that she had disappeared some unspecified time between six fifteen and seven. She had been wearing blue leggings and a pink T-shirt, but her mauve jeans were also missing, as were a flowery pink T-shirt and a pink hoodie with a kitten on it. She had definitely taken her pink rucksack. She had probably taken a couple of fruit bars, and possibly a banana. Basically, they were looking for pink – and maybe mauve. As they spoke, the men in the pub dispersed, and Will looked suddenly distracted. He picked up his jacket as if to go.

'Come with me,' said Duncan. They made their way to the door and he turned back to Freya. 'We'll find her.'

He and Will stood in the road together and Duncan handed him one of the two torches he kept in the boot of his car. The sun was slipping into the horizon in a fanfare of rosy pink, and the dark ridge of the hills seemed even darker against it.

'Let's try the barns. If she hasn't gone to Nadine's, she may have gone to find Gloria.'

Although he had already searched the barns earlier, Will followed him gratefully, happy, it seemed, to take instruction. They took the larger barn first at Hilary's farm, shining their torches into the straw in every enclosure. But the sheep had all long gone since lambing, and there was no sign of life at all. In the second barn, it was the same story. There were not as many nooks and crannies to explore and it was clear very soon that there was no one hiding inside. Duncan sighed. The broken slats let in the glowing pink of the sky, and the birds were singing with outrageous joy. At any other time, it would have been beautiful. Now the birds' indifference to their plight seemed callous. He wanted to shout at them to hush up, to show some respect, for pity's sake. But they just kept on merrily singing.

They called on Hilary at the farm, but she had been up to the field where Gloria and the other sheep were now grazing with their lambs and had seen nothing. She had been advised to stay put in the house in case Sophie turned up, looking for shelter as it got dark. They exchanged phone numbers. He and Will circled the farm for a while, looking in water troughs and turning over bits of corrugated iron propped against walls. Eventually they turned tail and headed back to the lane.

'Let's separate,' said Duncan, feeling that the area was becoming more immense the longer the shadows grew. 'I don't know where those men are going, but you go north and I'll go south. Keep in touch.'

It was getting dark now, and time to be really concerned. He could almost feel Freya's panic-fuelled heartbeat, although it was separated from him by thick stone walls and several fields. He walked at a brisk pace down the road, around the bend and towards the house. Then he went straight on by, and out towards the bus stop. He shone his torch helplessly into the bus shelter. It was useless. There was obviously no one there. Then he caught sight of something bright, lying at the base of the hedgerow just beyond the shelter. He bent down and shone his beam on it, then picked it up. It was a banana skin. He took in a quick breath. It was relatively new. There were no signs of decay, and on a day like this it would've started to blacken very quickly. This was a recently peeled banana, and someone had taken the trouble to drop it at the foot of the hedgerow rather than in the bus shelter. Sophie would have known to do that. She would have known that the banana skin would decompose and go back to nature. She would not have cluttered up the bus shelter with it.

Convinced she may have taken a bus, he rang Freya. There was a commotion as she checked in the pub, but it was clear that the last bus went at three minutes past six. She couldn't have taken the bus even if she'd had some bus fare. She was at home having tea until at least six fifteen, Freya was certain of it. He could hear the panic in her voice, in her breathing. 'But if she waited at the bus stop, it means she wanted to get away! What if she hitched a lift? What if someone stopped for her? Oh God!'

Duncan tried to reassure her. The landlord took the phone off her: 'Last bus is three minutes past six. Unless it was late. We'll tell the police, don't worry.'

He phoned Will to let him know about the banana skin, then started off again down the road. What if she had been trying to catch the bus? Who did she know in Cheltenham except him? Had she been trying to find him? Duncan felt pressed down suddenly by a flattening responsibility. Poor Sophie would have no idea how to find his flat in Cheltenham. She had been there once or twice, but she was only *six*. What sense did she have of areas of town? Lansdown, Tivoli, Montpellier, they meant nothing to her. Could she ask someone? Of course not, unless she had the address written down, which she wouldn't. And if she did ask someone (he imagined her asking a passing paedophile, 'Do you know where Duncan lives?') then it could be very dangerous indeed. He sighed again. The landlord had said he would contact the police. If she'd caught the bus – if it had been late – then the bus driver would know. They could check it out. Let them do that. He had to make sure she wasn't here, hidden somewhere behind a bush and terrified, or trying the long walk into Cheltenham on her own in the dark. For now it *was* dark, and there was no mistaking it. The glow from the horizon was little more than a dimming patch of turquoise, and the hedgerows were looming figures crouching by the roadside.

He chose to follow the Cheltenham road for a while, but he had no idea what sort of a head start she had had. Suppose she had left the house at half past six, she could be miles down the lonely road by now. He started to run, and he ran until he was out of breath. This was use-less. He would have to retrace his steps and go back up to fetch his car. But then he might see Freya and have to admit that he had found noth-ing, and he couldn't face Freya – ever – until he had found her daughter.

He rang Will, hoping he might be close enough to the pub to drive the car down to him, but Will was now in a truck with one of the men from the village. It was gone nine before he made it back. He felt guilty as he passed the house, wondering if Jack was okay, but he imagined Jack would be in touch with Will and Freya. He drove very fast to the place in the road he had reached on foot, and then more steadily, with his lights on full beam, most of the way to Cheltenham. As he cruised down the hill, the lights of the town glittered in the flat valley below. Each light represented a life or several lives: people watching televi-sion, talking together, drinking, winding down for the night. Soon the house lights would go off one by one, and all that would be left would be the street lights and the floodlit hotels and churches. People would be dreaming under the darkened roofs, and what about Sophie? Where would she be sleeping? Or would she be awake, shivering and terrified? Where could she possibly be? Eventually he turned round and came back, still scanning the hedgerows for a crouching child.

He left his car pulled up on the grass near the bus stop and stood at a nearby five-bar gate, looking into the blackness of a field. 'Sophie!' he shouted. 'SOPHIE!' He kept on shouting until his voice was hoarse.

His phone rang, an alarming sound in the darkness. It was Freya, breathless. 'The bus driver said the bus was a bit late and he thinks there was a small girl who got on the bus at Stonely. But he thinks she was with a woman. He thinks it was a woman, but it could have been a man. He can't remember!'

'Okay.' Duncan assumed a totally fake calmness. He surprised himself at how easily he kept that word steady. He must at least stay calm, because this might be all he could do for Freya. This might be it. But he could feel his ribcage pounding. 'Okay, we're going to have to let the police follow that line of enquiry. It may not be her. We have to continue looking.'

'But what if it is her? What if someone has taken her? She could be anywhere!'

'And it may not be her, so we mustn't stop looking. She could be crouching in a hedge somewhere, unable to find her way home in the dark.'

'Yes, but what if it *is* her! What can we do?'

Duncan made himself breathe deeply and steadily. He couldn't betray that he shared her panic. 'Someone in Stonely must know who caught the last bus. Ask at the pub. Ask Pete, ask everyone at the pub. Someone should know who had visitors today. Someone who came to play after school, maybe.'

'Yes! Yes, I'll do that. That could rule it out. Good idea!' He felt a tiny surge of relief at her last two words. 'Oh, and the police are going to bring sniffer dogs. It may be tonight. They've got Sophie's pyjamas, and the dogs are going to use them for her scent.'

'Good. A two-pronged attack. We'll find her.' He said the words manfully, but as soon as she hung up, a wave of hopelessness swept over him. He stood for a while, trying to steady his breathing, listening to it slice the silence of that strangely beautiful starlit night.

67

MELTING AWAY

Sophie has been watching a strange wafer-like white disc in the sky, and now realises that it is the moon. It has been slowly rising into the deepening blue as she's been walking along, making her escape. Behind the trees there is a band of flamingo pink, which softly merges into peach and then pale green before it meets the striking blue. She has been sitting on the little bench in the bus shelter for a few minutes while eating her banana. She is pleased to eat it, and it feels like a wicked treat, because she is not normally allowed to eat after tea, but now she is disappointed because it's gone. She leaves the shelter and tosses the peel into the hedgerow. Jack says that banana peels are buyer-degradable, so it will melt into the grass and become bits of earth. She eyes it gleaming brightly from behind some nettles. It doesn't look likely to melt, but then neither does Gloria's poo, and that melts into the grass like magic, and you never get to see it happen.

She wonders about buses. She has no money on her, but usually Mummy pays, and she imagines that children go free, so that's okay. Still, she thinks now that she may have missed the bus, as there aren't many.

She looks up the lane and then down it: a tunnel of green. She lets her head rock back and sees the evening light gleaming through the leaves. So many greens! She thinks of the crayons she would use at school to draw this. The lime-green crayon and the ordinary green. When she grows up, she will invent more crayon colours so that there are enough different greens to draw what she can see now. Lime green, light-coming-through green, underleaf green, moss green, beech-leaf green, oak-leaf green, ivy green. And then all the different grassy colours and flower leaves and caterpillars and things. She will also make sure there are more purples and pinks and extra red and flesh-coloured crayons in every pack, as they always wear down the quickest and get too short and stubby to hold.

She takes in a deep breath. The smells are lovely. Faint scents of bluebells and the garlicky smell from the white pom-pom flowers and the thick powdery waft of May blossom.

Sophie has been trying to work out how long it should take to be found. At first, she imagined that by the time she got to the end of the lane, someone – probably Jack – would have noticed that she was missing. This is because Jack usually plays with her for a bit before he goes off to use the laptop, although he has been playing with her less since he got his own. Yesterday he tore off Matilda's head and kicked it across the room. She smiled, but it didn't make her happy. She isn't really cross with Matilda any more. It's Daddy she's cross with. And Granny Sylvia.

Sophie climbs a gate and starts walking along the edge of a field. There is a star now, winking beside the moon. *He told me he didn't want another child.* She kicks the grass with her trainers as she walks. *Suddenly it's all Sophie this and Sophie that.* She can feel the hot tears burning her cheeks. Her nose fills up. There is snot running over her lips. The weird thing is, before Italy she could hardly even remember him. He was just a blur, and someone they all said was a good man. He was such a good man. That's what Mummy said and that's what Granny Sylvia said, but Sophie couldn't remember anything except the tupping and the empty chair on her big day. Daddy was a funny voice for one of her animals, a tupping ram with Matilda and an empty chair. And a threat.

The undergrowth is getting thicker and the light is going. Ouch. A nettle stings through her leggings. She takes it personally, like an extra insult. Duncan always says the sting is gone before you can count backwards from one hundred. She says, 'One hundred,' but can't think what comes next. She is thinking about Granny Sylvia saying that Daddy has just lost his memory, that's all. But she knows this isn't true. Daddy saw her. He looked her in the eye and whispered her name – *Soph . . .* – and then ran away.

Her daddy saw her and ran away.

She wipes her nose on her sleeve and is cross with herself, because she likes this top. *If Sophie hadn't been born, none of this would've happened.*

By now, Jack will have noticed. Surely. It's beginning to get pretty dark now. What if no one has noticed? Jack will have asked where Sophie is. He will. Or Mummy will have called her to clean her teeth. Mummy will be frantic. Or perhaps something has distracted her, like a phone call from Aunty Rachel. Perhaps she won't notice until she goes to bed. Mummy always pops in then to give her a kiss, and she pretends to be asleep because she likes to hear her whisper things like, 'Goodnight my little lamb, my sweet lamb.' No. Will and Jack and Mummy will all be worried. They will. It's not that Sophie wants them to worry, it's that she needs them to. She needs them to be very, very, very worried. It's okay, she tells herself, walking uncertainly in the darkness. She doesn't want them to find her too soon, because then Mummy will just hold her close and call her a silly sausage and it will all be over, as if she has just been a bit naughty or daft. She knows she is trying to get their attention, but it is for a good cause. It really isn't that she wants to be unkind, it's that she wants them to *listen* to her. She wants to be heard, and at the moment what she thinks doesn't seem to matter.

She comes to a stile and kicks it with her trainer. She doesn't want Daddy coming home again. Will told Jack that Dad could come home again because it's his house too and Mum can't stop him. And if Mum divorced him they might have to live in another house and go and spend the weekends with him. Will said *he* wouldn't have to because he was going off to uni, but Jack and Sophie would. She doesn't want to live in another house and spend the weekends with Daddy. Jack said he wouldn't spend the weekends with Matilda – he'd kill her first. Frankly, Sophie doesn't care about Matilda any more. It's Daddy she doesn't want to be with.

A bird is trilling sweetly from a bush. She slips over the stile and her face is aching from crying. She cries for two more fields and then runs out of tears. She is glad. It's too tiring. She's exhausted by all the crying and the self-pity. She puts down her rucksack and takes out her hoodie. It's getting nippy. After she's zipped it up she shivers. She listens. The birds have stopped singing. There are shadows thickening all around, varying degrees of darkness in the bushes and trees at the edges of the fields. She is tired and scared. She has no idea where she is.

Miss Dowling always says that if you get lost you should stay where you are, and someone who cares about you will come looking for you. If there are people around, ask a woman for help. If not, then find somewhere safe, and stay still.

Sophie stays very still. What if no one comes? She pictures Will ringing Duncan. Then Duncan will come. Duncan would find her. She hopes it's Duncan. Suddenly, there is a rustling ahead of her. A very tall, dark figure looms over her. Sophie can feel her pulse kick in her chest. If this is someone who knows her, why don't they say her name? She tries to stay silent and still, but she is panting with fear. She trembles out, 'Will . . . ?' but there is no reply.

The figure moves towards her and she turns at right angles and runs across the steep field. She runs and runs until she can feel her legs aching. She can hear someone running behind her, but still no one calls her name. Whoever it is, it's not a kindly woman she can ask for help. She scrambles over a gate and almost falls. She runs some more, then sinks to her knees. There's a pounding in her ears, like someone running. She wants to melt into the grass, right now, like Gloria's poo or the banana. All she can hear is the pounding, and all she can feel is the dewy grass and the pain in her limbs and the terror of someone's presence. She waits, shuddering, for him to say her name, but he does not. There is just a loud snort.

'Please,' she whispers. 'Please, don't hurt me.'

She clambers to her feet and starts to run again, but her foot finds no ground in front of it. She has reached the end of the earth.

It takes a moment to realise that she has fallen. Her elbow and her knees feel scorched; they have hit stones and the stones are underwater. *She* is underwater – except for her head and shoulders – heavy with the weight of it in her clothes. She moves slowly on all fours; her hands feel soft mud and sharp stones. She can't tell if she is still being followed. She must stay quiet. When she reaches for the bank and grabs at the undergrowth, something bites her! Ow! She pulls back in terror.

Ow. Ow. She can hear her own breath, heavy as a horse's snort. She feels the familiar burn on her hands and wrists. She's been stung – not bitten. These are nettles. She stifles a sob of relief and pain. Her palms are on fire. She picks herself up and wades through the water in trainers that feel heavy as bricks. Her leggings are glued on to her skin. She moves upstream and tries the bank again. Tree roots and twigs. She launches herself at the bank and pulls herself up. There is a lot of crackling and snapping, but she doesn't care. She has to get away. Then she slips back down suddenly on the buttery mud between the roots.

'Please,' she whimpers softly. 'Please, please.'

There is no kindness in the banks of streams. She has never thought this before, but the trees and their roots and the mud and the nettles seem to want to trap her out of spite.

She catches the scent of wild garlic and keeps lifting her heavy feet through the water. She will move towards its sweetness. There must be a softer piece of bank covered in leathery garlic leaves. She is shivering. The rucksack is leaden on her back. There must be some way out.

68

DREAMS OF LOST CHILDREN

God, all her life she had dreaded this. It was as if it was destined to happen to her sometime, careless, inadequate mother that she was. Over the past years she had managed to lose all her children for brief periods of time. She left Will in a department store once, totally forgetting that she had brought the buggy with her. It had only been for about five minutes, but it had been minutes of sheer horror. She lost him again a couple of years later, outside the primary school when she had been chatting to some mums, and had found him fifteen minutes later, stroking a cat down the lane. She lost Jack, aged two, at a village fete and found him leaning perilously low over a goldfish pond. She had taken her eye off a bouncy castle for two minutes to chat to another mum when Sophie had taken a notion, again aged two, to leave her brother bouncing and wander over to the hook-a-duck area at a very large summer fair. Each of the incidents had lasted such a short interval, and yet they had filled a huge space in her memory reserved for most dreaded experiences ever. There was nothing more guaranteed to shoot adrenaline into every branch and bud of your body, nothing more likely to rattle your ribcage with a pounding heart and heaving breath, than a missing child.

And there were the dreams, of course. In dreams, she had left babies in drawers and hedgerows and rivers; she had mislaid small children in

runaway buggies and cars and trains. She had watched them fall accidentally off cliffs and into streams and swimming pools and rip tides.
They had fallen out of boats, into the cages of lions and into schools of
hungry sharks. She had been quite remiss and careless, and had woken
up each time in a sweat of panic-stricken regret. Of course, she knew
that in these dreams they were only metaphors, symbols of ambitions
neglected. Lost children were cherished ideas she had allowed to wander
off, talents and possibilities she had put in jeopardy by taking her eye off
the ball. Forgotten babies were passions she had had no time to nurture,
despite her best intentions. Once, she had found her baby so emaciated
it had turned into a descant recorder, and then a twig. Doggedly she
had held it to her, wrapped in a blanket, and fed it spoonfuls of baby
rice, hoping to flesh it out and transform the little mite into what it had
once been before her neglect.

But this was no metaphor. Now she was faced with the real thing.
Sophie hadn't come to clean her teeth after tea. She was nowhere to be
seen.

Freya had arrived at Fiona's house before Nadine went to bed. She
had asked her as gently as she could about Sophie, but no doubt her
urgent voice and her greediness for information had made Nadine
uncomfortable. In the end Fiona had taken her daughter up to bed
and used the opportunity to talk quietly with her, while Freya paced
their downstairs rooms trying to look at pictures and books to distract
her. On a dresser in the kitchen was a framed photograph of Nadine and
her father. Freya knew that Fiona would have struggled to stop herself
removing it. It was Nadine's dad, after all. What a price girls paid for
the love of their fathers sometimes! Freya picked up the photograph
and scowled. She felt physically sick at the thought of what Reuben had
done to her own daughter. The repercussions would go on repercussing
for all of her daughter's life. And she would have to say he was a good
man, wouldn't she? She would not be a good mother if she ran him

down. She would have to wear a mask forever, and all because she had made a dumb move as a student. When would she stop paying for that?

Something was happening. She felt very odd. She made a dash for the toilet and was sick down it. She sank to her knees and coughed and swallowed the bile. She curled into a ball against the toilet wall and tried to let the tears come, but they wouldn't. Her hands were shaking, and when she tried to hug them, her knees were shaking too.

When Fiona came downstairs, she sat Freya down and made her sweet tea. She told her gently that Sophie had mentioned running away once to Nadine, but Nadine had thought she was just saying it. It was a few days ago, during the worst of the press interest. As Freya started to shake again, Fiona put a steadying hand on her wrist. 'And here's the thing: she said it was because she didn't want her daddy to come back and live with her.'

Freya covered her face with her hands. 'Are you sure? I thought . . . I thought she was angry with me for being angry with him.'

Fiona stroked her wrist some more, and Freya wondered what else Nadine had said. She must have looked at Fiona in alarm, because Fiona said, 'It seems that she is a bit . . . upset with you . . .' Freya groaned in misery and guilt. 'But not because of Reuben. She's upset because you won't see Duncan any more.'

69

HISTORY REPEATING ITSELF

It was ten past ten. A scream made him jump. It was a fox, wasn't it? Not a child? Jesus. The sound came again. Definitely the squawky scream of a fox. If Duncan stood still too long, he would have to accept that he was shaking, that he felt helpless, but that served no purpose. There had to be a logical solution. He had to think practically. He kept walking, the gentle swish of his long strides on the cooling grass giving him a calming rhythm. He had already wasted too much time on the conceited idea that Sophie would have tried to find him. *Him*, of all people, given the chaos he'd managed to cause her family, one way or another. If he hadn't even *taken* them to Italy in the first place, they would never have found out. They could all be blissfully remembering their father as a prince of charity and goodness, and Sophie would right now be tucked up in bed dreaming of otters. Otters. Were there any streams near here? No significant ones, he thought.

But he wasn't going to wimp out now, just because things were difficult. Freya had been very hard to fathom since they'd got back from Italy. Of course her life had been turned upside down. It had been devastated. All her faith in human nature had been challenged. She had been through the most unimaginable grief with her children. And her pride had been hurt. Bolstering Reuben and all his good works had been a prime feature of their time together. To discover, so publicly – in front of her children and in front of him – that he was clearly a man in a mask, well that would have humiliated anyone. But surely she could see that Duncan wasn't being smug? Surely she knew him well enough to know that he wanted to help? She hadn't given him much to go on lately. He had to keep reminding himself – or torturing himself – with memories of those long, happy walks together, those afternoons in bed, her skin, her joy, his sense of being necessary to her. But what if this really was the end? What if he had crossed a line, or all this grief was just too much for her, or Sophie was never found? If he couldn't be with Freya or the children he had grown to care for, what would be his legacy? His hair was already greying at the temples, and it was getting a little thinner each year. He had no children of his own. He would leave behind a couple of good architectural designs, a few watercolours, a cat. There had to be more to life, and he had glimpsed it. He had seen it in her face as she gazed at him in bed, in a 'thank you' from Will, when they looked at paintings in Florence, in the glee in Jack's face when he heard a nightingale at dusk with him, and in Sophie's face . . . Sophie's little face . . .

It occurred to him that he may have become less developed with time. He was less now than he had been as a boy. Perhaps he had grown backwards, or at least never been able to move beyond that point when his weakness betrayed him, when he had been too inadequate to step up to the mark, no matter how hard he tried. Now, standing lost in this field with not a single house light glimmering, he felt dizzy with the past. Twenty-seven years ago, at dusk. He had always enjoyed a summer evening walk with his mum and his brother. Usually his father came too, but sometimes he was too tired or too busy, and later his brother – although he was younger – found it all a bit uncool. So it was often just him and his mother, marvelling at the evening birdsong and the glorious red sunsets. 'I always think,' she said, 'that the lovely light where a sun goes down seems to beckon some wonderful new world, some new opportunity – I don't know, something amazing – waiting just over the horizon.' Her face had been all lit up in a peachy glow, and smiling. He remembered her smiling, delighted face. Sweet, calm. And it all happened so quickly, like a cloud going over. He had thought (how stupid) that she was joking for a moment, play-acting, although she wasn't one for dramatics. When she hit the ground and lay diagonally across the footpath, he knew this was something unexpected. 'Get . . . help,' she breathed, almost apologetically. And he had looked around at the long shadows growing across the fields, the dark density of the trees, and he could see no houses, not a glimmer of light to dash towards. He had stood, like he had stopped now, a creature stunned, as though running or any sudden movement would alert a predator.

There were no mobile phones back then – at least, not ones that people like them had for personal use. He had run, in the end, to the lane they had just left, and taken a direction they had never been in before, in the hope of some house or pub. But there was nothing. He had run on, helplessly, until he found a house with no lights on and no one at home. Finally, he ran all the way back home through the unlit lanes to his father, who called for an ambulance. Even then, he couldn't get the words out, didn't know the name of the nearest road.

They found her in the dewy dark, already cold. If he had known mouth-to-mouth resuscitation, if he had joined the Duke of Edinburgh's Award scheme like his brother – as his father had wanted him to – he would have learnt CPR in First Aid, he would have known what to do. But he had gone his own way. He had failed her. He had failed his lovely mother just when she needed him most. So much for trying to be independent, for doing his own thing. *That Duncan Swan thinks he's so clever.*

His phone rang. It was Will. 'Just to say, that girl on the bus: it was some guy from the pub's ex-wife and daughter up for the day. Mum's in pieces about it. So . . . anything happening your end?'

'No. I'll keep looking. Remind her the police'll be here soon with the sniffer dogs. It's going to be okay.'

'That's what I was going to say as well. They hope to be here later tonight, and they want us to stop looking in the fields and that, in case we disturb some evidence.'

Duncan shuddered. 'Okay.'

Evidence.

70

LAST CHANCE

Up ahead was an outbuilding of some sort. His spirits rose. He rushed forward and approached quietly. The smell of horse dung reached him before he entered. He cast the torch beam around. A brown horse eyed him lazily, as if it had been sleeping standing up. Then he heard a noise on the straw. He cast the beam again. It was another horse, raising its head in indignation at being stirred from sleep, although on closer inspection, this horse was steaming, as if it had just been for a night-time gambol. He did not like the look it was giving him, and then he realised it was Lottie's horse, Biscuit. Still, he was disappointed that there was no sign of a sleeping six-year-old. He cast the beam around again, just to be certain. There was nothing. He went back out and checked a very smelly wheelbarrow and behind some bags of straw bedding. Nothing.

Duncan had no real idea of where he was in relation to the house now, but the horses meant it must be walking distance, since this was where Jack came each Saturday. He resisted the urge to call Jack. What difference would it make? Right now, he just had to keep looking.

He looked up at the stars. Once, they had all been able to find their bearings by the stars. This seemed as remarkable now as the thought of birds finding their way back home after migrating. The same stars had shone down on their ancestors, but only on a clear night like this one. So clear, that there was a growing chill in the air now. It had been a sunny day, but a cool breeze had kept up, and it made the trees shiver, their lush new leaves sending out a loud swishing at intervals like the sound of waves breaking on shingle. Suddenly a white rabbit's tail made a fleeing zigzag path in front of him. He wondered if it had been disturbed by something, and he stood very still to listen. Nothing. Nothing, but then, a curious trill of birdsong. A robin. Triggered by his torchlight perhaps. The robin was the first to sing in the morning and the last to sing at night. Long after the final rays of sunlight, its cheery nocturne could be heard. Now it thought that the sudden light of a torch called for a bit of singing.

He crossed two more fields, calling Sophie's name as he went. The distant *woo-hoo-hoo-hooo* of a tawny owl seemed to follow his path as he began to climb slightly, and nearer the hedges he heard the panting, snuffly sound of a hedgehog out for a night-time stroll. The next field after that rose up quite steeply at first and then flattened out a little. Across it were dark mounds like small hay-bales, but as he walked along the edge by the hedge, he saw one of the shapes move – and then another. Then there was a faint bleat. He was in a field of sheep. As he shone his torch, he could see that some were standing and some were lying down. Quite swiftly the lying sheep started to get to their feet, as though a predator were approaching, so he swiftly turned off the beam. The lambs would be getting chunkier now, but still needed their mums and lots of sleep. The sentinel sheep would have lambs too. They must take it in turns, he thought, to be on lookout duty. He had caused havoc now. Another lamb bleated and then another. Then a great deep sheep bellow. They would all wake up. He wanted to say, 'At ease. There's nothing to worry about. As you were.' But instead he felt the need to bleat as well. 'SOPHIE!' he shouted. 'SOPHIE! SOPHIE! SO-PHIEEEEE!'

He sat down and put his head in his hands. The bleats were coming thick and fast. Then slowly, slowly, they trickled out until there was only one distant bleat. He listened. It was so far off. It was different. He strained to hear, lifting his hands away from his face and holding them stock still in mid-air.

'Dunking? Dunking? Is that you?'

He was on his feet and running. 'Sophie! Where are you? Yes, it's Duncan! Sophie!'

He put on his torch and moved it about. There, at a little distance yet, was Sophie, kneeling with her arms around a fat sheep. She stood up, clearly unable to see his face and squinting into the torchlight. He lowered the light and spoke more gently. Gloria knew who it was, though, and came trotting over to him, followed by her lamb. She headbutted him inelegantly, and Sophie came up behind her. Certain at last that this was Duncan, she leapt into his arms. 'Dunking! Dunking! I knew you'd find me. I *knew* you would!'

She was cold and sodden. She was shivering – or maybe it was him. His shoulders were shaking. He was crying. He tried hard to stop himself, but he couldn't. He buried his face in her shoulder and squeezed her hard, hoping she wouldn't notice. But there were sobbing noises and everything. He held on to her so tightly and for so long that Gloria lost interest and sidled away, and her lamb followed her.

'Let me phone Mummy,' he said at last, when he trusted himself with words. He stroked her hair while the phone rang, and she rested her head on his chest. 'Freya! I've found Sophie!' On the word 'Sophie' his voice broke up, and he had to say it again, and then there was a wild set of sounds down the phone, and he said he would bring her back. 'Where are you?'

'I'm in the King's Arms.'

'Well tell that king to put you down for a moment.'

'Stop! Have you really found her?'

'Yes! Wait there. I'll bring her to the pub.'

He stood up and lifted Sophie with him. They went back to get her damp rucksack. He looped it over one arm while she clung on to him, monkey-like, her arms around his neck and her feet around his waist. If he kept walking the way he had come, he would soon see the lights of the village.

'I'm glad it was you,' she whispered after a while. 'I'm glad it was you who found me.'

'Me too.'

'I hoped it would be you.'

Duncan thought about this. There were two pieces of information in what she said, and both were important. So, she had wanted to be found. She had wanted it to be him. What a wild goose chase she had sent them on. What a . . . He gave her a giant squeeze, and into the darkness of the steep lane he smiled.

When they walked into the pub, a great cheer went up. People he had never seen before slapped him on the back. Freya rushed over and flung her arms around Sophie, who transferred herself – monkey-style – to her mother. 'Dunking found me,' she said, her tired face alight. 'It was Dunking who found me.'

'Sophie, Sophie, my Sophie!' wept Freya, her voice going up an octave.

She hugged Sophie as if she might squeeze the breath out of her. She buried her nose in her little girl's hair and smelt her like the sweetest perfume in the world. Then she reached out an arm towards Duncan and smiled and nodded her tear-stained face at him. He came over and hugged them both, and Will joined in.

Pete handed Duncan a pint of beer. Someone told Duncan there was blood on the seat of his jeans. He realised his backside was probably bleeding. War wounds. He didn't care.

A policeman wearing a fluorescent yellow jerkin came in with a sniffer dog, asking which one was Freya. When he saw that Sophie was found, he grinned. 'That's the best news I've had all day!'

'Have a drink!' said Pete, leaning over the bar, a little tearful himself. 'On the house!'

'Thanks, but no. Not on duty. Okay if I sit here for a bit, though?'

'Of course,' said Pete. 'Fancy a bit of lemon drizzle cake instead?'

71

FORAGING FOR SCRAPS

When they got home, Freya slept deeply and peacefully with Sophie in her arms. In the morning, she found Duncan on the sofa. Breakfast was relaxed and late. She swabbed his grazes with lavender oil and felt a rush of lust as she applied it to his buttocks. After all the emotion and elation packed into the hours before sleep, her head was still swimming. She loved every precious inch of him with every inch of herself, except that things weren't the same as before. She felt free-floating, detached from herself, and had no certainty about anything any more.

The days that followed were warm and happy. Finding Sophie had blunted the horror of Reuben's treachery, and summer was beginning to fill the house with sunshine. They went on evening walks and Duncan stayed over most nights. Will told them all his good news and said he had officially accepted the offer. Freya was surprised that he hadn't mentioned it before. Had he thought she would try to stop him? She was pleased for him, but some part of her wondered why this little razor cut hurt more than the giant wound of losing him. Duncan made a special meal to celebrate. Two celebrations in one week.

Since Reuben's appearance in Italy and the chaos of her own and her children's emotions, Freya had found herself developing a slow, self-preserving numbness, as though she had injected herself with anaesthetic to avoid the pain of a tooth extraction or limb amputation. She found it both helpful and slightly repugnant, but she had no will to change the situation. The new indifference was easier than the pain, and that was enough for now. But it had taken Sophie's disappearance to reawaken the nerve endings: not pins and needles but cracks of lightning, boat-turning waves, hurricanes.

This morning, she had woken up to an uneasy feeling. She had dreamt she was packing a suitcase. She had hardly any time to do it and had no idea what to take. There was a terrible, sickening urgency to it. And . . . yes . . . when she followed the trail backwards to the dream before . . . there had been Will. He was walking away from her across a field – the field they often crossed at the start of their walks – and he was holding someone's hand: Renzo's, maybe. She was waving to him – not to get his attention, but a wave of goodbye. Even so, she longed for him to turn, but he didn't look back. He and his partner seemed to swing their joined hands in merriment, and she could see they were happy. She was glad. And yet . . . if he had just turned. She yearned for him to turn and return her wave.

All the emotion she could have felt for Duncan, for the resolution he had brought them, was now being swallowed up by something else. She wanted to melt into this new family warmth, this place of stability and peace. But the emotions sneaking around her were full of sly torment.

By the end of the summer, Will would have left. She wasn't ready. No one warned her. She felt there should have been a warning. Oh yes, he would come back and visit. Everyone said he would come back. But a whole era was ending. She was the child at a party who is just settling into it after a difficult start, only to be told it's home time. Already? That little bundle she had brought home from the hospital, the strange terror on realising she was being entrusted with him, alone; the years of curbed freedom, the open prison of maternal attachment and love; the heart-rending clinging at the school gates; the even more heart-rending sudden rejection that began with their embarrassment at the school gates and progressed to a generalised embarrassment at everything she did. She remembered Will's mortification at a parents' evening, when he was an angry thirteen-year-old, because she was wearing her old green coat. 'What's wrong with it?' she'd asked. 'Shut up,' he'd said, without moving his lips. 'Not now!' And later he'd revealed that it was so drab and didn't coordinate with anything: a black bag and brown boots and colourless earrings. The next parents' evening she had gone out the week before and bought some dark green earrings from the Red Cross shop. They were parrots, but that was not very evident. She had also matched the black handbag with black shoes. He had said nothing – until they got back. 'God, Mum, do you do it on purpose? You have to be the only mum who wears a pair of fucking dangling parrots in her ears. What were you thinking?'

In a few years' time she would get a text from Will saying, 'By the way, I'm married now. I didn't tell you because you would only have worn parrot earrings to the ceremony and embarrassed me . . . But I'm happy. You're welcome to visit . . .' And Jack. She had already embarrassed him. In ten years or so she would get an email saying, 'Me and Danielle have emigrated to South America to raise horses. It's amazing. You'll love it. I didn't tell you sooner because I knew you'd be upset and wail at the airport . . .' And Sophie, even Sophie would be embarrassed by her soon. No good recalling all the games they had played together, all the trust she had placed in Freya over the years. No, Sophie too would turn up one day with her partner and sit awkwardly at the kitchen table: 'Hey Mum, just so you know, me and Ted/Josh/Jacob/Kurt got married last week on a beach in Italy. You don't mind do you? We're so happy. I knew you'd just cry your eyes out if you came, so . . .'

Oh, it was such a feeling. So ordinary, so everyday, but so overwhelming. Something between grief and homesickness, a cold pebble in the throat the shape of a skimming stone, set horizontally, to stop any words coming out that could possibly articulate it, and to block any consolation going down. It was a bursting, suffocating, squashing, humiliating feeling, full of remorse and sorrow. She wanted it gone, but it trumped anything else she was able to feel.

One day during the week, when Duncan was still at work, Rachel phoned, and was able to reassure her sister about the house.

'Have you ever looked at the deeds? Obviously, Reuben never did.'

'No, I don't think so. Why?'

'Dad put the house in our name. Yours and mine. You and I are joint owners.'

'Not Reuben? Not at all?'

'No. And I don't want half of it. We can change the deeds now. Dad left me money instead, but he told me the house was in our names in case you divorced Reuben. He didn't trust Reuben. So, even if he is entitled to half your assets, which, frankly, I doubt, he would only have a quarter of the house to try for. I can help buy him out, if needs be. Unless someone else wants to . . .'

'No!'

'I'm just saying . . .'

When Freya put the phone down, she closed her eyes. What must her father have thought of her? It was good news, of course. It was wonderful news. But she was overwhelmed by that other piece of news that had slithered out from between the cracks.

When she thought about Reuben, she had to face something that made her shudder: that she had invented him. Not for Duncan's benefit, not just since Reuben's 'death'. No, right from the beginning, she could see now that she had made him up. She had inflated his small successes, exaggerated his few kindnesses, minimised his misdemeanours. In fact, he had rarely pleased her and had often made her ashamed. There had been very little to work with, but she was a true, doting female forager. She had made him up out of scraps.

But all this she had done unwittingly, so how could there be any certainty that she hadn't invented Duncan too? This wasn't his fault. He was caught in the fallout. She remembered Duncan's meekness and courtesy when he was being ticked off noisily by the Italian man for parking in the wrong place, and she began to cry. She cried and cried until her face ached. But still she didn't trust herself. For the first time in her life she found herself to be a mystery: shifty, unreliable.

72

NO LEMON

The following Saturday breakfast was jovial. Duncan proposed a walk later, and everyone seemed keen, although Jack made a point of saying that it would have to be before six, because he was meeting Danielle. Duncan and Freya exchanged covert smiles. When the children had left the table, Duncan picked up the book that Freya was reading for her book group. Fiona had persuaded her to join again since she was a new member herself. 'Ah, *Rebecca*,' he said, flicking through the pages. 'Interesting choice.'

'Yes. The dead spouse who won't go away.'

'How does it end?'

'House goes up in a great fire, I think. Don't go getting any ideas.'

'Don't worry.' Then, in a self-mocking tone he said: 'I just want to start a flame in your heart – or rekindle one, anyway.'

Freya looked down at the toast crumbs on the table, then got up and stood by the back door, looking out at the burgeoning flowers in the garden. He went to join her. Sensing, perhaps, that what she had wanted most from Duncan was some proof that he wasn't like 'all men', that he would move mountains for her, and that he may well have succeeded in proving this the night he found Sophie, he ventured a little confidence. 'So . . . what about the Freya who'd met the man she'd like to spend the rest of her life with?'

Freya felt both tender and apologetic. 'I don't need a man in my life right now.' She hadn't expected to say that. She didn't want to need a man.

'I don't want you to *need* me. I want you to like having me around.'

'Well . . . I do, but . . .' She looked off into the distance. She hadn't intended to mislead him with her warmth these last few days. She wished life could stay like this. 'Let's face it, Duncan, we both know there's no such thing as happy-ever-after.'

'No. No, I think I agree.' He didn't look as if he agreed. He looked baffled and a little awkward. The sun was warming them both as it rose high in a cloudless blue. 'But' – he took her hands and pushed them together – 'there *is* a happy . . . and there *is* an after . . .'

'I suppose . . .'

'So, here we are: after. And life will go on, after. Why not make it as happy as we can?'

'I'm sorry, Duncan. I don't think I'm ready.'

She hated herself for saying that. He didn't want to hear that cliché. He said nothing more, but turned away amicably. He was breaking up inside, and she could see it, but that is how he said goodbye: *amicably*.

She willed him to turn back.

'Aren't you staying for a walk?' she asked.

'Okay.' Smiling. Amicable.

The sound of car wheels on gravel interrupted their conversation. Freya's heart sank, but looking out of the kitchen window she could see an unfamiliar car. It was small, but brand-new. Before she had time to register the driver, who was facing away, Freya spotted the red mud along the bottom edges of the bodywork. Devon mud.

Sylvia swung into the kitchen like a diva late for her filming. 'You'll never guess what's happened! Oh Freya! Oh Freya! You've got to help!' And she burst into tears. In fact, as she slumped on to the living room sofa, it became clear that these were not the first tears shed that day. Her face was blotchy and her eye make-up had made dark rivulets down her cheeks. Freya went to put the kettle on, Duncan handed her some kitchen roll, and when they sat down, Sylvia lifted a panda face to them both.

'I don't suppose you have a gin or something?' She could hardly get the words out. She kicked off her court shoes and they stood like dramatic exhibits next to the sofa, one upright and the other on its side. Chunkables, who had been asleep on the sofa, trotted peevishly into the kitchen. 'With a . . . slice of . . . lemon.'

There was no gin, and no lemon. Duncan made her a cup of hot chocolate, and Sylvia sat and wept some more. 'There, sip it,' he said gently. 'That'll make you feel better.' Freya was impressed, but not surprised, by Duncan's kind gestures. And that thought struck her as significant. There was Sylvia, the woman who had so nearly ruined Duncan's life – and quite wilfully – and there was Duncan, offering her kitchen towel and hot chocolate. She might have sensed a tiny cracking in the walls of her giant dam at that moment, had her attention not been arrested by Sylvia's gigantic nose-blowing.

'Sylvia, whatever's happened?'

'Oh, I know I shouldn't be burdening you with this, not with all the problems you have and everything but . . . Well, I can't believe it. I just can't believe it . . .' They both waited, fearful of some new piece of news about Reuben. 'You'll find out sooner or later . . . so . . . the thing is I really don't think I deserve this. You won't believe it!' She started sobbing again.

'What? What is it, Sylvia?'

It was clear she was in genuine distress. She took in her breath in great heaving gulps, as if she were drowning. 'First I lose my son, and now . . . now . . . I lose my husband!'

'What? What's happened to Steve?'

'I can't bear it!'

'What do you mean? Is he . . . ?'

'He's left me! He wants a . . . *divorce*!' She spat out the last word with venom, as if it was a word she wanted to throw away as far as possible. It didn't belong to her.

Freya sat in a kind of stunned silence. Not because she was surprised that Steve should want to leave Sylvia, but because she couldn't imagine him finding the courage to actually do so.

'There was nothing – *nothing* – to suggest he was unhappy. Not a clue. Then he went out and bought me that brand-new car – a guilt gift, of course (I see that now) – and he was off. Not so much as a proper goodbye. No explanation, just "I can't do this any more," and he was gone. Took the BMW, of course, must've had it all packed up and ready to leave while I was at bridge. I mean. How pathetic! How cowardly!'

'Do you know where he's gone?'

'Oh, that's the worst part! He's only gone to stay with Ludo! *Ludo!* The one son I have left and he's . . . *using* him! *Poisoning* him against me! And I'm surprised at Ludo. I feel so betrayed!' She started to wail again. Freya and Duncan exchanged glances, from which they deduced that they had no idea how to handle this situation.

'I'm sure it's just temporary, Sylvia. Ludo wouldn't be able to turn his own father away. It's probably just for a few days until he finds somewhere to live.'

'Oh God! Somewhere to live! But he's got a home! He lives with me! He's always lived with me. He won't know what to do. He won't have a clue!'

Freya thought about Steve the last time he had been there, the evening Sophie went missing. They hadn't even told Sylvia or Steve about that. Steve had seemed a little bit defiant, but she would never have guessed at this. 'Things will settle down. Is there anything I can do to help?'

'Phone him! Phone him and talk some *sense* into him!'

'Wouldn't it be better to wait for the dust to settle?'

'What dust? Wait for him to go and live with some floozy?'

'I'm sure he isn't planning to—'

'Yes, that's what he says. He says there's no one else – he just "can't do this any more". Pah! No one else, my foot! There's obviously some-one else. Some woman has tricked him using her wiles. I know Stephen. He wouldn't be leaving me for nothing. He's got it all too easy living with me!'

She wouldn't stop ranting until Freya had promised to ring Steve at Ludo's. Then she kept on until Freya actually dialled the number. Freya went upstairs to be out of Sylvia's earshot. Ludo picked up and handed over to Steve. He sounded tired, but perfectly stable. There was no other woman, he insisted. There was just Sylvia, and he'd had enough. He had had enough for years now, but her behaviour since Reuben had turned up just pushed him over the edge, he said. 'I won't change my mind, Freya. I'm sorry if she's landed on your doorstep. She does have friends. She's always out with friends. I'm going to divorce her. She'll manage. I'm sorry.'

Freya went downstairs quietly. Sylvia looked at her so hopefully that Freya felt a wave of pity for her. 'I'm afraid he's not coming back. He wants a divorce.'

Sylvia let out a howl that brought the children out of their hiding places to the top of the stairs.

'Sylvia, I'm so sorry . . .'

'Sorry? You can't imagine! You can't possibly imagine how I feel!'

Duncan spoke up now. 'Well, I think she can.'

'And *you*! I know you've been divorced but there's *no comparison*! I've been married for forty-six years! *Forty-six years!* Don't you tell me – either of you – that you can *possibly* imagine what this feels like – because you can't! You have *no idea*!' She started sobbing again, and then let out a shriek. Chunkables, who had sidled over to her shoes, was now squatting over them and looking insolently at anyone who dared to watch him. When the shriek ended, you could hear the tail end of a trickle inside the upright court shoe.

73

THE LARK IN THE CLEAR AIR

Clearing up Chunkables's mess after Sylvia had gone, Freya caught sight of something in the waste bin that made her pause. She stood as still as a deer, waiting for danger to pass, staring at the thing in the bin whilst holding a pile of kitchen towel smelling of cat urine. At last she bent down and fished it out: it was Matilda. She had been discarded and stuffed head first under some empty yoghurt pots.

They went for their walk, just as they had always done before Italy. Even Will came along, occasionally thwacking the undergrowth with a long stick and stirring up the scents of early summer. They passed the pub, which had a chalked sign outside:

> DRINKS TODAY WILL COST YOU ZERO
> DUNCAN SWAN OUR LOCAL HERO!

Will threw his stick in the air and shouted, 'Yay! It scans!'

They crossed their usual field. The air was thick with pollen and reeked of wild garlic along the edges of the wood. Up ahead on the path Freya saw Sophie reach up her hand and slip it into Duncan's, and she saw that Sophie carried on talking as if nothing important had happened. She remembered what Sophie had said when she was reunited with her. *Dunking found me. It was Dunking.*

And then from nowhere, a skylark. It shot up through the air with its gorgeous and intricate trilling, and they all stopped and looked up as it hovered, miraculously, some hundred metres or so above the meadow. Showing off again, thought Freya.

'Did you know,' said Jack, 'that larks have been killed and eaten for hundreds of years? People would attract them to the corners of fields with mirrors and other lark lures, and then they'd be shot for sport, or netted up. The southern Mediterraneans still eat them.' Sophie was horrified. 'And the Victorians put the males in cages to hear their singing.'

Freya joined Sophie in lark empathy, and assured her that no one did that today.

'And did you know,' said Jack, on a roll, 'that larks are loyal? They are like swans: they mate for life. And did you know that a gathering of larks is called "an exaltation"?'

Freya had known this once, but she had forgotten it.

Everyone was in a cheerful mood. Exalted. She let the sun warm her face and felt the pebble slip a little. The high-pitched notes rang out in the clear sky and across the swollen hedgerows. She craned up to gaze at the lark. It seemed to her now that its wings trembled in earnest, straining to stay in the air, straining to impress its mate and keep the bond strong, trilling, fluting, singing its little heart out.

ACKNOWLEDGMENTS

I am indebted to my wonderful agent, Jane Conway-Gordon, and to my editors, Sammia Hamer and Victoria Pepe; also to Mike Jones, Sophie Wilson, Julia Bruce, and Rebecca Jaynes; and to Bekah Graham and the team at Amazon Publishing.

I would like to thank the writers Sue Limb, Rachel Joyce, Cindy Jefferies, Caroline Sanderson, Katie Fforde, Kate Riordan, Katie Jarvis, Jamila Gavin and Maurice Gran for their kindness and support.

As ever, I would like to say a special thank you to my daughters, Anna and Lucy, for their encouragement and for making me laugh, and to John for his constant support, warmth, wisdom, and cups of tea.

ABOUT THE AUTHOR

Jane Bailey is the author of six novels and a book of comic verse. Her first novel was shortlisted for the Dillon's Prize. She is writer-in-residence for Cheltenham Festival's First Story, which promotes creative writing in schools in low-income communities, and for Beyond Words, which takes creative writing to young people in Gloucestershire Hospitals. Jane lives in Gloucestershire.